DEBORAH SCHAUMBERG

An Imprint of HarperCollinsPublishers

HarperTeen is an imprint of HarperCollins Publishers.

The Tombs
Copyright © 2018 by Deborah Schaumberg
All rights reserved. Printed in the United States of America.
No part of this book may be used or reproduced in any manner whatsoever
without written permission except in the case of brief quotations embodied
in critical articles and reviews. For information address HarperCollins
Children's Books, a division of HarperCollins Publishers, 195 Broadway,
New York, NY 10007.
www.epicreads.com

Library of Congress Control Number: 2017938999
ISBN 978-0-06-265644-5

Typography by Jenna Stempel
18 19 20 21 22 PC/LSCH 10 9 8 7 6 5 4 3 2 1
❖
First Edition

For my wonderful daughters, Skylar Gina and Ryan Paige—I see the world anew through your eyes. And, of course, for my mom.

What is this dismal-fronted pile of bastard Egyptian, like an enchanter's palace in a melodrama!—a famous prison, called The Tombs. Shall we go in?
—Charles Dickens, *American Notes*

CHAPTER ONE
THE WORKS

This must be how madness begins. Traces of light or a shadowy haze around a person's face, meaningless images in my head, and then the fear, the all-consuming fear that at any moment they will come for me. For a long time I convinced myself that madness was not hereditary. I may have been wrong. I haven't told anyone, not even Father. To say it out loud would make it true, and I *don't want to be locked up with my mother.*

Through the slats on my window I scanned the street for crow-shaped faces, beaks of black. One day they'd come. My heart drummed against my ribs as I pictured them out there—as if I were thirteen again. I took a deep breath and yanked the laces of my corset until it squeezed my heart back into place. Tucking in loose strands, I hid my braid under a soft felt hat and threw on Father's military coat.

1

Sliding back the curtain separating my bedchamber from the shop, I was surprised to find my father splayed out on the floor. He usually made it to the sofa. Next to him was an empty bottle of gin, propped against the shiny metal of his mechanical leg, both of which seemed to blame the other for his fall. If Mother were here instead of in the Tombs, he wouldn't be drinking and I'd be going to school instead of to work. I pushed away the pointless thoughts as I placed a pillow under his head. Shutting the door quietly, I left through the side entrance leading to the hallway.

I turned the lock and spun around, bumping directly into a man in disheveled Union military clothing. "Oh!" I stepped back. "Pardon me."

He eyed me through long matted hair and, in a voice that sounded as if he had gravel in his throat, said, "Edgar in there, missy?"

"Yes, sir. But he's sleeping."

"I'll wait. Got no place else to be." I noticed that one sleeve of the man's jacket was empty, pinned across his body in a hollow embrace. He'd come to see my father about his arm, no doubt. Although Father's passion was clock making, and he used to be a machinist at the navy yard, he tinkered with mechanical devices of all sorts, including body parts.

With his other hand, the man skillfully pinched a wad of tobacco from a snuff tin, dropped it back into his pocket, then pressed the leaves into his cheek. His fingers moved with

2

the grace and dexterity of an illusionist doing a card trick. He leaned against the wall and closed his eyes.

Delicate morning light drifted in through the glass door to the street, softening the fringe of peeling paint and exposed patches of wood lath on the walls. But despite its honeyed glow, it was still a hallway laden with despair.

Survivors of the Civil War often had missing limbs. The war may have ended seventeen years ago, but it still hovered like a tattered shroud over the city, casting a bitter shadow. My father made sure I knew all the particulars. More than 625,000 men had died, many not much older than myself. He taught me about each and every battle, and all the Civil War insignia.

I looked at the soldier's threadbare forage cap. It had a red triangular badge next to a pin of crossed sabers. "Fourth Corps Cavalry, Division One?" I asked.

He opened his eyes and gave me a long look. Then he lifted his chin. "At your service, ma'am."

I nodded. "Good day to you, sir."

I waited until I was halfway down the block before turning to glance up at the roof of our tenement building. My falcon, Seraphine, slept there in a protected roost Father and I had built for her. I whistled to let her know I was leaving.

Trudging through the thin layer of gray slush that had appeared overnight, I pushed it forward with the steel toes of my boots. A first snow in October meant a long winter of coal to purchase, and as employment was harder and harder to come by, especially for a girl, losing my job was something Father and I simply could not afford. I dug my hands into the pockets of the boys' wool britches I wore and picked up my pace. I still had time to go by the school.

Maybe today I would have the courage to talk to Grace. We used to live next door to the Hammonds, but I hadn't spoken to her since I'd moved to the slums. Back then I didn't know there were tenements and factories only a few blocks over, or that one day I'd be relegated to their dingy halls.

As I approached St. Ann's, I ducked into the shadows to watch the flocks of girls flit by, chattering like little birds. Just as it did every day, my gut tightened at the sight of them. *Why do I torture myself like this?* But I knew why. I missed her. I had friends, but they were all boys. Girlfriends had a different bond, a special one. Then I saw her.

She was arm in arm with another girl. Their skirts were clean and pressed, and they marched along in their lace-up boots, confident of their position in society. They were probably discussing boys they hoped to be courted by. I remember Grace laughing at me for saying I wanted to go to college when I grew up. "Oh, Avery," she'd said, dismissing me with a wave of her hand. "You simply must marry, or you'll end up like that old spinster down the street, the one with all the cats." But even though we had different views on certain things, we'd shared all of our hopes and dreams with each other.

I removed my felt hat and smoothed back my hair. My nerves tingled, but she was usually with a larger group and today it was just the two of them. It used to be her and me walking to school, arms linked like that.

I peeled away from the protection of the shadows. "Hello, Grace."

The girls stopped and glanced at each other. Did she not recognize me? *Of course*—my work clothes.

"It's me. Avery." I smiled. "Avery Kohl."

The other girl, with a pointed face and a shiny black widow's peak, smirked. "My dear Grace, is *this* an acquaintance of yours? She looks like a river rat up from the pier."

Her laugh burned my cheeks, but I ignored the insult, sure that Grace would put this rude girl in her place. "Grace?" I pleaded.

But Grace dropped her gaze. Pointy Face tightened her grip on Grace's arm. "Let's go, Grace. She might have the pox."

Grace allowed herself to be led away from me, but not before she glanced up and I saw myself through her eyes: boys' clothes, dirt under my fingernails, drab hair from lack of brushing. It was no wonder she was embarrassed to admit she knew me.

I'd held on to the belief that one day things could go back to normal, that if Father and I worked hard, we could get our old life back. Or at least that my best friend would always be there for me, even if I had no money. That other girl was right. I was the lowest of the low—a filthy working-class rat. Even worse, I walked a razor's edge between that and living on the streets.

Tears burned in my eyes, but Cross Street Ironworks waited

impatiently six blocks away and I could not be late. Without glancing back, I ran—from Grace, the school, and the life I'd lost—until the pain in my lungs overtook the pain in my heart.

I smelled the factory soon enough—smoldering iron and sulfur, the kind of smell that makes your lungs itch and your tongue taste like rust. The Works, as we called it, ate up four city blocks and seemed to be growing, breathing out its hot, metallic breath, belching black smoke, and seeping yellow clouds into the sky.

A shadow raced along the cobblestones. I glanced up to see Seraphine circling gracefully, high above me. I whistled again. She responded with a long wailing scream. Then she tucked her wings and dove like a shooting star from the sky, faster and faster, until I lost sight of her between the buildings.

When I reached the entrance to the enormous redbrick edifice, I slowed to catch my breath and wipe away traces of my tears. Two tall windows stared down at me, but their grimy glaze masked the interior of the factory. Across the top of the building, Cross Street Ironworks was painted in large, once-white letters. Beyond the roofline, one of the stacks was visible, engulfed in its corrosive cloud.

Geeno came sprinting from the opposite direction, his thin coat damp in the places where he must have slept on it. I worried constantly about him living in a wooden shipping crate, especially when the temperature dropped. Once, I'd followed him to the box he called home. He was furious, and no matter how I'd pleaded, he would not take an offer to sleep on my sofa, so stupidly proud sometimes he reminded me of myself.

"Whoa, there," I said as he skidded into me. "You run the whole way?"

"Avery, you here." He took a deep breath, his shoulders relaxing. "I thought maybe you leave us, too, like Alexander."

I punched his skinny arm. "What? And miss the chance to boss you runts around? Never."

"Want to see a secret?" He looked up at me, his gap-toothed smile tugging at my heart.

If I was to be a rat, at least I was not alone. We were weld rats, and at nine, Geeno was the youngest. But he could hold his own. Geeno apprenticed with my father every Sunday, in the hopes that he would one day have a worthy trade. He was a natural tinkerer, quickly learning how a clock's hundreds of tiny parts worked together.

"Please?" he begged.

"Can it be quick?" I tapped my silver timepiece, a gift from my father on my sixteenth birthday and a constant reminder that his genius was wasting away like the sugar cube on his absinthe spoon.

Geeno nodded and removed from his pocket a large corked glass vial containing something shiny and black.

"What is it?" I asked.

He held it up as I squinted closer. With a sharp tap, it flicked its tail on the glass.

I jumped back. "Geeno! What on earth is that thing?"

He laughed, enjoying my reaction. "It's called a scorpion. My neighbor find it in his shipping crate. We checked; his crate is from overseas."

"It looks dangerous, Geeno. I don't think you should keep it."

"She half dead anyway." He slid it back into his pocket. "But I think I can fix her."

"Sure you can. Just do me a favor, don't let it escape."

As he pulled his hand from his pocket, a thin metal plate fell to the ground. I picked it up. It was a black-and-white tintype photograph of Geeno standing with his parents at the rail of a steamship. They had emigrated from Italy to raise Geeno in "the land of opportunity," only to die of consumption a week after touching foot on American soil. Geeno was left to fend for himself in the city.

The picture blurred, and for a moment I thought I saw another image. I blinked and angled it back and forth, but it appeared normal. My mind was playing tricks on me again. I handed the plate back to Geeno. He looked at it with a faraway sadness. Placing my thumb on his chin, I tilted it up. "What happened to them was not your fault, Geeno. Do you understand?"

His brows drew together as if he was making an important decision. Then he smiled up at me. "Thank you, Avery."

"Come on." I tousled his hair and pushed open the heavy

steel door, releasing a blast of heat. "Don't want to walk in late and upset the boss, now, do we?"

The boss's name was Roland Malice, a Polish ex-boxer. Legend had it he'd died momentarily in his last professional bout, but I knew him to be undefeated at the illegal matches held late at night on the docks behind the factory. His fists and forearms rippled with muscle. His hulking form tapered at the top to form a bald head, and a thick mustache twirled into long points on either side of his face. Everyone was afraid of him, even the coal runners, and they were the biggest of the bunch.

We stopped to grab our helmets from the row of pegs lined up on the wall above our crudely painted names. Mine just said "Avery." After my mother was taken and we fled Brooklyn Heights, Father made me stop using my full name, so no one could track us down. As if moving into the crowded ghetto wasn't enough to hide us.

I sighed as Geeno jumped up to reach his helmet. I was going on two and a half years now at the Works, six days a week, twelve, sometimes fourteen hours a day. We were here more than in our own homes.

Tony and Leo were already at their stations. Two helmets were left. One was Oscar's, late again, and the other, Alexander's, who wouldn't need his anymore.

Geeno wasn't the only one who missed Alexander. He got out, landed a better job as a welder for the Brooklyn Bridge project. The crew looked to me, being next oldest, now that he was gone. The weight of that sat heavily on my shoulders, especially as I was *not* myself lately.

I think it began midsummer, around my birthday. I'd come home from work to find Father crying. It unsettled me—his bowed head clutched in his dusty white hands. He'd tried to bake me a cake, but it was a lump of coal. His long, slender fingers that could work minuscule gears into intricate designs could not combine flour, milk, and eggs. "It's all right, Pop. I don't need a cake," I'd said, trying to console him.

"Yes, you do. And you need a mother." He'd shaken his head, spreading flour further into his hair. "You're sixteen now. I don't know how to raise a young woman. What prospects will you have? Your mother had everything under control. I cannot do this alone anymore."

Control was an understatement. My mother had a master plan, a plan to see me wed into a good family, one that could secure my future within the upper middle class. She'd cringe if she knew I was working, and in a factory, no less—a job for the coarse and uneducated.

That night I'd dreamt of my mother, screaming my name, pounding her hands bloody on the walls of her hospital room. It was a nightmare I'd had time and again these past few years, but when I awoke, something seemed to have shifted inside me. It started in small ways—random shadows flitting at the edges of my vision, an image flashing through my mind. . . .

Maybe I'm slipping into madness, just like her.

10

The sounds of the factory came rushing back. I closed my eyes and told myself, as I did every morning, *Just focus on your work*. I confronted my day—one task at a time.

Geeno and I logged our names into the time roll and headed toward our welding stations.

My heart warmed as I passed each boy's workbench—the brothers I never had. They made work bearable. Geeno was my little shadow. Tony, the oldest at fourteen, would stick his neck out for anyone. His brother, a newsboy over at South Ferry, got caught stealing, but Tony took the fall, so the court sentenced Tony to a year at the halfway house. Now he was escorted to work daily by the New York House of Refuge coach. Leo and Oscar were both twelve. Leo was a crackerjack-smart black boy, and Oscar, our lovable, mischievous Gypsy.

Just as I feared, Oscar's station was empty. The last time Oscar showed up late, Mr. Malice came down from the perch and bawled him out good. The perch hung like an oversize birdcage eighty feet above our heads. From there, Mr. Malice saw everything.

Each block of welding stations formed a crew. The kids in the other crews didn't talk to us because I ran ours and I was a girl. Besides, we had a black boy and a Gypsy. They shunned us all.

When Mr. Malice first hired Leo, even my crew was hesitant to work with him. I knew how that felt. No one had accepted *me* until I'd proved myself. So I'd volunteered to show Leo the ropes, and on his very first day he came up with a better way of holding the filler rod to produce a tighter seam. With that, he won the boys over—anything to make us look better than the other crews.

On one side of the plant, a giant belt moved pig iron to the new Siemens furnace. On the other side sat Bessie, the massive Bessemer converter. If Cross Street Ironworks was a living, breathing beast, then Bessie was her twenty-ton baby.

She stood on two legs with her potbelly slung low. The pig iron was dropped into her gaping maw. She'd get hotter and hotter, a low rumbling roar coming from inside her gut. We would feel the tension build as the air around her glowed like embers in a fire and the shadows turned purple. It was eerie. Then, impossibly, her immense bulk would flip completely over, blasting an orange volcano of fire and gas thirty feet into the air. Just as abruptly, she'd tip back and expel flowing white-hot liquid steel. She was something to behold, terrible and beautiful. The first time I saw her in action, I had a nightmare of her tearing herself loose, stomping out of the Works, and burying Brooklyn in molten metal.

Pulling on gloves and lowering my goggles, I flared up my arc welder and began to work. Sparks burst from the tip, heating the air so intensely I sucked air through my clenched teeth until my lungs adjusted. I found a strange satisfaction in creating the perfect weld. The speed and angle of the torch had to be just right to reduce slag and eliminate air bubbles in the weld pool. But it was more than that. I permanently joined things together. Nothing could tear them apart.

If only I could unite my own family as easily as I fused metal.

The loud grinding and clanging of machinery kept off normal conversation, but we'd learned to communicate without words. I was about to begin my third piece when I noticed Tony signaling.

Oscar sprinted toward us, pulling on gloves and helmet as he ran. Despite Tony's warning, he didn't see what was coming until it was too late.

Mr. Malice appeared in his path, holding a rod of steel like a baseball bat. I flipped up my goggles and started toward them. Halfway there, I felt Leo grab my arm. "Don't mess with Malice, Ave," he said, his eyes on Oscar.

I hesitated. Maybe Mr. Malice just wanted to scare poor Oscar—a thought pushed from my mind by the sickening crunch of steel on bone. Oscar collapsed, his legs knocked from under him.

Oscar bawled while Mr. Malice's booming voice echoed over the din of the factory. "You wanna come late? I'll teach you what happens when you cost—me—money!" He kicked Oscar with each word.

Oscar was bleeding from his mouth, trying to hunch into as small a ball as possible. I lost all sense of myself. "Stop!" I screamed. "For God's sake, he's only twelve."

Mr. Malice turned on me, his full height like that of a grizzly bear I'd seen at P. T. Barnum's circus. Glistening beads of sweat crowned his bald head. His small eyes, set into folds of fat, seemed amused, which scared me even more.

"When you're here, you belong to me." He spit on the floor. "You lackeys are lucky to have a job, you hear me? There's kids begging me for work every day, and I will not be taken for a fool." He glared at me, his voice a low growl. "Turn around, girl, and get back to your station."

But I couldn't leave Oscar.

"Please, sir. Oscar won't be late again." My eyes stung from the sweat running into them. "I promise."

Mr. Malice turned toward Oscar. "Oh, that's not all he did. Isn't that right, boy? Serves me right for hiring a gypsy." He raised his foot. He was going to kick Oscar's face.

"I said *stop!*" In that instant, everything was illuminated, surrounded by a halo of light, like when you squint into the sun. I clearly saw a dark gray cloud around Mr. Malice. I had no time to decide if it was real or imagined.

My anger compressed into a tight ball in my chest. I wished I could throw it at him like a knife. The air crackled with the sound of breaking ice. The hair on my arms rose up and a thunderous roar enveloped me. It felt as if something erupted from within me, cracking open my ribs.

The explosion threw us both back. Mr. Malice landed against a trolley loaded with tie rods, knocking it over. The deafening sound of metal crashing into metal reverberated through the factory. I hit the floor, my head smacking hard on the concrete, my last thought to wonder who'd tell my father I was dead.

CHAPTER TWO
THE NIGHTMARE

I opened my eyes to a hovering circle of concerned faces as all hell broke loose around me. The tie rods had fallen on top of the boss. The boys, seeing I was not dead, rushed to Oscar's side. He was still crumpled on the floor screaming, clutching his legs.

Two runners were dispatched, one to the livery for a horse cart to get Oscar home, and the other to fetch the ambulance coach to take Mr. Malice to the hospital. He lay unconscious amid the wreckage.

Tony reached out and pulled me up from the floor. As soon as I was on my feet, the foreman we called Scarface marched over and yelled, "Back to work!" He pointed the way, but the factory spun around me.

Tony seized me as my body swayed to one side. "Yes, sir," I

said. My skull felt like it had been cracked in half. "It's just that I'm seeing two of you, sir."

He swiped the air and huffed. "Ah, get on home, then. You'll damage the equipment. Don't come back 'til Monday morn, but mind you, come with yer head on straight or don't bother coming back a'tall."

"Yes, sir," I murmured.

"Either way," he added, "I'm docking yer wages for time off."

Tony was permitted fifteen minutes to walk me home. As we passed people in the street, flashes of light blurred my vision and sent pain stabbing through my head. I lowered my eyes, relying on Tony to guide me.

"Something must've set off that blast," Tony said. "Avery, are you listening to me?" He shifted, supporting my weight. "Try to remember."

I was trying, but my brain was spinning with thoughts that made no sense. "I'm sorry. I heard you. But my head feels like it's in a vise."

"We need to know what caused that explosion." He slowed his pace to match my dragging feet. "Malice is gonna blame us."

"I don't know what happened, Tony." It was not a lie, although I did feel I was somehow responsible. He shook his head, clearly disappointed. I kept my gaze on the street. "Did you notice anything?" I asked, wondering if he'd seen the fog gathering around Mr. Malice. "A flash, or smoke, maybe?"

"Nope. Nothing. The blast was huge, like the air was charged. No smoke though." We wove our way through push-cart vendors hawking their wares along the street. Stepping deftly, Tony added, "So long as Malice is in the hospital, that louse Scarface is in charge."

A boy raced forward, almost knocking into us. "Hey, watch it, chump!" Tony yelled.

I glanced at the boy and immediately regretted it. An image shot through my mind like a shard of glass, too fast for me to make out. Then another, from a man staring at me as he walked by. I cringed and covered my eyes, stumbling over my own feet. *These people must think me a drunkard.*

"You okay?" Tony tightened his grip on my arm.

I nodded. Tony was right; Roland Malice was bad enough, but Scarface was even worse. A power-hungry Irishman, Scarface had been at the Works so long his face had taken on the look of pitted metal, long scars searing his skin like jagged welds.

"You should rest." Tony sighed. "Can't believe Scarface gave you today and tomorrow off. Wish I didn't have to work on Saturday."

"You heard him. He's worried about the equipment, not me. Besides, he's not paying me."

"That piker will skin my beans, too, if I don't hurry." When we reached my building, he said, "I got to get back," and turned to go.

"Wait." I shielded my eyes with my hand. "Send for me if anyone's taking heat for this. Oh, and Tony, what did Mr. Malice mean when he said that wasn't all Oscar did?"

"I don't know, but whatever it was, Oscar sure paid for it good." Tony left me at my door and took off running back to the factory. I unlocked the shop and went inside. My father was out. On Fridays he mined the salvage yards for parts for his inventions.

My mind swirled with questions. I remembered the haze of darkness around Mr. Malice and the powerful surge within my body. *Did I somehow cause the explosion?* It didn't seem possible, but I'd felt like Bessie erupting. And the walk home was torture, the visions erratic.

I wished I could ask my mother about *her* visions. A long time ago, she'd tried to tell me. She'd been in bed with a cloth tied over her eyes. She often did this, said it kept her from "seeing things." In public she wore small spectacles with darkened lenses. Weeks earlier, the local Brooklyn Heights doctor had diagnosed her with "female hysteria" because she was prone to dizzy spells and melancholia.

Mother had asked me to sit with her. I was glad her eyes were covered. Sometimes when she looked at me, it was like she saw right through me.

"Avery, tell me about school. Is that nice Mrs. Bell helping you with your elocution?"

Earlier that day, I'd refused to read aloud in front of the

class with everyone staring, whispering hurtful things at me like *witch* or *devil's daughter*. Mrs. Bell had lashed my knuckles with a ruler.

"Mrs. Bell says I'm quite good at reciting Longfellow," I'd lied.

My mother had lifted the cloth and raised one eyebrow at me. I'd put my hands behind my back to hide the red welts.

"Avery, I think it's time I tell you about my visions. You need to understand what I'm going through." She'd pushed herself up onto one elbow. "Are children teasing you again?"

My cheeks flushed as I'd jumped up. "Yes. They tease me. Because of you. They say you're a mad witch." I'd run out the door, slamming it behind me. She'd never mentioned the visions again.

I felt the hole in my chest expand. *And now, I'm becoming the lunatic.*

Shrugging off my soot-stained jacket, I pulled my work gloves from the pocket and inspected them for holes. Small ember burns, but nothing I couldn't repair. These gloves, my helmet, and my goggles were my only protection. I had to take good care of them. Thankfully, nothing had been ruined in the explosion.

The thought of going back to work made me shaky inside. But I had to. And when I did, I'd either get beaten or fired. I wasn't sure which was worse. Welding was the only thing I knew how to do. I'd been at the Works since Father and I lost everything, and I was the best welder they had—now that Alexander was gone, anyway. Maybe that would count for something. Besides, if any blame was coming down on the boys, I had to be there.

I collapsed onto my bed fully clothed, hoping to escape my own thoughts. My head ached and my eyelids grew heavy.

I was a little girl hiding under the sofa. I watched Mama's lace-up boots pacing back and forth. She turned to answer a rapid knock on the door, the skirt of her dress sweeping over my arm. A man in a cloak and top hat entered the parlor, bringing with him a cold breeze that swirled around my legs. I tucked my bare feet under the hem of my nightgown.

A series of metallic clicks sounded—Papa's clock, about to begin its on-the-hour routine. This clock had a little Mama, a little Papa, and a little me, spinning in an endless ring-around-the-rosy. I counted the chimes. Eleven.

The man placed his hat and gloves on the table. His face reminded me of mine when I'd been crying: red-rimmed puffy eyes, blotchy cheeks. He folded his cloak over the arm of the sofa. Something concealed within its folds clunked against the wooden frame.

"Madame Kohl," he said, bowing his head.

"Mr. Edwards, what can I do for you?" she said.

I was supposed to be sleeping, not spying on Mama.

The man took a shaky breath. "Thank you for seeing me at this hour. It's about my wife."

"Please. Come sit." She motioned to two chairs near the fireplace. While he settled into one, she poured tea.

He cleared his throat. "I don't know what I am to do." He picked up the teacup, but his hand shook so much the spoon rattled wildly. He put the cup back on the tray without a taste.

Mama sat, hands folded in her lap. She looked pretty in her dinner gown, hair piled high.

The man shifted uncomfortably in his seat. "I believe she has . . ." He spoke to the floor. "How can I say . . . been unfaithful to me." He coughed as if the words hurt his throat. "I love her still. But my good name . . . Madame Kohl, you must understand—we have children. A man in my position . . ." His voice trailed off.

Mama leaned forward and took a slow sip of tea. Then she tilted her head and said, "Mr. Edwards, let us open our eyes and see, really see. Shall we?"

"But how? I heard you could help me, but now that I'm here, I don't know how you possibly can."

"Did you bring a photograph?"

The man removed a tintype from his breast pocket and handed it to her. I wished so badly I could see it.

Peeling off her lace gloves, Mama laid the photo on her open palm. She placed her other hand over it. It was so quiet I held my breath for fear they would hear it.

Their eyes met, and it was as if the man and Mama were seeing something that I could not. His eyebrows went up and then down. It was no more than a minute, but everything had changed. He sat up straighter.

"Ahhh." He nodded. "I thought I would go mad. I thought I must defend her honor, but now I see I was wrong. She is innocent and I am a fool. How can I ever repay you, Madame? Will you accept a note?"

"I do not want your money, Mr. Edwards." She stood, smoothing her skirt, and glanced at the photograph before handing it back to him. "She's very young, your wife. Be kind to her. Now, alas, it is getting late." She rolled her gloves back on.

"Yes, yes," he said. "I'll be on my way."

At the door he gathered his things, took her hand, and brushed his lips against the lace. Mama opened the door. He started out, then turned back to face her.

"I am ashamed of what I might have done." He reached into his cloak and removed a small gun. My heart skipped a beat. I'd seen Papa's Civil War musket, but this one was small enough to fit into my own hand. "I . . . I cannot go home with this."

Mama nodded. Without another word, he placed it on the table, donned his hat, and left.

She stared at the gun. The only sound was the *tick, tick, tick* of the second hand. My mother lifted the tiny weapon and brought it slowly to her temple. I wanted to call to her, but my throat squeezed shut. Then her eyes opened wide. She dropped her arm and held the gun with two fingers as if it was disgusting, as if it was one of Papa's oil rags. With her other hand, she pressed her hair back in to place and dabbed her face with a handkerchief. After she left, I heard her toss the gun in the rubbish bin in the kitchen.

I took a deep breath, my mind full of questions I was too afraid to ask. Sliding out, I ran to the window to see if the man was still there.

He was not. I squinted my eyes at the dark. One shadow shifted, just slightly, just enough to catch the circle of amber light from the gas lamp. Just enough for me to see its face.

It stood out stark white under long straggly hair. Small ratty eyes looked right at me, one of them catching the light oddly. The pointy nose tipped up on the end, like that of a skeleton. Its thin red mouth cut across its ghostly skin. I gasped, knowing even then that I would have nightmares of that white face. I was about to scream, but it raised a finger to its lips, like Mama did to shush me.

I jerked open my eyes, inhaling sharply. My mouth had gone dry. The nightmare felt lodged in my throat, choking me. My father had not returned, and every click of a gear and hammer of a chime made me jump. Dark shadows crouched in the corners of the shop.

I had to get out.

CHAPTER THREE
INK

I charged up the steep stairs, six floors to the roof of our building, and gulped the fresh air. The cool breeze soothed my searing headache and cleared away the sharpness of my dream.

Although Father was still out, he probably knew something had happened. Any time there was an accident at the factory, a whistle blasted out over the neighborhood, taunting spouses who lived in fear of its piercing sound. With all the moving machinery and scorching fire, it was not uncommon for a man to go down, but not the children. The welding area was considered safe. School would've been safer, of course, but no one liked to talk about that.

I missed school. I'd been foolish enough to think I might be the first in my family to go to college. My dream of attending Vassar women's college in the Hudson River Valley had slipped through my fingers like boiled bacon grease. Both an education and the security of an affluent husband were out of my reach now. The education was the loss I felt the hardest. I hadn't realized at the time that our social standing was so shaky or the slide into poverty so slick.

When money got tight, my father took me out of St. Ann's, where wealthy Brooklyn Heights children studied. As Grace made perfectly clear this morning, I no longer belonged to that world.

Then Father moved us to the tenements. We rented a one-room shop, divided into storefront and sleeping areas, in Vinegar Hill, the area named after a distant battle in Ireland. To me, it was just a sour taste in my mouth. My father hung a large clock outside the shop, and a sign saying New and Repairs, but nowhere did it say our name.

Somehow, the wounded soldiers found us anyway. Now Father spent more time working on his inventions than on selling clocks. His latest creation was a mechanical eye that could restore sight to Union soldiers who had lost one of their own. And every time one of his war comrades showed up, he stayed out drinking all night. I knew he never charged them for the gadgets he created, as if we could afford to be so generous.

I clenched my teeth. His kindness didn't bother me nearly as much as his obsession with a secret project, one he spent the rest of his time working on. Whenever I asked him about it, he evaded my questions. When I was little, his workshop in our old house was a place of marvel and wonder to me. Here, it was a mystery in the basement boiler room, kept locked away from all eyes, including mine.

Why can't he get a real job? I felt my blood heating, making my head throb all the more. I lifted the cord around my neck, absently playing with the trinkets I'd collected over the years. Among them were gears from my father's menagerie clock, the key to our old house, a silver ring from my friend Khan, and the *C* and *K* from my mother's Remington typewriter—her initials.

Looking out over the city from the roof of our building usually calmed me, the height a welcome respite from the dirty, crowded streets below. But tonight fear raced around my aching skull. *What is happening to me? Am I to end up cloistered away in the Tombs, like my mother?*

What I knew of the Tombs was no more than most. It was a notoriously awful prison for the worst criminals of the city. The basement housed an equally horrid lunatic asylum. The asylum's security officers wore masks that resembled the head of a crow, for no reason I could imagine other than to instill fear. It was cruel, to say the least. People were superstitious about crows, especially the old folks, who spit over their left shoulder at the sight of one. My father said it was stuff and nonsense.

A rhyme about crows suddenly came to me, one that Grace and I used to chant while we were skipping rope.

One for sorrow,
Two for mirth,
Three for a funeral,

Four for birth,
Five for heaven,
Six for hell,
Seven, you'll see the devil himself.

I'd never noticed the dark nature of our words. It was just a song we all sang. A chill ran over my spine, and I rubbed my arms briskly. Thank goodness for Seraphine. She kept crows from nesting anywhere near our building.

I took a deep breath and focused on the view.

To the east was the navy yard, tall masts in the river, abandoned dirigibles in the field, ribs exposed like dead dinosaurs. I wondered if one of the crumpled heaps was the balloon my father had piloted in the Civil War. To the west, the sun set through the construction of the Brooklyn Bridge, emblazoning it, as if the metal were still molten. South—the ever-growing thicket of buildings crowding the steeple of St. Ann's. And in front of me? I gazed past my work boots, propped up on the parapet, to the island of Manhattan, where my mother was imprisoned. It was beautiful from afar, but unless you were wealthy and lived uptown among the grand estates and wide boulevards, it was a pit of depravity and filth.

If only my mother had kept her visions to herself, the crows might not have taken her. Three years she'd been gone. My eyes burned and I felt the familiar ache inside my chest. My temples pulsed as the pain spread behind my forehead. I had to make this stop. *If I go mad, who will take care of my father?*

Seraphine chirped at me from her sheltered roost, bringing me back to the rooftop panorama. "I know, Sera," I whispered. "It's beautiful, isn't it?"

The view was the one thing I loved about Vinegar Hill. The river glinted shimmery gold. The nearby bridge tower seemed to belong more to heaven than to earth. A forest of sailships swayed and clanged in front of the blocky Manhattan skyline spiked by church steeples and cupolas. The tallest of them was Trinity Church. Its soaring spire and gilded cross welcomed sailors as warmly as any lighthouse beacon.

But most of all, I loved the airships. Tied up for the night, they hovered above the city like sleeping mammoths, the green glow of their mercury-vapor lamps visible in the night sky. I counted fourteen airships. They came in from all over the world. I imagined climbing aboard the steam-powered *Cloud Voyager*, the biggest, and setting sail for the West Indies or the Panama coast. I wished for somewhere warm, somewhere with color, away from the grimy gray buildings and congested streets of New York. Out there in the dusk, maybe my mother had the same wish.

The flapping of laundry lines being towed in rose from the narrow alley between tenement buildings, rusty pulleys squealing in protest, echoed by the buzz of women's voices as they caught up on the day. At least the reek of the air shaft seemed stifled by the cold. Built to bring light to the lower levels, it was used instead as a garbage chute to nowhere, and was filled nearly to the roof. Since we had a shop, our windows looked onto the street. Our neighbors, though, had fetid fluid leaking into their apartments.

I sensed someone behind me before I heard any sound. I spun around, nearly falling off the wooden bench onto the gravel rooftop.

"Khan. Why do you always sneak up on me?" I let out my breath. Thank goodness no visions invaded my mind when I looked at him.

Khan laughed. "Because I can, Little Bird." When we were kids, he thought my name meant birdcage. The nickname lingered.

Seraphine shrieked and hopped along the low wall. She loved Khan. He took something small and dead out of his pocket and tossed it to her. Quickly, she snared it with her sharp beak, then, gripping it with one claw, ripped it apart, swallowing it piece by piece.

He held up an oil lamp and studied my face, then carefully placed the lamp on the end of the bench. I hadn't realized it had gotten so dark.

Khan continued to stare at me, his intensity unnerving. "Why do you hide up here?" he asked, in his slow, deep voice.

"Whatever do you mean, sir? I am not hiding." I swept my arm toward the expansive view of the city. "I'm surveying my kingdom." When he didn't laugh, I looked across the water, in the direction of the Tombs. "I don't know. I can think up here."

He removed his hat, the worn brown Stetson he always

wore. "Heard the whistle earlier. Someone told me there was an explosion. I came as soon as I could. Are you all right?"

"It's . . . it's nothing," I stammered. "Banged my head pretty hard, is all." I rubbed the painful lump under my hair. "Good thing for my helmet."

"There's something else bothering you. Isn't there?" He spoke to me as if I were a child, even though he was only a few years older than me. "I know you too well, Avery. Tell me."

When I didn't answer, Khan sat down beside me and took my hand, his thumb absently massaging my palm. Down in the streets, he would never touch a white girl. But I'd known him my whole life, and up here on the roof we could be ourselves. Khan was my closest friend, really my only friend, other than the boys at work. A wave of pain cut through me as I thought of the disgust in Grace's eyes that morning.

Khan's full name was Khaniferre Soliman. At the Battle of Fort Pillow, Tennessee, in 1864, my father, a Civil War Balloon Corps aeronaut, saw a group of black slaves being gunned down as they tried to flee. So he disobeyed direct orders and landed his balloon in enemy territory. He'd rescued little Khan and his grandmother, but the rest of their family was killed. My father's discharge papers did not mention them or the black Union soldier he'd also managed to get to safety, only the fact that the balloon had been damaged beyond repair. In recognition of his bravery and heroism, my father lost his military pension and his right leg, shattered by Confederate fire aimed at the low-flying balloon.

Once, I asked my father if he regretted his decision. He'd placed his hand on his metal leg and said, "Had I left them to die, Avery, had I watched and done nothing, then I would've lost my soul instead of my leg."

My father had survived ground fighting in many of the war's bloodiest battles—Shiloh, Antietam, and Stones River. Ironically, when he joined the Balloon Corps, he thought he'd be safer. In his typically positive way, he told me a benefit of losing his leg was that he was spared fighting at Gettysburg, where over fifty thousand men had died.

I traced my finger over the black ink tattoo on Khan's muscular forearm. "This one new?" The complex design spiraled and swirled, connecting seamlessly with the rest of the patterns on his arm. They disappeared under the pushed-up sleeve of his muslin work shirt.

"Um-hum." He looked out over the river toward the city as the gas lamps sputtered to life, outlining the streets in a beautiful and intricate pattern—rather like his tattoos.

"She plan to cover your whole body?" His grandmother was systematically tattooing Khan in the ways of the old world. Among his people—descendants of the black pharaohs of ancient Egypt—he would have been a prince. With the knives he wore crisscrossing his body, he looked more like a rogue than royalty.

"It is who I am," he said.

Must be nice, I thought, *to know who you are*. These last few years I felt like I was living someone else's life, someone who scrounged for every penny, whose hands were dry and cracked from doing the wash and the cooking and the cleaning after welding all day. Someone who'd lost her mother and seemed increasingly disconnected from her father. And worst of all, someone who had, quite possibly, inherited her mother's madness.

I laid my head on Khan's shoulder. "Remember when we used to pretend you were Paul Revere and you'd flash a lantern at me from your house?" My old bedchamber window in Brooklyn Heights had a direct view of the wharf where he lived with his grandmother. "I wonder if I could see it from here, too."

"What does it matter?" Khan said. "I am not Paul Revere." As if he'd made his point, he stood, pulling me with him. "Come on, you're shivering."

Somewhere along the way, the streets had hardened Khan. I understood; it was survival of the fittest out there. Still, I missed the Khan who told me magical stories of his faraway ancestral land, tales passed down to him by his grandmother.

Sighing, I ran my hands over Seraphine's silky feathers and placed her on her roost. Before we headed down, I turned back to Khan. His brown skin gleamed in the moonlight. His mane of hair, braided into long thin tubes, brushed past his shoulders, and his golden-brown eyes, lion's eyes, made me feel warm and safe. I could trust him with my secret.

"Khan, I must ask you something." He'd known my mother

as well as anyone had. "Do you remember the things folks said about my mother? How they whispered about her, called her a witch?" I looked down at my feet as he waited for me to continue. "How after she was gone, no one mentioned her name, as if she'd never existed?"

As I spoke, other painful memories bobbed to the surface of my mind, like dead fish in a bucket. I recalled the shopkeepers' sympathetic stares and the hushed whispers of the neighbors. I felt tears on my face and swiped them away.

"I remember, Avery," Khan said.

"Well, I . . . I think I might have what she has. I don't even know what it is, but I'm scared." He was silent, listening. I wanted him to tell me I was wrong, that I was imagining it. He didn't. "What if . . ." I took a deep breath. "What if *I'm* going mad, too?"

There. My secret was out. I almost flinched, as if the crow men could swoop out of the sky and snatch me from the roof.

Khan looked at me for a long while. "I was beginning to wonder if you'd turned to stone in there." His smile lifted me momentarily, but my heart did feel like stone. He took my face in his hands, wiping my tears with his thumbs. "My *ouma* says fear itself does not make one weak, only the denial of it."

This was the old Khan talking now. His hands were warm on my face. I looked up at him, the gold of his eyes dancing in the flickering light. My breath caught in my throat. His face was close. I let my gaze fall to his full mouth, the strong jaw shadowed with stubble.

When did my friend become so handsome? As kids we'd pretended one day we would marry, but I'd never really thought of him as anything other than a friend. *So, why is my skin tingling under his touch?*

Distracted, I removed his hands from my face and went over to the parapet wall. I rested my chin on my fists and stared out into the darkness. The hour after twilight, when night cloaked the streets and the lamplighter had not yet made it to our area on his rounds, the shadows were as thick and black as coal tar. They oozed into crevices and puddled in the alleyways. The only light came flickering warily from the windows facing the street.

"What brought these feelings on now?" Khan asked.

"It started around my birthday," I said. "I . . . I began to see things. After the explosion today . . . it was dreadful, worse than ever. I know this sounds absurd, but I fear I may have somehow caused the explosion. And this afternoon I had the strangest dream, one I think I've had before. There was a hideous man. He—"

I was about to describe the dream to Khan, but the words caught in my throat. Something shifted in the shadows below.

CHAPTER FOUR
A COIN FOR A BOY

I fixed my eyes to the spot where the darkness seemed to lengthen into a pointy beak-like shape. The hair on my arms rose. "Khan," I whispered. "Come here. Do you see anything across the street?"

He leaned over, squinting. "No. There's nothing there."

I pointed. "Near that alley."

He shook his head. "Avery, this dream you had is giving you paranoia."

Whistling drifted up from the street and a little bobbing light approached: the lamplighter. He lifted a long pole with a wick on its end, touching it to the gas lamp. *Poof*, the lamp sprung to life. The shadows shrank back as if afraid of the light. There was nothing there.

"I could have sworn . . ." I rubbed my strained eyes. "Never mind." Now that the darkness was dispelled, people emerged from their homes. "Thank you for coming to check on me, Khan. What would I do without you?" His friendship for me had never wavered. Once again I recalled my encounter with Grace. If I'd been dressed in finery, would she have treated me differently? I was the same person on the inside, wasn't I?

"Will you be all right alone?" He pulled me into a hug. I felt the muscles of his chest tighten.

"I'm fine," I said, leaning into his embrace, although I trembled when we made our way down the stairs.

"I have business in Manhattan tomorrow, but I'll come by again soon."

I watched through the window as Khan left. Then I lit all the oil lamps, chasing away the shadows within the shop, but even that did not calm my nerves. To keep busy, I wound the clocks and organized my father's tools, swept the ashes around the stove, and wiped spots off the glasses. With nothing left to do, I picked through leftover chicken pie. And still Father did not return.

The ticking of the clocks seemed to grow louder with every passing moment. I decided I did *not* want to stay here alone. My father's favorite tavern was only a few blocks away, and this was not the first time I'd have to persuade him to come home. But it bothered me that I was afraid. I was acting like a child. Khan was right—the nightmare had shaken me.

I grabbed a coat and hat to hide my hair. Then I snuffed the lamps, locked the shop, and headed north. The night was crisp and clear. Coarse salty air gusted from the river, chilling the tip of my nose. I dug my hands into my pockets, keeping my head down as I walked. It wouldn't do for a girl to be out by herself this time of night, at least not a respectable one.

The streets of Vinegar Hill degenerated with each hour that passed. Barroom brawls often tumbled out onto the sidewalk, and sailors, sunburned and intoxicated, staggered into the streets. Although Manhattan had the most notorious gangs, here in Brooklyn we had ruthless river pirates who made the nearby docks a treacherous place at night.

I walked in the shadows, skirting the amber pools of light from the gas lamps. People ignored me; probably thought I was one of the homeless who huddled in doorways and hunted through rubbish bins. Darkness offered obscurity. I laughed at myself. *One moment I'm afraid of the shadows, the next I'm seeking them out.*

At the intersection of Plymouth and Pearl, I peered around the corner and sucked in my breath. The monstrous Brooklyn Bridge tower loomed above like a cathedral in the sky, the moon shining through its gothic arches. On one side of the street were two pubs overflowing with sailors, dirigible pilots, and stevedores from the navy yard. On the other side was the new opium den, brass doors flanked by onion-shaped burners, smoke infusing the air with an exotic odor.

Word on the street was, the government was soon going to

prohibit Chinese immigration. Of course, this made the dens more popular. After all, who would feed the addiction if they shut down? I was glad my father did not go there, but I didn't understand the ban; I'd seen the massive arm and torch of a statue that was being built to welcome all immigrants. Industry certainly seemed to be booming with the available labor, and neighborhoods flourished when immigrants moved in, opening shops and ethnic markets.

The doorman at Sweeney's Saloon recognized me, despite my hat and coat. He tipped his flat cap and spoke in his thick Irish brogue. "Me eyes must be playing tricks on me. How are ye, Miss Avery? Ain't been here in a while, now, have ye?"

"Good evening, Mr. Craig. I'm trying to find my father. Have you seen him?"

"Aye, I did. Ye just missed him." He pointed. "Headed up the street with that bloody rough-looking black friend of his."

"You must mean Mr. Thorn."

He nodded, his scowl revealing exactly what he thought.

"He looks intimidating," I said, "but Mr. Thorn's a good man."

"Think what ye like, but anyone packing steel and lead like that's looking for trouble."

It was no use arguing and no use looking for my father, either. If he was with Jeremiah Thorn, who knows where he'd be? I thanked Mr. Craig and turned back toward home, the walk feeling longer now.

"Mind yerself out there," Mr. Craig called after me. "If he comes back, I'll tell'm yer scouting for him."

I walked fast, eager for bed. I still had a headache, but at least I wasn't seeing things.

Halfway home, a tall coach, pulled by four black horses, clopped by me. It came to a stop ahead. I glanced behind, then back toward the coach. The block was deserted except for a group of boys squatting around a tin can, flames licking up toward their fingerless gloves. Acting on instinct, I ducked into a darkened doorway. The horses huffed plumes of cold mist and scraped their hooves impatiently.

Hair rose on the back of my neck. Something seemed strange about the coach. It was unlike any I'd seen before. The driver, perched on a high seat up front, wore a hooded cloak instead of the typical livery. But it was the exterior cladding that was most curious. The coach appeared to be made of riveted black metal and had wheels cast of iron. No wonder it required four horses instead of the usual two.

The door opened. A well-dressed man in suit and derby emerged. I pressed back deeper into shadow. The man stepped toward the boys, who looked up, ready to flee. They were glued in place by a purse jingling in the man's palm, restraining them better than if he'd held a gun.

"Come on over here, boys," he said, holding the purse up. "Who wants to earn a fifty-cent piece?"

They glanced around as if unsure, but I knew what they

were thinking. That much money could buy a pound of mutton chop and a dozen eggs.

"I am a doctor. We are testing citizens for a rare psychological condition," he continued. "It only takes a moment. Doesn't hurt at all."

The tallest of the bunch strode over. "I'll do it," he said.

The man pocketed the purse and reached into the coach, pulling out a metal contraption. He fitted it onto the boy's head. The rest gathered close to watch. I couldn't tell what it did, but after a moment the man told the boy he was done and removed it.

"Where's my coin?" The boy held out his hand.

"You'll get it. After all of you are tested."

The boy pushed one of the others forward. "Come on, do it," he said. "Don't be a chicken. I didn't even feel it."

They lined up. One by one, the man tested them, saying nothing. When he was finished, he put the machine away. I heard him talking to someone concealed within the darkness of the coach. "Yes, sir," he said. "Worked just like you said it would." Then he counted out seven coins from his purse.

But there were eight boys.

He threw his arm in the air, tossing the coins away from him. "Thank you very much, boys. Here you go!"

The coins rolled over the cobblestones. The boys, whooping and hollering, clambered over each other to find them in the dark. They did not see the man grip the arm of one of the boys, or hear him mutter roughly, "You're coming with us."

"No! I won't!" The boy kicked and thrashed. His hat fell off his tight curly hair.

I was about to yell out when two more men jumped from the coach. The boy went rigid, as did I. The men wore black-beaked leather masks with round lenses fitted into the eyeholes, like morbid crows, like the men who took my mother.

Some of the boys looked up then, and the tall one yelled, "Hey! What do you think you're doing?" As he spoke, he pulled a knife from his belt.

The doctor turned toward him. "Your friend has a condition that requires hospitalization. Here's his money." He tossed another coin at the tall boy. "He won't be needing it."

While he spoke, the men in masks seized the boy, lifting him by his arms. Coming to his senses, the boy opened his mouth as if to scream, but one of the guards clamped a hand over it and shoved him into the coach. The doctor climbed in after them, and the driver whipped the horses. With a jolt, the coach surged forward. The boys jumped back, eyes wide. The tall one bent down, furtively pocketing the extra coin, while the others stared after the coach, terror written across their faces.

On the side of the coach, the curtain slid back. A head poked though the open window to glance back at the boys. The face was illuminated by the coach's lantern. My breath caught in my throat. Something began to creep inside me, a mashing of imaginings and memories. I felt disoriented, dizzy, the same feeling I got when waking from a dream and not knowing what was real.

It's him. It was the man outside my window when I was young, his white skin and straggly hair unmistakable. The man from my nightmares.

CHAPTER FIVE
ABSINTHE

I couldn't sleep. His face was engraved on the inside of my eyelids, and a cold numbness cloaked me like a sticky, invisible veil. I shivered in my bed, staring at the door.

After the coach left, I'd run home, thoughts spinning around and around my brain. The man with the white face was with the men in crow masks. *Does that mean he also works at the Tombs?*

The inner workings of the Tombs were a mystery to me. My father had been inside. He'd visited my mother exactly six times, and each time I'd pleaded with him to take me along. He'd always refused, saying it was too dangerous for me. And where was he now? I'd likely caused an explosion, for goodness' sake. Whatever was happening to me was more hazardous than going into a hospital to see my mother, even one as vile as the Tombs.

I must go see her, I resolved. *She's the only one who can explain these visions to me.* This time I would not take no for an answer. *I will make him take me tomorrow, and if he refuses, I will go myself.* I had no work tomorrow and, unfortunately, neither did he.

My muscles tensed at a scraping sound outside. The door to the shop banged open. I leapt up, snatching my knife. A figure stumbled in, a string of curses giving away his identity as he collided with the furniture. He rummaged around the cupboards, looking for something—his pipe, no doubt. I let out my breath. Through clenched teeth, I said, "It's on the sideboard," even though I did not want to help him.

"Oh, hello, love," he slurred. "Wash you doing up?"

"You *must* be joking," I said.

The curtain screening my bed was pinned up from corner to corner, creating a diagonal slice of moonlight on the floor. The shop clocks ticked and twanged like dogs wagging their tails, as if they were happy to see him. I felt like telling them all to hush up.

"Joke? Hmm, I did hear a funny one—"

"Pop! Where were you?" I yelled. "I went to Sweeney's looking for you. You're drunk and I need to talk to you—it's important!" I thought he'd be worried about the accident at the ironworks, that he'd be worried about *me*. Instead, I'd spent the night wondering where *he* was.

"Whoa, whoa." He waved his hands about. "Jush give me second."

"Pop, please tell me you didn't spend all our money." I crossed my fingers.

"Nah, we got plenty . . . we got each other." I saw his dark silhouette, arms outstretched toward me, and knew he was smiling. It softened my resolve to be mad at him. I knew why he did it. I knew the anger and helplessness that burned inside him. On top of that, tonight was his and Mother's wedding anniversary. I knew all that, but it was no excuse to get stinking drunk.

A match flared in the darkness, then the even, puffing flicker of a pipe. Sweet, dark, caramel-cherry smoke slithered by my nostrils. Another match and the kerosene lamp sparked to life. He looked terrible, hat askew, hair sticking out. When we used to go out, ladies acted frivolously around him. It wasn't just his handsome face; it was his boyish charm. How I hated to see him this way. His bright blue eyes were watery. His rugged face, so dashing, battle scars and all, now seemed worn and weary.

He sat hard onto the sofa, awkwardly trying to remove his prosthetic leg. I noticed he was wearing the one the government had issued him after the war, not the one he'd made himself. This one was a primitive three-section chunk of metal that never fit him correctly, creating sores on his thigh stump. His own design was a multi-geared mechanical work of art.

"I thought you didn't use that one anymore." I put down my knife and went to help him. I should've let him struggle.

He leaned back and spun his hat through the air, somehow landing it perfectly on top of his tallest clock. "Thank you, sweets. Jush wait till you see my other one." He hiccuped. "I'm making some modifications."

Kneeling in front of him, I undid the leather straps. The leg clanged to the floor.

"Pop, I saw something tonight . . . something terrible." I closed my eyes, recalling the awful scene. *That poor little boy.* If they had discovered my hiding place, it could just as easily have been me. My father took my hand, listening intently as I continued. "I saw a black metal coach pull up to a group of boys. A doctor said he wanted to test them. When he finished, two men in crow masks jumped out and grabbed one of the boys. They took him."

"No! A young boy?" His blue eyes opened wide.

"There was someone else in the coach—horrible looking. I've seen his face before. I . . . I thought it was a nightmare, but it must have been real. I remember him looking up at the window of our old house. I think I was no more than six. . . ." I took a deep breath, trailing off. Maybe smacking my head had loosened something in my brain.

"You're safe now, Avery. Come here." He pulled me to him, wrapping his arms around me. His voice sobered momentarily. "If they are trolling the streets, we must be careful."

My shoulders shuddered. Next to him on the sofa, I let myself relax into his strong embrace. "Yes," I whispered. "But who is he? If he's the same man I saw when I was little, then he must have watched Mother for years before she was taken."

"I wish I knew," Father said. "Never seen him at the hospital."

"Pop, they were testing for a . . . a psychological condition. What do you think they meant? Do you think the boy they carried off is like Mother?"

He leaned back, closing his eyes. "I honestly don't know."

His breath grew heavy. He was falling asleep fully dressed. I smelled the alcohol on his breath, like anise and camphor.

"You said you gave up absinthe, Pop." The green liquid made him absolutely dysfunctional. "I know it's your and Mother's annivers—"

His eyes opened a slit. "Oh no, you don't," he said, patting my cheek. "Lesh not talk about your mother anymore. Lesh talk about you. How's my sweet Avery? Every day you look more like her, you know."

"I thought you didn't want to talk about her?"

"No." He turned away, but not before I saw his eyes well up. "I don't."

I stood and helped him off with his frock coat and single boot, as my mind went back to another anniversary.

I was ten years old. My father told us to don our finest clothing. I actually wore a dress, even though I hated dresses. I could hardly move in them, let alone run. I didn't understand why girls were forced to wear them, although my mother looked beautiful in her long gray gown, touring hat tied under her chin. And Father was positively dapper in a tweed suit and derby.

"Pop, do you remember when we went to Philadelphia for

the Centennial Expo?" I asked, as I hung his coat by the door.

"Hmm, 1876, your first time on an airship," he mumbled.

My father had booked passage on the sleekest airship I'd ever seen, the *SS Hollister*. We rode to Philadelphia in style. It was the most magical day of my life. A thirteen-acre building of glass and steel, Machinery Hall, trembled when the towering Corliss steam engine on display was fired up, its thirty-foot flywheel spinning with ease. We saw things we never thought possible, like Alexander Graham Bell's telephonic device, which allowed conversation with someone far, far away; the Otis Brothers steam elevator lift; the forty-two-foot-tall arm of the forthcoming Statue of Liberty; and a slice of a fifteen-inch-diameter cable that John Roebling said would support a sixteen-hundred-foot suspension bridge, the longest in the world. I laughed. "Remember how we refused to believe a bridge could span from here to Manhattan Island?"

"I shtill don't believe it." He smiled. "By jiminy, I haven't thought of that in years. Remember the food? We ate ourselves sick."

My mouth watered at the thought of the fat German sausages, of steaming Turkish lamb stew and drippy caramel apples. Both of us quieted as the smells and sounds of the day washed through our memories.

On the ride home, Father had made us a promise, a promise I stupidly believed. He swore he would one day build his own airship and we would explore the world together, a family adventure.

"Avery, I'm sorry about . . ." He shook his head slowly. "About everything. You deserve better."

It was another moment of clarity in his drunken stupor. Now I was the one with teary eyes. I felt sorry, too. Sometimes I felt like I was the adult and he, the child. But I loved him that way. And before she was taken, so had Mother. He'd never been one to worry about money for coal or food. He was content to tinker away, making exquisite clocks for people far and wide. He told me that before the Civil War, he'd even been commissioned to design a clock for the Central Park Menagerie. It would've been marvelous. He'd built a model. Different animals popped out each hour of the day, waltzed around, and then climbed a ladder to a hatch above the twelve.

The war put an end to all that magic. The little metal animals danced in the shop until dust choked their gears and rust hardened their movement, the unfortunate zebra forever stuck with his rear end poking out of the hatch.

For some reason, I got it in my head that it was a countdown. As each of my father's clocks broke down, he and my mother moved further away from me. He'd clearly lost the will to maintain them, or was he intentionally letting them go, as he'd been forced to do with my mother? I bit my lip. *He's lost hope.* I had to make things right before the rest of the clocks stopped ticking forever. I looked around the shop. Twelve left.

Once again I recalled the young boy taken by the white-faced man. There was something sinister going on at the Tombs, something involving others besides my mother. But what?

"Pop, wake up. I want to ask you something about tomorrow."

"Tomorrow? That reminds me." He looked up at me, raising his eyebrows. "I have an interview tomorrow." He tapped his thumb on his chest and smiled. "At the brand-new Pearl Street Station. They're hiring men to run wire under the city. How d'you like that? Electrification comes to the masses."

"What? That's wonderful, Pop!" I smiled and clapped my hands. "I'm sure they'll want a man of your talents. But you need to get some sleep so you'll be fresh in the morning."

I'd heard tell of Thomas Edison's new project. There was an article in the *New York Times* when the power station opened last month. Edison supplied ninety or so customers in Manhattan's busy First District, including the *Times* headquarters, with electrical illumination. Soon he planned to add hundreds more. This was our chance. If Father could get a job there, we'd have a regular income.

My father's eyes closed, and his head slumped forward. The request I'd been waiting to discuss with him jammed up inside me. He could not take me to the Tombs tomorrow. He needed this job.

But I could not wait another day to see my mother. There were no visiting hours on Sunday, and if I asked for time off after what had happened at the Works, I'd get fired for sure. I had to talk to her about these visions before I caused another explosion. It had to be tomorrow.

I lifted Father's good leg and covered him with a wool

blanket. Then I carried the lamp to my bedchamber, unhooked the curtain, and extinguished the flame. As I settled back onto my bed, the sound of his snoring oddly comforting, I thought about how often I used to spy on my mother. Until today, I'd forgotten about the times I'd hidden under the sofa in hopes of seeing her late-night guests. More memories drifted in. I recalled a woman who'd lost her baby, a dying old man, a couple with marital conflicts . . . the list went on. Each time, whether they came filled with anger or despair, they'd left happier, more content.

My mother seemed to have been helping people. And yet, it must have been the cause of her fragile mental condition, her hysteria . . . her madness. A cold quiver shook my shoulders. I needed to know what was really going on.

I wished I could ask Khan to accompany me. But it was not possible. Unbeknownst to my father, I'd followed him to the Tombs twice before I'd started working every day, so I knew there was a sign affixed to the door. Both times, Father had ripped it down and tossed it into the street. After he'd gone inside, I'd picked it up. In bold letters it read "White Visitors Only."

No, I would have to go to the Tombs alone.

CHAPTER SIX
THE FERRY

Just when the smooth rocking motion of the ferry began to lull me to sleep, we hit a wave and my head bumped against the rail. We were already a good distance from the Fulton Street terminal on our way to Manhattan, on my way to the Tombs. I wiped my sweaty palms on my trousers and fiddled with the trinkets of my necklace hidden under my shirt. *Am I truly going through with this?* I had to. I had no other choice.

I'd told my father I was going to work. He'd barely noticed when I left, busy as he was getting dressed for his interview. The absinthe must have taken its toll; he'd gulped down a raw egg mixed with bitters for breakfast. But it was nice to see him in a suit again.

I tilted my head back, inhaling the salty breeze. The partial skeleton of the new Brooklyn Bridge loomed overhead, dark filigree against a milk-white sky. I squinted up at the structure. Impossibly tall stone towers disappeared into the clouds. Roebling's steel cables were strung between them, mooring Manhattan Island to Long Island. Each side of the suspended carriageway was desperately reaching toward the middle, like the arms of some monstrous but delicate beast. Amid the cry of seagulls I heard the continuous clanging of metal and the ceaseless grinding of machinery.

When a dark fleck streaked across the sky, I wondered if it was Seraphine chasing gulls. She was never far. I guessed my friend Alexander was up there somewhere, too. Eighteen men on the construction teams had died already; I prayed for his safety.

The ferry jumped and quivered its way across the East River, billowing black smoke behind it. The passengers rode standing room only, crowded together for the crossing. Finely clad men and women jostled against sooty chimney sweeps, construction workers, and farmers lugging potato sacks or squawking chickens in rattan cages for the Saturday markets.

The steady chug of the steam engine soothed my nerves. No one noticed me, dressed as I was in boys' britches and hat. I hid my blouse and corset under one of Father's wool aeronaut officer jackets stripped of its shoulder brass and insignia. I mapped out the route to the Tombs in my head, going over the turns once more.

Just then a commotion started up among the passengers.

Loud, angry voices rose above the drone of the engines. I twisted around to see.

A man in a top hat with a bushy mustache argued with a young stable hand, who yelled back at him while trying to calm the anxious horse at his side. The boy's voice softened when he turned from the man back to the horse.

"Shhh," he whispered. "It's all right." He stroked the dapple-gray mare as she strained her head up and down against her bridle, fear exposing the whites of her eyes.

I felt a constriction in my chest, and my vision momentarily blurred. I sucked in my breath as my sight cleared. Everything was backlit with shifting shades of light. Around the man with the mustache, a murky outline formed. I recognized the pulsing, darkening fog, eerily similar to what I'd seen just before the accident at the Works. I was keenly aware of every second ticking on my timepiece and the blood racing through my veins. An explosion on this boat would kill us all. I gripped the rail to steady myself.

The stable hand was surrounded by a hazy gray glow, which flickered between dark when he confronted the man and light every time he touched the mare. In spite of my pounding heart, I found this fascinating.

The crowd backed away from the horse's stomping hooves. They pressed into me, blocking my view. *Something bad is going to happen.*

Pushing to the front, I watched as the quarrel escalated—it

seemed the horse had been chewing on the man's coat. The man's fists tightened on the wooden handle of his umbrella; he shook it as he shouted, then raised the umbrella over his head, threatening the cowering lad.

As he readied himself to strike, he glanced past the boy. Our gazes fleetingly locked. Light exploded behind my eyes, and I saw the man's thoughts like a memory in my own head. The visions ripped through my brain: His boss firing him. His wife crying. Voices raised. His young son hiding in the closet. The man's fear of not providing for his family. *His fear*—triggering senseless anger.

Squeezing my eyes shut, I rubbed them hard. *What's happening to me?*

When I opened them, the man was staring fixedly at me. His arm was frozen midswing. His eyes filled with confusion, and I knew he'd seen the images, too—his own memories played out before him. He shook his head like a dog shaking off fleas. Then he swung.

The umbrella smashed down onto the boy's shoulder. Set free from the boy's hold on its reins, the horse reared up, knocking a basket of chickens from a farmer's arms. As the basket broke, a flurry of squawking, terrified birds flapped into the air. A large woman, presumably the farmer's wife, berated the man with the mustache. With one hand gripping his injured shoulder, the boy jumped up and grabbed for the reins. He gently coaxed the horse back against the rail. Calming her, he pulled a carrot from his coat and held it under her fuzzy, reaching lips.

Swift action on the part of the deck crew ensured no one else was injured and the loose birds were contained. They escorted the man with the mustache to another part of the boat. I slunk into the crowd as the other passengers expanded back into their places and their own thoughts.

I leaned over the side. The turmoil in my head and the swaying of the ferry made me queasy. Taking a deep breath, I relished the cool misty spray on my face.

When I looked up I saw I'd made it to Manhattan, the pestilent heart of New York, pulsing with its poisoned blood.

CHAPTER SEVEN
BOJANGLES

It was a long walk from South Street Seaport to the Tombs. I had plenty of time to figure out what I was going to say once I went inside. Each time my father had returned from visiting my mother, I'd grilled him with questions about her condition and her quarters. He'd told me she had her own room, thank goodness, as I needed to speak with her privately. He'd also said they had her on medication that made her groggy and unresponsive. I hoped she'd at least be able to answer my questions today.

Gray skies threatened a storm, but the brisk wind also carried away the stench from the gutters. The city teemed with people. Women in long dresses and layered petticoats wicked up mud and grime from the street as they stepped around piles of horse manure and refuse. I was glad I wore thick-soled boots and wool britches. Even when we could afford dresses, I'd cringed every time Mother made me wear one. They were usually long poofy things that restricted my movements and made me feel silly. Today, with my hair pinned up under an old wide-brimmed slouch hat and my necklace hidden, I easily passed for a boy. Just in case, my jacket concealed a knife tucked into the back of my leather corset.

The incident on the ferry had left me shaken. I did not fabricate the images I'd seen. *How is it possible to see someone else's thoughts?* I forced myself to keep walking. Whatever these visions were, they were getting worse. At the thought, a fresh wave of guilt, along with memories of that awful day three years ago, swept over me.

At thirteen, I'd been old enough to stand up for my mother, old enough to fight for her. Instead, I'd worried about what the neighbors would think, what my friends would say. I watched, frozen, as four men in crow masks entered our home. When Father reached for the gun he kept hidden under the table, I watched as they pried it from his fingers. One of them restrained him as the other jabbed a needle into his arm. Seconds later he was unconscious next to his soup bowl. My mother struggled as they covered her nose and mouth with a rubber cone, muffling her screams. Attached to the cone was a bag that looked like the inflated bladder of a cow. One of the men squeezed it slowly; as he did, my mother's frantic eyes glazed over. She fell into a quiet stupor.

They glanced at me as they tossed some papers on the table

and escorted her out. My hand still held a trembling spoon midair, its liquid dribbling down my arm. "He'll wake soon enough," I heard one say, through his mask.

The crows left my father a hollow man. The bit of spirit he'd retained after the war was lost that morning. He went to Tammany Hall twice to fight for my mother's release. After the first visit, he was fired from his job as a machinist at the navy yard. After the second, two men in suits came with papers saying our home hadn't been properly financed and took it away from us. Furious, Father told me that Tammany Hall was part of a "corrupt political machine." They either turned a blind eye or supported what was going on at the Tombs. Either way, he gave up. He stopped going. He stopped fighting. I overheard him tell Khan he was afraid the next thing he'd lose was me.

Mother had been locked up for three years now. *For what?* They said for medical studies; they said they were helping her. I knew that to be a lie. Father said she seemed to be getting worse under their care.

The most direct route to the Tombs skirted the edge of Five Points. My father had warned me to stay away from the area, and indeed, the closer I got, the dimmer the daylight became. A disarray of horse-drawn drays and food carts lined the curb. The streets seethed with menace. Dark alleys whispered of gang rapes and brutal murders as I rushed past.

Here, crossing a street could mean crossing a border from one gang territory into another. The Whyos, a band of Irish thugs, and the Monk Eastman Gang, made up of Jewish criminals, were the largest. People lived and died for control of the streets.

There *was* a police station in Five Points, but it was known as the Slaughterhouse, the most corrupt precinct in all of New York. I didn't know if it was the October air or my fear giving me chills. Sticking to the shadows, I did my best to remain inconspicuous.

Across the street, a group of black men and boys surged by, whooping and hollering. I lowered my hat and turned to cut down an alternate route, but I recognized one of the jackets.

It can't be. Then I looked closer. Khan walked slowly, surveying the pack. For some reason, he paused and began to turn in my direction. I darted around a corner before he could see me.

Safely hidden, I leaned against a wall of old clapboard siding, paint peeling off in delicate curls. The building felt like it was leaning back on me, as if it were too tired to hold itself up in its decrepit state. Nearby, a group of kids in dirty rags shot marbles by the corpse of a dead horse. I heard the buzzing of flies and cupped my hand over my nose and mouth to block out the foul odor.

Khan said he had business in the city. Was it with this group? It looked like a gang. I gritted my teeth. I didn't have time to find out; I had to get to the Tombs.

I ran the rest of the way.

Finally, I stood within sight of it. Gray soot-covered stone ate up an entire city block. The proportions were so large that the building looked, from afar, like a one-story structure, but it actually housed four floors of prisoners and, below that, the decaying subterranean hospital. The prison was called the New York Halls of Justice and House of Detention, but everyone knew it as the Tombs, both because it was modeled after an Egyptian mausoleum and because the official name of the hospital was the Temple of Mind Balance Studies.

I took a deep breath. Horses and carts crowded the boulevard, drivers shouting. A few blocks away, the rattle of the Third Avenue El bounced between the buildings. The air, charged with the coming storm, smelled like grease and rotting hay.

I looked up at the thick black clouds to see the nose of an enormous airship sliding across the sky directly over my head. It came to a stop above the Criminal Court Building next to the Tombs. In a flurry of ropes and activity, it moored to the iron spikes that extended up out of the roof. Then it slowly sank down until the sleek boatlike structure attached to its belly rested on top of the building.

Must be hunkering down for the storm. Or maybe that's how they transport prisoners. A bridge connected the two buildings. The Bridge of Sighs, it was called, where prisoners saw their last bit of freedom.

I knew I had to do this, but I couldn't get my body to listen to my brain. My feet grew roots into the cobblestones, and my heart beat like a wild animal.

All at once the clouds opened up, pelting me with bullets of rain. I had to move or get soaked. Just missing a teetering four-horse omnibus, I bolted across the congested street and up the steps of the prison to the protection of the entrance portico. Four massive stone columns carved with papyrus stalks held the roof high above my head. The main entrance to the prison, flanked by a police officer on each side, dominated the center of the porch. The double doors stood at least twelve feet high. A family under black umbrellas approached, nodding to the officers as they entered. Two men in top hats came out. Strangely, the entrance to the prison was more inviting than that of the hospital.

I proceeded to the far end of the portico and faced a rusted iron door with T.O.M.B.S. etched into the stone above it. I'd stood in this very spot, heart aching with desire to see my mother, but I'd never before breached the formidable stone walls.

The handwritten sign admitting only white people was once again posted on the door. I glanced over both shoulders, then quickly tore it down. A little smile stole across my lips as I tossed the crumpled note into a puddle. My father would be proud.

I entered, and the door closed behind me with a resounding thud, smothering out the world. The vestibule, a square room of large stone blocks, was lit with flickering lamps along two sides. The tall ceiling disappeared into shadows, giving the room an underground feel that further heightened my foreboding.

Unlike the police officers outside, dressed in standard blues, the Tombs guard was uniformed all in black. He sat on a chair too small to contain his bulk. To his right was a desk with two items on its dusty surface: a metal vase holding withered stems attached to mildewed red-black lumps that made the room smell like a funeral; and the guard's mask, one of those horrid crow masks. I'd never seen a guard without one, and although it stared at me sideways like the severed head of a bird, I was glad he wasn't wearing the demonic thing. *But why isn't he?* As if in answer, I noticed smoke curling up from his right hand. I must've caught him on break.

I squeezed my fists as I inched toward him.

The guard was massaging his temples with his other hand. He stopped and glowered at me as I approached, glancing at his mask as if considering the effort to retrieve it. Everything about him seemed unsettled, not only his wavering eyes but the quiver of his cigarette.

I wanted to turn around and run, but my feet stumbled forward anyway. My mind muddled around for the words I'd meant to say.

"My . . . my name is Miss Greene, sir," I said, through the lump in my throat. My father told me he used the name Greene when he came. Mr. Isaac Greene—friend of the family.

He turned to his desk, took a shaky drag of his cigarette, then mashed it back and forth on the wood top. He opened a drawer and wrote something on a yellow card.

"I'm, uh, here to see a patient?" I tried not to make it sound like a question, but it did.

Still he said nothing, though his eyes tightened.

"My father was supposed to—"

He cut me off. "Name?" he barked, his voice echoing around the empty room.

"Miss Greene—"

"*Patient's* name!" Spit flew from his mouth.

"Oh." I tried to steady my jittery voice. "Cassandra Kohl, sir. She's in—"

"I know where she's at." His brow furrowed deeper. He scribbled on the card again and tossed it onto the desk. "I know exactly where she's at." As he said this, he leaned forward over his large belly and looked me up and down. A shiver flared between my shoulder blades. Maybe this wasn't such a good idea.

He stood, towering over me.

"Open your jacket. Arms out."

Oh no, the knife! I'd meant to hide it outside, but the sudden rain flustered me. My hands shook as I unbuttoned my jacket, my heart pounding so loudly I was sure he could hear it. Sweat formed along the brow of my hat.

He placed his huge paws on my shoulders and ran them to

my wrists. As his hands slid down to my waist, his face took on a disgusting leer. Mortified, I looked up at the ceiling as he stooped and slid his hands slowly along my legs. Then he stood up with a huff.

Thank God, he's done.

"Turn around," he said.

Slowly, I turned so my back was to him. I faced the entrance, seriously contemplating running for it.

"Arms out," he ordered.

I held my breath. His hands reached up under the back of my jacket.

"Well, well, well . . . what—have—we—here?" he said, drawing out each word.

I spun back around. His lips twitched with grim satisfaction. "I . . . I was alone. It's just to protect myself, sir," I said with mounting hysteria.

Horribly, he smiled, revealing squares of grimy yellow teeth. "What'd you plan to do with *this*, huh?" He slid the knife partway from its sleeve. It was a primitive Nubian dagger with a curved blade and leather-wrapped handle. "Looks old. Where'd you get it?" he asked, testing its weight in his hand.

"It was a gift," I said in a ragged whisper, "from a friend."

"I doubt it. Maybe you stole it." In one quick motion, quicker than I would have thought a man his size could move, he grabbed my wrist and pinned it behind my back. My hat fell to the floor, letting my braid tumble down.

I screamed. Pain shot through my shoulder. He leaned his face close to mine. His rank tobacco breath slid into my nostrils.

"You know what we do to thieves in the Tombs, huh?"

A sob escaped my throat.

"I might be lenient though . . ." He sneered, his eyes unlacing my corset.

"Please, sir . . ." He was so close I saw the red veins in his pale watery eyes. Tears blurred my vision as a dark cloud surrounded him, like the darkness I had seen at the Works and on the ferry. All my senses felt heightened. My pulse raced. Foul as the air was, I took a deep breath to calm my beating heart, and as I did, the visions came. Slowly, snippets of this man's life swirled through my head. An orphan. Unwanted. Taken in by horrible foster parents. Beaten. Living on the street. Learning to fight. Learning to hate. His only friend a mangy dog named Bojangles. Bojangles dead.

Desperate, I didn't realize I'd said the name out loud. "Bojangles."

The guard's glazed eyes shifted back to mine. "What? What did you just say?"

My arm screamed in pain. I blubbered out the name again. "Bojangles. I'm sorry he died, sir." My mind raced for any sort of connection, and then I remembered my dog, Jinx. "I had a dog when I was young," I whispered.

He nodded his head and slowly, as if he wasn't sure what to do, let go of my wrist. Confusion and sadness played across his features. I watched the murky haze retreating, softening, dissipating. To my surprise, he sat down, laid the knife on the desk, and rubbed his eyes.

I wasn't sure if I should say anything. Afraid to move, I stood, catching my breath. With the arm of my jacket, I wiped the sweat dripping down my face.

In a raspy voice, he said, "He was a stray—skinny as a bitch. We found each other, living under the Ninth Avenue El."

Why is he telling me this? Yet it confirmed the images I'd seen were memories, private memories. It was hard to believe.

"Bojangles was sweet—sweet as candied yams, you know?" He looked up at me for the first time, and I quickly nodded.

"Bo would wait for me at the back door of the White Horse Tavern, where I worked. One night, some blokes I knew came in and, don't you know it, we got tanked up good. We left and stayed out most all night. Must've passed out. When I woke up, it'd snowed two feet. By the time I came round to my senses, it was too late. I found him, all right. I found Bo frozen solid to the stoop. His face . . ." The guard cleared his throat. "His face still looking up at the back door."

He didn't speak again. He didn't ask me how I knew about the dog. By the press of his mouth, I could tell he felt bad about the way he'd treated me. He picked up the yellow card, slid it into a sleeve, and held it out to me. Then he pushed a button on the wall, and with a slow grinding noise, the metal door behind him slid open.

Hesitantly, I stepped forward and took the card. I picked up my hat and stuffed my hair under it. He waved me on, his eyes lost in the past. I didn't dare reach for my knife.

At the end of the hall, another guard in black waited. This one wore his mask, and even though I could not see his eyes, I felt them glaring right at me.

CHAPTER EIGHT
THE GOOD DOCTOR

The guard tilted his head as I approached, a birdlike motion that seemed to fit his ominous mask. When I got closer, I heard his shrouded breathing and saw his eyes through the dark glass lenses. He held a gloved hand out for the card. Pulling it out of the sleeve, he gave it a quick glance, then narrowed his eyes at me.

My skin prickled as he closed the accordion gate, shutting us into the lift. As he pulled the release mechanism, a steam generator hissed to life above our heads. I heard the grind of gears clicking into place as we descended.

We passed the basement level to Sub-Basement One. Out of the corner of my eye, I stared at the strange gun sticking out of the guard's holster. It wasn't like any of Father's weapons. This one, made of brass, had a chamber attached to its side, which held a glass vial filled with amber liquid. My father had told me it was a tranquilizer gun. The sight of it was as unnerving as the masks.

The guard's beak-like profile made my skin crawl. I smoothed my features, trying to calm the rolling feeling in my stomach.

We exited into the lobby, if you could call it that. It looked more like an underground cave. It smelled damp, and the stone walls were marbled with strings of green algae. Three hallways branched out of the main space, a tangle of tubes and wires clinging to their low arched ceilings.

"Wait here." I jumped at the guard's request.

Although the air was cold, I began to sweat. My father had told me a little about the layout of the asylum, but nothing he'd said had prepared me for the disquieting and grisly reality. A clock on the wall ticked out loud seconds, instructing me to run. A reeling sensation overwhelmed me, squeezing at my throat. My eyes darted around the murky space. I reached for the comfort of my knife before I remembered it was no longer there.

The guard approached the desk where a nurse sat watching us. Instead of a proper nurse's dress, she wore a sleek white coat that buttoned diagonally from shoulder to hip. A wide apparatus-laden belt cinched it tight around her waist. Cut low in front, the coat extended almost to the floor, covering all but the toes of her boots. The guard leaned over the desk, clearly eyeing her breasts.

The skin of the nurse's face was pulled taut under her

goggles. It was a wonder she could smile, but she did more than that—she actually laughed at his muffled comments and coyly adjusted her starched white cap. *Do they know how disturbing they look?*

As if they'd heard my thoughts, they simultaneously glared in my direction. She handed him the visitor log and a pencil.

"Sign your name." He pointed. My hand shook as I wrote *Miss Olivia Greene.*

The guard escorted me along the central hallway, the sound of his boots echoing around the narrow space. We turned down one corridor, then another. Here and there the new electrical bulbs hung bare, connected by drooping wires. It made sense that government buildings would be among the early installations. I disliked the weak, pale light they emitted. I tried to mentally keep track of directions, but the dimness and lack of signage made it impossible.

Along the halls, nurses walked pale vacant-eyed patients and doctors strode with purpose, their noses buried in leather-bound notebooks. I noticed the nurses all wore the same dark goggles, but the doctors' goggles seemed to be a source of personal pride. Some had mirrored or iridescent green lenses, while others had intricate arrays of smaller lenses, or instruments that could be flipped down in front.

The metal doors along the way were closed tight, except one, which I glanced into as we passed. It looked to be some sort of operating room. Large mechanical arms hung above a thick wooden slab with straps at the top and bottom. The guard rushed me by before I could see more.

Finally we stood in front of SB 1-12, my mother's room. The guard unlocked the door, peeked inside, then stood stiffly against the hallway wall, a few feet away. I removed my hat and found myself wringing it like a rag as I entered and closed the door.

The acrid smell of her room reminded me of the dishwater thrown onto the street outside the sixpenny eatery kitchens, astringent and moldy. Everything was white, including the bedsheets, which rose and fell with her breath. Behind her, an instrument ticked a steady rhythm, like a slow beating heart. A bulbous glass inside a metal cage dripped fluid through a rubber tube and into the vein of her arm.

My stomach knotted at the thought of my mother's life within these walls. No windows, no sunlight. She used to study the sky, said we could tell a lot from the clouds. If she wasn't crazy when she came in, this place was enough to drive her there.

She was sleeping, tightly tucked under the sheets. I watched her for a moment, so peaceful, so beautiful, her auburn curls fanning out around her creamy pale face. I'd always wished I had her stark beauty. My features were similar, but I had my father's coloring: plain brown hair, olive complexion. My mother reminded me of a porcelain doll, except for the dark circles now staining the skin below her closed lids.

I bowed my head as a dreadful thought came to me. *What if she doesn't know who I am?* I'd changed so much these last three years, and she's being medicated, just as Father had said.

I went to her bedside and sat next to her. Placing my hand on her shoulder, I gave a gentle shake. "Mother, wake up."

Her eyelids fluttered but did not open.

"Please, wake up," I repeated. "Mother, it's me, Avery." Nothing. I shook her again. "Mother, please . . . I must talk to you. Would you like some water?" I poured a cup, then slid my hand behind her head, gently lifting it off the pillow, and held the cup to her lips. The water dribbled down her chin as she swallowed. Tears welled in my eyes.

I laid her back down and glanced at my timepiece, every second pulling at the knot in my stomach. I'd forgotten to ask how long I could visit, but I had a feeling the guard outside the door would not wait long. On a shelf below the table, I found a hand towel. I dipped it in the water and pressed it to her forehead and cheeks. "Mother, wake up." I dared not raise my voice lest the guard hear me.

Blinking, she glanced blearily around the room. "Avy," she whispered. "Avy, is that you?"

"Yes, it's me. I have to talk to you. Please, Mother—please try to focus."

A tear slipped from her watery eyes. "I've . . . missed you, Avy."

I reached my arms around her and lifted her to me. The

sheet slid down and I saw her hands, wrapped in gauze. I recalled my dreams—had she been beating the walls?

Gingerly, she put her arms around me. The rubber tubing moved with her. I'd forgotten how much I craved her touch. Her head rested on my shoulder. My eyes stung, and before I could stop it, a deep choking sob gripped my lungs.

This place, this hospital, it's killing her. I buried my face in her hair. All the confusion and fear of the past twenty-four hours churned inside me. All the years of feeling loss, and guilt, and even betrayal, swept over me, shaking my body with uncontrollable tremors. I wanted her to hold me and tell me everything was going to be all right, like she used to when I was small. But she was not capable of that, at least not now. I cried until I felt empty inside.

At last, I whispered into her ear, "Mother, I'm seeing things. It's happening more and more. Please tell me . . . am I going mad?"

I felt her head shake ever so slightly. "Avy . . ." Her voice was faint and rasping; she took long breaths between her words. "You're not . . . mad. You're . . . an aura seer." She swallowed hard. "A healer—like me." The effort seemed tremendous as she fought the fog that gripped her. I felt her chest lift, heard her breath in the back of her throat. "Go . . . to the Gypsies," she whispered. "Find . . . Niko." Her head rolled to the side as if it was too heavy for her. "He has a—"

Whatever else she intended to say was cut off. Her arms fell limply to her side.

"Mother, wait! What's a seer?" She remained silent. I laid her down. As I did, the sleeve of her nightgown pushed up. Around the metal needle taped near the inside of her elbow, her skin was mottled with bruises. I slid the other side up. The same injuries.

My poor, poor mother. I covered my mouth with my palm. *What are they doing to her?* I thought about a time when I was young and developed a terrible fever. The doctor had used a tool to open my vein and let the blood flow into a bowl. The treatment had left me similarly bruised. *Are they performing bloodletting on her?*

I wiped my own face with the damp towel, forcing myself to stop shaking. She said I was an aura seer, a healer. I wasn't sure what she meant, but . . . *I'm not mad. I'm not mad.* A chilling thought seized me. *If I'm not mad, then neither is she.*

I tried to swallow, but my throat constricted. *If she's not insane, why are they keeping her here?* My heart felt like it would burst.

I'd seen aura-reading booths at the Gypsy festival. Maybe that was why she wanted me to go there. I would go, and I would find this person, this Niko.

A loud knock on the door made me jump. Out of habit, I grabbed my hat and stuffed my braid under it.

The knob turned, and a stocky goggled nurse plodded in, leaving the door ajar. She smiled at me with oversize horse teeth.

"Well, hello, dear," she said, an English accent coloring her words. "Is this your mum?"

"Oh, no," I said. "Friend of the family." I gripped my mother's bandaged hand. "She's . . . she's sleeping," I stammered.

"Must be hard on you to see Mrs. Kohl like this. But don't you worry, the good doctor is taking care of her. In fact, the front desk told me he planned to stop by. To my surprise, they said he'd like to meet her visitor." She lifted her chin and nodded. "Doesn't make the rounds anymore, being as important as he is and all. You should be honored. He'll be here any moment."

My mother's hand stiffened. Though she lay still, I saw a bead of sweat break out along her hairline. The muscles of her jaw clenched. *She's afraid*, I realized. *She's afraid of the doctor.*

The nurse busied herself with the charts hanging at the end of the bed. Before I could decide whether to flee, I heard footsteps in the hallway. The doctor stepped into the room, his crisp white lab coat and pressed suit at odds with the straggly hair hanging from his scalp. My body went frigid. He wore no goggles, and when he looked down at me, his eyes bored into mine. His left eye, in particular, looked dead, as if its spark had gone out, and the lid puckered around it like the skin of a rotten apple. He was tall, but it was his face, his white waxen face, that sent quivers down my arms. His skin was pulled tight over his lips, which seemed to be painted on, a thin red line. It was one thing seeing him at the window of a coach but quite another meeting him face-to-face in a small room. I couldn't breathe. I couldn't tear my eyes away.

He spoke. His voice, high and scratchy, chilled me to the bone. It was as if his vocal cords had holes in them. He eyed me like a lab specimen. "Ah, I had a strange inkling . . . a young lady coming here all alone. I recognize you now—Cassandra Kohl's daughter. I am Dr. Spector. My, you've grown up." My tongue, a dry lump, was unable to utter a word, and his cold stare told me it would be useless to disagree. His grating voice continued. "Last I heard, you and your father left town. I've never seen your names on the log before. And now I know why, Miss Olivia Greene, and judging from previous logs, your father is Mr. Isaac Greene. Clever." He ground his teeth. Under his breath, he muttered, "Incompetence."

Dr. Spector smiled, if you could call it that, a slit across his face. "May I ask you a question, Miss *Kohl*?" Without waiting for a response, he said, "Do you understand why your mother is here at this esteemed asylum? Do you know what we are treating her for?"

I shook my head no, afraid to say the wrong thing and not trusting my voice. The doctor took a step closer. I noticed his eyebrows were drawn on and his eyelashes seemed to be missing. The air in the room felt heavy in my lungs.

"She is a rare case, your mother. We are studying her particular form of hallucinatory degeneration and have recently discovered it is, quite possibly, hereditary. The mind is a delicate instrument, wondrous at times, but her condition, left unchecked . . ." He stroked his pointed chin with a gloved hand as his gaze raked over my mother. "Well, let us just say it is critical to get the proper treatment. Tell me, Miss Kohl, have you ever seen something that was not really there?"

"No," I blurted out. "No. Never." I gave my mother's hand a squeeze, trying to tell her without words that I loved her. Then I let go and took a step toward the door. I did not want to leave my mother but I had to. "Please excuse me, sir, but I'd best get home. My father is waiting."

The doctor held up his hand, stopping me. "Miss Kohl, before you rush off, I would like to do a harmless test on you. I have developed a device to detect conditions such as your mother's. If we catch these mental infirmities early, we can stem their advance on the brain. I'm sure your father would approve. For your own safety, I must make sure you are not harboring this illness." He stepped into the hall and nodded to the guard. "My technician will escort you to the testing room. I will prepare, and meet you there."

With that, he strode from the room. The nurse beamed at me, as if proud the good doctor was taking the time to test me personally, no matter that I'd lied to her about this not being my mother.

The guard entered and clutched me by the arm. "Nothing to be afraid of, miss," he said through his crow-shaped mask.

This can't be. "Mother? Mother, what's happening?"

"She can't hear you," the guard said. "Come with me, please. As the doctor told you, it's for your own safety." He forced me toward the door.

"Go along, dear," the nurse said. "Mustn't keep the good doctor waiting."

I tried to turn back toward my mother, but the guard held

me tight. My mind froze. *They are going to test me. They are going to lock me up.*

Behind me, I heard the nurse cry out. The guard spun, taking me with him. My mother lay half off the bed, the nurse desperately trying to hold her up. A rivulet of blood dripped onto the floor from a hole in my mother's arm.

"She ripped it out!" the nurse screamed. "Don't just stand there. Help me get her back onto the bed!"

The guard dropped my arm in his rush to help. In that moment, my mother lifted her head and her eyes found mine. Breathlessly, she mouthed one word: "Run!"

For a split second I hesitated. *How can I leave her like this?* But the fear in her eyes forced me into action. I spun through the door and ran in the direction opposite to the one Dr. Spector had taken.

At each door I passed, I grabbed the knob and tried it. Locked. They were all locked. Terrified, I kept going. I had to keep going. The blood pounding through my veins drowned out the sound of commotion behind me. Nurses stepped back, pulling their wards aside to avoid a collision as I hurtled down the hallway. One called out for me to stop, another tried to grab my arm, but I swerved away, almost tripping over her as she tumbled to the floor.

The end of the hall loomed ahead. I was trapped. There was one more door, and I rammed into it. It opened into a mechanical room. I slammed the door shut, my first thought to hide amid the machinery. But as I raced to the far side of the room, I saw a door. I opened it slowly and peeked out. The hall was dark, deserted.

I swept through, once again trying doors as I went, this time cautiously, quietly. The third door opened to a stairwell. I sprinted up. My lungs ached, but I was afraid to slow down.

Counting the flights, I stopped at the ground floor. I held my breath and peeked out. Beyond was the iron door to the entrance vestibule. Looking in the other direction, I saw the guard standing by the lift. He did not see me. I could make it.

I gave myself a moment to get ready, then sprinted forward.

"Stop! Stop!" the guard called out.

I slammed into the iron door—it didn't budge.

CHAPTER NINE
STILL AS STONE

Frantically, I stabbed at the button on the wall. The door slid open. Ahead of me I saw the exit to the street. I saw freedom, and I ran toward it.

A piercing alarm blared directly overhead. Across the vestibule, another door banged open. The black-masked guards flocked into the space like a murder of crows.

The guard who'd told me about his dog jumped up from his chair, startled by my sudden appearance. As I sprinted by his desk, I swiped my knife off the top. He was too slow to hinder me, but from across the vestibule I heard a high-pitched command, "Stop or we'll shoot!"

The exit was too far. I skidded to a halt, raising my arms in the air. *I'm caught.*

I swiveled just enough to see guards fanning out. From

the middle of the black swarm, Dr. Spector emerged. Guards flowed around him like an oil slick. My muscles stiffened. The barrels of five of the strange tranquilizer guns were pointed directly at me.

"I do not want to hurt you or your mother," Spector said. "I can help you." He glanced at the guards and nodded. They lowered their weapons.

He's lying. My mother told me to run. It was now or never, while the guns were down. I ducked my head and raced toward the exit.

"Sedate her!" Spector's command echoed around the small space.

A *pop*, and something whizzed through the air. A dart hit the wall, the vial exploding in a spray of liquid and glass. Another shattered to my left. I felt my boots slipping on the mess. Before I knew what was happening, I fell, shards of glass ripping into my hands and knees.

The crows advanced. I stumbled up and smashed my shoulder into the entrance door, forcing it open.

Tripping down the steps outside, I ran from the Tombs, hoping to get lost in the bustling traffic. I had one foot on the sidewalk as the other hit the street. A sudden shout from a carriage driver stopped me in my tracks. A team of horses thundered by, but not before a huge horse clomped down onto my foot. Searing pain crumpled me to the ground. The iron-edged wheels of the wagon cut across the cobblestones, spewing mud into my face. A few inches closer and the wheels would have severed my legs.

I felt dazed. Rain splattered my eyes. Blood trickled through my fingers. Splayed on the sidewalk, I heard the door of the Tombs crash open. A breeze whipped my hat into the gutter. Thoughts of my mother ripping a hole in her arm so I could escape slapped me to my senses. For her sake, I had to move. Now.

Ignoring the pain, I tucked my knife into the waistband of my trousers and pushed myself up. I hobbled across the boulevard, dodging horses and trams. The rain soaked my hair and blurred my vision. The cobblestones were slick beneath my feet. Ahead, I saw a dark alleyway between the buildings. I rushed toward it, bumping into pedestrians, ignoring their angry looks. When I rounded the corner, my foot gave out. I fell again, losing precious seconds I needed in order to flee.

But in the next moment, I felt myself swept up and shoved into a deep, shadowed alcove, my face pressed against the cold stone. My breath caught in my throat as a hand wrapped around my mouth, sealing in my scream.

Tightening my muscles, I tried to fight, to elbow or kick, but his grip was like a vise. Remembering my knife, I slid my hand slowly toward it. I almost had it when my attacker tilted back my head, exposing my neck. I expected to feel cold steel at my throat, but he leaned forward and, instead, I saw his white teeth flash a smile.

I looked up into the golden eyes of Khan. He released my face but kept one powerful arm wrapped around my shoulders and the other around my waist. His body, pressing against my back, completely shielded me from view.

"I'm being chased. We have to run," I cried, craning my head to look. "They're coming."

"Shhh," he murmured. "They will not see us."

"Khan, these are trained guards." My heart hammered in my chest. "They have guns."

"Trust me, Avery. They will pass us by."

And then I heard them. They were splitting up. Some guards ran ahead and some came into the alley. *We're in plain sight!* I wriggled, trying to compress myself further against the wall.

I felt the warmth of Khan's mouth at my ear. "Be still," he whispered. "Be as still as the stone."

The clicking of boots made my legs go weak. Behind me, I felt a change in Khan's body. His breathing slowed, became long and deep. He bowed his head, veiling me under the curtain of his ropelike strands, rain dripping off their tips to run down into my blouse. And then I knew what he meant by being as still as stone. It felt like he was melting into the wall and taking me with him. My heart did an erratic dance, but I could no longer feel his, beating against my back. It was as if he had slowed his heart.

The guards came right past us, their boots scraping the street. One had a club that he tapped rhythmically as he walked.

I watched their beaked shadows move slowly along the stone. But they did not stop. They did not even hesitate. Khan was right. They passed by us. It was as if we had disappeared.

We stayed like that, silently waiting, until the guards were long gone. Then we melted into the crowds and made our way through Manhattan. The rain lightened to a steady drizzle, but it didn't matter—I was already soaked to the bone.

Working for a shipbuilder gave Khan use of some of the boats, and when we reached the waterfront, he led me to an old fishing scow with peeling paint and a rusted railing. A tall black steam pipe stuck out of the top of the shedlike wheelhouse. Inside, I found a seat atop a pile of braided ropes that stunk of fish, while Khan lit the boiler. The puttering engine came to life with a puff of smoke. I couldn't think. I couldn't wrap my mind around all that'd happened.

Crossing the East River by ferry was difficult enough, but maneuvering through the river traffic in a boat dwarfed by tall clipper ships with sails higher than buildings, and four-story steamers whose giant paddle wheels churned the water to a foaming froth, was a jarring experience. The bellows and blasts and clanging of bells set me on edge. I flinched at tugboat toots. The bustle of New York Harbor, the busiest port in the world, was worse than the bedlam of Manhattan's streets.

Once safely across, Khan and I scurried toward the shop. Even though we were on the other side of the East River, my muscles tensed at every shout or crack of a whip.

I shared the short but shattering conversation I'd had with

my mother. I also told Khan about Dr. Spector, and the incident on the ferry. For some reason, I didn't mention the Gypsies. I still wasn't sure how I felt about that.

"I can't believe you went in there alone." Khan stopped and stared at me. "Why didn't you ask me to go with you?"

"Let's keep moving," I said, my boots splashing in the mud. "And I would have, Khan, but they don't allow black visitors into the Tombs."

He puffed up his cheeks and blew the air out. "Right. I should've known."

When we reached the entrance to the shop, I placed my hand on Khan's before he turned the knob. "Khan, what was going on in Five Points? I saw you there with a group of boys."

"Avery, we are not talking about this now. Not after all you've been through. Look at your hands. They're still bleeding."

I opened my mouth to disagree, but the door swung open before I could say more.

Khan shook my father's hand. "Thank goodness you're here, sir. Avery's hurt. I have to get back to the city." He said goodbye and disappeared around the corner. I couldn't help but wonder if my question was the reason he'd slipped away so quickly.

Inside, my father flipped his sign to Closed and locked the door behind us. Then he went to the windows facing the street and pulled the blinds shut, cutting off the slanted late-afternoon light.

"Avery, what happened?"

"I went to see Mother."

"What?" My father took a step back, eyes widening. "Sit at the table. Tell me everything."

While I spoke, he opened the cupboard and pulled out a metal bowl, a glass, and a bottle of gin. Then he set a pot to boil water. I started with my ride on the ferry and finished with my escape. "It was horrible being in the same room as him, this Dr. Spector," I whispered.

I'd never seen Father so angry. The vein at his temple throbbed. "Avery, how could you be foolish enough to go into the Tombs? I've told you time and again how dangerous it is. By myself, I didn't arouse suspicion, but a young girl visiting? They'd suspect it was you." He poured a shot, downed it, and slammed the glass on the table. "You see this?" He smacked his mechanical leg. Once again he wore the brilliant prosthetic he'd built for himself. Hidden between the multitude of gears and gauges was a long-nosed gun. "This is for the first crow that lays a hand on you. But I can't protect you if you go waltzing into their nest. And now that they know we didn't leave the area, we'll have to be extra vigilant. Why didn't you tell me what you were planning?"

"I'm sorry," I whispered. "I was afraid. I thought I was going crazy. I'm having visions. I wanted to talk to Mother as soon as possible. And . . . and I wanted you to get that job."

"Bloody hell, child." He placed a towel under my hands. "What am I to do with you? Come on, let's clean you up."

When I was dry, in baggy trousers and one of Father's large shirts, I sat back down at the table. I sipped the steaming cup of beef tea, a healing practice my father retained from the Civil War infirmary. In the minutes I'd been gone, he looked as if he'd aged. He rubbed the bridge of his nose as he spoke.

"All these years I'd hoped it wouldn't happen to you, too. You have to bury this thing, Avery. Pretend nothing is happening to you. Never tell anyone about these visions. Do you understand?" He pulled my chair closer and put his arm around me, sloshing gin onto my back. I didn't speak, or mention that I'd already told Khan.

In a deflated voice, he said, "I went for the interview—sober as a judge, I might add. They took one look at me and laughed. They told me a man with a metal leg should not work with electricity." He started to chuckle, but it turned into a groan, which he stifled with another swig of gin. "Why did I let her do it? This is my fault . . . all my fault."

"Let her do what? What's your fault?"

"How . . ." He leaned away from me, closing his eyes a moment, then pulled his shoulders back as if bracing himself. "How is she?"

"You never told me just how bad it is in there for her. You were right, she's heavily drugged, and she must have hurt her hands because they were bandaged up." I clenched my jaw. "But now we know she's not insane, we have to get her out of there."

"I always knew. And don't you think I've tried?" He stared down at the bottle clutched in his hands. "I have tried everything."

"You knew? All this time? Why didn't you tell me? You let me believe—"

"What? And have you think she's a witch or a freak, as people said? You showed no sign of having these visions, Avery. I did what I thought best for you."

I blew out my breath. He was right, there was a time I had thought of her that way. "Pop, I have so many questions. Can't you tell me more about the visions? We should go to the Gypsies, as Mother said." His blue eyes were the hue I imagined the oceans of warmer climes to be, clear and light, so unlike the dark water surrounding Manhattan Island, the angry waves that I'd crossed to escape the crows and Dr. Spector.

But those beautiful eyes hardened at the mention of the Gypsies. "No. You will not go anywhere near that camp."

"But maybe they—"

"That's final, Avery." He stood up, swaying. "Pretend these visions do not exist or they will get you into trouble. And as I told you, stay far away from the Tombs and the Gypsy camp."

I bowed my head, knowing I'd angered him.

As he stomped off, he mumbled, "You have no idea what those Gypsies are capable of."

CHAPTER TEN
SECRET NOTE

On Monday morning, as I dressed for work, there was a knock at the front door. For a moment I panicked—*the crows?* Gripping my knife, I lifted a window slat just enough to see out. Then I let out my breath; it was a Union veteran in full regalia, as if he'd worn the same clothing since the war. I unlocked the door and let him in.

Father came over, and I heard him say, "Up and about early, eh, Mr. Cranford?"

Maybe my father was right. Maybe the soldiers *were* the only ones who could find the shop, but we couldn't hide inside all day.

I could dawdle no longer; I had to get to work. I kissed Father goodbye.

"Be careful," he said. It was the most he'd spoken to me

since our conversation two days earlier. All day Sunday he'd been tight-lipped, refusing to say anything more about the Gypsies or explain his comment.

I grabbed my felt hat on the way out, sad that I'd lost my father's slouch hat in the city. The walk to work set me on edge, my heightened awareness making me feel twitchy and frayed. I took the shortest route to the Works, certainly not passing St. Ann's. I doubted I'd ever go by there again. And I checked behind me every few moments to ensure that I wasn't being followed. By the time I arrived at the factory, I was a bundle of nerves. At least once I was inside, the crows couldn't find me. They wouldn't think to look in there.

Once again I gazed up at the two helmets left on the wall. Oscar wouldn't need his for a while. I felt a lump in my throat. Maybe that was the way of it. Maybe the Works would burn us up and spit us out, one by one.

As I headed to my station, I heard snippets of conversation about the explosion. Some men pointed at me. I looked at my feet to avoid their eyes, but I did hear someone say that Mr. Malice was back from the hospital.

A blast from Bessie sounded. The monstrous mill shuddered to life, fires stoked, iron lined up like food in a trough. Steam built up. I squeezed my fists. "You need us," I said under my breath. "Without us, you'd decay into a rusty relic."

There was a tap on my shoulder. "Who you talking to, Ave?" Leo must've walked in right after me.

"Huh? Oh, no one. Myself." I laughed, shaking my head. "You scared me, though. I thought maybe you were *him*." I lifted my chin toward the perch above our heads. "Have you seen him?"

"No, but we're keeping our heads low just in case," he said. "Heard he was all bandaged up. Ave, are you okay?" He noticed my hands wrapped in gauze.

"I'm fine, Leo." I put my helmet on and smiled at him. "I better get to work."

At my workbench, I organized my tools. Battery connected to carbon arc welding gun; flux tin open and within reach; helmet and gloves secured. I checked my previous welds for root cracks or bead holes. Welding, to me, was an art. Go too fast and the bead is brittle, too slow and it slags over the metal. I became so focused when I worked, sometimes I'd look up to see men on all sides leaving for the day.

I checked the first tab on the pile. Tabs were red cards with instructions from various sections of the factory. Runners dropped them into bins according to the size of the job. They were once organized by due date, but everyone wanted theirs done immediately; it was impossible to satisfy the demand. Now, we did large orders first. Small ones had to wait.

Since we were so close to the navy yard, much of our work came from there. I lifted a circular portal window. Its steel frame required welded hinges. I laid the parts out, lowered my goggles, and flared up my torch. I held the filler rod at a precise angle as I drew my gun across the metal, sparks flying into bright orange arcs before fizzling out. When I finished, I inspected the work. Perfect. No seaman would experience leaks from this porthole.

I was about to move on to the next tab when the second foreman, a man I'd never spoken to before, ran up to me. He was tall, with lean, wiry muscles, and might have been good-looking if it weren't for the years the mill had put on him. I'd heard he was a fair boss, respected by the machinists' division he headed.

"Miss Avery." He removed his cap and pushed the matted hair off his forehead. "Heard what happened on Friday. Me and the men, well, we wanted to say we're sorry about your friend." He smiled, crinkling the leathery skin around his eyes. "How's he doing?"

I was astounded. Two years and never a word until now! I raised my goggles. "Mr. Matteo, sir, thank you for asking." Behind him, I could see Tony, Geeno, and Leo watching. "I don't know how he is, but I think Mr. Malice may have broken his legs."

Mr. Matteo squeezed his fists. I saw a flash of anger in his eyes. This was the face of a man who'd seen terrible things and had buried them deep inside. "Well, tell him we're pulling for him."

"I certainly will," I said. "Thank you, sir."

Mr. Matteo pulled an envelope, smudged with black

fingerprints, out of his pocket. He handed it to me. "From Mr. Malice." Then he slipped a folded piece of paper out of his pocket. "And this is from my guys. For Oscar," he said, pressing it into my hand before he tramped off.

An uneasy feeling settled over me. I stared at the dirty envelope. This was it. I was getting fired. *I won't open it.* I stuffed it in my pocket. I peeked into the folded note. Inside was a ten-dollar greenback. Two weeks' salary! I'd have to get it to Oscar. If his legs *were* broken, he'd be missing lots of work. I braved a look at the perch. I was employed only so long as the note in that envelope remained unread.

When the lunch whistle sounded, Tony came over to get me.

"Come on, Avery, take a break and eat, will ya?" He held a lunch sack in his fist. "I saw Scarface roaming the stations. Has he said anything to you?" Tony scowled.

"No, but he watches me. Like he's expecting me to cause another explosion."

As we navigated through the machinery of the work area, some of the men eating lunch at their stations glanced up at me. One nodded, another gave me a half salute, one a quick smile. Word must have gotten around about my altercation with Mr. Malice. These tough men who hated having women and children in the workplace were acknowledging me for the first time. Warmth swelled inside me. For the moment at least, I'd earned their respect.

Leo and Geeno were waiting for us by the door. Leo pointed

at my foot. "Are you sure you're all right, Ave? You're limping."

"It's nothing. Us weld rats are tough, right?" I chuckled. I'd wrapped my foot with linen and laced my work boots tight to keep the swelling down.

Geeno nodded, giving me one of his precious smiles.

We stopped by the recently installed drinking fountain, taking turns sipping water from a metal cup that hung from a chain on the side. Wealthy people and temperance activists donated water fountains for poverty-stricken areas of the city in hopes of discouraging alcohol consumption. Ours, with a stone back and basin, had the word *BOGGS* cut into the top.

Leo pointed up at it. "What does it say?"

"Boggs—I've seen him in the papers," Tony said. "Some rich bloke who says he wants to help us 'less fortunate' saps."

"Well, I ain't complaining." Leo smacked his lips and swung the cup on its chain.

I stole another glance at the perch. "I'm sure Mr. Malice is thrilled, too, given how he's always forbidding the men to drink alcohol on the job."

A workman approached us. "Come on, move along. This isn't a social watering hole." I'd noticed him before, ushering men back to work. No doubt Mr. Malice was afraid we'd take too many water breaks now.

We usually ate lunch on the docks behind the factory. I sat, dangling my legs over the choppy waters of the East River. Nearby, a row of wooden tables was already full of workers. We weren't allowed to sit with them.

"Here," I said, handing the envelope to Tony. "It's from Mr. Malice. You read it." Tony was the only one on our crew, besides myself, who knew how to read.

The boys gathered around, as anxious as I to find out what the note said. Tony slid his pocketknife along the edge and pulled out a slip of paper. He read, speaking quietly so the men behind us would not hear.

> *Miss Avery,*
>
> *An inspector from the Brooklyn Gas Light Company is to verify the factory does not have any gas leaks that could have caused the explosion. For your sake, I hope you are not in some way responsible. But seeing as you chose to stick your nose where it does not belong, you may have Oscar's tabs on top of your own.*
>
> *R. Malice*

Tony handed the note back to me. "Who does he think he is? You had nothin' to do with it."

I gave him a weak smile. My stomach felt queasy. I'd caused that explosion somehow. Hopefully there was no way for Mr. Malice to pin it on me.

"Yeah," Leo piped in when I stayed silent. "He's lucky *you* weren't hurt."

"I'm just happy I still have my job," I said.

Tony put his hand on my shoulder. "I'll help you with the extra tabs, Avery."

"I help, too," Geeno added. Leo nodded in agreement.

"No, Mr. Malice told me to do the extra tabs and—"

"Avery," Tony said. "Us weld rats stick together, remember?" He smirked.

I smiled at the three of them. "Thank you. I'll divide them up. We can likely finish during lunch." I wished I could tell them what was going on, but I didn't know if I could begin to explain it. Besides, they were safer not knowing. I kept thinking about the fear on my mother's face after she ripped the needle from her vein, the blood puddling onto the floor.

"Oh, I almost forgot." I pulled out the folded-up paper. "Look what else Mr. Matteo gave me. His crew chipped in for Oscar." I showed them the banknote.

Tony let out a low whistle. "Hey, what's this?" He took the piece of folded paper and opened it all the way. It was a printed poster. He and I read it to ourselves while the boys waited for us to tell them what it was.

"It's nothing," I said, opening my eyes wide at Tony.

"Yeah—nothing. Just scrap," he agreed.

I did not want them to know Mr. Matteo had covertly given me a notice announcing a secret meeting of the Amalgamated Association of Iron and Steel Workers. It was going to be held one evening next week at a warehouse on Wallabout Place. *Is he inviting me to attend?* I quickly stuffed it back into my pocket. I would never go—the very idea was preposterous. Union unrest could only lead to trouble. If Mr. Malice caught wind of this meeting, I was sure he'd fire every employee involved.

Then, I thought about the pride I'd felt when the men recognized me for standing up to Mr. Malice. Mr. Matteo must really believe in the idea of a union if he was willing to risk his job for it. If enough people joined, the unions would grow strong. What if they were strong enough to make a difference? Would that make it worth the danger?

The boys and I ate at our stations for the next few days, working our way through the extra tabs. I didn't tell them I was also staying late each night. I couldn't ask them to do that. But when I left work each evening, I ran home as fast as my injured foot allowed. Being out on the street alone filled me with dread. I was hypersensitive to every movement or sound from behind.

I barely saw my father, as he spent more and more time working in the basement. We exchanged pleasantries when we crossed paths, but his eyes were sunken and faraway. I gnawed at my fingernails. I should never have gone to the Tombs.

When Khan knocked on the door Friday evening, I felt a rush of tension release from my muscles. I hadn't realized I'd been wound up tighter than a clock spring.

We went up to the roof. Seraphine hopped back and forth on the wall, trying to get Khan's attention. I winced as I loosened my shoelaces. The top of my foot and side of my ankle had turned black and blue. Thank goodness for the steel in my boot or the horse would surely have crushed my foot.

"Sorry I didn't come check on you sooner," Khan said. "I've got too many irons in the fire, as they say, and I can only stay a few minutes. Are you all right?"

"No," I said, "I'm not. It was horrible, running out and leaving my mother there. Khan, all these years I thought she was insane." I folded my arms over my knees and laid my head on them. "I've been so wrong. And my father? He's still furious—he barely speaks to me." I held back the tears trying to form in my eyes. Three years she's suffered in that place. I balled my fists until my nails dug into my palms, the prickle of pain a welcome distraction. "I wish I could talk to her again, Khan. She said she and I are aura seers, healers. I don't even know what she meant. Dr. Spector must want her because of this, but why?"

Khan shrugged. "I can't imagine," he said.

My mother's words about going to see the Gypsies echoed in my mind. My family used to visit their camp on the twenty-first of June for the Midsummer's Eve festival, the same night as my birthday. We'd last gone three years ago. After what happened that night and the next, I swore I'd never set foot in the Gypsy camp again. Besides, my father forbade it.

But my mother had told me to go. How could I ignore that? And Oscar was there. I could check on him at the same time.

A shiver along my skin reminded me there was someone else at the camp I might see, but I tamped that feeling down, thinking only of Niko.

If Father won't answer my questions, I decided, *I'll find someone who will.*

"Khan, there's something I didn't tell you, but it might be important. My mother said I should go see the Gypsies. There is someone there I should talk to."

"The Gypsies?" His eyes lit up, and a wide grin spread across his face. "I can certainly help you with that, Little Bird. I know the Gypsies well."

"You do? How is that?"

He laughed. "You'd be surprised at the connections I've made. You don't work for the leading steamboat builder in New York and not meet all kinds of folks."

"All right, but please don't mention anything to my father. Tomorrow's Saturday; he'll be out late. He won't even know." I spoke wildly, grasping at straws. "Maybe the Gypsies can tell us something that will help get my mother out of the Tombs."

A sinking feeling settled over me as I fiddled with a gear on my necklace. I couldn't believe I was about to disobey my father *again*, after angering him so. But this wasn't happening to him, it was happening to me, and he'd refused to help.

Khan flipped open his pocket watch, then jumped up. He adjusted his hat and held out his hand to pull me up. "I have to go. Let's talk tomorrow."

He disappeared into the darkness, leaving me to fetch the lantern.

"Wait," I called out after a moment. "Tell me how you hid us from the guards!"

But there was no response. I wished I'd asked him before he'd rushed off.

When I got home from work Saturday evening, there was a note on my door. It said,

Meet me at the overlook by Plunder's Neck at half past seven. —K

Plunder's Neck. I shuddered. I'd have to go into the marshland. It must be the latest location of the Gypsy camp.

CHAPTER ELEVEN
THE GYPSIES

I followed a path through the forest, thick with pine needles, the sinking sun slanting through the trees. Seraphine clung to the heavy glove that protected me from her razor-sharp talons. My mind drifted to the night three years ago—the last time we went to the Gypsy camp as a family. It'd been much closer to the border of town back then but still had felt a world away. I recalled every detail.

It was my thirteenth birthday and the Midsummer's Eve festival; the night felt magical. The monstrous bonfire, visible for miles, infused the air with the smoky scent of applewood and laurel. Every breeze held the promise of hot buttered popcorn, wispy sweet spun sugar, or fried cinnamon dough. Revelers and performers alike concealed their faces behind elaborate masks. I wore a green tunic adorned with feathers and leaves, iridescent fairy wings, and a green velvet mask over my eyes.

In one tent, a blindfolded woman in red hurled knives, one after the other, to land—*thunk, thunk, thunk*—inches from a man she'd pulled from the audience and told to stand very, very still against the wall. My parents were so engrossed in the demonstration they did not see me slip away.

A small tent surrounded by torches caught my eye. I entered quietly, not wanting to disturb the show in progress. A boy in a double-breasted waistcoat and the mask of the Greenman—or was it Shakespeare's Puck?—faced the crowd. He asked a woman to dance for him. She laughed and refused.

But the strangest thing happened. Clearly against her will, she stood and began to dance. Faster and faster she twirled, a stringless marionette. She shrieked. Her husband, presumably, yelled, "Stop this nonsense!" and stomped forward. He raised his fist to punch the boy—but clocked his own jaw instead. He fell onto another man, and a brawl broke out. People backed up to watch or hastened out of the tent.

Amid the commotion, the boy was perfectly still, staring at me. He had thick wavy brown hair and eyes that sparkled behind his mask. I moved toward him, no longer hearing the tumult of shouts and shoving. The only sound was the ticking of my timepiece and my own shallow breath.

When I reached him, he took my hand in his, bowing deeply to press his lips against it. His hair fell across his face, softly brushing my arm. A wave of heat rolled up my neck, and my face felt hot behind my mask.

Still bent over, he looked up at me. His eyes took my breath away: deep blue with flecks of violet, like stars reflected on water, like the kaleidoscope my father made me as a little girl.

"I've been waiting for you," he said, his tone playful, "so very long."

I shook my head, trying to break the spell. "You seemed to be having fun in the meantime—at the expense of others."

A flicker of amusement lifted the corner of his mouth. He stood. "Today is your birthday, is it not?"

He was taller than me, and he watched me through the lock of hair that fell across his mask. I didn't want to give him the satisfaction of being right, so I ignored his question. "What is your trick?" I demanded.

He laughed. I noticed his dimples and perfect teeth. "It is no trick, my lady love." I realized he still held my hand. He was so close I could smell him, like muskwood and spice and the scent of the bonfire. "I can make you do anything I want," he said, flashing me a crooked smile.

I pulled my hand away and raised my chin, glad of the mask. "I highly doubt that."

His smile was taunting and contagious. "I won't, though," he said. "If you promise to come back tomorrow night."

I suddenly felt reckless. "And if I don't?"

"I will make you kiss me," he said, leaning closer. "Right now."

I didn't know what came over me then. Maybe it was the

magic of the night. Or maybe I knew, deep down, that I would probably never see him again. I whispered, mostly to myself, "You can't make me do something I already want to do."

I looked up into his face—the smooth skin, wild hair. He had an untamed look about him, and I felt myself drawing closer, lost in the mysterious eyes behind the mask. I felt his breath. As I closed my eyes, his lips pressed gently to mine. His kiss was soft, tentative at first. My pulse quickened. I knew both of us felt a current, like water flowing between us. His mouth became urgent. His hand brushed my neck. Heat coursed through my body. I was on fire. He pulled me closer to him, until I could not tell if it was his heart I felt or mine. They beat in perfect unison.

I let go of the world. But in the next moment, reality came crashing down around me. I heard my father shout, "Avery!" as he burst into the tent.

The crack of a branch underfoot broke off my daydream, but it was one I'd relived often.

The Gypsy camp came into view, its saturation of hues unlike anything in all of New York. The billowy silk tents glowed in the dusky sky, reflecting in the dark waters of Jamaica Bay like magical lanterns. I named the colors in my head—fiery crimson; turquoise pool; dreamy yellow, like the sun encased in gauze. By comparison, my world was gray.

The Gypsies kept to themselves, the Midsummer's Eve festival and their brief trips into town to sell copperware or tinsmithing services being the exceptions. But it was the Gypsy women who folks journeyed to see. They told fortunes and sold charms. People were both fascinated and terrified by their knowledge.

I looked at my timepiece. Eight o'clock. *Damn.* Where was he? Khan was never late.

It'd taken me over two hours to get here, first hidden under the hay of a farmer's wagon, then walking—or rather, limping—the rest of the way, with Seraphine swooping in to keep me company. Brooklyn became a very different place out in its far reaches, a wild place called the Flatlands. Buildings gave way first to rolling hills and farmsteads, and then finally to old-growth forests and marshland that could swallow you whole.

And yet, somehow, I felt safer out here in the desolate dark than in the crowded streets of Manhattan Island, where crow men and street gangs lurked. The only structure I'd passed since I left civilization was the wall of stone surrounding the Cemetery of the Evergreens.

A figure emerged from the mist, his long black coat flowing out behind his broad-shouldered silhouette, unmistakable in his Stetson hat. I set Seraphine free and grinned as she flew straight at Khan, causing him to duck. My little huntress was also a prankster.

"You're late," I said.

"Nice to see you, too, Little Bird."

"Don't call me that." But I smiled as I punched his arm.

He pushed me back. "Oh, so now you're tough! Lucky for you I showed up to save you last Saturday."

"What?" I huffed. "You're the one who's lucky. I was this close"—I held two pinching fingers out in front of his face—"to slitting your throat."

"Ha!" He laughed, and soon I was laughing, too. He glanced down at the Gypsy camp. "I realized after I sent the note that I should have come to get you. I didn't think. I've had so much on my mind lately."

"I've noticed." I remembered Khan with the gang of boys in the city.

He rubbed his bristly chin. "Next time we'll come by boat. It's just that I was nearby. . . ."

"Never mind. But you have to tell me now—what was that . . . that thing you did?" I thought back to how close the guards had been. "It was like we disappeared!"

"It is just something passed down to me." He shrugged.

"Your grandmother taught you how to do that?"

"Yes. I suppose it's like when an animal hides in the forest. You think they're gone, but they are right in front of you, invisible to your eyes because you do not know how to look."

I shook my head, not understanding or believing it could be that simple.

Khan put his arms around me. "I'm glad I wasn't far away," he said. "Avery, promise me you'll keep your wits about you. It's been a week now; have you seen any men in crow masks?"

"No. My father is convinced no one can find us in Vinegar Hill. He doesn't even have his name on the shop. But Khan, how did you know I was in trouble at the Tombs?"

"You won't believe it. I happened to look up and I saw Seraphine doing frantic loops over the building. I knew something was wrong."

"You're right, that is unbelievable—and lucky." I dropped my gaze; our boots were touching toe to toe. "Well . . . thank you. You saved my life."

"It was my pleasure." He grinned. "Really."

The way he said it made heat rise to my cheeks. I remembered the feel of his muscular body pressed up against my back, his tattooed bicep rippling under my palm . . . how later I could still smell him on me, sweet, like cloves and earth.

Flustered, I turned away and started toward the camp. "Khan, you never told me what you were doing in the city."

"We don't have time for this, Avery," Khan said, walking by my side. "Do you want to talk to the Gypsies or not?"

"Yes, I do. And I want to see Oscar."

"Good. I spoke to a Gypsy friend of mine. She's willing to help you—"

"What?" I stopped walking. "You already told someone? Don't you think you should have asked me first?" Resentment smoldered under my skin. "Khan, I've been agonizing all week about whom to trust. My father would be upset if he knew."

"Avery, I'm sorry." Khan let out a long sigh. "I should have asked, but you said you wanted answers and my friend is something of an expert on visions. You can trust the Gypsies. Your mother told you to come here, for goodness' sake."

"Yes, but my father has kept us hidden, all this time, by being careful. I jeopardized that by going to the Tombs without him. I just don't want to do anything else that will put us in danger."

"I understand, but your father is also hiding from *you*. You tell me how he's always in his workshop or out drinking."

"You have nerve, saying that." I took a step back and glared at him. "My father saved your life."

Khan hung his head. "You're right. I am indebted to your father. But Avery, you obviously have some kind of rare ability that he can't help you with. You said this started around your birthday? It's been four months! I think you're afraid to embrace what you can do. Instead, you're letting it control you."

Khan was right; I did keep things inside. I always had, especially things I was afraid of. I supposed I was like my father in that way.

He cupped my chin gently in his hand, the touch of his fingers on my skin sending flutters down my neck.

He nodded toward the camp. "Are we going to do this or not?"

The colors were even more brilliant up close. A soulful harmonica tune floated by on the breeze, the sound entwined with soft singing in another language, but I couldn't see anyone in the darkness. The air was thick with the smell of campfires that flickered in the distance, and roasting meat—pig, perhaps. My mouth watered. My father and I'd eaten stewed potatoes and cabbage all week.

"Looks quiet, doesn't it?" I said.

Khan held up his hand and whispered, "Don't be fooled. You surprise any one of these folks—men, women, and children alike—you can expect a knife in your throat before you say 'good evening.'" He cupped his hands to his mouth and made a sound like a whippoorwill, waited, then did it again.

A moment later, a flap lifted in the side of a red tent and a striking girl emerged, holding a kerosene lantern in one hand and a slender cigar in the other, its bright red tip flaring in the dark. Her black dress matched the long hair cascading from under a silk top hat, of the kind men often wore. As she sauntered closer, I noticed she moved with feline grace. I immediately felt awkward.

"Salut, Khaniferre." She had a robust accent. Without a glance in my direction from her black-rimmed eyes, she leaned in and kissed Khan on the mouth. My cheeks burned again as he placed his hand familiarly on the small of her back. From the way he looked at her, I knew he must've been completely under her spell.

I couldn't blame him. Her sweet perfume swirled around me, making me dizzy. Feeling uncomfortably aware of my boys' trousers and oversize military jacket, I looked down at my boots: practical, yes, but *that* was how a woman dressed. I saw that her bustle allowed just a peek of red lace under the folds of her dress.

Khan politely removed his hat. "Katalina, this is Avery, the one I was telling you about."

I tightened my jaw, picturing him sharing my secrets with her. She turned, and I realized she was probably only a few years older than me, perhaps Khan's age. *He must think of me as a child compared to her.*

Katalina held up the lantern, purging the shadows I so liked to hide in.

"So naive," she said. "So full of power."

Does she mean the visions? I didn't feel full of power.

"All right." She passed the lantern to Khan. "We start tonight, yes?"

"Start what?" I asked.

"We are going to help you, teach you to control your power so you can get your mother out of the Tombs." She made it sound so simple. "In exchange, you are going to help us."

"But you don't understand," I said. "I had no idea . . . there are so many guards."

She looked directly into my eyes. "Oh, but I do understand, more than you can imagine." After one last puff of her cigar, she dropped it and smashed it into the dirt with the tip of her boot. Holding out her arm to me, she said, "If you want your mother back, you have to trust me."

What choice did I have? I trusted Khan, and he vouched for her. "All right," I said. "But I want to see Oscar first. And my mother told me to speak with a man named Niko."

Katalina tucked my arm in hers, leading us into the camp. "You must mean my father. His name is Nikolai Moralis. Alas, he is not here at the moment. I will tell him. So, you are an aura seer. You are seeing energy around people, yes?"

"Energy?" I shrugged. "I'm not sure."

"Bah." She swiped her other hand through the air impatiently. "We start at the beginning. The first thing you need to know is that auras are energy, the life force around living things." She glanced at Khan, who nodded.

"See?" he said. "I told you Katalina knows about this."

Katalina grinned like a satisfied cat. I got the feeling she was trying to impress Khan.

"The aura is essentially an emotional map of the body," she continued.

I thought about the times the visions had been more forceful—on the ferry, at the Works. Usually there was strong emotion involved. "I think I can tell how someone is feeling when I see their aura clearly."

"Describe to me what you see."

I thought for a moment. "It's like a shifting glow around a person. Sometimes dark, sometimes light. Mostly shades of gray. And changing, flowing from one shade to the next."

"No color?"

"No. No color."

"That is unusual. Well, think of what you see as a person's vital energy. Many cultures have a name for it. In ancient Egypt, it was called the *ka*, the spark of life. Chinese medicine refers to the *chi* that flows around and through the body, and the Hindus use the word *prana* to describe this life force."

"Katalina, how do you know all this?" I had never heard such terms.

"I have learned from my father. He is an authority on the second sight. He has traveled the world in search of such knowledge."

After the confusion of the last few days, it felt good to talk to someone who knew what I was experiencing—even if I didn't understand all she was telling me. "At the Midsummer's Eve festival, there's always an aura-reading booth. Is that the same thing?"

"Yes, a few among us have the ability to see a person's aura and tell a little something about them. It is more common than you know. But from what Khaniferre says, I have a feeling you are something different, something more. He told me about the explosion. I know of only one other with a powerful gift like yours, and even he cannot do that."

"May I please speak with this person?" I asked eagerly.

Katalina's arm tightened in mine. "No, I am very sorry, you cannot," she said. "He is gone."

I thought back to the guard with the dog, Bojangles. "Sometimes I see their memories."

"Are you sure?" When I nodded, she said, "Hmm . . . that is rare indeed."

"I just don't understand why my mother is being held captive."

"We will talk more after you visit with Oscar." She led me along. "We are almost there."

The night sky glimmered with stars. Small torches had been lit around the camp. We passed animal pens and horse stables. Ornately painted wagons were interspersed among the colorful tents. We stopped in front of a wagon surrounded by bright red flowers. Its decorative sides sloped out toward the top.

"Welcome to the apothecary," she said. "Please do not step on the poppies." A candle in a glass mason jar illuminated a set of fold-down steps. "Oscar is in there with the herb doctor. Prepare yourself. He is not well."

She put her hand on Khan's chest when he moved to catch up with me. "Goodness, must you follow her everywhere like a devoted dog? She will be fine without you. You can wait here and keep me company," she purred, leaning her body into his.

Khan took her wrists. "Sometimes, Katalina, you let your words fly a little too freely."

"Humpf." She pursed her lips.

Just what is their relationship? I wondered, as I entered through a Dutch door.

The apothecary was a wonder to my senses. The dark wood was waxed to a high polish. Candles flickered along the sides, revealing a plethora of cabinets and cubbies, all of which held tiny glass bottles and tins. They tinkled like bells as I meandered through the spice-scented space. Through a gauzy curtain at the far end, I saw a tall, thin man hunched over a wooden bunk built into the side. Both he and the bed were draped in colorful fabrics.

A low moan escaped from a lump under the sheets.

"Oscar?" I whispered.

The herb doctor glanced up, then motioned for me to enter. He had a sharp nose and high cheekbones tattooed with lines of runic letters. One eye was covered with an elaborate monocle strapped over his shaved head, the other was so green it sparkled like an emerald. There was an otherworldly air about him, as if he were made of ancient stardust. It was impossible to tell his age.

Oscar was clearly sedated. The left side of his face was swollen with bruises, and his legs were splinted with wooden boards. He groaned and shifted, as if the pain reached into his dreams.

"Will he be all right?" I fidgeted with my necklace.

"I cannot yet tell," he said. "Both legs are fractured, but with this one"—he pointed to Oscar's right leg—"the bone punctured the skin."

My stomach did a little flip. The herb doctor continued, "We will watch for infection. If it gets ugly, we must amputate."

Poor Oscar. I imagined him waking to discover he only had

one leg, like my father. I placed my hand on his arm. It was hot. "Don't worry, you're going to be all right," I whispered, hoping it was true. "Where are his parents?"

"Oscar's mother and father died in a fire when he was very young."

"Oh, I'm sorry to hear that." I paused, not sure what else to say. Then I felt in my pocket and pulled out the bills. "Some of his coworkers donated money to help him out." The boys and I had added what we could to the collection.

"Very kind." He nodded and tucked the notes between two jars. He adjusted his monocle so that his eye appeared to be three times normal size. Rubbing his chin, he deftly removed something dried and twisted from a tin. "This is arnica root. Mash it into a paste with hot oil and apply it to your injured foot."

I looked down at the ugly yellow-brown root. "How did you know about my foot?"

But Oscar moaned again, and my question evaporated in the thick fragrant air. The herb doctor swiftly dropped the gauze between us, dismissing me to attend to his patient.

CHAPTER TWELVE
THE MYSTIC

Khan stayed behind with some Gypsy boys as I followed Katalina through the maze of tents and caravans. He seemed comfortable within the camp. Obviously he knew Katalina well. After seeing him in Five Points and now here, I was beginning to wonder what else I did not know about my friend. I hated the way this mistrust made me feel inside, jittery and cold.

Small campfires, surrounded by laughter and music, animated the darkness. It felt warm and welcoming compared to life in the tenements. But did the Gypsies live in any place for long? I knew all too well that they could pack up camp in a day and disappear.

As if she were reading my mind, Katalina launched into a story.

"The Romany people are of the old country. We came to America in hopes of a better life. We came here for roots." I liked her soft lilting accent, the way she rolled her *r*'s. "What we found was a country divided. White people against black. Children working like adults. Street gangs. Immigrants living in poverty. We found a people broken apart from each other. We came to a nation so caught up in building itself, it forgot its own heritage. It forgot the old ways." She stopped and looked at me. "It forgot its magic."

We had walked to the far end of camp. A blue tent sat just a few feet from the water.

"We are here," she said. "Do exactly as the mystic says. Open your eyes." She placed the tip of her long fingernail on my forehead. "And your mind."

With that, she pulled the flap of the tent back and disappeared into the dimly lit interior. I heard her speak in a hushed voice to someone inside, heard my name. My hands felt clammy. I wiped them on my trousers. I had to do this for my mother. Taking a shaky breath, I followed.

"Katalina?" I whispered. She reached for my hand and pulled me forward, then raised the wick of a lantern on a table, spreading soft light into the space.

The walls and floor were covered with fabrics and worn tapestries in shades of blue. Sweet incense smoked the air. A young waiflike girl in a filmy white dress looked up at me with huge pale-blue eyes, so pale they were almost white. I'd never seen a ghost, but if I ever did, I imagined it would have her diaphanous appearance. She was exquisite-looking, ethereal.

On one side of the tent, a gap in the tapestries revealed a

small candlelit bedroom. Within, an old man sat on a pillow. He was perfectly still, except for a long gray beard moving ever so slightly with his breath.

Katalina extended her hand in his direction. "That is Yoska Torre. And this"—she pointed at the girl—"this is his grand-daughter, Hurricane."

Hurricane looked younger than myself: thirteen, maybe. "Nice to meet you, Hurricane."

A tiny smile stole across her lips as she dropped her chin shyly.

Katalina turned to leave.

"Wait," I said. "How long will he sit there? And why is he called 'the mystic'?"

Katalina laughed. "Yoska is one of the elders and quite deaf. Hurricane is the one I call 'the mystic.'"

"Oh," I said, stunned.

Hurricane lifted her head and smiled, seemingly pleased by Katalina's nickname, as if she cherished Katalina's approval.

Katalina grinned. "Do not worry about disturbing Yoska. When he is meditating, nothing can wake him, not even a real hurricane."

The girl stood on tiptoe and whispered something to Katalina, whose eyes widened momentarily. Before I could say another word, Katalina whisked up her skirt and swept away. I did not like the secrets.

An awkward silence settled around us. "So, what exactly *is* a mystic?" I asked.

Hurricane gestured toward a tufted chair next to the table. "Please sit," she said, in a delicate voice. She tucked her silky cropped hair behind her ear. It was milk white, like her skin. "I'm not a real mystic. I just do energy work like my mum used to do, so I'm told."

"Oh." I didn't want to pry, even though I was curious about her mother. "Katalina said I see energy. Is that why she wants me to meet with you?"

"Yes. I might be able to help you focus and strengthen your sight. But first, I must cleanse the space." She lit a bundle of dried herbs bound in twine on fire, then blew it out and waved it through the air. "Sage," she said, as the smoke dissipated. "It clears away negative energies." Then she tamped it out. "I will guide you through a meditation by placing my hands on your energy centers. Relax and close your eyes. It doesn't hurt." She stood in front of me.

I closed my eyes, feeling awkward, but her voice was soft, hypnotic. "Relax your shoulders. Focus on your breath, in . . . out . . . long and slow, in . . . out . . . With every breath, relax your mind. If a thought comes to you, let it go, like a leaf in a stream, drifting away."

As she spoke, I tried to slow my breathing. She positioned her hands on my head.

"Imagine a third eye here." She gently touched the center of my forehead. "Visualize your breath entering through your third eye."

Too many thoughts popped into my mind. I heard the hiss

of the lantern; an itch on my shoulder made my skin twitch. *This is impossible. How do I stop myself from thinking?*

Then I pictured my mother, the blood running down her arm. Taking a deep breath, I tried again. Hurricane lifted her hands and put one lightly on my throat, one on my upper chest. "I sense constriction here, around your heart."

I exhaled long and deep, and felt my body relaxing.

The skin under Hurricane's hands tingled. There was a lurching sensation, as if I was falling. The feeling unsettled me, so I opened my eyes. When I did, I saw Hurricane in a luminous field of light. Our arms, our legs, were all surrounded by a vibrant light, flowing from me into her, her into me. I turned my head, the light trailing like liquid from my eyes. The old man across the tent sat in a glowing pool of light. A shiver coursed through my body. Did we all share the same vital energy—the same life force, as Katalina called it? The idea filled me with wonder and surprise. *What if . . . what if we are all connected?*

My head fell back; my eyes rolled up. Then I lost sense of my body. There was no need of it. I was pure energy, expanding outward. Looking up, I saw beyond the tent to the night sky. It was a feeling unlike any I'd ever experienced, as if I could expand out into the stars, into the universe. *Am I dreaming?*

Hurricane squeezed my shoulders. I didn't want it to end, but she shook me hard. I gathered back into myself. My eyelids felt heavy, and I closed them for hours—or maybe only seconds. When I forced them open, everything looked normal.

Hurricane sat across from me, studying me. Tear tracks glistened on her cheeks.

I whispered, "It was beautiful. I didn't know it would be like that."

"Neither did I."

"How did you do it then?" I asked, confused. "That light . . ."

"I didn't do anything." Hurricane stared at me, tilting her head. "You did." She slid a handkerchief from within her sleeve and dabbed at her face. "I didn't see any light, but I felt it. It made me feel, I don't know . . . content, happy inside." She propped her head on her fists. "Did Katalina tell you how I got my name?"

"No, she said nothing about you."

"I'm told that when we came to this country, my mother fell in love with an American and got pregnant. On the day I was born, a terrible storm was sent to punish her sin. Papi says the storm stole my color. My mother named me Hurricane. Romany people are superstitious of those like me. Albinos are said to bring misfortune."

"That's stuff and nonsense, as my father says." I'd never heard that word, *albino*. I reached out and gently touched her hand. "You mustn't believe that. You're beautiful. Where *is* your mother?"

"She must've been frightened of me, too. She ran off to live with my father on a commune called Brook Farm. I have no memory of her."

"Oh, Hurricane. I'm so sorry. I know how hard it is to be without a mother."

She pressed her lips together for a moment. "She left her diary. I've read it a thousand times. They called themselves Transcendentalists. It's from her diary that I learned how to do energy work."

I thought of Geeno and the sadness he felt over losing his parents. I told Hurricane the same thing I told him. "Hurricane, if you can't remember her, you must have been very young. You mustn't blame yourself."

She nodded. "Papi says that, too." She took a deep breath and let out a long sigh. "Let's try again, shall we?"

We spent two hours working on my focus. What I needed was my welding gun; I seemed to have no trouble focusing at work.

As we finished our session, I said, "Thank you, Hurricane. I feel like I'm gaining a little control."

"Your second sight is strong. I wonder why it took so long to manifest, though." She glanced at the diary. "My mother's notes suggest that trauma or shock can hinder our energy flow."

I thought about the years I'd spent not wanting to end up like my mother, denying what was happening to me, burying it inside. Then I remembered Dr. Spector, lurking outside our house. "Do you think seeing something that terrified me when I was young could have had this effect?"

"Possibly. When did you start having visions?"

"After my sixteenth birthday. But it wasn't until I saw Oscar beaten that I felt something open up inside of me, like an eggshell cracking apart."

"Is that when you caused the explosion that Katalina told me about?"

"Yes, exactly," I said.

"I think we should do this again soon. Especially as Katalina wants you to be strong enough."

"Strong enough for what?"

Hurricane sat back, her eyes darting to the entrance. "Maybe Katalina should tell you. She . . ."

"What is it?" I'd suspected Katalina was not telling me everything. "I need to know, Hurricane. Strong enough for what?"

"To . . . to save Indigo, if he's still alive." Hurricane looked down at her hands. "Don't you remember the last time you were at the camp?"

"Of course I remember." My stomach clenched. "It was three years ago."

"Yes," she said, her voice barely a whisper. "The Midsummer's Eve festival."

"That's right. But how did you know?"

Hunching her shoulders, she said, "You kissed a boy you shouldn't have. His name is Indigo, and . . ." Her white-blond eyebrows drew together. "You quite possibly cost him his life."

CHAPTER THIRTEEN
KALEIDOSCOPE

I marched down the dirt road. Khan knew better than to speak to me after I'd flown into a rage at Hurricane's accusation. My shouts, as I'd stuffed my hair into my hat and stormed out, had even startled deaf Yoska.

Now, at last, I knew the boy's name. It fit him.

I thought back to that night. Before my father had dragged me out of the tent, Indigo had whispered in my ear, "Swear you'll come back tomorrow. I need to see you."

I had disobeyed my father, just as I'd done tonight. I'd gone back.

Yet, when I'd arrived, the Gypsy camp was deserted. The remnants of the fair lay strewn across the grass, smoldering embers of the bonfire trailing smoke into the air. They'd disappeared. He knew I'd come back, and still he'd left. I'd cried all the way home, my thirteen-year-old heart aching from his slight.

I was angry with myself for storming away from Hurricane. If I wasn't such a pawn to my emotions, I could have discovered what else had happened. I'd just been so incensed that she thought a kiss from me could cost Indigo his life.

It was going to be a long, miserable walk home. Luckily, Khan had thought to bring a lantern. I heard a rushing sound behind me, as Seraphine landed expertly on the shoulder of my jacket. As usual, she relaxed me. After a while, I slowed my furious pace and yelled out to Khan, "Slowpoke." To salt the wound, I added, "I'm going to trip up here with no light. Can't you walk a little faster?"

With the lantern attached to his pack, Khan's shadow bobbed like that of a drunken giant. He caught up quickly. "Ah, so you're ready to tell me what the hell happened?"

"No," I huffed. "I don't want to talk about it."

"Suit yourself," he said, walking by my side now. He started whistling a ditty to the beat of our steps. I loved that about Khan. I never had to explain myself to him if I didn't want to.

The sounds of the night penetrated my thoughts. An owl hooted; the trees whispered in some ancient but familiar language. My mind began to uncoil. I looked up at the velvety black sky, pierced by a thousand pins of light.

At my side, Khan tilted his head, listening. I heard it, too: the unmistakable tromping of horses. Someone was coming up the road. We stepped to the side as a two-horse covered stage-coach jingled up and stopped. The driver, sitting on a high bench in front, glanced down.

"Sure is late to be out walking. We're up from Canarsie Landing to Fort Greene." He nodded toward the road. "How far you boys going? I could give you a ride."

Khan stifled a laugh. I kept my head down and kicked his foot.

"Sure thing, mister," Khan said. "We'd appreciate it. We're headed your way."

I pulled my hat lower and remained quiet. Folks would not think highly of a girl out alone at night with a boy, let alone a white girl and a black boy. I shook Seraphine off my shoulder; she disappeared into the night.

The driver watched, rubbing his chin. "Well, I'll be. Falcon, right?"

Khan answered for me. "Yep, raised from a chick." He blew out his lantern as we climbed into the coach. Khan respectfully removed his hat, but I didn't dare. I was glad of the one small lantern up front, which kept the bulk of the carriage in shadows.

The moment we sat down, I felt the tension. A well-dressed man and woman were in the seat across from us. They stared at Khan. Clutching her valise to her body, the woman leaned over and whispered something to the man.

Khan sighed. "Think I'll ride in back," he muttered.

I wasn't about to let him ride alone. I jumped up, following him out and around to the rear of the coach. We climbed up onto the jump seat.

"Are you all right?" I whispered as the driver cracked his whip and we started off.

He rubbed the back of his neck. "How about a spot of bourbon?" Reaching into his coat pocket, he pulled out a pewter flask. Pressed into the metal was the image of a balloon above a battlefield: the Balloon Corps.

"Is that my father's?"

"Yes, war-pocked and all. He gave it to me on my eighteenth birthday." He took a long swig and held it out to me.

My father had engraved Khan's full name on the back, along with the date. Over two years ago, not long after I'd been forced to quit school. I took a drink, and started coughing. The amber liquid burned its way down my throat to rest like a hot coal inside my stomach. Somehow it felt good, the heat radiating through my body.

We leaned our heads back to gaze at the stars as we passed the flask back and forth between us.

"Khan," I said at last. "I want to ask you something. And this time you'd better not give me the runaround with your vague answers, you hear me?"

He nodded. "Yes, ma'am."

I glanced at him. "And wipe that silly grin off your face."

He lifted his hand and wiped his mouth down into a frown, mocking me.

"This is serious, Khan. What was going on in Five Points?"
Am I slurring my words?

"You don't give up, do you?" He rubbed his forehead.

"Khan, it looked like . . . like a street gang."

"What?" His eyebrows shot up. "I am not in a gang."

"So tell me then," I whispered. "Khan, I'm your best friend. But you've been very distant lately."

"Those young men you saw me with came here to work. But you know better than anyone the conditions in the factories and mills." He frowned, a shadow in his eyes. "I hate how many hours you put in at Cross Street."

"Mr. Soliman." I pretended to fan myself. "You sound like a musty old man who believes a woman's place is solely in the home." I laughed, the alcohol making me feel flighty.

"Far be it from me to tell you that, Avery. I know you wanted to get an education." He reached over and ran the back of his hand along my jaw. My breath shortened. "You're beautiful *and* smart." No one had ever said that to me before. I was quiet as he continued. "Those men are trying to form a labor union, but as you can imagine, they face a lot of resistance."

"A labor union?" I grabbed the side of the seat as we went over a rut in the road. "Khan, I forgot to tell you. Some men at the Works are also involved with a union. Secretly, of course. It's impressive, given how dangerous it seems."

"Yes. I know." He nodded. "Avery, I didn't want to burden you with all this when you're so worried about your mother."

The words seemed to draw him back to himself. Khan lifted the flask in the air. "To your mother," he said, taking a sip and then handing it back to me. It was almost empty.

"To my mother." I drank, feeling the warmth spread into my chest, feeling bad for doubting Khan.

Khan whistled. "Not bad for a first-timer."

"Family trait." I laughed. It felt good. A breeze caught my hat and I grabbed it before it blew away. My hair tumbled free, fanning out in the wind. I snuggled closer to Khan, enjoying the rhythmic sway of the carriage. "What about you and Katalina? The two of you seem close." I cursed my quick mouth; I sounded like a jealous shrew.

Khan raised his eyebrows, a bemused smile on his face. "We're good friends. I've known her a long time. I helped repair her father's boat."

Maybe Gypsy girls are simply more open in their affection.

Khan put his arm around me. "Are you cold? Your hands feel like ice." He lifted my hands to his mouth and blew warm air into them. "Mmm, you smell good, like honeysuckle."

His breath tickled my wrist, sending a fluttery feeling through my stomach. I looked up into his warm, tawny eyes. A shiver trembled down my back. I'd always felt safe in his strong arms, but this was different. I couldn't get my head around what my body was feeling—my stomach in knots, my breath shallow. I wanted the touch of Khan's mouth on mine. Was it the alcohol muddling my thoughts? He was my best friend, my safety net.

Would kissing him change all that? Was this my way of erasing the thoughts of the Gypsy boy?

My necklace poked Khan in the chest, breaking the moment. He lifted the leather cord. "What is all this stuff you wear?"

"Memories . . . things I love . . . things that are special to me. It's silly, I know." Laughing, I held up a ring. "Remember when you gave me this?" My voice sounded slow and fuzzy.

He smiled. "I do, actually. What was I, nine?" I nodded. Khan's eyes focused inward. "It was a promise ring. I'd wanted to marry you, before I knew it was taboo." He reached into his own shirt and pulled out a chain. Dangling from it was a tiny silver tube. "It's a kaleidoscope," he said.

"Oh! I've never seen a miniature one."

"It was my mother's. She . . ." He took a deep breath. "I'm told she gave it to me before she died. My *ouma* said it reminded my mother of the world's beauty when everything around her was ugly." He held it up, squinting. "Can't see it in the dark, but the patterns are made from all kinds of seeds. She intended to plant them one day, when she was freed from bondage."

He slid it off the chain and placed it in my hand, wrapping my fingers around it. I looked at the intricate designs etched into the silver. "Khan, I can't."

"Keep it for me, then. We'll plant the seeds together when your mother is free from the Tombs."

"Thank you," I whispered. I bit my lip, feeling the trace of tears in my eyes. The coach slowly came to a stop at a deserted station at the edge of town. "Must be Fort Greene. We won't have far to walk from here."

I tucked the kaleidoscope into my pocket and prepared to jump down. At that moment, the well-dressed couple stepped around the rear of the coach. Their eyes opened wide at the sight of a black boy and a white girl huddled together.

The woman sucked in her breath. "Scandalous!" she hissed.

I don't care, I thought recklessly. I gave her a cheeky grin as I hopped down, Khan's hand in mine.

CHAPTER FOURTEEN
LOST TIME

I woke to the clamor of a hundred ticks and tocks. Khan once said the sound would drive him crazy, but I loved it . . . usually. After so many years living with Father's creations, I didn't think I could handle silence.

Today, though, my head throbbed with every click of a gear, every swing of a pendulum. I rubbed my forehead. I should've made one of Father's concoctions, but couldn't stomach it.

I'd had another vivid dream. I was Seraphine, flying above the city, circling the updrafts to go higher and higher. I was free. Powerful. A hunter. I cocked my head at a flicker of movement below, something darting into the street. Tucking my wings, I dove. Wind rushed by, faster and faster, until everything was a blur around me, my eyes locked on my target. Inches above the street, I knew to snap out my wings, snaring the prey in my talons. In the same instant, I would swoop back up into the sky. But something was wrong. My wings, pinned tightly to my sides, would not open. The street came up to meet me, fast, and I smashed full force into the cobblestones, my brain exploding out through my third eye.

I leapt out of bed. Sunlight bathed the shop in a warm glow. My father's alcove was empty. He still made his bed like a soldier, tight as a drum. He was at morning mass, no doubt. Every Sunday he lit a candle for my mother.

As angry as I'd been last night, I knew I had to talk to Hurricane and Katalina again soon. The Gypsies were my only chance to learn everything I could about my visions, and to help me figure out how to get my mother out of the Tombs.

When I'd stumbled in last night, my father had raised his eyebrows at me knowingly and made me a cup of wild sage tea for my queasy stomach. I didn't dare tell him I'd gone to the Gypsy camp, so when I pulled the arnica root from my pocket, I had to lie to him, again. My stomach had twisted at how easily the deception slid off my tongue. "Khan got it for me. He learned it from his grandmother." We'd made the poultice and applied it to my foot.

I peeled the hardened gauze off my ankle, gently circling my foot. The pain was gone. Even the purple bruise was fading. The arnica had worked like magic.

Stuffing a chunk of soda bread in my mouth, I threw my father's long wool infantry coat over my nightshirt and slipped out the side door. I made a quick stop in the hallway bathroom, which we shared with the Olson family. We were lucky; many tenements on our block did not have indoor plumbing. Then I headed up the stairs to the roof to check on Seraphine, the vestiges of the dream still haunting me.

The cold bit into my bare feet as I stepped out onto the roof. I held my breath as I lifted the canvas flap over Seraphine's roost. *Ki-ki-ki-kee*, she chirped, happy to see me, as always. Stroking her brown-and-white speckled feathers, I imitated her sound. She ducked her head and repeated it back to me, making me smile.

I'd inherited the young peregrine falcon the day Old Man Lorenzo started spitting blood into his handkerchief. He'd lived upstairs and had a crackling sense of humor; he was the one who wanted me to call him that—"Old Man Lorenzo." I'd spent hours in his apartment helping him with his birds. He had all kinds, but Seraphine was my favorite. Caring for Seraphine was the only thing that got me through the horror of losing my mother and moving to Vinegar Hill.

In between terrible coughing fits, he taught me how to train and feed her. When he died, she'd disappeared for two full days. I thought she was gone for good, but she came back to me, and as she grew, she learned to hunt and feed herself. Our neighborhood certainly had fewer rats, thanks to her. *Now she's a part of me*, I sighed. *If I lose her, I lose part of myself.*

"It was just a dream," I whispered, pressing my lips to her

soft head. I went over to the low wall enclosing the roof. The sun-warmed ledge at the bottom felt good on my frozen feet.

The street below was coming alive. Sunday was a day to be outside in any weather, but today it was all the more spectacular. The morning sun cut through the brittle October air, melting the fine layer of frost and bouncing off the light fabric of the airships flying over Manhattan Island. Crisp sounds reached my ears: horses clopping on the cobbles, newsboys shouting headlines, the far-off clanging of the bridge construction. From my elevated vantage, I looked down on feathered hats and bonnets strolling arm in arm with fedoras and derbies and toppers on the way to St. Ann's or Plymouth Church. *My father should've made hats instead of clocks. We'd never be hungry then.*

Seraphine flew to the wall, and together we watched the bustle below. I noticed some pedestrians pointing into the dark alley across the street. A young boy cried as his mother pulled him briskly away. Two men emerged from the shadows; people dodged them, lowering their heads to avoid eye contact. I knew why. It was their masks, their crow-like masks.

They angled toward the large clock jutting from the wall above our store. I heard them banging on the door and put a hand on my chest to still the pounding of my heart.

They've found us. I was trapped. I couldn't leave the building barefoot, in a nightgown. Seraphine, sensing my distress, started to twitter and screech. I grabbed her leather hood and secured it over her head, obscuring her eyes. She puffed out her feathers and calmed down.

"Shhh," I whispered to her. "Stay quiet now."

Crouching behind the parapet, I slowly peered over the edge until I was staring directly down at the crows. In addition to their beaked masks with goggle eyes, they wore black wide-brimmed hats and long black leather coats. They rapped again on the glass front door to our shop. One of them tried the knob and found it locked. They scanned the street. I ducked out of sight as one tilted his head to look up. Then I heard glass shatter, followed by the sound of the men crashing their way through the shop.

I stayed huddled on the roof until my legs were numb, images of the crows bursting out onto the roof flooding my imagination. When I dared peek down again, I saw that they were leaving. I let out my breath. My hands shook and my teeth chattered.

Amidst the glass strewn across the sidewalk were pieces of wood and metal and a myriad of elaborate gears. Our entrance clock lay in pieces, another moment of time lost to me forever; another omen of my broken family.

The crow-guards crossed the street. Just then I saw my father, walking obliviously toward them, his mechanical leg reflecting in the sunlight every time he took a step. He'd taken to wearing a long coat to conceal it, but as he moved, it showed anyway. With the guards' backs to me, I beckoned, hoping to catch his attention. He had his head down, as if deep in thought, but as he got closer he looked up, somehow sensing their presence. From the way they picked up their pace, I could tell they knew exactly who he was. Without taking his eyes off them, my father lowered the brim of his hat and slid his hand slowly down the side of his metal leg. He was going to pull out his gun. I had to stop him before something terrible happened.

Frantically, afraid to yell out, I tried to signal him. I jumped up and down, waving my arms in the air. I had to get his attention.

An idea hit me. Quickly, I removed Seraphine's hood and pointed at my father. Recognition sparked in her eyes. She leapt from the wall and swooped down toward him. It worked. The movement caught his eye, and he saw me on the roof beyond. He held up his forearm as Seraphine came in for a landing, skimming the tops of the crows' black hats. The guards jumped back. I couldn't hear what they said, but I could tell they were furious.

One of them lunged forward and kicked out Father's good leg. Seraphine took off into the air as he fell to the street with a loud clatter. I cringed, biting my fist, as the other guard stomped on my father's arm with his heavy black boot. They stood on each side, pinning his arms wide. People backed away.

Isn't anyone going to help him? The taller one pushed back his leather coat to reveal a rifle. *No! I should've let my father shoot them.* He shoved the barrel into my father's face and said something, nodding toward the shop. Whatever my father said must have angered him more. He slammed the gun into my father's nose; blood spurted out. They said something else and then stepped back, releasing him. As one, they turned on their heels and disappeared into the shadows of the alley, leaving my father bleeding in the street.

By the time I raced down, Mr. Meyer and his young son had helped my father home. When Mr. Meyer spoke, he wouldn't look me in the eye. It could have been my bare feet and night-gown, but I got the feeling he was scared of us.

"Miss," he said, "my boy, Abe, will go fetch Doc Walters. I . . . I have to get on home."

"Thank you, sir," I said, as I hooked my shoulder under my father's arm. Relieved of his burden, Mr. Meyer scurried away, crunching through the glass on the sidewalk.

Despite his broken arm, now dangling uselessly at his side, and the blood dripping from his nose, my father crushed me to him. "Avery, I thought they'd found you." He winced with pain between each breath. "When I saw you on the roof . . ." Tears welled in his eyes, but it was the fear in his gaze that unnerved me. "I don't know what I'd do if I lost you, too."

At those words, all the hurt and anger I'd felt for the last week melted away, leaving the residue of shame. "I'm fine, Pop, but you need to sit down." I navigated him through the narrow shop to our small living area in back. Easing him into a chair, I gently extricated myself from his grip, poured water on a towel, and wiped his face. The bleeding had stopped, but his nose was obviously broken and he had a nasty black circle embedded into his cheek from the barrel of the gun.

"What did they say to you?" I looked around at the mess they'd left: furniture overturned, two more clocks smashed. My heart ached at the sight. Father's clocks defined the life I'd once had like a song from my childhood, and these would never again play their rhythmic staccato tune. They'd ripped down the curtain of my sleeping alcove.

"They asked about you," he said. "I told them you'd run away with your lover and, last I heard, you were living on a farm down south, making babies."

My mouth dropped open. "No. You did *not* say that."

"Yes, I did. Clearly they didn't think it was funny." He smiled. I was relieved to see the twinkle in his eyes. We had a long-running joke about how I was the least ladylike girl he'd ever known, and unlike with other young women my age, getting married and having children was the last thing on my mind.

"How did they find us?" It had been over a week since my escape from the Tombs. I had hoped we were safe.

"I don't know. They must have put out feelers."

"Why can't they leave us alone?" I squeezed my fists.

"Avery, they won't stop until they lock you up like your mother." He shifted uncomfortably, holding his injured arm. "When you mentioned Spector's name to me last Saturday, it sounded familiar. Took me some time, but I figured out why.

Open the top drawer of my desk. You'll find a packet of papers."
I dug them out and set them on the table. "This is the spurious
document they gave me when they abducted your mother. Look
at the signature."

I picked up the tattered sheet. *Temple of Mind Balance
Studies* was emblazoned at the top. Scanning the print, I saw
*involuntary admission . . . hallucinatory degeneration . . . rare
psychological condition* and *term of commitment—indefinite.*
Right below, in fancy flourished script, was his name: *Dr. Ignatius Spector—Executive Director.*

"Oh my God. He's in charge of the Tombs." I felt momentarily light-headed. To steady myself, I righted a chair that lay
on its side and pulled it close to my father. "You said you'd never
seen him there when you'd visited her before. I wonder why?"

"When would one run into the executive director of *any*
organization, my girl? I think you got very unlucky, and clearly
a young girl visiting alone is uncommon." My father scratched
his jaw. "After I dug up the admission order and saw his name,
I had a war buddy ask around. The only things he could tell
me were that Dr. Spector became head of the Tombs hospital
in 1864, and that he's from down south somewhere. It wasn't
until around the time they took your mother that anyone
started catching sight of his guards. Seems their masks were
his idea. Spector must have friends in high places—maybe the
police or Tammany Hall. But that doesn't explain how he can
afford his own militia. Someone must be backing him. The man

is shrouded in secrecy." My father looked down at his arm and winced. "What the devil is taking the doctor so long?"

I got up and poured him some water. My whole body was trembling. "Why do you think they wear them, the crow masks?"

"Fear, maybe. I know they scare the dickens out of people. Avery," he said suddenly, his voice growing solemn. "Promise me you will never go near the Tombs again."

I dropped my head. *How can I promise that?* "But Pop—"

"It's my fault your mother is in there," he said, cutting me off. "I'd never forgive myself if they took you, too."

"It's not your fault, Pop! Please don't say that."

"It is." He paused. "Your mother and I hoped you wouldn't have visions, like she does. But it *is* my fault they took her away. This is something I never told you, but I . . . I'm the one who encouraged her to help people, to make her special ability known." My father's eyes took on a faraway look as he continued. "When I met your mother, at St. Joseph's Military Hospital, she was only eighteen, just a couple years older than you are now. I'd lost my leg and I was dying. She nursed my body back to health, but my mind was on the brink of an abyss. She used her gift and somehow helped me heal, after the horrors I'd witnessed. I loved her from the moment we met. But her family, old money New Englanders, had given her away to the Sisters of Charity when she was young, told her the devil was inside her. They told her she should never have children."

"That's horrible. Is that why I've never met her family?"

He nodded. "It took me a long time to convince her to stop hating herself. After you were born, I suggested she help other people the way she'd helped me. They came to the house. For a time, I thought . . . but I was wrong."

I laid my hand over his. I wanted to explain the energy to him, what it felt like to see it, but I barely understood it myself. "You did the right thing." He looked up at me, his eyes searching mine. "Besides." I smiled. "I wouldn't be here if you hadn't saved her from the nunnery."

The crinkles around his eyes, the ones I loved, deepened. "Avery, I'll figure out a way to get your mother out. They can't hold her forever. But right now, you have to hide. It's not safe for you here." He glanced down at his useless arm. "They said they'd be back tomorrow. I'm to give you up."

"What? What about you? You can't stay here, either." It was as if the crows were pecking at my heart. "Pop, they'll hurt you again."

"Begging your pardon, miss." My father and I spun around, startled by the deep voice behind us. Dwarfing the shattered doorway was Jeremiah Thorn. "But they've got to get to him first." He let out a robust, rolling laugh. "And they're sure not getting through me."

Although Jeremiah Thorn was generous with his devil-may-care demeanor and wide smile, which filled his stubble-shadowed face, the spark in his eye also held a dare, and he moved with the powerful grace of a caged lion.

My father's face lit up. "Well, well, look who's here."

Jeremiah entered, ducking below a clock hanging from the ceiling, military boots rattling the gadgetry of the shop. His worn leather adventurer's hat held a pair of old brass goggles at the band, and as he approached, he opened his dusty canvas coat to reveal a small arsenal strapped to his body. "At your service, and as you can see, I come prepared."

He pulled off his right glove and clasped my father's hand. A look passed between them that spoke of their history. I knew that under his left glove was a hand made of shiny metal, a streamlined mechanism of meticulous beauty. The gears and cogs and perfectly hinged fingers my father forged for him moved as nimbly as if they were made of flesh and bone.

Putting his glove back on, he said, "Edgar, tell me the other guy looks worse than you." He laughed again, closing the toggles of his coat. "My cousin saw what happened here, came running to get me. From the looks of this place . . ." He scanned the room. "It's like we're back at war. Miss Kohl." He tipped his hat at me. I liked his easy manner, the way he dissolved the tension in the room.

"Mr. Thorn," I said.

A head poked out from behind Jeremiah. "Ahem, did one of you summon a doctor?"

Jeremiah stepped aside. Doc Walters was a short round man with spectacles that he regularly pushed up his piglike nose, who always smelled like the peppermint candy he sucked on to cover the smell of alcohol on his breath. Wispy white hair clung to the sides of his bald head as if it knew it was fighting a losing battle. He glanced around at the mess and craned his head to look up at Jeremiah. "Oh my, Mr. Kohl, what has happened here?"

"It's a long story, Doc. This here's a war friend and patriot," my father said. "May I present Officer Thorn, of the United States Colored Troops, Twenty-Ninth Regiment, and rabble-rouser extraordinaire."

"Ha-ha! Seems to me you're the one stirring up trouble now," Jeremiah said.

"Sure does, doesn't it?" My father turned toward me, his face paling. He shut his eyes and leaned back. "Avery, pour us a little something from that bottle in the cupboard, would you please?"

I retrieved a bottle of Old Tom gin and poured three glasses. Jeremiah picked up two, holding one out to Doc Walters. The doctor's eyes shone. "Oh, well," he sputtered. "Normally I don't imbibe, but I suppose one taste can't harm."

My father held his glass in the air. "Here's to my wife. God, I miss that woman." He tossed the shot back and sucked air through his gritted teeth. "Gentlemen, if you'll excuse us, I have to speak with my daughter. Doc, I'll be using that bed over there." He pointed to his alcove on the other side of the shop.

"Oh yes, yes, of course." The doctor placed his empty glass on the table. "I'll prepare my things." He waddled over, pushing the curtain aside. Jeremiah strode back to the entrance and stood there, arms folded, scanning the street. He was right. Nothing could get past him.

"Trust me, Avery, they will not catch me off guard again. Now get dressed quickly and pack some things," my father whispered. "Do you have somewhere you can go?"

"But, Pop." I couldn't lose them both. "You can't. What if they take you?"

"Avery, it's you they want. It's this thing you and your mother can do." A bead of sweat broke out on his forehead. "Please, tell me you have someplace you can stay."

Where can I go? My mind reeled. I didn't want to endanger anyone else. Khan lived at the wharf with his grandmother, Leo with his family. I couldn't put them at risk. Tony was at the halfway house—they'd never allow me entry. I thought about asking Katalina if she could put me up, but I couldn't do that to my father. It was bad enough I was visiting the Gypsy camp at all.

Then it came to me. I knew exactly where to go. Someplace only I knew.

CHAPTER FIFTEEN
SCORPIONS AND DRAGONFLIES

Struggling with my heavy pack, I made my way around to the waterfront on the far side of the navy yard. Every long black coat made my heart skip a beat. The crows could be anywhere. I'd stuffed as much as I could into my father's canvas knapsack, shuddering as always at its dark stains—blood that wouldn't wash out. Where I was going, I would need to stay warm. I just hoped I remembered how to get there.

On my left, I passed the Havemeyers & Elder sugar refinery, the largest in America. The huge squat buildings hunched along the East River, awaiting ships to carry sugar to craving people everywhere. The air smelled sickly sweet, like burnt cookies.

I'd once tried to get a job there. I remembered the sticky resin coating the floor, the way it stuck to the bottom of my boots when I was pushed out the door. I'd sought work at many places before I was hired at Cross Street Ironworks. Roland Malice, the only factory owner who would hire a girl, had examined my hands. Said he could tell a good welder by their hands, something about dexterity. And if I was going to dress like a boy, he'd added, I might as well work like a boy.

I spent the next hour traversing the streets. My stomach grumbled; all I'd eaten was a penny pie I'd bought off a cart vendor. Nothing looked familiar. I'd been here once, so I'd thought I'd remember. What if I was wrong?

Backtracking to the corner of First and River, I sat on my pack and pulled out a hunk of bread. I hoped my father was all right. The curtain hadn't masked the agonizing groans of the bone-setting procedure. Jeremiah Thorn, true to his word, made sure no one came in.

A loud blast from the refinery startled me. If I didn't find my destination soon, I'd be sleeping on the street. Near the giant coal bins, crammed between the warehouses, were abandoned shipping crates piled two or three high. These wooden boxes had grown into a city for the homeless and destitute. Geeno lived somewhere in there, but I was afraid to ask for directions. From afar, if I kept my head down, I passed for a boy. Girls didn't wander alone.

I remembered Geeno's crate being at ground level. Did the inhabitants move about, or claim ownership of their spot? Hopefully, the latter. I walked slowly past each crate. They had makeshift doors and windows cut into the wood, some bedecked with oddly out-of-place lacy curtains. The air, thick with factory smoke, stung my eyes as I tried to peer into the dim interiors. Entire families made homes here. A group of dirty children played jacks in the alley, oblivious to the miserable living conditions. Three men stood around a table, cards laid out on top.

Think, Avery, think. Despite the cold, I began to sweat, the comforting bulge of my knife the only thing keeping me calm. The crates all looked the same. I approached the far end of the row, dreading the thought of starting over. Something crunched under my boot—a hairy spider. I squealed and jumped back, then glanced around, worried someone might have noticed my outburst. Head down, I quickly paced back up the narrow street.

Wait. There was something strange about that spider. I ran back. Stooping down, I flipped it over. It had seven normal legs, but in place of the eighth was a segmented piece of wire connected to three tiny interlocking gears embedded in the larger section of its body. Looking closer, I saw several other partly mechanical dead bugs nearby. I thought of Geeno showing me the scorpion he wanted to "fix." It had to be him.

The nearest crate was as long as a railroad car and just as dark. I held up the oilcloth flap covering the doorway, as my eyes adjusted. "Geeno?" I whispered. "It's me, Avery."

Inside was a narrow room with a cot on one side, a moth-eaten chair, and a box-crate table. It smelled strongly of coffee and I wondered if I was wrong, if someone older lived here. At the far end I noticed a door, half my size. A thin line of light flickered under it along the floor. I crept forward, gripping the hilt of my knife, and knocked.

A flexible metal tube snaked out through a tiny hole in the wood. I drew back as it pointed itself up at my face and then whisked back inside. I heard bolts sliding and locks turning. The door opened to Geeno's sweet smile. He rushed out and hugged me around the waist.

"Avery! Why you here? How you find me?"

"Geeno!" I hugged him back. "Let me be the first to say, finding you is not easy." I let out a long sigh. "But that's why I'm here."

He made me sit while he built a fire in a small potbelly stove in the corner. A pipe vented smoke through the outside wall of the crate. No wonder he didn't freeze to death. Quickly, Geeno brewed up some thick black coffee and pressed a cup into my hands. It tasted surprisingly good. Apparently, he lived in a coffee-shipping container, and some cargo came with his home—to the tune of fifteen cases.

I told him as little as I could without fabricating more lies. "So, after someone broke into the shop, my father asked me to find a safe place to stay, in case they return. Is it all right if I stay with you for a while?"

He straightened his shoulders. "Don't worry, Avery, no one find you here. I guess this means I can't work with your pa today. I just getting my things ready to go."

"Thank you, Geeno. And yes, you will have to wait until

his arm is healed and we know it's safe there." I paused, then blurted out, "I saw Oscar yesterday. He's terribly ill."

"I know," he said. "Leo tell me after they drop him off at the Gypsy camp. I hope they do not chop his leg off."

"That would be horrible. But I think he's in good hands. The herb doctor has some secret magic." I nodded toward the back. "So what's in the other room?"

Geeno's face fell. "I try to help some little creatures but . . ." He looked down at the floor. "I kill them. They not at all like clocks."

I'd never seen him so sad. "Geeno, it's not your fault. You can't fix a living thing."

"But they hurt. They need someone to help them."

I wondered if Geeno's desire to help the broken creatures stemmed from his parents' death and his life alone here. I wished he could go to school, have a mother to take care of him, cook for him. I wished he had a little magic in his life.

"I show you?" He stood and pointed to the small door.

"Sure, you go first." I hoped the scorpion he'd shown me wasn't running loose back there. I ducked to follow him in, and he locked the door behind us. The candlelit room was similar in size to the front room, but shelves lined both sides and a long wooden table ran down the center. "Geeno, what is this?"

"It my treasure," he said, beaming. The shelves were crammed with scraps of metal, gears of all sizes, old clocks and instruments, spools of wire, and coffee tins filled with screws and nuts and bolts. I even recognized some old metalworking tools, similar to the ones we used at the Works. Now I understood all the locks.

"Where did you get all this, Geeno?"

"Most in the trash," he said. "Oscar, he give me some, too."

"Oscar?" I thought back to what Mr. Malice had said the day of the explosion. "Geeno, what if Oscar was stealing from the factory?"

"No way." He shook his head and laughed. "I doubt Oscar that stupid."

I wasn't so sure. "Geeno, you and I both know it's hard to live on our salary. I bet he could make a pretty penny selling tools like these."

"I guess." He shrugged. "Oscar has been bringing me food, but he say the vendors gave to him."

If Oscar *had* been stealing to feed Geeno, he'd probably saved him from slipping through the cracks of the street and into the sewer below. I hunched my shoulders under the weight of my shame. I'd been more concerned about rekindling my friendship with Grace than taking care of Geeno.

"Look here." Geeno stood at the table, pointing to a row of glass mason jars. Each had a metal top poked through with breathing holes for the insect within. Some also held bits of grass or dried fruit. Bending down, I scanned them one by one—a hornet, a spider, the scorpion I'd seen earlier, a dragonfly, a grasshopper, and a giant beetle with iridescent green wings. "I find them," he said. "Well, the scorpion, my neighbor Tom, he find that. But they all hurt. They need help."

I didn't know what to say. Clearly, helping these insects meant everything to Geeno. *How can I tell him it's not possible? How can I tell him he shouldn't try to save them?*

A flit of movement caught my eye, and I noticed another dragonfly in a shallow box on the table. Geeno had fabricated two of its four wings. They were beautifully crafted out of paper-thin segmented copper. Fitted around the insect's abdomen was a silver tube, some sort of patch where it was hurt, I supposed. Attached to the tube were gears linking the wings to it.

The dragonfly's wings trembled pathetically. I pulled out a stool and sat quietly, my heart breaking for the bug as well as for the young inventor. Geeno sat across from me, his big brown eyes filling with tears. I took Geeno's hand. We watched the dragonfly struggle.

The dragonfly would not give up. I thought about its will to live, its life force, its energy. *I wonder . . . ?* I turned the box so that I was facing the insect's eyes, huge turquoise orbs that covered its entire head like a helmet. I relaxed my breathing and focused on my third eye, the way Hurricane had shown me. Instantly, I saw everything bathed in light. The glow flowed around the dragonfly's body . . . its legs . . . its wings . . . everything except its metal parts.

I pushed energy into those parts. I imagined them as one

with the whole, working together to complete the insect's body. The dragonfly jerked. Light began to flow around the gears and mechanical pieces. Soon it encompassed the entire insect, metal parts and all.

In that instant, the dragonfly zipped up into the air. It whizzed past Geeno. He leapt up, clapping. "Avery, you fix it! You fix it! How did you do it?"

"I can't explain it. I . . . I can't believe it worked." I stared at the flying insect. "But you're the one who fixed it, Geeno, not me. I just gave it a little push."

Despite my words, my heart swelled with a lightness I'd never felt before. *It truly is a gift.* If this wasn't magic, I didn't know what was. "Did you see it, Geeno? Did you see the light?"

Geeno tilted his head, smiling. "No, but Cyrano was dying like the others, and now he perfect." He skipped around the room after the glittering dragonfly.

"It's beautiful." I wondered if this was what my mother had felt every time she'd helped someone. This was worth everything, worth being looked down on by the neighborhood ladies who'd called her a witch behind her back, worth not being invited to tea or meetings of the Brooklyn Heights Society Club. *This must be part of being a healer like my mother.*

The dragonfly settled atop Geeno's mop of hair. I laughed, pointing, making it take off again into the air. Swiftly, it circled back and landed on his arm. He burst out in giggles. Geeno's laugh was like music. I wanted him to always be this happy.

"Avery, you fix them all?" He picked up the glass jar with the scorpion.

"*We* fix them, Geeno. I can't do this without you, remember?" I glanced at my timepiece. "But before we do, are there any runners around here? I need two."

Geeno left and returned moments later with two skinny kids in tow—his friends Simon and Shane. Their bright eyes twinkled as they eagerly took two cents each to run written messages, one to the wharf where Khan lived and worked: *Meet me at the Northside Pier in one hour. I'll be at the fishmonger's stall.*

Geeno told me the fishmonger was the busiest vendor in the market—a good place to hide. The other message was to my father. Since we'd gone into hiding, we'd come up with a way to write messages in code. I wrote *DSOANFOETBWEOCRAR-RYEIFAUML*.

It looked like jabber, but was quite easy to understand if you read every other letter start to finish, then again, beginning with the second letter: *Do not worry. I am safe. Be careful.*

Then Geeno and I worked side by side on the insects. It was as mysterious as it was magnificent to see each glow with new life, accepting their metal parts as if they'd been born with them.

By the time I left to meet Khan, Geeno had a living mechanical menagerie crawling and flying around the room. He gave each insect a name, and for some reason I couldn't explain, they all seemed to know who he was. They followed him around as if he were a bizarre Pied Piper. It made me cringe a little, but he promised they would stay in the workroom.

I broke into a run, smiling ear to ear. People were sure to think me simple, but I didn't care. Warmth radiated through my body. I still couldn't believe what'd just happened, what I'd done. Somehow, the world looked different—shinier, more alive. *What other wonderful things are possible with this gift of mine?*

CHAPTER SIXTEEN
IMPALEMENT ART

Khan helped me down into the boat. "Are you feeling okay? You have a funny look on your face." He started up the engine.

"It's nothing." I wanted to keep this feeling inside, like an exquisite secret, like a hidden mystery. I suddenly remembered another secret feeling—how much I'd wanted to kiss him last night. Heat warmed my cheeks. I looked away, feigning interest in the design of the boat. "This is lovely." I rubbed my hand along the smooth wood. "I've never seen anything like it. I was expecting an old rattletrap like you had last time."

Khan beamed with pride. "She's a steam-driven skiff. And she's fast."

The enclosed front end of the boat was long and sleek, made of glossy varnished wood. An open seat in the middle was just enough for two people, and behind us a large engine with a tall black flue pipe puttered out plumes of smoke. Khan adjusted some knobs on the brass instrument panel and turned the wheel, backing us out.

"Do we have to go around Gravesend to get to the Gypsy camp? Out into open water?" I asked. The East River was bad enough. I did not want to brave the bay, steam skiff or no.

"No, I know another way."

We cruised north along Brooklyn's industrial riverfront, passing the immense factories lining the shore. Khan turned into an inlet where a sign read Newtown Creek.

As we sliced through the water, I told Khan how the crows had come to the shop. "They broke my father's nose and arm."

"Son of a bitch." Khan reached down and squeezed my hand, rubbing it with his thumb. A tingle ran up my arm. "Avery, you can't go back there. You'll stay with me. My *ouma* will love it. She hasn't seen you in a while."

"Khan, I can't do that." I let go of his hand to hold on to my cap as the wind picked up. "I can't endanger your grandmother— or you. I have a place to stay, a safe place. Don't worry." I knew he would anyway. His brows drew together in a deep furrow. "Can you check on Seraphine for me, though? And my father."

"Of course." Khan flashed me a tense look. "I don't know many men like your father, Avery. Don't worry. He'll be fine. He's tougher than I gave him credit for."

The creek got smaller and smaller, until we were ducking our heads under low-hanging branches, the *chug-chug-chug* of the engine putting me in a pensive mood.

When I looked up, a vaporous fog clung to the water, the afternoon sun tinting it orange. In the distance a stone wall blocked our way, but as we neared, I saw it arched over the waterway. Once on the other side, a strange quiet descended upon us. Huge pine trees blocked out the light, and through the mist creeping up the bank, solemn faces stared down at us.

"Khan," I whispered, relieved to see the faces were made of stone. "What is this place?"

"Strange, right?" He glanced around. "We're cutting through the Cemetery of the Evergreens." He slowed the boat to navigate the narrow passage. "The reservoir is up on the hill. There's talk of filling in this stream, but for now, it's the best way across Brooklyn. Not too many people know about it."

"Oh, I've never been inside this place." The cemetery was built to alleviate overcrowding at the old Brooklyn churchyards, though many complained it was too remote. Squinting between pockets of mist, I saw it was eerily beautiful, a place of rolling hills and lush greenery—just not a place I wanted to dwell in. I was glad when we exited through the arch on the opposite side and left the cemetery behind. Soon we pulled up to Plunder's Neck, the base of the Gypsy camp.

The Gypsy scouts must have seen us coming. Katalina met us at the dock in a long red dress, top hat pulled low on her brow. The shade of her lips matched her dress, which puffed out below her waist over a lofty bustle.

Out of the side of his mouth, Khan said, "Glad I didn't have to squeeze you into the boat dressed like that, Little Bird." I laughed, secretly happy that Khan appreciated my practical, if boyish, outfit.

Katalina kissed Khan hello. When she turned away, his glance flitted toward me. "Well, I know you two have a lot to discuss. I'm going to catch up with the boys."

Katalina watched him go, a pained expression on her face. In a soft voice, she said, "*Chudato* Khaniferre." Then, seeing my puzzled look, she interpreted, "It is the word for 'mysterious.'"

"Do you love him?" I spit out, before I could catch myself.

She removed a thin cigar from a pocket of her dress and lit it. "Why do you ask?"

"He's my best friend, and I was wondering if the two of you . . . No, never mind; it's none of my business."

She blew a puff of earthy-sweet smoke into the air. "I do not think Khaniferre is the type for settling down. Come." She led me into her tent. There was a large area for shows and, through a curtain, a plush bedroom draped in velvet and silk. All the while, I pondered her inscrutable words. Did Katalina have feelings for Khan that were not returned? But she was so perfect. How could he refuse her?

Katalina pointed to a settee, tossing her top hat aside. "I would like to discuss your encounter with Hurricane. Please sit. Let me explain." As I settled myself, anxious for some answers, she tapped her cigar ash into a brass tray. "Indigo is my younger brother."

"Your brother?" I had not expected that.

"Yes, and when I met you, I hoped you were the girl Indy told me about three years ago." She took a long pull on the cigar. "And then Hurricane recognized you."

"I knew it. Was she there that night?"

"Yes."

"I don't understand." I folded my arms. "What did Indigo say about me?"

Katalina sat by my side. I could smell her floral scent, jasmine and rose, weaving through the clove-infused smoke. "On the night of the Midsummer's Eve festival, Indy came to me and said he had met a girl who completed him. He said he had met his soul mate."

My breath caught in my throat. "But . . . but I came back the next night. He was . . . everyone was gone."

"Yes." She hung her head. "He was thirteen. Naturally, I thought he was being dramatic. Indy has always been playful, a trickster. I did not take him seriously. I wish I had." She set her cigar down before continuing. "He wanted to go after you that night, when your father dragged you from him. He swore something bad would happen, said he needed your help. You see, he has a gift like your own and he can recognize it in others, even if they do not yet know it in themselves. He saw the gift of second sight in you that night. He kept saying over and over that he needed you."

"Needed me?" I remembered him being cocky, so sure of himself.

She nodded. "And I would not let him go to you. Later

that evening, men in masks besieged us. They shot Indy with a tranquilizer dart, obviously aware of his special power and preventing him from using it. They beat him." Katalina took my hand. "There was a cruel leader. He looked to me like a pale rat. White-faced." She shuddered.

"Dr. Spector." I felt a weight press onto my chest. "He's the man from the Tombs." Even here, far from the cold shell of the Tombs, a chill settled over my shoulders like a wet shawl. "Spector watched my mother when I was a little girl, before he took her. I saw him once, outside my window." I wondered if he'd followed us to the Gypsy camp. What if it *was* our fault he'd come here? Maybe Hurricane was right to blame me.

Katalina nodded. "Yes, Dr. Spector. We believe he has watched others as well, people who showed signs of a gift. It is possible he came to our festival before. Everyone wears a mask, so we would never have known."

She continued in a shaky voice. "Spector asked about you, if you had 'the sight.' Indy lied to him." Katalina crossed her heart. "He swore you did not." A sob broke through her control. Instinctively, I wrapped my arm around her. She stiffened but did not move away. "They held me. Made me watch. Spector turned a metal iron in the flames of the bonfire. Then he—" A low moan escaped her throat. "He branded him, Avery. He ripped open Indy's shirt and branded his skin with the image of a crow. I'll never forget my baby brother's scream, the smell . . ." Her eyes were haunted. When she spoke again, it was from an unimaginable place in her mind. "His flesh still burning, they took him away. They attacked anyone who tried to stop them. My father almost lost his life that night. It was the last time I saw Indy."

"Mercy, Katalina!" I squeezed her hand. I waited until she had gathered herself, my mind a whirlwind of thoughts. "Have you tried to visit him? My father was able to get in under a fictitious name."

"Gypsies do not have the same rights as you and your father. They would never let us in."

"I'm sorry. So that's why you packed up and left." I leaned forward, resting my head in my hands. All this time I'd thought Indigo had played a cruel trick on me. Instead, he was locked up in that vile asylum. "They took my mother one week later. But why?"

"We do not know. We heard of others who were taken around the same time as Indy and your mother. Spector must have been watching and waiting, deciding when to make his move." She let go of my hand and crushed her cigar into the ashtray. "We came back, ready to fight. We set up a watch on the Tombs. By then he'd increased the size of his militia. As of yet we do not know what Spector is planning. I fear one day soon we will find out." Grim-faced, Katalina looked at me as if she was trying to see into my soul. "Avery, you are the only hope we have of getting into the Tombs."

I was beginning to understand. "You want to use me as bait?" I didn't appreciate the idea much.

"Bait? No. But if an opportunity arises, we must be ready.

Indy foresaw this evil coming but had faith that you could help him." She looked down at her black laced boots. "I did not believe him. I will not make that mistake again. And we will do nothing until we know we can protect you. If you can get inside the Tombs and use your ability to cause an explosion, then maybe we can get them out." Katalina pressed her hands to her face, wiping away the sadness.

"Katalina, I wish you'd told me all this as soon as Hurricane recognized me. Of course, I will do everything I can for your brother."

"You are right. We must trust each other, yes?" Then she rose and held her hand out to me. "And you. No running away again."

I took her delicate hand, and she pulled me up. "I can ask the same of you," I said.

"*Touché*. Have you been practicing the techniques that Hurricane showed you?"

"Yes, they're helpful, but I'm far from controlling anything." I touched my necklace and thought of my father. "Something happened yesterday, Katalina. Two men in crow masks came to the shop. They accosted my father."

"Aye, they are looking for you, then. It is good you will come here by boat from now on. This location is much more secluded than the last, but we cannot take a chance of them following you. We no longer hold the Midsummer's Eve festival. It is too risky." She tilted her head, studying me. "Avery, can you defend yourself?"

"Well, my father showed me how to shoot a gun and do some hand-to-hand moves with a knife."

"Good. And *my* father should be back from our sister camp on Long Island later this week. I sent a runner, who has since returned with news. Father is anxious to meet you. In the meantime, he has tasked me with teaching you my particular skill, which I have not shared before." She lifted her chin. "Of course, you will never be as good as I am." She laughed, lightening the mood.

Intrigued, I followed her back to the large room. She opened up a panel in the wall, revealing a host of knives and two crudely drawn human-sized body outlines covered with splits and cuts. She wrapped a leather belt several times around her waist and slid knives into the belt loops until she wore at least two dozen.

Removing a strip of fabric from her bodice, she held it over her eyes. "Will you do the honors?"

I'd seen her do this before! "That was you!" I cried, amazed. "My parents were watching your show the night I met Indigo."

A smile stole across her lips and she squared her shoulders. "Impalement art. You get a front-row seat, no charge."

I secured the cloth over her eyes, then sat on one of the benches to watch. Graceful as a cat, she turned to face the painted people. She bowed her head dramatically as she removed two knives with her right hand. Then, quick as a flash, she swung her arm. With a loud thud, the blades landed simultaneously on each side of the head, a sliver of space between the outline and the knives. I held my breath as Katalina hurled the rest, forming a precise line around the body. Never once would she have nicked an actual human.

I clapped. "Katalina, you're amazing!"

She held one last knife. In a split second, she flung the knife toward the other outline, so hard I felt the impact of it in my feet. It sank deep into the wooden heart of her victim.

"That felt good." She laughed, removing the blindfold and tucking it away. "They do not let me kill the volunteers from the audience." She unbuckled the belt. "Your turn."

I laughed, but my stomach felt queasy at the thought of throwing a knife at someone, aiming to kill. "I can't throw like that, Katalina."

"Bah." She tugged me to my feet and wrapped the belt around my waist. After yanking the knives from the wood, she loaded them into the loops. "First I will teach you the technique, and then you practice." She put her hands on my hips. "Left hip slightly forward," she said, and pushed it there. "Hold the blade like this. Ah, not so tight. Relax. Step forward and bring your arm around." I made the move in slow motion. "The key is the wrist. Cock it back and forth." She stepped back and lit one of her skinny cigars. "That's it."

As if I could remember all that. I focused. Step forward— arm back—hinge wrist—release.

The knife tumbled through the air, smacked the wall, and clattered to the floor. I tried again, with the same result.

"Relax your shoulders," Katalina said. "Do not grip so tight."

Over and over I threw the knives. Not one stuck in the wall, and my arm was starting to ache. Katalina retrieved the knives and loaded me up again. "Try slowly. Do not throw so hard. The knife is sharp. If the point hits, she sticks," she huffed. "I told my father this would be impossible. Keep at it. I am going to scrounge up some supper for us."

Despite Katalina's doubts, I continued practicing. I threw at least a hundred more times. Most of the knives fell to the floor, but a few stuck haphazardly in the wall, even if they weren't anywhere near the targets. After a time, I heard a rustle behind me and spun around to see Hurricane watching me.

"If you knew how awful my aim is, you wouldn't sneak up on me like that," I said.

"May I talk to you?" she asked. We went to the bench and sat down. "Avery, I said some things last night that I shouldn't have." She blew her bangs up into the air. "I apologize. I do want to help you."

"Thank you, Hurricane. I overreacted. I've been on edge with all that's going on. Katalina told me you were there that night. Why didn't you say so?"

She shrugged. "I wasn't sure if Katalina wanted me to." Then her shoulders slumped. "She barely has time to talk to me anymore. She's teaching you to throw? I've asked her a hundred times; she always says no."

I realized Hurricane resented me. Maybe she thought of Katalina as an older sister. It made sense, as she'd never had a mother. "She's only doing it because her father made her. Hurricane, you've been a great help to me. I couldn't do this without you. Katalina truly admires your ability."

"She does?" She sat up.

"Oh yes." I smiled. "Why else would she want me to work with you?" I certainly did not want to add to Hurricane's feelings of alienation. "Would you please tell me what else you know about energy? Did you do energy work with Indigo as well?"

"Yes, he had his own obstructions to manage. Indigo spiraled down into a dark place after their mother died." She tucked her hair behind her ears.

"How did Indigo use his power?"

"I honestly don't think your abilities are anything alike. His felt . . ." She frowned, searching for words. "Harsh, almost hostile. But to me, yours feels quiet, like . . . like a mother's love."

I smiled. I liked the sound of that.

"Indigo can control people, make them do things," Hurricane said. "But as far as I know, he never saw memories. I'll talk to Mr. Moralis when he returns; see if he knows more."

"I can't control my visions. They just happen, usually when there's turmoil around me. I most assuredly cannot make people do things. I don't believe my mother could, either."

"Well, she certainly had Mr. Moralis wrapped around her

little finger." The minute the words escaped, Hurricane slapped her hand over her mouth.

"My mother?" It took me a moment to grasp what she meant. "Hurricane! What are you insinuating?"

"Please don't say anything to Katalina," she whispered, glancing back to the tent's entrance, "but I think your mother was Mr. Moralis's mistress."

CHAPTER SEVENTEEN
VIOLENCE IN THE STREETS

Hurricane told me that she'd seen my mother secretly visit Mr. Moralis on numerous occasions in the months leading up to the Midsummer's Eve festival. "I didn't know who she was until I saw her come into the tent with your father. A moment later, your father snatched you away from Indigo."

"Don't be ridiculous." My mother would not have told me to come find Mr. Moralis if she was having an adulterous affair with him. But I had a bitter tang in my mouth. I asked Hurricane if she'd said this to anyone else. She had not. "Good. I don't want you spreading false accusations about my mother."

But later, as I lay in my little cot in Geeno's crate, doubt crept into my mind like a troublesome weed. *Is that why my father wanted to keep me from the Gypsies?* He'd reacted so strongly when I'd mentioned them. I did not like the thought of my mother hurting my father in such a way. My mother would never do that. *Or would she?*

I went to work every day at Cross Street Ironworks, the boys and I doing our best to keep up the heavy workload. Now that I was staying with Geeno, I had to tell him I was working late. He insisted on helping, so I swore him to secrecy and let him stay. After the whistle blew at the end of each day, we said goodbye to the others, lingering until they left. We finished the day's tabs together, then crept home, hiding in the shadows of the street, only stopping to pick up food. My guilt ebbed somewhat as I ensured Geeno ate a hearty meal each night. The hot potato man always saved us leftover goods before he packed up his pushcart for the night.

The people of the crate village had punched a hole in the top of the refinery's colossal steam boiler, creating a spray of hot water. We all used it to wash up. Monday and Tuesday night, after scrubbing the soot and grease from my skin, I met Khan at the pier to go to the Gypsy camp. I spent hours honing my focus with Hurricane and my throw with Katalina.

But Wednesday night, I told Khan I was too tired. Instead, I left Geeno and headed toward Wallabout Docks. I tried to talk myself out of my foolish curiosity. On the one hand, I told myself, *I'll sneak in, just to listen. No one will recognize me.* On the other, I argued, *Am I insane? If someone rats me out, I'll lose my job!* But I kept walking.

The street was quiet. I pulled out the paper to make sure I had the correct address. At the top it said, *Attention Working-men! Secret Meeting of the Amalgamated Association of Iron and Steel Workers, Wednesday at 7:30 pm. Corner of Wallabout Place & Keap Street.* I was in the right place, but the meeting started half an hour ago. Was it over?

On the corner was an old brick warehouse. From the navy yard beyond, I heard the sound of water slapping against the wooden ships, and the clang of rigging moving in the wind. The large arched wooden doors marching around the building were all closed tight. I scanned the darkened windows. On the fourth floor, I saw light flickering behind the glass. They must be up there.

Attached to the side wall, I noticed a steel stairway, its switchbacks rising upward, similar to the stairway at the Works. I could climb up and peek into the window. No one would see.

As carefully as I could, I climbed the stairway, stopping whenever it creaked or whined. Near the top, men's voices reached my ears, but I couldn't make out their words. I had to get closer. Finally, I peered over the windowsill.

There were maybe fifty men gathered, lanterns lighting the space. I recognized a few. They sat on chairs, listening to a speaker on a box in the center of the circle. His fist pumped the air, and his clear voice brimmed with passion. "We've heard it before, 'We mean to uphold the dignity of labor. To affirm the nobility of all who earn their bread by the sweat of their brows.' Well, now is the time! Join with me, my brothers, to end this involuntary servitude, to end the grievous conditions under which we work, and to show the big industrialists they can no longer tyrannize the common man."

This was greeted with whoops of affirmation. When the room settled, the man spoke again. "In exactly one week from tonight, we will show them our power, we will show them our unity. We will strike!"

A chant started, spreading throughout the room. "Strike! Strike! Strike!"

The steel workers were planning a strike. I couldn't help but feel a sense of pride in these men, in their devotion to the cause, but what did it mean for the boys and me? I'd heard enough. I hastened my way down the stairs and sprinted back to Geeno's. I did not tell him what I'd seen, but I fretted we'd be swept up into the danger that lay ahead.

The next night, I anxiously made my way toward the waterfront to meet Khan. I had yet to see Nikolai Moralis. Katalina assured me he would be back from his travels by the end of the week. It was hard to wait. I was desperate for answers about him—and about my mother.

The streets were particularly crowded. I pulled my hat lower but kept my eyes and ears vigilant. I was surprised I didn't see Khan sooner. One moment I was alone; the next, a strong arm wrapped around my shoulders, forcing me into a darkened alley. A mangy dog glared at me from the other end as if I'd come to steal whatever it was shaking back and forth in its teeth.

By this point, I knew to whom the arm belonged. "Khan, you scared me half to death. We have to stop meeting this way." I stepped back, laughing, but his face remained serious.

"You'll be glad we did. You were about to turn the corner into a street full of angry protesters."

"What are you talking about?"

"It's a rally. From what I've seen, hordes of workingmen are marching tonight for the Knights of Labor. They're up in arms about the rape and murder of those two young sisters who worked at the shirtwaist factory. Apparently it was their employer, Norman Bale, who did it. They arrested him today. The Metropolitan Police are out in force, hoping to contain the mob. If we turn north on Seventh, we should get ahead of them."

Sweat seeped into the back of my shirt. I quickly told Khan about the secret meeting of the steel workers.

"Avery, why do you put yourself in situations like these?" he huffed.

"I don't know. I tried to talk myself out of it, but this involves my job—the people I work with, Khan. I had to find out what's going on."

"Well, I'm glad they didn't catch you spying on them." Khan unbuttoned his jacket, his knives a comfort to us both.

"I'm going to walk a little ways behind so I can watch out for you."

"All right." I removed my knife from its sheath and slid the blade into the sleeve of my coat so I could hold it inconspicuously. Then I stepped from the alley and headed north, hugging the building. There was no sign of the rally, but the side streets were overrun with men hooting and hollering.

Rallies and strikes were rarely peaceful. My nerves felt raw, exposed. I flinched at a shriek from an organ-grinder's monkey; I spun away from a grasping woman begging for a handout for the baby bundled in her arms.

When we reached Seventh Street, the crowd thickened, clogging the area. They obstructed buggies and carriages. Drivers whipped the poor horses, which had nowhere to go. Here, sagging clapboard structures looked as dirty and broken-down as the people sitting on their stoops spitting brown tobacco juice onto the sidewalk.

I took a deep breath as we turned the corner. We were almost to Kent Avenue, the last street before the docks. A line of people waited along the sidewalk for the rally to pass. We wove to the front. The street was clear. They'd closed it off to horse carts and coaches; even the vendors were nowhere in sight. We just had to cross the street and disappear into the crowd on the other side.

Easier said than done. I leaned forward and looked toward the head of the rally. The men were closer than I'd hoped. Dusk was settling in, long rays of light reaching between the build-ings. I took a deep breath and stepped onto the cobblestones, Khan right behind me.

A nightstick came down, blocking my way.

"Can't cross here." A police officer stared down at me. "We're keeping people off the streets."

I nodded and stepped back onto the curb. Somehow the con-gestion behind us had become a solid mass. The rally advanced forward. In all my life, I'd never seen anything like it.

The men were packed so tightly they looked like a swarm of sticks and signs and fists. The ground trembled with their advance. There was something noble about the unions, though. The workers risked everything to stand up for what they believed in, just as my father had done when he'd disobeyed orders in order to save Khan and his grandmother.

The police officer in front of me pushed us back as hun-dreds of officers came marching in neat rows from the opposite direction, toward the union members.

Cold claws seemed to dig into my spine, squeezing the air from my lungs as I struggled to remain calm. The space between the protesters and police rapidly diminished. They were less than ten feet apart when Khan hauled me back into the crowd. Something exploded behind us, almost knocking me down.

Chaos broke out. Smoke plumed into the air. Khan wrapped his arms around me, shoving his way through the panicked, screaming people. I held on to Khan with all my might.

I jerked as gunshots rang out from behind. More screams.

When we were finally out of the fray and far from the commotion, Khan held me for a long time. "I can't go to the Gypsy
camp tonight," I said, as I sobbed into his shoulder. I didn't
understand why there was so much violence. *Is this really the
only way for people to make themselves heard?*

CHAPTER EIGHTEEN
DEAD CROW

On Friday evening, I set out once again to meet Khan at the Northside Pier. As soon as he saw me, he hugged me tight. We'd spent most of the previous night huddled in the back booth of a tavern. Getting up for work this morning had not been easy.

"Did you see the papers today?" he said, pushing off from the dock. "Two policemen and four workers dead."

"It's hard to miss. The newsboys are shouting it from every corner." I stared into the fathomless depths of the river. Our boat ride that night was quiet, haunted.

As he navigated the dark waterway, Khan softly sang a song his grandmother had taught him. "Babylon's falling to rise no more. Oh, Babylon's falling, falling, falling. Babylon's falling to rise no more." His words gave me chills.

At the Gypsy camp, I met Hurricane in the blue tent of

the elders and spent the better part of an hour trying to clear my mind. It was more difficult today, given the curious elders huddled around us, watching. Just as I began to get control over my frenzied thoughts, Katalina's loud voice broke the silence. She entered with a gangly boy in tow. His mop of hair hung over his face and his ruddy cheeks suggested he'd been running.

Katalina had the boy by the ear. She addressed the elders. "Pardon the interruption, but Pesha has been caught lighting fires—again!" She glowered at the boy. "We do not tolerate arson, Pesha. And within the confines of this camp, it is inexcusable."

"Who are you to tell me what to do, Katalina?" Pesha scoffed. "Just because your father is head of the camp, you think you can order me around?"

One of the elders approached them. "Pesha, this is very dangerous."

"Don't worry. Soon as I save up some money, I'm leaving. I'd rather live in the city anyway." He spit on the floor.

As the elders discussed what to do, Hurricane cupped her hand to my ear. "Can you see his aura, Avery?"

I shifted my gaze and saw a dark swirling cloud around Pesha. Tentatively, I nodded.

"Get him to look at you," she murmured.

I called out his name. "Hey, Pesha."

When he looked up at me, images flooded into my head, of Pesha being picked on by some of the other Gypsy boys. They called him a sissy and a scalawag. I saw him shoved, knocked to the ground.

Hurricane spoke softly, so no one else would hear. "Focus, Avery. Push your energy toward him."

Without looking away from Pesha, I did as she instructed. I thought about Geeno's insects, what I'd done with them. I imagined radiant light flowing through my third eye, flowing toward Pesha, flowing into him. His dark energy began to lighten, shading to gray. Still looking at me, he straightened his shoulders, and the muscles of his face relaxed.

But when a tear slipped down his cheeks, he flushed and looked away, swiping at it with his sleeve. His head hung low; his aura began to darken once more.

"Wait, Pesha," I called. But it was too late. He tore himself from Katalina's grasp and disappeared through the flap of the tent. The elders followed Katalina out, still caught up in a heated debate over his punishment.

"What happened?" Hurricane asked.

I smiled at her. "I think I understand now why my mother called us healers; it's not in the physical sense, but of the emotions. If only I were better at this, I believe I would have been able to help Pesha. I saw his memories, Hurricane. I saw where his spirit needed healing."

Hurricane squeezed my hand. "That's beautiful, Avery. What a special gift you have."

I felt my muscles relax after the intensity of the last few days. I'd started to heal Pesha's energy. *I affected his emotions,*

I thought, recalling the single tear that had escaped his eyes.

All I needed was more practice.

Khan and I traveled home in the pitch-black of night. Although Khan swore he had the waterways memorized, I was half convinced he could see in the dark like a cat. Often, the darkness frightened me, but tonight I welcomed it. It made me feel safe.

We made our way in silence, my mind racing. Could I learn to use my gift as my mother had? Was it possible?

In the last week, Geeno's rickety crate village had become my refuge. The people were nice, although they kept to themselves. I'd even warmed to Geeno's mechanical pets. We'd managed to add to his collection a small mouse whose shredded body Geeno had saved from the mouth of an alley cat.

By Saturday evening, Khan and I were both exhausted from the late nights and the fear of running into crow men. When we entered the Gypsy camp, we gratefully followed our escort to a fire circle, where Katalina and a few other men and women were eating roast rabbit and leeks.

I sat on a stump and let out a long sigh. Katalina took Khan's face in her hands. "*Piramneja . . .*," she said, which sounded very endearing. "Eat. The two of you look like a pair of sodden rags. We have a saying—you try to jump over your own shadow."

Khan smiled wearily. "I love your Romany proverbs, Kat."

We were given plates of food and some hard ale. Khan absently tossed tidbits of his food to the dogs that hovered outside the circle of flames. *He has a big heart*, I thought.

Katalina swiped at his arm. "Do not waste meat on those mongrels."

Khan glanced at me and winked.

"My father has returned," she announced. "He would like to speak with you later, Avery. Shall we practice with the knives while we wait? I watched you on Tuesday. Your skill is improving . . . a little. Hopefully you are developing your muscle memory. You will need it when you do not have time to think."

"My father said the same thing when he taught me to fight."

Katalina laughed. "Good. The women of your country most certainly do not know how to defend themselves."

I hated to leave the fire, but I did want to practice. As I stood to follow her, a commotion erupted at the camp's entrance. We heard the thud of horses charging down the dirt road, but at first saw only a cloud of dust and gravel. On all sides, the Gypsies sprang into action. Khan was right; they were armed to the hilt. Even the women and children carried weapons and organized themselves like an army. Most of them threw on some kind of intricate metal armor: helmets, face masks, armbands or breastplates with weapons attached. It was impressive. They certainly were not going to be taken by surprise like they were when the crows came for Indigo.

We gathered at the open field, where a bonfire was lit, and waited for the riders. Khan and I stayed at the back. A ring of men and women with long bows, arrows notched, lined the inner circle. Seeing them side by side made me realize how advanced the Romany were in their acceptance of women. Here were women with power of their own. Warriors. I stood on tip-toe to see Katalina, feeling a flush of pride. She was my training partner, my mentor. Perhaps my father had felt this way about some of his army comrades. The thought of my father wrenched my heart.

A passage opened through the throng, allowing in a pair of huge black horses. Each carried a rider and a bound captive. The two Gypsies rode bareback and dismounted gracefully. They were dressed in flowing black pants and tunics; if it weren't for the light of the bonfire, they would have disappeared into the night like shadows. Even their faces were covered with black cloth. Nothing showed but their eyes.

From one horse they untied a body that slumped to the ground like a sack of potatoes, landing with a sickening thump. From the other, they ordered the captive down. He had his back to me, then fell onto his stomach, groaning.

Katalina came forward as the two riders removed their head scarves.

"Since her father is the ruling elder," Khan whispered to me, "she assumes authority until he arrives." His teeth flashed briefly in the dark. "As you can see, it is a role she relishes."

With her foot, Katalina rolled the body onto its back. I gasped. He wore the unmistakable crow mask of the guards of the Tombs.

CHAPTER NINETEEN
LIKE FATHER, LIKE SON

"What did you bring us, Horatio?" Katalina asked, her black-lined eyes gleaming in the flickering light. She lifted another crow mask from Horatio's bag and held it up. "Two crows?" She turned on him, furious. "And why did you bring them here? Do we want to summon the rest, to slaughter our people?"

"Katalina, hear them out," a man from the circle shouted.

"Bah! We send young fools to watch the Tombs and they bring us back a prize?" Katalina was pacing like a wild cat. "And what do we do with them? Ah? Had you thought about that, Horatio?"

"Katalina, you do not understand. We followed them, as we were told, but this one"—Horatio pointed to the immobile body on the ground—"he tried to kill that one. Called him a traitor."

The other Gypsy horseman stepped forward. "We couldn't

watch a man murdered and do nothing. We . . . we saved his life."

"For what, Lucas?" Katalina screamed. "Let them kill each other, for all we care! Let them do our job for us. Now, if we do not kill the fat one over there, he will report back to Spector." Horatio and Lucas looked down. Katalina pulled a knife from her skirt. "Come here, Lucas." She placed the blade in his hand. "You must kill him. He cannot leave the camp alive."

A ripple of remarks flew around the circle. Some of the Gypsies yelled out, "No! Wait for Nikolai!" while others shouted, "Kill him!"

Lucas held the knife and looked searchingly at the group. The fat guard cried out weakly, "No! Please!"

"Khan, you have to say something. That man is hurt and unarmed." I shook his arm.

"I know." He nodded and moved toward the bonfire, shouting, "Katalina, stop! Lucas, please, put the knife down."

The guard looked up as Khan pushed through the front line. I caught a glimpse of his face. It was the guard who had told me about his dog, Bojangles.

"Wait!" I yelled. "I know that man."

A hush stilled the crowd. Lucas froze, and then slowly backed away.

The guard managed to get himself up onto one elbow. He fixed his eyes on me, his gravelly voice barely a whisper. "It's true. She came to the Tombs to . . . to—" He broke into wet coughs and spit blood to the side. "To see her mother."

"So?" Katalina was tapping her foot, watching me. "It is of

no consequence. This man will put us in danger."

"He's not like the others." I wasn't sure why I said it. I just felt it to be true.

"I see. You expect us to spare his life because he remembers you? The crows are all searching for you." Katalina turned to face the circle of her people. "Do you recall what happened last time? If he lives, he will return with Spector."

"No." The guard crawled pathetically toward Katalina. "I told Jason I wanted to quit. I thought he was a friend. But he tried to kill me." He turned to look at the masked dead man a few feet away, but the sudden movement overwhelmed him. He laid his face in the grass and rested a moment, then turned his bloodied, swollen eyes to me. "I can help you," he whispered, and passed out.

Katalina sighed. Sensing her indecision, I spoke quickly, "Katalina, please, let him tell us everything he knows." There was something else, something I knew would sound outlandish, but I had to try to explain it to her. "When I saw this man at the Tombs, I saw his energy, and yes, it was dark. But I think he wanted to change. I *saw* his energy change." I moved my gaze across all the eyes focused on me. "We need him . . . and he deserves a second chance."

As I scanned their faces, I saw a tall, thin man walking through the crowd. People stepped aside to make way for him. If I thought it was quiet before, now it was eerily silent, as if everyone held his or her breath. Even the dogs and the horses were still.

Katalina, Horatio, and Lucas stood, heads bowed, as the man approached. His voice was one of authority. "I am afraid you have lost your way, Katalina. I stayed back to see how you would handle this situation. I am not at all pleased. Do you expect revenge to satisfy your heart?"

"I am protect—"

He held up his hand, silencing her. "A leader must not use her own hatred to steer others."

"It's just that—"

His head snapped up. The burning look he gave her stopped her words midstream. She looked down and murmured, "Yes, Father."

Nikolai Moralis pointed toward the dead guard. "Horatio, Lucas. You saved a man's life tonight. Be proud, but do not forget the life you took. Prepare his body as if he were one of our own. And Katalina, I would like you to administer to this man here. He needs attention."

Bossy as ever, she ordered two husky men to lift the guard. Khan rushed to help. The crowd dispersed; some came forward to offer assistance, while others went back into the camp.

Mr. Moralis approached me. Removing his hat, he placed his hand on my shoulder. When I looked up into his eyes, I realized they were familiar. His eyes were like Indigo's, dazzlingly blue-violet. I felt unsteady. Hurricane's inference about this man and my mother came flooding back to me, but I forced my heart to still. *I will not let her absurd notions fluster me.*

"You are a brave young woman, Avery. I am Mr. Moralis."

He held out his hand to shake.

I understood now why the Romany followed him. It wasn't his tall, sinewy stature or his dark, handsome face or piercing eyes. It was the magnetism he possessed, a charismatic allure. With a midnight blue flowing shirt, long beard braided with beads, and black hair tied back with a cord, he looked every bit a Gypsy king. "I'm glad to finally meet you," he said. "Come, sit with me."

I followed him to a large tree trunk near the bonfire. We were alone now.

"You are not afraid to stand up for what you believe," he said, his eyes fixing me with a steady gaze. "But I sense self-doubt within you. Tell me, what stands in your way?"

Considering everything that had happened in the last few days? I tilted my head back and looked up at the stars. "I *want* to save my mother, but I'm afraid. Every time I see Spector's face, even if I picture it in my mind, it fills me with crippling fear." I sighed. "Even the crow masks terrify me. Katalina and Hurricane tell me I have power, but I don't know how to use it." I held up the leather knife belt. "What good is all this if I'm not strong enough?"

He clasped his hands and rested them on his lap. "What do you think makes one strong?"

"Well, I seem to have trouble with the idea of killing someone." I laughed; it sounded silly, but it was true. "If the moment came, and I had a chance to get my mother out, but I had to kill someone? I don't know if I could do it."

"And you think that makes you weak?"

"Yes. I'd like to be more like Katalina. I mean, what she did tonight was different. That man wasn't threatening her. But I know she'd be strong enough to kill the monster who took Indigo, who took my mother, without a moment's hesitation." I fiddled with my necklace, rubbing the familiar items between my fingers. "I'm hoping my power, as she calls it, will make me stronger."

"Avery, I know someone with a gift akin to yours. Both of you have much inner strength."

I wondered if he knew I'd met Indigo. "Do you mean your son?" I asked.

He looked at me and smiled. "No, actually. I am speaking of your mother, Cassandra."

Hearing him refer to her by her first name gave me pause. It seemed more than cordial, bordering on impolite. Come to think of it, my mother referred to him the same way. "My mother? She told me to find you."

"Yes, I know. Let me explain how I met her. Many years ago, just before she and your father were wed, your mother came here seeking knowledge, knowledge she'd heard I could give her."

I stared into his bright blue eyes. Mr. Moralis had a fierce intensity about him. I understood my father's apprehension over Mother's friendship with this man. *Had it been more than friendship?*

"Your mother," Mr. Moralis continued, "was raised to believe she was cursed, that a demon possessed her soul. Before agreeing to marry and have children, she desperately wanted to understand her abilities. As it was, her parents not only refused to attend the wedding service but sent a priest to tell their daughter that if she were to become pregnant, the infant must be killed."

I gasped. He was talking about me. My father had omitted that detail when we'd talked about this. "How could anyone do such a thing?"

"It is more common than you would imagine," he said softly. "People fear that which they do not understand. I told her everything I knew, but it is I who ended up learning from her." He stared into the fire. "Anyone can make people do things they do not want to do, even without the special gift of the seer. People use power or strength to bend wills. Tonight, Lucas almost killed a man, even though he did not want to. True strength, Avery, lies with those who can make people see the *right* thing to do."

He looked at me again. "You speak of my son." His voice took on a harshness I hadn't heard before. "He has the power to make people do anything he wants. But he is not like you or your mother. He cannot heal their hearts." He pressed his lips together and took a deep breath. "I believe that is why this Spector wanted him so badly. His power can be very, very dangerous."

A shudder passed through me, thinking of what Spector

would do if he had a power like that.

"I have traveled to places where ancient magic and spirituality still live on in the cultural traditions, where wonder is woven into the very fabric of the people's lives."

As he spoke, I felt myself drawn to the fire—its heat, the crackling glowing logs. I watched the flames lick the air, hungering to consume, their brilliance making the night all the more velvety and dark around us. I imagined my mother sitting here, feeling the same confusion, listening to Mr. Moralis speak.

"My wife had an extraordinary gift. Indigo inherited it from her." His jaw tightened as he grew silent.

"I'm sorry," I said. "Hurricane told me something happened to her."

"It was an accident. A terrible accident." His eyes flicked in my direction, reminding me again of Indigo's. But now they looked pained. "Avery, you and your mother are aura healers. It is a rare gift. Your power is in helping people, healing their spirits. But your gift will not help you save your mother. Katalina is wrong. I do not want anyone else hurt. You should stay away from the Tombs. I'm so sorry."

I felt my throat tighten. I'd been hoping he would tell me how to strengthen my power so that I could help my mother. "No, please don't say that. My mother told me to find you—"

"Because she knew I would try to talk you out of going back into the Tombs. At least, that is my belief."

"But what about the explosion? I can learn to use that,

develop it somehow, can't I?" I was desperate.

Mr. Moralis slowly shook his head. "I spoke to Hurricane this evening. In all likelihood the explosion was due to the long years you spent burying your abilities. With the shock of Oscar's beating, the energy literally exploded out of you. It is not likely to happen again."

My eyes stung, but I blinked back my treasonous tears. I would not prove myself weak. I would not prove him right. Instead, I stood up and paced back and forth in front of the fire. *Why did my mother tell me to find him if she just wanted me to stay away?* She could have told me that herself.

"Mr. Moralis, please, there must be another reason why my mother sent me here. I don't know what she was trying to say, but I can't believe . . ." Then I remembered her words just before she passed out. "Is there something you have? She was starting to tell me what it was." He remained silent. I pushed on recklessly. "I almost gave up on her once. Have you given up on Indigo? Will you leave him in the Tombs to die if there's a chance—"

"No!" He stood up. "Never!" Again he stared into the fire, stroking his beard. "Let me think. . . . Something I have?" His eyes lit with sudden realization. "Of course! Three years ago, I asked your mother to come see me. I had found something during my travels that I wanted to share with her."

Once again, I felt uncomfortable with the familiar way in which he spoke of my mother. I imagined my father finding out that Mr. Moralis had sent for her, a married woman, in order to share his secrets with her. And when she came, Hurricane saw them together. Hurricane had seemed to regret saying anything. *Did she tell me all she saw?*

He turned toward camp, speaking over his shoulder. "Wait here. It is ancient magic. And trust me when I tell you, you have never seen anything like it."

CHAPTER TWENTY
THE PERCH

Monday morning, I opened my eyes and stared at the low ceiling of the crate, thinking about the assemblage of other crates above my head. Apparently they were sturdy enough to stack without fear of toppling. I wished we were not at the bottom of the pile, although the top seemed just as perilous, given the shaky ladders leading upward. And one nor'easter could easily topple the upper crates.

I glanced over; Geeno was sound asleep. I didn't know how he did it. My body ached from the flimsy cot. And with the clicks and taps of the mechanical creatures moving around in the other room, a sound night's sleep was out of the question.

As always in the morning, my thoughts went to my father. *Is he safe?* Khan checked on him as often as he could. Apparently the crows had come to the shop a few times, but Jeremiah

Thorn's scouts warned my father of their approach, allowing him to disappear until they left. He spent the rest of his time locked in the basement, continuing to work on his mysterious project.

Khan hadn't been able to take me to the camp on Sunday, and as it was too risky to go by land, I'd agreed to wait until tonight. I was anxious to get back. It felt like valuable time was slipping through my fingers.

I'd waited by the bonfire Saturday evening, until Mr. Moralis returned holding a wooden box that looked so old it was a wonder it hadn't rotted through. Its stained, blackened surface was covered with crusty barnacles like those on the bottom of boats. Mr. Moralis sat down, a gleam in his eye, placing the box on his lap.

"On an expedition to the Empire of Brazil, I met a shaman," he said. "I stayed with him for a time, and he taught me much about energy seers. Ancient civilizations used crystals to channel energy, to harness and amplify it. When I left, he gave me one of these crystals. In legends of old, they were called Lemurian Seeds or God Stones. Some were carved into skulls or spheres. This one is very old—and very powerful, so I'm told."

Unlatching the box, he'd removed a thick smoky-clear stone, like ancient glass, faceted to a point on one end. He held it almost reverently in both hands. There *was* something beautiful about it, something unearthly, the way it caught the light of the fire, of the stars, almost as if it was lit from within. He was right; I'd never seen anything like it.

His voice shifted to a whisper. "When your mother held this stone, she said she felt its vibration."

I carefully took the stone from him, running my fingers over the surface. It was polished smooth except on one side, which was lined with ridges. It was the length of my forearm, and my fingers could almost encircle it. But I didn't feel any vibration. I didn't feel anything at all. "Are you sure this is what my mother wanted you to give me?"

He nodded. "It must be."

I shifted into my second sight. Still nothing. "It's beautiful, but I don't understand what it's supposed to do. How is it magical?"

"Supposedly, in the hands of the right seer, this stone will reveal ancient knowledge or expand your energy in some way. Your mother is the only seer I know who has ever felt anything from it. I hoped it would work for you. Maybe as you learn of your gift, the crystal will respond. I'll keep it for you. When you come back, you can try again." He put it back into its box, frowning.

Back in Geeno's crate, I felt a tickle on my arm. "Avery, time to get up." I must have fallen back asleep. I opened my eyes to the sight of Geeno getting ready to pounce on me.

"Whoa, there," I said, smiling. "This cot is not strong enough for two."

I pushed aside thoughts of the crystal as I dressed. I had to trust my mother. She'd wanted me to have it for a reason—I just had to figure out why.

Geeno and I stealthily made our way to the Works, every step darkened by thoughts of black-cloaked figures.

When we arrived, we saw Leo sitting on the steps outside the door, his face wet with tears.

"Leo, what's wrong?" I sat down next to him.

"Scarface fired me." He sniffed and wiped his nose on his sleeve. "He said people don't want to work with a Negro anymore. And they won't drink from the fountain if I do."

"What? That's terrible!" I put my arm around him. "It's not right." Maybe this was provoked by the riot. "Any chance your folks will let you go to school?"

He shrugged. "I don't think so. We need the money." He stood up. "I'd better go. 'Bye, Ave. 'Bye, Geeno." Leo walked away, head hung low.

A hot ember burned in my chest. Maybe Khan could find him some work. The flame continued to build as I set up my station. It wasn't fair. Leo was good at his job. The uneasy feeling I'd had watching the rally returned.

As the only girl, my position was probably just as vulnerable as Leo's. I noticed an envelope leaning against my welding gun. It was the same stationery as the one Mr. Matteo had delivered last week.

I glanced around as I picked it up. No one seemed to be watching me. After a moment, Tony caught my eye and came over. "Did you see Leo? He wanted to say goodbye."

I nodded, afraid that if I talked about it, I'd cry.

He spied the envelope clutched in my hand. "Is that from Malice?" I knew Tony and I were wondering the same thing: *Am I about to get fired?*

"I think so." I slit open the envelope, pulled out the note, and read aloud.

> *Miss Avery,*
> *The investigation is concluded. I would like to see you in my office immediately.*
> *R. Malice*

Tony nodded up at the ceiling. "The boss wants to see you up there?"

"This can't be good." I looked up at the perch. None of us had ever set foot inside.

"I'll come with you." My heart swelled—Tony, always willing to sacrifice himself.

"No, Tony, you can't. If I'm getting fired, I don't want to take anyone down with me." I took a deep breath. "I have to do this alone."

"All right, Avery. Good luck," he said.

Whatever was going to happen, it'd be worse if I kept Mr. Malice waiting. Tony and Geeno stopped work to watch me go. My boots felt heavy, as if I'd welded metal plates to the soles. I dragged them toward the far side of the mill, where an iron stairway crisscrossed its way to a point eighty feet up the concrete wall.

I gripped the handrail and started up. The metal treads were corroded through in places. The wall bolts dripped rust like orange tears. My legs got shakier with each switchback of the stairway.

At the top platform, I made the mistake of looking down. My knees wobbled. I still had to walk across thirty feet of narrow metal catwalk with only a thin guide wire on each side. Pushing damp hair from my face, I grabbed the wires and shuffled onto the bridge. Of course, Mr. Malice had a private steam-driven cage elevator, or he'd never make it to his office. I wondered what he'd do if it jammed, picturing his bulk navigating this walkway. The hysterically funny image eased my fear a bit. Another catwalk spanned out from the opposite side of the perch but was off-limits, as it passed directly over Bessie and her incinerating volcano.

Taking slow, careful steps, I made it across. Sweat trickled down my back, fed by the haze of heat rising up from the furnaces below. The thrum of the machinery pulsed through my body; the blood quivered in my veins. I lifted my hand to knock, but stopped when I heard Mr. Malice talking.

"That's preposterous! I refuse to do that to the people in my employ." I couldn't hear a response. A second passed, and then Mr. Malice bellowed, "I don't care who you are! If you attempt it, I'll alert the authorities!"

To whom is he speaking? And what do they want him to do? At least Mr. Malice was standing up for us. When a few minutes went by with no other discussion and no one emerging,

I knocked tentatively on the door. Mr. Malice barked, "Enter."

The door grated against the metal floor as I pushed it open.

He was alone, when I'd expected someone to be with him. Was he talking to himself? It took me aback and I fumbled my words. "You wanted . . . you asked to see me?" My mouth felt dry. "Sir," I added quickly.

There were windows on three sides of the room, file cabinets bursting with papers, and an iron box that said "Security Safe" on it, looking heavy enough that I wondered how it did not fall through the wooden floor. To my right was the gate of the elevator; in front of me, a cluttered desk with Roland Malice sitting fatly behind it. A bandage covered his bald head. Another cradled one of his meaty arms. He held up his good hand, indicating I wait as he finished reading some papers.

I glanced at the wall next to me, which was covered with newspaper articles and photographs—the entire history of Cross Street Ironworks, laid out before me. Built by Roland Malice's father, Tyber Malice, a fierce-looking mountain of a man, it was one of the largest iron mills in the country. Tyber Malice still owned it. There was an article on Roland, describing how he took over daily operations of the mill a year after his boxing career ended abruptly. He'd been prematurely pronounced dead at a heavyweight match. I recalled the rumor I'd heard when I first started at the Works, the stories that he'd died in the ring and come back to life. *So it's true.* I squinted at the caption under a photograph of him posing with a girl. The Polish Punisher, he was called. The girl looked sad. I wondered who she was.

A large hand slapped over the picture. I jumped and spun around, bumping into Mr. Malice's sling. He winced and glared down at me.

"I'm sorry. I'm so sorry, sir." I sucked my breath in through my teeth, forcing myself to tilt my head and look up into his eyes. He could crush me with his one good hand.

"She's very pretty, the girl in the picture," I said. "What's her name?"

His eyes narrowed, and for a moment I thought I'd made a huge mistake. Frightened, I closed my eyes and focused on my third eye. When I opened my eyes again, my second sight took over, filling the room with a light only I could see. My mind surged with images, memories. The girl from the picture begging Mr. Malice not to fight, telling him she would leave him. Roland's face and body pounded. Roland's jaw cracking. Spitting out blood and teeth. Hitting the mat, his eyes slits in the purple pulp that was left of his face. Somehow, waking up six months later in a hospital bed, his girl long gone, nobody knew where.

I sensed his confusion as he stared down at me. Although the memories had played across his mind, he did not know I'd seen them as well. I blinked, clearing my sight.

"Yeah, well, that was a long time ago," he said, removing his hand from the photo. "And none of your damn business." He stepped back. "I called you up here for a reason. Is there anything you'd like to tell me about the explosion, Miss Avery?"

"What do you mean, sir?"

"The investigation was inconclusive. A cause cannot be determined. There are no gas leaks." He glared at me. "I'm giving you a chance to tell me if someone purposely set off a charge in my factory."

I stiffened. "Sir, I don't know how the explosion happened."

His gaze never wavered. "I will not tolerate trickery or theft amongst my employees."

"No, sir."

"Miss Avery—" But we were interrupted by a ringing sound from across the room. "Eh, what now?" Mr. Malice mumbled, lumbering toward his desk. He picked up a brass cone hanging from a sleek wooden box mounted to the wall. When he held it to his ear, I realized it was one of Bell's telephone machines, the first I'd seen since the Centennial Expo. He must have been on the device before, as well.

While he was talking, I turned back to the photographs. I was overcome with the desire to test my skill. Maybe I could somehow heal Mr. Malice's spirit. Pressing my hand to a tintype photograph of Roland Malice and his father, I closed my eyes, just the way I remembered my mother doing.

Images floated through my mind. I saw Tyber Malice and Roland arguing. Roland agreeing to fight. His father telling him that if he lost, he was to give up boxing and take over the factory. Roland sleeping. Tyber Malice pouring something into Roland's water jug. Tyber Malice laughing as he bet big money on the other contender to beat Roland.

Mr. Malice was drugged. My mind spun. Mr. Malice's own father let him be beaten nearly to death and caused his love to leave him, just to get what he wanted, to have his son take over the factory. *And* he made money off the fight. *These are Tyber's memories.* I'd seen my mother retrieve memories from a photograph. For a moment I felt giddy with delight. Then I jerked my hand away.

Thank goodness, Mr. Malice was still talking into the machine. Did he know what his father had done? I certainly did not want to be the one to show him. But with a father like that, I was beginning to understand why Mr. Malice was so cantankerous.

He hung up. Holding his ribs, he eased himself into his desk chair, picked up the papers on his desk, and slid them into an envelope. "Where was I? Oh yes, did you know Oscar was stealing from me?" He ran his finger along the bandage on his head as if it itched.

My fears were confirmed. "Mr. Malice, none of us knew, I swear. We'll pay you back."

He glanced up at me, as if surprised by the offer. "No. That's not necessary. But I don't care how good a welder you are. If something like this happens again, you're fired. Am I making myself clear?"

"Yes, sir." *He thinks I'm a good welder, then?* I realized the answer mattered to me.

Mr. Malice gazed out the window at the city of machines

below. "A very important client just rang me up. He needs his work finished by tomorrow. You are to be personally responsible for the welding tabs under the name of Richard Morris Hunt. Stay as late as you must to complete them." He looked at me a moment. "That's all. You may go."

"Thank you, sir. You can count on me. Sir, there is one more thing—"

"Stop. I know what you're going to say. And I know Leo doesn't deserve it, but damn it, I've got to keep the peace with the other employees. A word of advice: you keep sticking your nose in other people's business, it's going to come back to bite you." His voice got louder. "That will be all."

"Yes, sir."

Yet as I closed the metal door behind me, I heard Mr. Malice say, "Her name was Angelica Post."

Back at my station, I got right to work. If I was going to finish my current tabs and the ones for Mr. Hunt, I'd have to make haste.

All in all, the meeting had gone better than I'd expected. *I think Roland Malice has a heart after all—deeply buried, yes, but in there somewhere.*

The boys came to visit one by one, as I knew they would. Without stopping work, I repeated what had happened. I told them about the articles on the Works and Mr. Malice's career-ending fight, watching the astonishment dawn on their faces. But I avoided any mention of the things I'd learned using my second sight.

I barely heard the end-of-day whistle, but I saw the boys cleaning up their stations and the men lining up to sign the time roll. Tony and Geeno approached my workbench. They were filthy, as was I. When they lifted their goggles, it looked as if they had masks over their eyes, the areas where the layer of fine black soot hadn't touched their skin.

"See you tomorrow," Tony said, flipping his thumb back toward an officer from the House of Detention standing by the door. "Can't keep the long arm of the law waiting."

"See you tomorrow," Geeno and I said simultaneously.

The factory shut down with jarring abruptness. The great machines shuddered to a stop, the massive conveyor belts ceased their endless loops, and the haze began to settle around us. We heard the occasional sizzle and pop of hardening steel. Lanterns lit the perimeter of the factory and the perch, but the afterglow of Bessie was enough light to work by. She remained blistering hot all night until they fired her up the next morning. Sparks flew up from her boiling guts for hours. I imagined that from up in the perch, our welding guns looked like two shooting stars in a night sky.

When I glanced up, I saw the blocky silhouette of Mr. Malice watching us.

After an hour or so, Geeno and I sat in the shadows, taking a water break.

"Almost done," Geeno said.

"Yup, I'm starving. What say we pick up something for supper on the way home?" I took a long drink from a canteen I'd filled at the water fountain. Glancing at my timepiece, I said, "Too bad Mauricio will be closed up for the night." Mauricio was our favorite pushcart peddler. He only spoke Italian but was so animated in his sales of *spaghetti caldo* that people flocked to his cart. But by now many vendors would already be back at the pushcart stable for the night.

"Let's finish up." I put on my helmet and was about to lower my goggles when a cold draft slithered over my shoulders. "Wait." I held up my hand and listened. Across the factory we heard a door slam, the scrape of boots on the concrete floor. I pointed to the cluttered space under the worktable. "Geeno," I whispered, "hide."

"Avery—"

"Shhh, not so loud." I crouched next to him. "I'll be right back."

"It probably one of the men, forgot something," he said, voice low now.

"Probably, but either way, don't move." He nodded and ducked under the table. I didn't want to alarm Geeno, but something felt wrong. My neck tingled. It did not sound like someone who knew his way around the factory.

I crept along the welding stations. It was easy to stay hidden behind all the equipment. Getting closer was risky, but I had to see who it was. I stopped and listened again. More footsteps, methodical and slow, paused every few feet, presumably looking for something . . . or someone.

There was another noise, a quieter one. A swishing, like fabric. It fanned out around me so that I couldn't pinpoint its location. But it was close.

A cold sweat dampened my neck. I lay down and rolled my body under a low metal shelf. I tried to be quiet, but my goggles, pushed up onto my helmet, tapped the bottom shelf as I went under. On my back, I held my breath as the swishing sound came toward me. The hem of a heavy black cloak licked the length of my arm. Through the holes in the metal shelf, I clearly saw a crow-shaped mask.

Please, Geeno, don't move, I prayed. Dust and sweat burned my eyes, but I dared not breathe. It seemed like an eternity before I heard the swish of the cloaks fading. There was more than one crow skulking about the place. Carefully, I rolled onto my stomach, preparing to jump up and run. But I heard them moving farther off into the factory, and I crept back toward Geeno. He looked at me, tight-lipped and still. I wedged in near him, where I had a view out, putting my finger to my lips.

The steam elevator hissed to life. I shifted to see. The crows stood at the base, waiting, while the lift ascended toward the perch.

Mr. Malice must have heard it. He looked out the window. I was too far away to make out his expression.

The passenger became visible in Bessie's glow. I saw a white face through the bars of the cage. *Spector!*

Come on, Mr. Malice, I thought, *don't go soft on me now. If you're ever going to pummel someone, this is the time.*

The elevator stopped. Through the windows, I saw Spector speaking with Mr. Malice. A few moments later, the back door opened and Mr. Malice stepped out onto the abandoned catwalk. I could hear him now, voice raised.

"Look, I don't know who you are and I don't care, but as you can see"—he pointed down at the factory floor—"she's not here." He hesitated and then added, "In fact, I fired her." He held his bandaged arm in the air. "She caused an accident, so I fired her today."

He was lying to cover for me, and talking too loudly. He wanted me to hear his warning.

"No. I have no idea where she went. Now get out."

Spector emerged from the office behind him. I knew he said something, but unless he shouted like Mr. Malice, it was impossible to hear.

Mr. Malice's jaw dropped. "*He* sent you? Why would—"

Spector lifted his hand. I clearly saw the outline of a tranquilizer gun. And the next second, I heard a *pop*.

Mr. Malice cried out, a dart embedded in his chest, "What the—"

I held my hand over my mouth, fully expecting Mr. Malice to lose consciousness or fall to his knees. But he just stood there, arms slack, face expressionless. Spector spoke again, and for some reason, Mr. Malice turned and made his way further out onto the catwalk. I heard it creak and groan beneath his weight. *Where is he going? He can't go out over Bessie.*

A sickening feeling crept into my gut. I ducked out to get a better look, despite Geeno desperately trying to wave me back. Mind whirling, I closed my eyes and fought to focus on my third eye. It was hard to do, my concentration scattered and elusive. But when I opened my eyes, I saw something terrible, something I'd never seen before.

The aura around Spector was unfathomably dark. Long tendrils stretched away from him like black eels, sliding along the catwalk, slithering toward Mr. Malice.

What's happening? Mr. Malice continued to shuffle forward. He was eighty feet in the air, directly over Bessie. Somehow, Spector was controlling him, I just knew it.

To my horror, Mr. Malice unclipped the guide wire. With a loud twang, it snapped free, dangling from the bridge. Without hesitation, Roland Malice stepped off the catwalk into the air.

He fell in complete silence and what seemed like slow motion. Bessie's large opening received him with nothing more than a hot sigh.

I screamed.

CHAPTER TWENTY-ONE
BESSIE BABY

Vaguely, I felt pulling on my arm, but all I could see was Bessie, silently digesting her evening meal. It was wrong. She was his baby. I heard crying and realized it was my own.

Shattered, I turned to see what was shaking me. Geeno. He was saying something, but I couldn't hear him over the thumping in my brain.

A whirl of black rushed toward us. *The guards.* They moved so fast it was as if they'd learned to fly like crows. My mind sprang to the danger we were in. *I have to get Geeno out of here.*

"Run!" I yelled.

A flood of relief washed over Geeno's face. "That's what I say."

I sprinted, clutching his hand in mine. We twisted and

turned, trying to outrun the swishing cloaks and hammering boots behind us. The sounds were getting louder. They were gaining on us. But I knew this place like the back of my hand. *Think!*

The main entrance was out, as it might also be guarded, but there *was* a place we could hide, if we could get to the Siemens furnace room. "This way," I hissed, taking a sharp right turn. I heard Geeno cry out, and I spun around. One of the crow-guards had his other arm. Without thinking, I caught up a pair of sharp metal-cutting shears from the station next to me and hurled it at the guard. I missed him entirely, but my missile embedded deeply in the wooden table, pinning his cloak. Geeno wrenched his arm free and we bolted.

Ducking down an aisle stacked high with crates, we looped back around toward the elevator, which was descending from the perch. We'd lost the guards for the moment, but we'd have to be fast or risk running into the murderer in the elevator.

"Come on, Geeno. We're firing up the Works." I shoved him ahead of me. "Faster!"

Spector's white face stood out starkly in the darkness over our heads. His mouth was curled into a sadistic smile. I was in a nightmare—the sudden sense of dread, spiking adrenaline, disorientation. Only seeing Geeno's little body running ahead of me kept me from crumbling to the ground.

We were almost there. The elevator was still twenty feet or so above us. We skidded to a stop at the control panel door.

"You start on the left." I fished for my key, mingled with the other trinkets on my necklace. Everyone at the Works was given a key to the control panel, to shut the machinery down in an emergency. I'd never had an occasion to use it before. My hand shook as I tried to jam the key into the lock but dropped it in my haste. "Bloody hell!"

"Here, let me." Geeno shoved his key in, swinging open the steel cage door. Memories of our instruction kicked in as I pushed knobs and pulled levers. At my side, Geeno did the same. We turned on anything that moved—the belts and the trolleys, the iron depositors, the jets of the water-cooling tanks, the Siemens furnace, and Bessie. Within seconds, the ironworks had exploded to life in a cacophony of turning gears, hissing steam, clamor, and commotion.

We locked the control panel door so they could not shut the equipment down again, and turned to run. The elevator came to a stop.

"Avery Kohl." A cold whisper entered my brain. "I've been searching for you."

I froze. My whole body began to tremble.

"You are sick. You need my help. Come with me. I will take you to your mother," he assured me.

It's a trick, I told myself. *He murdered Mr. Malice.* The only thing separating me from Spector was the elevator gate and a few feet of space. His crisp gray suit hung oddly on his skeletal frame, his top hat too formal. His clothing was a mask, too, I realized, as if the finery could hide the evil. My sight flickered, and I saw his true nature unfold. The energy of others appeared to me as vaporous, smoky clouds that shifted from black to gray to white. Those auras were malleable, and I knew people had the ability to change them, to own them. This was something else entirely. The smog surrounding Spector was so dense it was devoid of light, darker than black. It moved and writhed like a monstrous octopus, infused with a life all its own.

His eyes bored into mine, and I felt the unnatural tentacles curl around me, trying to penetrate my soul. I stood transfixed as he slid the gate of the elevator open and took a step forward. He was so close I could see his small teeth, outlined in black as if they were rotting in his mouth. "Come with me, Avery Kohl."

"Avery?" The small sound of Geeno's voice broke the spell I was under. I spun, grabbing Geeno's arm, and ran.

Behind us, I heard another *pop*. *He's firing at us!* I dragged Geeno into the Siemens furnace room, the sound of the machinery drowning out everything else. Geeno tripped again, dragging at my side. "Come on," I whispered. "Almost there."

On hands and knees, I crawled under the coke oven, pulling Geeno through to the conveyor belt, which exited through a small hole in the wall, just big enough for Geeno and me if we laid ourselves flat on its surface. "Lie down! Watch your hands and feet."

Geeno climbed onto the moving belt and lay on his stomach. I jumped on behind him and was about to lower my head when I saw something sticking out of his leg. It was an ampule of murky liquid. *No!*

"*Hold on, Geeno! I'm right behind you.*" I ducked my head as the conveyor belt took us through the wall and tilted up, up toward the coal reservoirs. Below us were the great rollers that flattened steel into thin sheets. If we fell, there would be nothing left of us to find.

Geeno's arms went limp. I wrapped my fingers tightly around his ankle and slid my body forward over his legs. I felt the belt quiver below me as it angled more steeply. We were going higher. "Don't move, Geeno." I gripped the glass tube and yanked. Geeno cried out. "It's all right," I reassured him. "Just hold on."

Once we were over the metal grate floor, I jumped off and ran to catch up to Geeno. Throwing my arms around him, I lifted him off the belt and carried him into the coal runner's station, where we huddled against the wall. We'd wait until they gave up looking. We could hide here all night if we had to.

Geeno's head lolled to the side. I made a pillow of a burlap sack and removed his helmet. "Avery, what hap—" He tried to speak but his eyes fluttered closed.

"You'll be all right. You'll be all right," I repeated, stroking his cheek. Lifting the strange ampule, I studied the swirling liquid inside. *Please don't die.*

From up here I had a direct view of the perch but could not see down into the factory. As I stared out, trying not to think about what had happened, Bessie released a cascade of fire, sparks raining down onto the factory floor like fireworks.

I thought of all the times I'd heard Roland Malice talking to her. He'd yell, "Come on, little lady. You got it, girl," or "Show us your stuff, Bessie baby," as she prepared to tilt her enormous body.

"I'm sorry, Mr. Malice," I whispered. "Goodbye."

I must've fallen asleep. My eyes felt swollen, caked with sweat and dirt and dried tears. I rubbed them open, to darkness. Something wasn't right. It took me a minute to realize that the factory was quiet. I looked at my timepiece. Half past five.

Did the crows break into the control panel and switch everything off? I wasn't sure, but somehow I knew they were gone. I could no longer feel the chill of their presence. They must've thought we'd escaped to the streets.

"Geeno, wake up." I peeled my arm out from under him. Pressing my face against his chest, I felt him breathing, but he was out cold. I had to get him to the Gypsies. The herb doctor would know how to counteract Spector's poisons.

Luckily, Geeno was light enough for me to carry. I hoisted him up. It was slow going, and I stopped every few feet to listen. The only sound came from Bessie as she crackled and hissed.

On the main floor, I passed the control panel. It was still locked. Strange. How was the factory shut down? I stared up at Bessie as I continued toward the rear entrance. Now I'd really have nightmares about her. A tear slipped down my face and fell onto Geeno's. I needed to talk to my father. We had to report the murder of Roland Malice to the police.

Then I remembered what my father had told me about Tammany Hall and the police. They were all corrupt. Besides, who would believe me if I told them what'd happened? *I'll end up in the asylum for sure or worse, hanged.*

I laid Geeno down and ran to the workstations. I grabbed our coats and put away our tools so it would appear as if we'd left for the day. Then I sprinted back to Geeno, catching a glimpse of a piece of black cloth with the shears still lodged in the middle of it as I ran.

After the long night, I felt weak and disoriented. I was bent over, recovering my breath, when the oddest thing happened. Even though I knew we were alone, I felt like someone was watching me. When I placed my hand against the wall, I could've sworn it sank into the metal. For an instant, I had the distinct feeling of fingers interlaced with mine, and jumped back, looking at the place where my hand had been. There was nothing there.

Gingerly, I touched the wall with the tip of my finger. Solid as ever.

I have to get out of here. If I hadn't recently convinced myself I wasn't mad, this would have sent me over the edge. Lifting Geeno, I made my way to the sliding door that led to the rear docks and rail terminal. Padlocked. I'd have to go out the front and around the entire building. I started in that direction, but behind me I heard a loud click. I whirled around. The lock was open.

"What the hell?" I yelled at the factory.

It was as if the Works was helping me. I looked around again, half expecting to see the ghost of Mr. Malice. I even closed my eyes and focused on my third eye. Everything was exactly as it should be. Static. No energy that I could see, other than that surrounding Geeno and myself . . . until I looked up. Above the door, a set of numbers on the wall glowed for a brief second.

I sat Geeno on a chair, pushed a crate over, and stood on top of it. Reaching up, I ran my hand over the metal surface of the wall. The numbers were raised, as if pressed out from behind: 8-13-21. *How strange.* I'd never noticed them before. Then again, I didn't usually come out this way.

Geeno groaned. I jumped down just in time to stop him from falling off the chair. Forgetting everything else, I lifted him and removed the lock. The door slid easily along its metal track. Before shutting it, feeling silly but grateful, I whispered into the space, "Thank you, Mr. Malice." Just in case.

The cold night air felt good after the heat inside. I stayed in the shadow of the building and made my way around to the side, where the all-night pubs ensured plenty of hansom cabs would be hovering like flies.

My only chance was to get Geeno to the wharf where Khan

worked and pray he could get us to the Gypsies in time. I dug forty cents out of my pocket and approached the first cab in the line. It was a typical hansom, the driver sitting up high on the back of a buggy just big enough for two. The buggy was open in front but had a roof and three sides to hide us. His horse bobbed its head at my approach.

"Excuse me, sir." I tried to sound as grown-up I could. "My friend is ill. I need to get to the wharf along Furman Street as quickly as possible."

"You got money?" I showed him the change. The driver had several missing teeth and a threadbare top hat, but the horse looked to be in good condition. And I couldn't afford to be particular; the crows might be lurking nearby.

Getting Geeno in was easier said than done. I found a blanket under the seat and covered him up, my sack serving as a pillow. The streets were quiet, the *clop-clop-clop* of the horse the only sound. I realized I still had my helmet on, so I tossed it by my feet and ran my hand through my hair. It was nice to feel the cool breeze on my face.

So much had happened since I'd caused the explosion at the Works. And now Roland Malice was dead. What was going to happen when the men showed up for work in a few hours? My life was spiraling out of control, the words of a madman— *Come with me, Avery Kohl*—etched on my brain. No matter how hard I tried to block them out, I heard them again and again.

I kept nodding off, lulled by the rocking motion of the buggy and the darkness of the streets. My mind sifted through thoughts randomly. I wished I could curl up in my bed and sleep, and wake tomorrow to find it all a terrible dream.

The way to the wharf took us around the navy yard. A choking heaviness came over me as we passed the entrance to my street. I gripped the sides of the buggy, torn between jumping out to see my father and telling the driver to whip his horse to a run. The shop was a dangerous place, especially as Spector had also found Cross Street Ironworks.

As we turned a corner, warm light swelled over my face. I sucked in my breath. A spectacular sunrise peeked between the tenement buildings, tinting the sky pink and purple. The East River shimmered in the distance, illuminated by the dawn.

My mother had not seen a sunrise in three years. What would she say it was trying to tell me? I allowed a small kernel of hope to enter my heart as the long slanted rays drove out the shadows. I would talk to the guard from the Tombs today. He'd said he could help.

With or without the Gypsies, I would come up with a plan.

CHAPTER TWENTY–TWO
WELD RATS

Sunrise was no quiet time on the Brooklyn waterfront. We turned up Furman Street into the loud congestion of early morning traffic, on the street, on the river, and up in the air. Tugboats lined up next to great sailing ships with two-hundred-foot masts, yards of sailcloth, and miles of rigging that snapped and clanged in the wind. Massive tramp steamers carried coal or cargo from around the world. Impossibly tall floating grain elevators were towed up to large brick warehouses that lined the docks, and the factories beyond spewed ash into the yellow-black clouds.

And everywhere the airships, casting rippling oblong shadows along the water.

I lifted Geeno out of the cab—my arms were tired now; I couldn't carry him much longer—and paid the driver. Where was Khan? Was he working outside this morning? I scanned the area, but he was nowhere in sight. A gilded sign outside his building read John Englis & Sons. Englis was an old-time ship builder. Khan said he'd built the first of the Union's gunboats, the *Unadilla*, in just forty-eight days at the start of the Civil War.

I stepped through the two-story sliding wood doors into the cool, dark interior. The smell of freshly sanded pine hung in the salty air. Four or five men looked up; thank goodness, one of them was Khan. He ran over.

"Avery, what are you doing here?" He lifted his work goggles and grabbed Geeno, laying him on a pile of sandbags. "What happened?"

"Khan, he found me." I looked around, lowering my voice. "Spector came to the factory. He murdered Roland Malice. He shot Geeno with a vial of liquid." I took a deep breath and wiped my forehead. "We must get him to the Gypsies right away."

"Man alive! I'll be right back." Khan sprinted over to a group of workers sanding the tall wooden ribs of a ship. A man with white hair and eyes like the sea looked us over as Khan spoke.

"Let's go," Khan said, hurrying back.

"Wait! I've got to get word to Tony. He will be worried sick when we don't show up for work. Do you have a runner?"

On the way out, Khan flipped a coin to a scrawny boy and relayed the message. *Geeno is ill. I'm taking him to the same place as Oscar. From A.*

As we came within sight of the Gypsy camp, I prayed it wasn't too late. We carried Geeno to the apothecary, where I told the herb doctor what had happened and gave him the sealed glass dart containing the rest of the liquid. Khan had already disappeared, off in search of Katalina.

On my way out, I checked on Oscar. He didn't look good. Still sedated, his skin had taken on a yellowish tinge and red lines streaked up one of his legs. I closed my eyes and squeezed his clammy hand. "Don't give up, Oscar," I whispered. "And just in case you heard the herb doctor say something scary about your leg, I want to tell you my father's metal leg is fantastic, even has its own gun. My father will make you a replacement, if it comes to that." Oscar's hand remained limp and lifeless as I tucked it under the colorful throw.

Outside, I sensed a difference in the camp. It was quieter than usual, and the few people there eyed me suspiciously. My legs felt barely able to hold me up. Geeno and Oscar were like little brothers to me. I knew I shouldn't have let Geeno stay late with me. This was my fault.

I felt a pair of arms encircle me. Katalina gave me a hug, then held me out by the shoulders. "*Sar zhal-pe tusa! Mishto zhanes sar te nashaves la bedatar!* Using the skills I taught you, of course."

"Katalina, you know I don't understand what you're saying, don't you?"

She laughed. "I said, '*Salut*, friend. You know how to get out of trouble.' But you look like a vagabond chimney sweep. What do you see in this welding business, anyway? So dirty, bah."

I thought about what I must look like with my soot-streaked face, my hair matted down. She was right; my clothes were black from crawling through the coal room. Every inch of me was filthy, but I didn't care. Mr. Malice was dead; Geeno and Oscar were hurt. I felt as beaten as Mr. Malice's old punching bag hanging in the storeroom.

Khan put his arm around me. "Easy, Katalina. She's had a long night."

Katalina pushed Khan away from me. "Off of her, then. She needs a hot bath and a long rest."

I woke up in a nightshirt that I assumed belonged to Katalina, red sheets silky on my skin. It had been a week since I'd slept in a real bed. I didn't want to get up.

The last thing I remembered was Katalina and another young woman, Mariana, leading me to Katalina's red tent. I was scrubbed in scalding and perfumed bathwater, my hair combed through and oiled, my nails brushed, and my skin massaged with something that smelled like honey. They'd fed me Romany tea, cinnamon saffron dough, and eggs with cascaval cheese. It'd been years since I'd felt this clean and this full. I didn't have female friends in my life anymore to braid hair or share secrets with. I hadn't realized how much I missed it.

After I'd eaten, they bundled me in a hooded wool cloak and made me tell my story over and over again as, group by group, people crammed into the tent to hear it. No one, not even the herb doctor, believed Spector had controlled Mr. Malice. The consensus was that he'd sedated him so he could push him off the catwalk. I'd argued that Spector had not been close enough to push Mr. Malice. Mr. Malice had jumped on his own. But no one paid me any mind. And it wasn't until I fell asleep midsentence that I vaguely heard Katalina yelling at everyone to get out.

Clutching the sheet around my body, I sat up. I was alone. Candles had been lit and clothing laid out on the red sofa. Freezing, I tiptoed over. Katalina had set out one of her black dresses and some boots. The only items that belonged to me were my leather corset, my knife, my necklace, and my helmet. I slipped on the underclothes and leggings and pulled on the dress, buttoning it up the front. The bustle was sewn in, so there was no avoiding it. Grimacing, I patted my enlarged derriere. The upper dress was tightly fitted, while the skirt had soft layers cascading down from the padded encumbrance in back.

I never understood the bustle or the dreadful crinoline. I remember climbing inside my mother's hooped cage crinoline when I was small and pretending it was an American Indian hut. It was so large that I fit easily. The bustle had been getting smaller, however, until recently. Now it seemed to be expanding again.

Grabbing some hairpins, I walked to Katalina's full-length mirror and stopped short. I stared at my reflection, lifted my chin, and straightened my shoulders. For some reason, my face looked more like my mother's, and it was not just the clothing.

What is it? I leaned closer, squinting. We both had hazel eyes and slightly wide noses, but it wasn't that. There was a quality to my expression I'd never noticed before, a softening of the eye, maybe, or a set to my jaw. Could it be the visions? Could it be that we saw the world the same way? I wasn't sure, but whatever it was, it warmed me inside. I pinned my hair the way she used to, as a tear slid down my cheek.

I missed both my parents. I had not seen my father since that Sunday morning when the crows broke into the shop, over a week ago. *When will I get the chance again?*

Stepping gingerly on the wobbly little heels, I went out into the crisp air of early evening. Tonight, the camp was alive. People were stoking fires, skewering meat for roasting, sharpening weapons, or gathering animals from the nearby pastures.

I saw Khan in the distance, talking to a group of young men, and headed over. He glanced up as I approached, then snapped his head back again and watched me, his mouth hanging open. The other boys smiled and removed their hats.

"Who are you?" Khan asked. "And what have you done with my friend Avery?"

Heat rose to my cheeks. I'd always tried so hard to be inconspicuous. The attention was unnerving. "My clothes are being

washed. These are Katalina's. Are we going to see the guard?"
When he didn't answer and continued to stare, I said, "Khan,
stop acting like a simpleton."

He smiled, turning to the Romany boys. "Excuse me, gentlemen. The lady needs my assistance."

He held out his arm for me, bowing his head.

"Oh, for goodness' sake . . ." I rolled my eyes but took his
arm, as I did need help navigating in these heels. "Khan, be serious. Spector found my house and where I work. Who's to say he
won't come here next?"

"Apparently, Mr. Moralis thought of that. He's already
started sending people to their other camp. Luckily, even this one
is pretty remote. Most people presume it's all swamps out here."

Katalina hustled over, taking my other arm. "I figured you
for basic black, yes?"

"It's a bit snug." I fumbled with the dress, trying to cover up
my cleavage. Katalina's waist was tiny in comparison to mine.

She lifted an eyebrow. "You hide behind your boy's disguise. Be proud of who you are. You look beautiful."

Why can't I look beautiful in whatever I choose to wear?
I smiled, though, knowing Katalina meant well. "Maybe when
women's clothing is considerably more comfortable."

Katalina laughed. "Are you feeling better?" she asked.

"I'm fine, thank you. How's Geeno?"

"He will be all right," she said. "Come, there are people we
must see."

"Is it the guard?" I asked.

"Not yet." Katalina led us toward the center of camp. At twilight, the camp took on a magical feel. It reminded me of the Midsummer's Eve festival. The branches of a grand oak in the distance glittered with candles hung in mason jars. It was eerily beautiful, like flocks of lightning bugs.

Katalina pointed to two boys sitting under the tree. "Your friends came to find you. Meet Khan and me at the dock when you are through."

I couldn't believe it. Neither could they. As one, Tony and Leo stopped talking and stared at me.

Then they jumped up, wiping off their trousers. Leo spoke first. "Ave, I almost didn't recognize you without your work duds. You look nice."

"Thanks, Leo. It's good to see you. Any luck finding employment?"

He shook his head.

"What are you both doing here?"

Tony cleared his throat. "You won't believe me when I tell you what happened this morning. I got your message first thing. The runner was waiting for me at the factory. About an hour after we arrived, the police rushed into the Works and shut us down." His eyes opened wide, as if he still couldn't believe it. "They questioned everyone, then told us all to go home until further notice. Mr. Malice has gone missing, and they suspect foul play."

I swallowed hard, but kept my mouth shut. I did not want to involve the boys in anything. *The less they know, the better.*

He continued, "We heard there was blood on some of the equipment."

I cringed, thinking of Bessie's blast.

Tony ran his hands through his hair. "I found Leo at his home. We wanted to check on Geeno and Oscar. How are they doing?"

I hated to lie to them. "Geeno has a fever. He'll be fine. But I don't think we should disturb him. Oscar is still very ill, too."

"All right," Tony sighed. "I've got to get back anyway, in case the House of Refuge finds out the Works shut down and wonders where I am. Thanks for taking care of them, Avery. Tell them we stopped by. Us weld rats have to look out for each other, right?"

It felt horrible, but once again, I had to lie. If I told them what was going on, they would want to help, especially Tony. It broke my heart to do this, but I saw no other way. "Listen, I'm glad you're here. You should know that I won't be coming into work for a while. I want to help nurse Geeno and Oscar back to health, and there's some . . . some trouble with my mother that I must deal with."

There. At least it wasn't too far from the truth. I squeezed my lips together, not wanting to cry. But there was no stopping the tears. I felt my throat tighten and closed my eyes as they watered up.

Neither spoke, but Leo came over and hugged me tight.

"I'll come see you just as soon as I can." The sound of my words rang hollow in my ears. I placed my hands on Leo's tight curls. My stomach felt hollow. "I'm sure the authorities will sort everything out. The Works will reopen soon enough." Maybe this would prevent the strike from happening next week. I hoped so; I didn't want anyone else to get hurt.

Tony nodded solemnly. From the corner of my eye, I saw Hurricane approaching with the old box containing the crystal.

"Hello, Hurricane. These are my friends Tony and Leo. Boys, this is Miss . . ." I turned back to Hurricane. "Do you go by Miss Torre, like your grandfather?"

Her cheeks reddened, and she looked down at her feet. In a hushed voice, she said, "No, just Hurricane." Tony was the one to get past the awkward moment. "Pleasure to meet you, Miss Hurricane," he said.

Leo beamed.

She peeked up at them, her pale blue eyes sparkling through her white lashes like sunlight on the river.

Then Tony turned toward Leo. "Come on. If we can't see Oscar or Geeno, we should head out."

I hugged Leo again, and then Tony. I whispered in his ear, "Tony, don't bring him back here. It's too dangerous."

I felt him stiffen. "All right, Avery. But please send for me if you need anything—anything at all."

My stomach churned as I watched them leave. It was for the

best, but I felt like I was losing yet another part of my family.

When they disappeared into the woods, Hurricane handed me the box. "Mr. Moralis said to give you this. What is it?"

"It's a sacred relic. But I have no idea what to do with it."

She stared off in the direction the boys had gone. "I wish I had nice friends like that."

"Hurricane, I'm sure there are boys and girls here that would love to be your friend."

She tilted her head. "I don't think so. They're leery of me. Katalina is the only one who talks to me. Or, she used to."

I did not miss the implication that it was my fault Katalina spent less time with her of late. But I let it go. "Don't give up, Hurricane," I said softly. "You have to open yourself up so other people can get to know you."

As soon as I said it, though, I thought, *I'm a hypocrite.* Apparently, I'd spent my whole childhood burying part of myself without even realizing it. If I hadn't been so afraid of being like my mother, I could have learned about her visions earlier. My behavior must've hurt my mother terribly. Again, I pictured her in the Tombs, her glassy eyes, the blood on her arm. *I just hope I get a chance to make it right.*

Hurricane and I continued to the dock in time to see Khan off as he departed. I was told I could stay in an unused caravan near the apothecary, close to Geeno. Katalina and Hurricane accompanied me through the camp. The waxing moon, almost full, gave the surrounding trees a silvery cast.

"If you need more clothing, there are some garments inside," Katalina said. "I told the herb doctor where to find you if your friend Geeno wakes, and I will have your belongings sent to you when they are clean. Get a good night's sleep, Avery. Tomorrow we must finish packing up the camp in case the crows come looking for their own. We have sent scouts to warn us at the first sign of them. Khaniferre will get off work early and return to help."

"Katalina, has the guard awoken yet? He looked very badly injured."

"No. But if he does not wake on his own, we will use salts. He *will* talk to us tomorrow. There is no time to waste." She swiped her hand through the air. "Bah! Here we are, nursing our enemy back to health when we should be burying him along with the other one. It sickens me."

Hurricane opened the door and lit a lantern inside, then they left me by the steps of a tiny but ornately painted bow-top wagon. When I entered, it took my breath away.

The Gypsies were truly the most artistic, creative individuals I'd ever known. Here was a storage wagon with a spare bunk for visitors, and it was decorated as if they were expecting Queen Victoria herself to stop by. One side had built-in drawers of dark polished wood with gold inlay; the other had orange velvet benches flanking a potbelly stove backed by a wall of colorful mosaic tiles. All the walls and the ceiling were painted bright red with gold accents. And in the rear, red velvet curtains were swagged over a plush bed piled high with colorful pillows and quilts. *They will have to pry me out of here with a crowbar.*

I sat on one of the benches and carefully removed the long crystal from its container. I held it in the flickering glow. A fractured rainbow of light bounced around the little room as I turned the crystal in my hands. Although the effect was dazzling, the crystal held no special power that I could see or feel. Discouraged, I put it away.

There was a knock on the door. When I opened it, a small bundle sat on the steps. Inside was all of my clothing, cleaned and pressed, and—thank goodness—my boots. My feet ached from walking in Katalina's heeled shoes all evening. I laid out my corset, knife, necklace, and coat and opened the top drawer on the left. Wrapped in tissue paper were delicate dresses of every color. Another drawer contained tights and shifts. I tried the right side and found what I was looking for: a pair of sturdy wool britches, without holes like mine, a clean white muslin shirt to wear under my corset, and, just to irk Katalina, a man's fedora. At the last minute, I added a pair of spats to keep my boots clean. Then I changed into a shift and buried myself under the soft pile of quilts on the bed.

I couldn't get the image of Mr. Malice falling into Bessie out of my mind, or the horrible scene that had led up to his death. A few things struck me as odd. What were the numbers on the wall above the door? And before I'd gone into Malice's office, he'd been talking to someone on the telephone device.

He'd clearly been angry about something to do with the employ-ees—us. He'd said he'd alert the authorities if the person he was talking to did something . . . but what was it they wanted to do?

What he'd said to Spector echoed in my thoughts: "*He* sent you?" Who was he referring to? Did someone send Spector to kill Mr. Malice? And if so, why?

CHAPTER TWENTY-THREE
THE GUARD

Morning came too soon. I dressed wearily and headed toward the apothecary, stopping first at a fire to have some breakfast. When I arrived, Geeno was sitting up, watching a spider spin a web in the corner. "Avery, guess what," he said. "The herb doctor say he is going to make me a monocle like his. It makes everything look close-up."

"Geeno, I'm so happy to see you're awake. How are you feeling this morning?" I handed him a hot roll.

"I'm tired, but Oscar looks bad."

I glanced toward Oscar's bunk. "I know, Geeno. They're letting him sleep so he can heal. I'm glad you're all right, though. Your pets are probably wondering what's happened to you." He looked so small, so pale.

"I hope they no eat each other." He smiled, but his smile

quickly faded—as if he'd been pretending all along. His eyes met mine searchingly. At that moment he looked older than his nine years. "Avery, is Mr. Malice dead?"

I sat down next to him and pushed the hair off his forehead. "Yes, Geeno, he is."

"Did that bad man do it?"

I nodded. I'd hoped his memory of the events that brought us here would be foggier.

"Is he going to come after you?" He laid his head on my chest.

"He might try, but we'll be ready, Geeno. Don't fret. I just need you to worry about getting better, nothing more." I looked up at the spider. "Have you found some creatures in need of your special services?" I had to keep things light or he'd end up with the same nightmares I've had all my life.

"*Our* special services. We heal them together." He closed his eyes and within minutes was fast asleep again.

I spent the day working alongside the Gypsies. We crated dry goods, gathered firewood, and honed weapons. The rest of the tents were disassembled and packed into wagons. By midday more families had hitched their caravans to their horses and headed out to the camp on Long Island. Katalina told me it was in a beautiful hamlet known as Dick's Hills, after the founder, Dick Pechegan, and it was very safe, as it was difficult to get to. Lucas and Horatio had gone back to their surveillance of the Tombs. By the time I spotted Khan's boat pulling up in the late afternoon, I was anxious to speak with the guard. Khan wanted to be there when we questioned him.

"I'm glad you're here," I said as he docked.

"Yes, when I'm on deliveries I get them done quickly so my afternoons are free." He laughed. "I see you're back to your regular attire." He lifted a canvas tarp off a wooden box. "I have a surprise for you."

I heard her even before I saw what he was uncovering. "Sera!" I called, bouncing on my toes. She shrieked even more loudly at the sound of my voice. Khan lifted her out and handed her to me. I felt the familiar warmth radiating through my chest when I held her. She had her hood on. I stroked her feathers and she responded with her *ki-ki-ki-kee*.

"Thank you, Khan. Thank you so much. How is my father?"

"I couldn't get inside. I recognized his friend Jeremiah Thorn outside the shop. He told me your father is hiding out in the basement permanently now."

I pouted. *Are they bringing him food and water? Is he taking care of himself?*

"Jeremiah gave me a parcel from your father, and I found this attached to Seraphine's leg. What is it?" He held up a small metal tube.

"My father and I trained Seraphine to carry secret notes. Sometimes he'd send her to the Works to find me. She's an incredible tracker." As I spoke, I removed Seraphine's hood and tossed her up into the air. She flew in ever-higher circles. I shielded my eyes to watch until she disappeared into the dusky orange-streaked sky.

Khan handed me a packet wrapped in brown paper, and the tube. His eyes were warm. "Remember when I saw her circling the Tombs? She must have been tracking you then."

"Yes! Of course." I nodded. Popping open the tube, I saw a piece of rolled-up paper. It always amazed me that my father could write in such tiny letters.

The note simply said *M.T.Y.L.T.T.* I smiled. Even in the midst of pandemonium, he remembered. "It means he loves me 'more than yesterday, less than tomorrow.' It's engraved on my timepiece—see?" I showed Khan the back.

Next I unwrapped the parcel. Inside was another note, wrapped around a little clock. This one was written in our secret code. I deciphered it for Khan.

> *Hi, Buttercup,*
>
> *Khan relayed incident at Ironworks. Sorry about Malice, even if he was a mean old curmudgeon. Wherever you are, stay put. Crows out in force. Don't worry—men keep me well hidden while I complete my finest project. I promise I will get us out of here.*
>
> *Love,*
>
> *Your sober father*
>
> *PS: Found this clock while clearing out shop, remembered it was your favorite.*

At one inch tall, the marvel I held was the tiniest grand-father clock in the world, complete with a swinging split pea–sized pendulum behind a little glass door. My father once told me he'd made it for the mouse that lived in the shop. My throat tightened, and the feeling spread into my chest. *Father's clearing out the shop. Is this the last clock, then?* I held it to my ear. *Tick-tock, tick-tock.*

I didn't understand why my father still made promises to me, promises I knew he couldn't keep. He was so caught up in his big project that he could not see how bad things really were. Maybe it was Father's way of coping, but I was through with living in denial. I swallowed hard, folded the paper around the clock, and tucked it into my pocket.

Khan cleared his throat and rubbed the back of his neck. "I missed you last night, Little Bird." He took my hand. "Were you all right staying here?"

"Of course. Please don't worry." I smiled up at him. "But I missed you, too."

Khan looked around the camp, his brows drawing together. "Wow, there's little left for me to do. Looks sort of sad without the colorful tents."

Mr. Moralis walked out onto the dock. Khan released my hand to shake his. "Horatio reported back this afternoon," Mr. Moralis said. "There's a search under way for the missing guards. Now that you're here, we're planning to revive the one we have."

As we followed Mr. Moralis, Khan told me the Works had

reopened. "I spoke with Tony. The police could not find a body, so for now that foreman you dislike—what do you call him?"

"Scarface."

"Right, Scarface. He's running things. Apparently he asked Tony where you and Geeno had gotten off to. Tony played dumb."

"Khan, I forgot to tell you, but when I was getting Geeno out of the factory, I saw three numbers on the wall with dashes between them: eight, thirteen, and twenty-one. What do you suppose they are?"

"Could be the combination to a safe. Most businesses have a safe to protect important papers from fire. I know Mr. Englis has one with a combination lock on it. It'd be foolish to put the numbers on the wall, though." He chuckled.

"Hmm, that must be it. Mr. Malice had a safe in the perch. This sounds strange, but I feel like Mr. Malice was trying to tell me something. Maybe it has to do with the safe."

Khan snorted. "Nothing about you surprises me anymore, Avery. Now you're telling me Mr. Malice reached out to you from beyond?"

I scrunched up my face. "My goodness, you're right. Please, forget I said that."

We arrived at one of the few caravans left. Unlike the others, this one had bars on the windows and a heavy steel door. Two burly men stood by the entrance, smoking cigarettes. They stepped aside as we approached. Katalina and Hurricane were waiting by the steps. I was pleased to see that Katalina held Hurricane's hand. Hurricane worshipped her so.

Mr. Moralis stared directly at Katalina. "Let us hear the man out. Do not do anything rash."

"Rash? Do not slit his throat, you mean?" Katalina swiped her finger across her neck.

I winked at Hurricane and she beamed back at me. I thought Katalina was joking, but apparently her father did not think so. He held out his hand, asking her wordlessly for her knife.

The herb doctor stepped outside. "The salts worked. He is ready to speak with you. I must go finish packing up the apothecary."

The guard stood up shakily when he saw us. He had a crimson line around his neck where the other guard had tried to strangle him with a cord. He eyed Katalina warily. Mr. Moralis spoke first. "What is your name?"

"Nelson Lemming, sir."

"I am Mr. Moralis. I believe you've met Miss Kohl." He extended his hand toward the others. "My daughter, Miss Moralis; Mr. Soliman; and Miss Hurricane. Do you understand why your presence here has caused such turmoil, Mr. Lemming?"

"I believe so." He took a few steps back and wrung his hands together. "I've heard about the boy that was taken from your camp, and is being held at the Tombs."

Katalina flew across the room. "That is my baby brother,

you imbecile. Do you know what they did to him? Do you?" If her father hadn't disarmed her, Nelson Lemming might've had a knife in his heart. She screamed in his face, "They branded him like cattle! How do we know you were not there, hiding behind your crow mask?"

The guard held up his arm. "I wasn't! It wasn't me!"

"Enough, Katalina." Mr. Moralis guided her back to a bunk and sat her down. "If this is too emotional for you . . ."

She shook her head. "No. I want to stay. I want to hear what he has to say."

Hurricane sat next to her, and I next to Hurricane. Khan stood by the door. Mr. Moralis continued, "You said you want to help. How do we know we can trust you?"

Nelson Lemming shook his head. "Just let me go. I swear I won't tell a soul. I'll leave the city. Whatever you want."

Hurricane whispered to me, "Avery, see his aura. Focus as hard as you can."

I squeezed my eyes shut, but my mind was a whirlwind. Just seeing the guard again made my head buzz. Hurricane took my hands. She whispered, "Use your breath, in, out, nice and slow. Calm your mind."

"All right." I lowered my shoulders, relaxed my breathing, and focused on each breath in and each breath out. As random thoughts popped into my head, I pictured them floating away on a river. Soon my mind felt calmer. I slowly opened my eyes and saw the room with my second sight. As I looked around, I realized all of us were highly charged, our auras various shades of gray. I relaxed my breathing again, and my own energy became infused with pure white light. I pushed that light toward Nelson Lemming.

He glanced at me with a strange expression, and I saw snippets of his life. I saw his dog Bojangles again. I saw his fear of Dr. Spector, of the other guards. I saw the argument he'd had with the dead guard. "What they're doing is wrong," he'd said. "We have to get out now, before it's too late." I saw the other guard turn on him, punch him, call him a traitor, wrap a steel cord around his neck.

As he continued to look at me, his aura changed, softened, lightened. He let out his breath as if he'd been holding it and sat down. "I do want to help." He glanced up at Mr. Moralis. "I can't rightly explain it. I'm ashamed of some things I done, but it's not just that. I can't be a part of what they're doing anymore." His eyes met mine. "There are bad things going on in the Tombs. I was going to leave, if Jason hadn't tried to kill me. I'm not a religious man, but I believe this here happened for a reason. Please, let me help."

I nodded. I accepted that he'd changed. I'd seen it happen with my own eyes. "I believe him," I said, and whispered to Hurricane, "It worked this time. Maybe because he was already trying to change. Thank you."

Hurricane squeezed my hand. "Well done."

Mr. Moralis looked at Katalina; she nodded, as did Khan.

"All right, Mr. Lemming. We are choosing to trust you, because we need your help." Bending over so that his face was closer, he lowered his voice. "If you lie to us, you endanger our lives. I will not kill you, but I swear this: You will find yourself bound and gagged and on the next freighter to Romania, where you will be imprisoned in a work camp for the rest of your life. You will wish you were dead. Am I perfectly clear?" I hadn't heard Mr. Moralis use that tone before, or imagined such a threat. It made me wonder how many others among the Gypsies' enemies had met a similar fate.

Lemming shifted in his seat. "Yes, sir."

Crossing his arms, Mr. Moralis took a step back. "Good. Tell us everything you know about the Tombs."

Lemming cleared his throat. "The Tombs started out as a hospital for the criminally insane, an adjunct to the prison. The lower levels were abandoned because of water problems—flooding, you know. But just before the end of the Civil War, Dr. Spector reopened them. I was a prison guard at the time. Some of us were transferred, given different uniforms, told the mask was important because of the type of work Spector was doing. And we had to sign a vow of silence about anything going on at the Tombs."

In a lower voice, Lemming said, "Dr. Spector takes folks like your mother into the lab." He wrung his hands together. "I hear terrible screaming. He's performing some kind of experimentation. I'd have quit sooner, but I need the money." His eyes slid to the floor. "I'm sorry. I stood by and paid no heed." His voice strained as he tried to get the words right. "But I couldn't stand it anymore. I . . . I told Jason. I thought he was a friend, but when I told him it wasn't right, what Spector was doing, well, you already know what he did."

Khan took a step closer. "What kind of experiments is Spector doing with them?"

Lemming shifted again as Khan took another step in his direction. "I don't know." He shook his head. "I swear, I don't know."

Khan bowed his head and pressed his palm to his forehead in frustration.

My knees felt weak and my breath was shallow, as if I were breathing through a thin tube. I was glad I was sitting down. Khan handed me his handkerchief. "Avery, are you all right?"

I dabbed the perspiration from my neck. "I need some air." I walked over to the door and stuck my head out, inhaling cold air deep into my lungs. I turned back. "I have to get my mother out of there, Mr. Lemming. Please. Can you think of a way to get her out?"

"And Indigo!" Katalina added.

Before I could think better of it, I said, "And we must find a way to stop Spector."

Khan stared at me as if I'd gone mad.

I clutched my hands to my chest. "He's taking children off the streets."

"The place is a fortress," Lemming said, "and they've increased security after you got away. You'll never get back in." He rubbed his chin again. "Spector rarely leaves anymore; the only time I know of for sure will be for the All Hallows' Eve masquerade."

Mr. Moralis exchanged a look with Khan. "What is this masquerade?"

"Spector's benefactor is hosting it for his patrons." Lemming looked up at us. "There's big money backing Spector's operation."

"Do you know the names of any of these 'big-money' benefactors?" Mr. Moralis asked.

"No, but I see the fancy carriages that pull up for his meetings at the Tombs, and he pays better than any other boss I've ever had. I guess that's why the guards never leave. He buys our loyalty—and our silence."

Later, looking out over the home of the Gypsies, as it converted from a camp to a traveling caravan, I thought about our meeting with the guard. I'd wanted so badly to speak with him, but we'd not learned anything useful. And now I could not erase the image of my mother's screaming as Dr. Spector took her into his lab.

CHAPTER TWENTY-FOUR
BEST FRIEND

Early the next day, since Khan and I had to retrieve some things from Geeno's crate, I begged him to go with me by horseback instead of by boat. We borrowed two horses from the Gypsies and rode into the woods. The familiar swaying motion brought me back to happier days. I missed riding. We used to own a horse named Luna, a dapple-gray mare. I'd ride her whenever Father didn't have her hitched to a cart delivering clocks or hauling stuff from the salvage yards. I remembered the smell of her when she'd rub her soft muzzle on my face, like sweet hay and sunshine. Father had sold Luna, along with most of our fine possessions, when we'd fled Brooklyn Heights to hide in the slums.

We cleared the trees; my horse began to trot. Misty morning light blanketed the flatlands. I eased from a posting to a swinging motion and transitioned her to a canter.

"Race?" I challenged.

Khan grinned. "You're on."

I leaned forward, lifting from the saddle, my weight in my heels. My horse lengthened her stride, picking up speed. The hood of my cloak flew back. I glanced sideways, to see Khan gaining on me.

Just then I heard Seraphine's shrill cry and looked up to see her soaring through the sky above. "I'm coming!" I leaned further forward, spurring my horse on. It was as if she'd been waiting for me to ask. Faster and faster she ran, the wide-open field calling her. The cloak whipped behind me. Hooves thundered the ground; sweat glossed her flanks. I was flying, the closest to Seraphine I'd ever been.

My face flushed. At the edge of the field I eased the mare back to a walk and tilted my face toward the sun.

"Whew, I needed that," I told Khan as he caught up to me.

"Yeah, me too. Except the losing part." He laughed. "Avery, I have a confession to make." I turned sideways to face him. He tilted his head. There was a solemn yearning in his warm amber eyes. "I miss the old days, too—when you and I were young and we thought we would always be together."

Warmth spread through my chest. Impulsively, we reached out and held hands, our horses trudging along, cooling down. I took everything in—the trees, bright red and orange; the clod of the horse's hooves on the earth; the contrast of the warm sun and crisp air; the tingle in my hand where it touched Khan's.

We neared the edge of Brooklyn proper and let go before someone saw us. We had to find the Gypsies' stable. At any other, we risked having the horses stolen, a common problem in these parts.

After turning over the reins to the stable hand, we worked our way through the crowded streets to Geeno's crate in the industrial sector. We unlocked the back room, gathering my meager belongings and all of Geeno's things. Then we carefully wrapped his insect jars in newsprint. The only escapee seemed to be the partly mechanical mouse, which had chewed through his box and disappeared.

"Can you imagine the look on someone's face," I said, "if they find that particular rodent in their mousetrap?" I chuckled at the thought.

"I wish I could've seen it." Khan looked at me with an awed expression. "A mouse? That's unbelievable, Avery. These all are."

We layered each wrapped jar in burlap to keep them extra safe, and Khan placed them in a large satchel. When we returned to Fulton Street, the bustling center of town, we peeked around to make sure the coast was clear. It wasn't. Three crow-guards were heading straight for us. By their aggressive stride and the way they surveyed the street, I knew they were hunting. *Hunting for me.*

My throat constricted. A feeling of vertigo rushed over me.

Khan jumped into action. He ducked into a doorway, pulling

me with him. Just as before, he pressed his body against mine and bowed his head. Khan was as immobile as the wooden door to my back. It grew eerily quiet around us, and even though it did not make sense, I felt as if we were no longer there. The guards marched by. Both the guards' proximity and Khan's flustered me.

We waited until they were gone, then bolted toward the stable.

We rode back to camp on edge. I'd begged Khan to teach me his special cloaking skill, but he assured me that, like my second sight, it was something he was born with. By the time we arrived, Mr. Moralis had sent the elders, along with most of the women and children, to safety. The rest of the men stayed behind to finish the work of moving.

As the sun dropped, so did the temperature. I rubbed my arms as we went over to the caravan where Katalina and her father stayed now. They'd spent the day further questioning Nelson Lemming. We did not want to set him free until we had all the information he could give us—especially true for Katalina, who did not want to release him at all.

It was Katalina who ushered us in. Hurricane sat at the table with Mr. Moralis, quietly peeling potatoes. She brightened when I smiled at her. Horatio and Lucas arrived a short while later. Khan gravely informed them of the crows we saw in town.

Mr. Moralis's eyes hardened. "We have learned more about

this event Spector is attending on All Hallows' Eve. That's only five days from now. The invited guests are strictly men, high-society men, supporters of Spector's work at the Tombs." Mr. Moralis poured himself a glass of wine. "Would either of you like one?" He glanced at Khan and me. "You look like you could use it."

We shook our heads no. I was already sick to my stomach just discussing Spector.

Mr. Moralis continued, "Apparently the guests will all wear masks and an insignia—a gold ring, shaped like the claw of a crow. The guards have been told to seize any man entering without the ring. Lemming also said there will be courtesans from the House of the Scarlet Ascot, to entertain the guests."

Lucas whistled. "Sounds like some party."

Katalina smacked him in the chest. "You think it is nice? Go ask one of those girls what they think, eh? Fool."

"I used to know a couple of girls there. They're tough as nails," Khan said, then must have realized how it sounded. "But . . . it's been years since I've seen—"

"I should have known!" Katalina pounced on him before he could finish. "I will be angry with you later, Khaniferre."

Khan removed his hat and wiped his forehead. I was not as surprised as Katalina seemed to be by Khan's disclosure. He told me he knew people in all walks of life.

"Well, that's it then." Lucas ran his hand through his hair. "The guard has not provided us with any useful information."

Mr. Moralis began to pace. I could see he was trying to work something out in his head. He stopped and sipped his wine. "There may be a way we can get into that party—one of us, at least. Lemming said he had to go back to collect his pay, then he planned to skip town. Assuming we can trust him enough to let him go, he is going to need his cloak and mask to get back into the Tombs, but we still have the others, belonging to the dead guard. Someone may slip in disguised as a crow-guard."

We all registered the same look of surprise. *That could work.*

Horatio stepped forward. "I will do it," he declared.

Mr. Moralis ran his hand over his long beard, rolling each bead in his fingers like my mother used to do with her rosary. "All right. I don't like it, but it's the only way I can think of to learn more. Of course, no one says anything in front of Lemming that might reveal our plan. We don't know for sure if we can believe him."

With that decided, we headed outside, to the smell of game turning on the solitary spit. Khan took my hand, leading me away from the group. We walked along the edge of the shore, the voices of the others fading to a pleasant background sound. My stomach growled, but I knew Khan wanted to talk. I wondered if he knew how much Katalina cared for him, even if she refused to admit it.

I played with my necklace. *I'm sure she's noticed we are gone.*

We came upon a fallen tree to sit on. The still water of Jamaica Bay mirrored the sky, reflecting each star. It looked like the edge of the world, as if you could jump into the darkness and float among the stars. I picked up a stone and threw it into the water, shattering the illusion, sending ripples twinkling across the surface.

Khan's fingers interlaced tightly with mine as though he was afraid to let go. "Are you all right?" he said. "You seem disheartened."

I looked up at the night sky. "I feel like I've learned so much, Khan, and yet we know nothing of Spector's purpose. I can't imagine what we can do to get my mother or Indigo out of the Tombs or to put a stop to Spector's plans. Mr. Moralis is sure I can't re-create an explosion."

Khan's thumb grazed the inside of my wrist. "I know." Then he turned to face me. "What's it like to see an aura?"

I wished I could explain it so he could understand. "Lonely," I said. "Like no one else sees the world as I do. Do you ever feel like an experience isn't real—no, that's not the word—like it isn't authentic, unless you can share it with someone else?"

"I think so," he said. "But I want you to *try* to share it with me. Try to explain it, Avery. It feels as if there's a part of you that's a secret, that I don't know you as completely as I did before."

"All right." I took a deep breath. "When I focus, I see light around every living thing. And with people, at least, the light changes all the time. It's as though I see their emotions."

He shook his head. "Look at me and tell me what you see."

"Khan, I don't know . . . I shouldn't. Memories come to me. It's strange."

"I don't care. I want you to. Besides, I'm curious." He smiled and shifted, as if preparing himself to be studied. I felt as he did in that moment, that we had drifted apart. I missed the time we used to spend together.

"All right," I said.

I closed my eyes for a moment, focusing on my third eye, directing my energy to that spot. "There's light surrounding us," I said, opening my eyes and staring at him. "It's pale, not dark, so I can assume neither of us is angry or heated. From what Katalina tells me, others see auras in many colors, and the colors have different meanings. But what I see is different. I see auras in hues of gray. They change and flow and join with the auras of other living things around them. It's so hard to explain, Khan." I looked around. A soft glow surrounded Khan and me. The trees glowed silvery in the moonlight. A fish flashed by like a shooting star. The world shimmered and pulsed with soft, natural energy. Even the ground glowed, every blade of grass outlined with light.

I breathed it in. I ran my hand over the dandelions crowding the base of the log. The light flowed between my fingers, melding with that of the flowers. It was indescribable. I felt a rift open between Khan and me as I struggled to put my experience into plain words.

Khan watched me. "You're right," he said softly. "I can't even imagine what it must be like to see that. This Indigo fellow, Katalina's brother—I suppose he can see it, too?"

"I suppose." The light around Khan began to darken. I looked into his eyes and saw what he was remembering: the day after my thirteenth birthday. Khan listening to me while I told him about the boy I'd met. How the boy had disappeared. I'd cried into Khan's shoulder and he'd put his arms around me, comforting me.

"Khan, were you jealous?" I blinked, clearing my sight.

"I didn't like seeing you hurt."

With that, Khan took me in his arms. I nestled into the warmth of his chest, like when we were kids, shielded momentarily from the cold night air. Safe. He pressed his lips to my forehead and murmured, "Avery, my little bird, I talked you into coming here and now I just want you to fly away. Far, far away." He tilted my chin up. His golden eyes, the color of turmeric spice, searched mine, as if he wanted to see into my soul. Then he slowly pulled my face toward his. I knew he was going to kiss me. I wanted him to. I wanted his mouth, his strong arms, his smooth tattooed muscles touching me. But most of all, I wanted to feel close to him again, the way I used to. The way I did today when we'd held hands.

Khan's lips were warm and soft. I closed my eyes, slid my arms around his neck, and kissed him back. He tasted sweet and familiar, his kiss excruciatingly gentle. My heart pounded faster. His hand wove into my hair. His lips moved slowly, parting mine, his tongue lightly teasing. It felt as if all the bottled-up emotion from everything we'd been through was embodied in this one kiss. I wanted to stay in the moment, to let go, but my stomach flipped over, warning me to stop.

I can't lose my best friend . . . my oldest friend. He means more to me than this. I pushed gently away.

I felt his breath on my tingling lips. "I'm sorry," he whispered. "I know we shouldn't." His long lashes brushed my cheek. "It would be impossible for you and me—"

"Shh." I pressed my finger to his lips. "Khan, I hope you know that my hesitation has nothing to do with the color—"

"You don't need to explain. And trust me, Avery, I know you better than you know yourself. You are not one to bow to conventions of society. It's one of the things I love about you."

My chest swelled with warmth. Except for my second sight, he did know me so well. I touched my lips to his, a quick kiss, then lifted them in a smile. "I love you too, Khan. But right now I need to focus on one thing—the Tombs."

Behind us, I heard the snap of a twig. I sat up. "Did you hear that?"

"Hear what?"

I spun around. The woods behind us were thickly layered in dark shadows. My ears strained to hear the footfall of someone stepping stealthily through the leaves. In the distance I heard the Gypsies around the campfire, talking and laughing, the soft nicker of the horses, but the woods were dead quiet.

My intuition prickled, a stark reminder of the danger closing in on me—crushing me like a corset made of metal.

CHAPTER TWENTY–FIVE
HOUSE OF
THE SCARLET ASCOT

My sleep was robbed by a dreadful dream. I was at a hellish carnival party and Dr. Spector was the ringmaster. There were cages of grotesquely deformed people in a long mirrored hall, at the end of which was a red curtain, drawn tight. Behind it I heard my mother crying. When I parted the curtain, my hands came away covered in blood, sticky and dark. I ran through and found myself in a shadowed boudoir. There was someone in the bed. As I approached, I saw a flash of tattooed skin. It was Khan—he was under the sheets with a woman.

I sat up. Sweat dampened my brow. I'd grown used to nightmares, but these shocking illusions made my cheeks flush. I'd never seen a man naked, and to imagine seeing Khan with a woman disturbed me. The feel of Khan's kiss came back to me, and I touched my lips, remembering.

Shaking off the strangeness, I draped a wool blanket over my shoulders and set off to find breakfast. As I approached the fire, my heart skipped a beat. Geeno sat on a log, eating porridge. I ran to him. "Geeno! You're better." I was about to hug him when I noticed the big eyes of a bug staring at me from the top of his head. "Oh! Don't those things fly away?"

"Nope," he beamed. "They stay with me always."

"That's amazing." I sat down, scooting a little farther from him just in case. "How are you feeling?"

"Much better. Avery, I made you a surprise." He reached into a small burlap sack. "Well, it really for you and Seraphine both."

He handed me a small mechanical instrument attached to a leather wrist strap, and a leather hood clearly shaped to fit Seraphine's head. Unlike the one I already had, this one did not cover her eyes. On top were four tiny gears spinning around a spike of copper.

"What is it?" I examined the device on the wrist strap: a set of interlocking gears and a hand above a dial, though it didn't show time. The face was that of a compass.

"You wear this." He buckled it onto my wrist. "And Seraphine wears the hood. It shows you always where Seraphine is, even if she far away."

"Geeno, are you certain?" I could tell by his proud smile he was. "How does it work?"

"The dial point to her when she have her hood on. It uses

magnets. Look." He placed the hood on two of his fingers and ran around, waving his arm as if he were flying. I looked down; sure enough, the little needle followed him wherever he went.

"Geeno, I don't know how to thank you. When did you have time to make this?"

"Your father helped me get it started. It was in the things you brought back. I plan to give it to you the other night—I know how much you love Seraphine."

I shook off the blanket. "Come here, my little inventor." I picked him up and swung him around in a circle, not even caring about the bug clinging desperately to his hair. "One day we must show my father that it works. He will be as delighted as I am." It was then that I noticed the apothecary cart was gone. "Geeno, when did the herb doctor leave? Why didn't you go with him?"

"He left early this morning. He wanted me to go, but I told him I wanted to stay with you."

I hugged him close. "Thank you, Geeno, but I wish you hadn't done that. It would've been safer for you to leave."

I left Geeno by the fire, my fingers fishing for Father's Union pin strung on my necklace. I missed him. He would be so proud of Geeno. The chill of the morning held fast, and by late afternoon, a light snow had begun to flake down from the sky. The caravans that were left seemed leeched of their bright colors, as if the world were fading.

Even Katalina dressed in dull gray as we worked side by

side brushing down a horse. She asked me if I was feeling better. "I noticed you and Khaniferre were quiet when you finally joined us at the campfire last night."

"Oh, were you looking for us?"

"No, I ate with my father before you arrived. Father is as disappointed as I am with our progress. When I saw Khaniferre this morning, he said you were upset last night."

"Yes," I agreed, but I couldn't meet her eyes. "I was. I'd hoped we'd learn more from the guard, and I'm terrified for both my mother and my father. Khan wanted to talk; he worries about me."

"Did he say anything about *me*?" She bit her lip.

"He's concerned for us both." I did not want to give Katalina false hopes about Khan's feelings, not when she clearly cared for him—and deeply. She sulked away.

I spent time working with Hurricane. With her encouragement, I tried holding the crystal, rubbing its smooth surface, talking to it, but nothing had any effect. It was just cold quartz in my hands. When Hurricane left, I sat on the steps of my temporary lodging, my hands in front of me. I focused until white light surrounded them. I didn't think I would ever tire of seeing this beauty, or of the feeling of connection it sent through me. But what I wanted right now was to be able to re-create the explosion I'd caused. Even though Mr. Moralis said it was not possible, it was the one thing I felt could actually help us. I tried building up the energy; I tried throwing it outward. Nothing worked.

Katalina returned with a new bounce in her step. "Come with me," she whispered. "I want to show you something."

I followed her to her caravan. Once inside, she locked the door behind us. On the bed were two beautiful wigs, one blond, one red. "My mother was fond of wigs. I dug these out of her trunks."

"Why, Katalina?" I sat down, curious to find out what was going on.

"Just hear me out." She held her hands up as if expecting me to run—which made me want to. "When I spoke with Khaniferre, I also questioned him about his *friends* from the House of the Scarlet Ascot," she said, emphasizing the word *friends*. "He swore they were not love interests, but he did mention their names. I have sent one of our runners to deliver a calling card to them. I introduced myself as Isabella Moore, acquaintance of Khaniferre Soliman. I told them I, and a friend, have interest in joining the house, and to expect us at their place of residence on October thirty-first. I am counting on them needing as many girls as possible for the party. Other than having to bribe the little runner to help me write the note in English, it is a brilliant plan, yes?"

I knew Katalina's reading and writing were poor, but now I knew she was also crazy. "What are you talking about? Expecting us . . . ?"

"You and I will meet these girls and go with them. Avery, do you not see? This is our only chance to find out what Spector is doing, *and* to discover those supporting him." She put her hands on her hips. "We must go to that party! In disguise, of course—red for me, blond for you." She pointed to the wigs.

I jumped up. "You're mad! Your father will never allow it." It was a preposterous idea!

"No one will know, except Horatio, of course, and he is afraid of me. I swore him to secrecy. Besides, he will be there with us should anything go awry."

A hollow feeling opened up in my stomach. "Katalina, these girls are prostitutes. What if . . . you know . . ."

She let out a long sigh. "Men like window dressing at their parties. The houses show off their girls, let them flirt and tease, but that is it. After all, they want the men to come back for more—and *pay* for it. You have four days to decide. If you will not come with me, I will go alone. The day after the party, my father will move the rest of us to the camp on Long Island. We will never get another opportunity like this. At least accompany me to Rosalinda's today when I buy a dress," she pleaded.

I couldn't let her go alone, and I needed a distraction. My mind was a stew of jitters. I fretted, gnawing at my nails while Katalina told her father she and I needed to get some womanly supplies for the journey and we would hasten back. "We will go straight to Rosalinda's," she explained. "Horatio will accompany us, to keep us safe."

That afternoon Geeno ran down to the dock to see us off. I squeezed him to me. He tilted his head back and said, "Can't I come with you? I don't want to stay here alone."

"You're not alone, Geeno. Hurricane is here, and Mr. Moralis. They'll look after you. I'll be back before you know it." Hurricane had refused to go to Long Island without Katalina. Maybe she and Geeno would become friends if they were stuck here together.

He blinked, holding back tears. "Hurricane doesn't talk."

"She's shy, but she's very sweet. Give her a chance—she'll come around. You know what? I need your help. Seraphine also hates it when I leave. Will you look after her for me?" I reached into my pack and pulled out the leather glove. "She's heavy. Do you think you can hold her?"

Geeno nodded excitedly. I whistled, and Seraphine flew toward us from a nearby tree.

"Hold up your arm, Geeno." I slid my glove over his hand and forearm—a little big, but it would still protect him. Seraphine reached out with her thick claws, landing gracefully on his arm. He stroked her back while I secured the hood over her eyes.

"You right, she heavy," he said, giggling.

"See that field over there?" I pointed to a clearing in the trees at the far end of camp. "Take her there and you can watch her hunt."

Geeno carried Seraphine toward the far field, beaming. He'd forgotten all about my leaving.

Katalina and I climbed down into the boat with Horatio and we puttered out into Jamaica Bay. I held my thick hooded cloak tightly at my neck. The gray sky sapped the daylight. But the snow remained light, the flakes glowing green in the light of the overhead airships. I tilted my head back, letting the snow kiss my cheeks and lips. How I wished I were up there in an airship, looking down.

We moored at one of the few quiet docks in Manhattan. Rosalinda's was a Gypsy-owned dress shop not far from the waterfront. Horatio waited outside for the runner who was to meet us here with a reply from Khan's friends at the House of the Scarlet Ascot.

Rosalinda herself ushered us in with a flurry of hugs and kisses.

Hands on hips, Katalina said, "Rosie, we need attire for a fancy soiree." Like a tornado, Katalina gathered gowns and accessories in her arms. On the way over she'd convinced me to try some things on as well in case, by chance, I changed my mind about the party.

Rosalinda's head bobbed. "If you don't wear it, my darling, you can send it right back."

They hastily cinched me into a stiff canvas corset, the whalebones pressing into my ribs. Over it, I wore a dusty rose dress and a long gray velvet overcoat. It was reassuringly modest, considering Katalina intended to pass us off as courtesans. She was striking in red-and-black stripes, a black cloak, and a matching jaunty top hat.

"The crowning touch," Rosalinda said, as she pinned a beautiful gray felt hat on top of my head. It was wrapped with silk and had a net of black lace that veiled my face. "It's called a birdcage veil."

Perfect, I thought. *Khan would have a laugh at that.*

Taking our parcels on credit, we pulled up our hoods and stepped outside. It had gotten dark, and Horatio was nowhere in sight. But the Gypsy runner was waiting for us.

Katalina gave him a coin, then broke the seal and handed the message to me.

"'Dear Miss Moore,'" I read. "'We would welcome the opportunity to introduce you and your friend to our proprietress. Coincidentally, we have a large event that very evening, and she is in need of additional consorts. Come in your finest. We look forward to meeting you. Sincerely, Mercy Thoreau and Delilah Sweet.'"

"What did I tell you, eh?" Katalina boasted.

It worked. I couldn't believe how assertive and clever Katalina had been. But even though I'd agreed to let her get me a dress, by no means would I go to that party.

Katalina leaned against the brick storefront. "I am sure Horatio will be along at any moment." She lit one of her cigars, puffing smoke into the already gray sky. "Avery, remember when you asked me if I love Khaniferre? I owe you the truth. I do. I only wish he felt the same for me."

"Have you told him?" I asked softly.

"No." She glanced sideways at me under the brim of her hat. "I know he is your friend, but please do not say anything."

Why did I kiss him? I thought. *I betrayed Katalina in her own home. If she were to find out . . .*

As if materializing from our thoughts, Khan stepped onto the sidewalk, breathing hard. He'd clearly been running. He was with Horatio. I knew from their expressions that something was wrong.

Khan glanced over his shoulder. "I was sent to find you, the three of you. Let's get off the street so we can talk." We slid into the shadows of an alley. "They raided the camp. Spector, the crows . . . two men are dead."

Katalina gasped. "My father! What has happened to my father?"

"He got away." Khan looked up at me. "As did Geeno. They took the guard with them, and they . . ." He swallowed hard, as if he could not get the words out of his throat.

Katalina stepped forward. "What is it?" She grabbed his arm. "What else?"

With eyes seeking forgiveness, he said, "They captured Hurricane."

CHAPTER TWENTY–SIX
SADIE-MAE

We stumbled in shocked silence through the gloomy streets of the city, twilight darkening around us. For thirteen blocks, we followed Horatio, delving deep into a part of Manhattan I'd never thought I'd see. It had many names, most popularly the Tenderloin, but it was also called Satan's Circus and the Modern Gomorrah. As bad as Five Points was, with its gangs and its violence, it was still a neighborhood where people lived and worked. The Tenderloin was a playground of pure debauchery and filth. There were more brothels, nightclubs, gambling casinos, and saloons concentrated here than anywhere else on the island of Manhattan.

Once in the thick of it, we wove through narrow, seedy lanes, stepping over piles of waste, a dead pig, and slumped bodies of drunken undesirables. A few detestable worms propositioned Katalina, until she drew a knife from her skirt and held it openly clenched in her fist. My stride faltered at the sight of a young girl leaning on a lamppost, the glow highlighting her heavily painted face. Her skirt was pinned up to exhibit a shameful amount of leg.

My heart pained at the sight. "Why, she must be younger than Hurricane!" I whispered to Katalina. She nodded, huddling closer to me.

Behind the girl was a woman in tattered garments. She addressed the men of our group. "Messieurs, my daughter can pleasure ya. She's a virgin."

I sucked in my breath. The mother's skin was covered with open sores, one of her eyes looked eaten away, and she wore a nose made of metal tied to her face.

Khan shook his head and we hurried by. In a low voice he said one word that explained the horror of what we'd seen. "Syphilis."

"Mr. Moralis's cousin runs a hotel near here," Horatio explained. "He'll put us up for a few nights." There were eleven Gypsy men, plus Mr. Moralis. We were to meet them at the hotel.

Finally, Horatio pointed across the street to a dilapidated three-story wooden structure. The roof bowed so much in the middle, the dormer windows tilted toward each other. "Is it safe?" I asked.

"Best we got," Horatio said.

A tall, sturdy-looking prostitute lounged by the entrance. When I got closer, she looked me up and down and said, "You can put your eyes back in your head, girlie." My eyes *did* widen; her voice was that of a man. Ducking my head, I hastened inside.

Somehow, I managed to climb three narrow, creaky flights to a cheerless, shabby room. Geeno and I would stay together, Katalina with her father. I shook all over as I huddled with Geeno in our cold bed.

Night slipped away, then day, then night again. Geeno brought back food that went cold on the nightstand. I could barely eat in this repulsive place. My thoughts twisted and turned. Two Gypsies murdered. In all likelihood, Hurricane was in the Tombs—a living death. *Why? Does Spector mean to question her about my whereabouts?* My world was ripping apart at the seams, as was the city around me. I wanted my father.

Khan came to check on me. Nothing he said could ease the anguish I felt over Hurricane's capture. "I'm sorry. I know you've spent a lot of time with her lately." He squeezed my hand.

"So what now?" I muttered. "Is Horatio still planning to sneak into the party?"

"Yes. The guard would be an imbecile to admit he told us anything. They'd kill him for sure. And we need more information."

Later, there was another knock. "Avery, may I come in?" Katalina sat down. "I wanted to see how you are doing."

I looked out the grimy window. "Katalina, all around me, terrible things are happening."

"You must not blame yourself, Avery. We have a saying: *Te praxos man le mosa opral, sorro trajo pe'l changa simas.* It means, 'Bury me standing, I have been on my knees all my life.'" She leaned in, her dark eyes on mine. "The Romany people have always faced persecution. We will no longer stand idly by."

"I left Geeno there. What if they had taken him as well?" The thought alone brought a wrenching to my chest. I couldn't lose him, too.

"My father tells me Geeno did not get caught, because he was in the field with your falcon. You probably saved him." She set her jaw. "The party is tomorrow night. As you know, Horatio is going, and I intend to as well. My father has gone to the camp to retrieve our things. He plans to go back again tomorrow for the rest. He will not notice I am gone until it is too late to stop me."

I rolled onto my back. "The crows didn't take anything?"

"No. They swept through, guns raised, asking where you were. When they knocked my father out, Hurricane spit out that you had gone to the city with me. It would have been better for her if she had not opened her mouth, but she was scared." She shook her head. "The two men were killed trying to protect her. Luckily, we had hidden the mask and cloak. If they had seen that, they may have slaughtered everyone. They checked the caravans and left with Hurricane and the guard, presumably to track you down in the city."

"Spector must have been surprised to find the camp so empty."

"Yes." She flicked a cockroach off the nightstand. "Horatio found the box with your crystal intact, and he retrieved the wigs and Geeno's bugs as well. Geeno was worried about them."

She fixed me with her eyes. "I do not think you are up to coming to the party, but I wanted to see how you felt. As I said before, if you cannot do it, I will go alone."

I wiped my face. This pain I felt inside would never go away. Part of the bleak and desolate landscape of my mind wanted action, demanded it, no matter how frightful it was. I'd come this far—how could I stop now? If there was a chance of discovering how to put an end to this, I had to take it. Spector had to be stopped.

I pushed myself up. "All right, Katalina. I'll go with you."

Katalina grinned. "Then you need to eat."

The day of the party, I found myself staring out the window, studying the sky for signs as my mother used to do. But the gray clouds were thick and all-consuming; they gave nothing away. Which suited my mood. My blood felt icy in my veins, and no amount of hot tea could warm me.

I'd convinced Khan to take Geeno to work with him—get him out of this seedy place. And luckily, Mr. Moralis was still at the camp. Katalina came to my room and we quickly dressed. I cinched her corset and buttoned up the back of her dress. "I'm scared, Kat. And everyone will fear the worst when they discover us missing." The nickname made me feel closer to her, and right now I needed to feel close to people. As if sensing my feelings, she leaned her head against me.

"I am scared, too, Avery." My eyes widened. I'd never heard Katalina admit to being afraid of anything. "Leave a note on your bed saying we had to get out of this dismal flophouse for a few hours and not to worry. We will explain *after* we have information to share. Together we can do this, yes?"

"I hope so." I'd decided that Katalina had built a hard protective shell around herself. Being allowed in through the cracks felt special. It lightened my chest and would, hopefully, get me through this night.

We adjusted the wigs and hats, then donned the long hooded cloaks to hide our clothing and quietly left with Horatio. He had the crow-guard uniform in a large sack for later. I moved as if in a dream, my mind unable to think past the next step my feet had to take, my nerves jumping, quivering under my skin.

Horatio had secured a hansom cab to take us to Spring Street. The dress was heavy, the bustle cumbersome. Every breath was squeezed through my tightly corseted rib cage. I did like the hat, with its veil of netting hiding part of my face.

We disembarked in a genteel, well-lit neighborhood. "This is the red-light district?" I whispered.

Horatio nodded. "The high-end one, of course. Good luck," he said as he headed off to the house of the masquerade.

I'd made us calling cards. On Katalina's I'd written *Isabella Moore*, and mine said *Grace Hammond*. I enjoyed the irony of using my ex-friend's name in such absurd circumstances.

Katalina knocked on a fine but unassuming entrance. A small panel in the wood slid open. Katalina presented her calling card and the door swung open to reveal a dimly lit hallway.

The doorman extended his hand toward a staircase. "Up one flight, if you please. Second door on the left."

As we made our way up, I noticed the thick runner silenced our footfall. When Katalina knocked on this door, it opened to two beauties in exquisite finery. One, tall and thin, dark straight hair cut across her forehead, was all angles and lines. She wore brocade and burgundy. The other was made of softness and curves. She wore a gown of pale blue and had gossamer blond hair. If I didn't know better, I would've thought them high-society ladies like those my mother used to entertain. When I saw their faces, though, I realized they were probably the same age as Katalina.

The blond one visibly brightened. "Mercy! They're here!" She spoke in a soft and whispery southern accent. Taking Katalina's hands, she continued. "You must be Isabella. I'm Delilah Sweet. And this is Mercy—Mercy Thoreau."

"Pleased to meet you. May I present my friend, Grace Hammond?" Katalina turned to me.

I smiled as Mercy nodded. "Come in. We are almost ready to leave," Mercy said. The room beyond was ornate, the huge canopy bed at its center draped in thick damask. The flowery wallpaper, heavy drapes, and ornate rugs looked luxurious in the dim lighting of the gas lamps, but as my eyes adjusted, I saw the stains, watermarks, and threadbare corners. The room was like an elderly woman with thick powder and heavy rouge masking her aging face. "How is Mr. Soliman?" she asked. "It's been a while since we've seen him around our neck of the woods."

Katalina visibly relaxed, exhaling quietly. For the first time, her smile seemed genuine. "Oh, Mr. Soliman is just dandy."

Katalina was better at pleasantry than I. She prattled on about nonsense as the others got ready. I hoped my anxiety didn't give us away.

Delilah mistook the meaning of my quietness. "The House of the Scarlet Ascot is just up the street. It's a real classy joint. Sadie-Mae, the proprietress, runs a tight ship. She'll be expecting you. And since y'all are new, she'll expect you to be shy, so don't get too jiggy about it."

Mercy pinned on her hat. "Whatever you do, do not drink the alcohol. Just pretend to sip at it. The drinks at these parties are often laced with laudanum, and I've seen girls get themselves into a pickle."

The four of us walked up Spring Street to the House of the Scarlet Ascot, Delilah chattering the whole way. Tonight, All

Hallows' Eve, the streets were anything but quiet. There were couples in masks and finery on their way to parties, and glowing jack-o'-lanterns watching us pass. A parade threaded its way through the district, led by a giant skeleton held up with poles and trailed by sudden bursts of firecrackers.

Halloween had always been a festival of mystery and magic when I was young, but tonight I jumped at every sound, and my jaw hurt from clenching it. Tonight Halloween was the ghastly and frightful time it had set out to be, like a sorcerer, weaving a strange spell over me. I had to be careful.

Our destination was a gracious town house, well maintained on the exterior, and although improper women sashayed up and down the street, none lingered in front of this house. A heavily made-up woman met us at the door. My first impression was not one of size, although her gaudy dress was enormous; it was of a combination of bawdiness and an underlying sense of violence. She was a fox in a henhouse. Her cheeks had round circles of rouge on them, and she eyed us through heavily caked lashes. Her perfume stung my nostrils—rotting roses and talcum powder.

"Good. Right on time, girls." She glanced at a locket watch on a chain around her neck. It disappeared into the cleavage of her ample bosom when she dropped it. She must have caught my gaze, because she pushed her shoulders back and smiled. "We can't all be endowed with such plentiful womanly gifts, my dear."

Mercy introduced us. "Madame, these are the friends I told you about, Grace and Isabella."

"A pleasure. I'm Mis' Sadie-Mae." We nodded as she stepped aside. "Don't stand there letting in the cold. Come on in, girls."

I rubbed my thinly gloved hands together as Katalina and I entered the foyer. I curtsied. "I'm Grace. Grace Hammond. It's nice to meet you."

"How old are you, Grace?" Sadie-Mae asked, as she appraised me from head to toe.

"Sixteen, ma'am."

She smiled, her eyes twinkling with delight. "That's good, Grace, very good. They like the young ones."

Katalina introduced herself as Isabella Moore. Sadie-Mae walked in a circle around her, clucking her tongue in approval. "Isabella, you were born for this line of work."

Sadie-Mae's house was elegant: marble floors, rich wood paneling, and ornate gas sconces emitting a warm glow. It was a place for respectable men to visit. She ushered us into the parlor, which was richly done in toile and gilt mirrors, where the other girls were gathered. Some stood talking; some lounged together on tufted velvet sofas. The colors of their dresses were so varied, the girls looked like a bouquet of exquisite flowers. They caressed and embraced one another, their movements languid and sensual. It was quite risqué. My insides shook; I hoped no one would talk to me.

A murmur swept around the room as we entered. Delilah smiled and took my hand, walking us toward the back.

"Fancy, isn't it? Y'all won't come upon a finer house. They've got a clientele of rich and famous gentlemen. I had a bit of a grind with Grover Cleveland himself, before he was running for governor of New York, of course."

"Attention, girls." Sadie-Mae clapped her hands. "As you know, this is a very important evening. Our house was chosen out of many." She puffed up her chest. "And it was chosen because we have never, you hear me, *never* given up a secret. Men know that what happens here stays here. Rumors don't start. Wives don't come a-knocking. Powerful men could be ruined by one slip of a sassy tongue." She glared at each of us in turn. "Whatever you see at this party is forgotten the moment you leave." Her glare melted away, and she smiled like a mother hen. "Be proud you are part of the House of the Scarlet Ascot. Remember, you are representing my good name, so behave properly. Line up and I will dismiss you one by one. The coaches are waiting outside."

The girls quickly got into a single-file line. Sadie-Mae ran her hands down sleeves and along bodices and even knelt down to feel under dresses.

"Y'all don't fret," Delilah whispered. "Sadie-Mae wants this evening to go off without a hitch. Says it could be her ticket to future business."

After Sadie-Mae performed her search, she tied a red lace

mask over the face of each girl and dismissed her to the waiting conveyances. Other than expressing displeasure at a flask strapped to one girl's leg, which she tossed aside, Sadie-Mae made no comments. After my turn, the three of us waited at the door for Katalina. I watched her through the red lace over my eyes.

Katalina shot me a troubled look as Sadie felt under her dress. Instead of rising, Sadie gathered the material and lifted it up. Katalina had her knife belt wrapped around her thigh, with three sharp blades attached.

Mercy gasped, and Delilah gripped my arm.

CHAPTER TWENTY–SEVEN
THE HALLOWEEN MASQUERADE

"Isabella," Sadie-Mae hissed. "What in heaven's name do you think you're doing?"

"Just in case," Katalina stammered, "in case someone tries to hurt me."

"Tsk, tsk, tsk. Hold your skirts up, Isabella, and don't you dare move." She unfastened the belt. Before Katalina could protest, Sadie-Mae whipped the belt back and forth across her legs. I cringed at each crack of the leather. Katalina sucked in her breath.

Sadie-Mae smiled lovingly at her and placed a plump palm on Katalina's cheek. "No one hurts my girls, except me. But if they do, you keep your trap shut. Understand?" She smoothed Katalina's dress back into place and, as if she were speaking to an ill-behaved child, shook her finger. "It is not nice to threaten a paying customer. It's bad for business. You're lucky I like your pluck, or I'd throw you back out on the street."

Katalina bit her lip as Sadie-Mae tied the mask on her face. The entire ride she sat simmering, like a pot left to boil.

My mind drifted to Hurricane. *What is she going through at this moment?* I adjusted my dress, tugging at the waist to ease my breath. The weight of these clothes echoed the weight pressing down on my heart.

Delilah leaned forward to peer through the window curtains. "The party's at the Tredwell mansion. Since their mother, Eliza, passed, the three sisters let it for special events. I hear it's fancy."

"How far is it? I feel claustrophobic in here," I said.

"Only six blocks. Y'all know the Bond Street area near Washington Square Park?"

Just then, the coachman shouted, "Whoa, whoa." He pulled the horses to a stop. I caught my breath as the coach door opened to the black-eyed mask of a crow-guard. My hand shook as he helped me down.

A dense fog had settled over Manhattan. Yellow orbs lined the streets where gas lamps hovered on faintly visible posts. I squinted up, but even the airships had disappeared in the vaporous night sky. We'd arrived at a stately redbrick estate with an arched entranceway. All the drapes on the tall windows appeared to be drawn. Another crow-guard stood by the front door. He, like the others, wore the familiar black cloak and black brimmed hat. I peeked at each in passing, trying to recognize Horatio, but there was no way to tell if it was him. I couldn't even see their eyes.

We entered a shadowy vestibule, the mist creeping in at our feet. A man with a silver carnival mask shaped like the moon took our coats and hats and silently extended his hand to the even darker parlor beyond. Two crows stood flanking the passageway. They nodded to a guest who held up a hand bearing the gold crow-claw ring.

Peculiar music—violin, maybe—drifted through the two-story space. Exaggerated shadows, cast by the flickering gas chandeliers above, danced along the undulating surfaces of the black-draped walls. Tables along the periphery held vases of bloodred roses. It was too dark to see how many men were there, but all of them were dressed the same: black tuxedo, long black hooded cloak, and a carnival half-mask, grotesque and monstrous, covering everything but the mouth. Black-suited waiters hovered around the periphery of the space. I noticed they wore no masks. As I passed one, he offered champagne on a silver tray. I gasped and stepped back: he stared ahead with milky-blue eyes. I approached another—the same. All of them were blind.

My hand shook as I accepted a glass. I was about to take a sip but remembered what Mercy and Delilah had said about the laudanum. They had disappeared into the party with the rest of Sadie-Mae's girls. A soft bubble of talk and laughter bobbed about the room. It could have sounded pleasant if it didn't look so nightmarish. Katalina and I stuck together, doing our best to avoid eye contact.

"Are your legs all right?" I whispered as soon as we were alone.

She nodded and hissed, "I wanted to catch up my knives and cut that woman."

"Kat, what were we thinking? These people . . . this place . . . it's far too dangerous." My fingers felt numb from squeezing them so hard. A cold dread slinked up my spine.

She nodded. "I fear you may have been right. But I will not leave without some answers."

Two men, their silver masks glinting in the candlelight, barred our way. The first, his mask shaped like a bizarre baboon face, took my hand and bowed low, brushing metal-lic teeth from the half jaw across my glove. "May we have this dance?" he said.

"Oh." I turned at Katalina. My mind raced. *What do I say?* Katalina gave me a fierce look. I turned back to him, setting my untouched drink on a table. "Yes, that would be lovely."

The other man, with the mask of a fox, bent to whisper something in Katalina's ear. She laughed and tilted her head coyly. *Sadie-Mae was right; she's a natural. While my insides are quivering like gelatin.*

The baboon held my hand up as he escorted me through the crowd to the dance area in the center of the room. A beautiful piano waltz floated around us as he placed his hand on my lower back. *Thank goodness for large dresses.* At arm's length, we began to move. I did my best to follow his lead. The fox spun Katalina away, and they vanished into the clusters of other dancers.

"What is your name, dear girl?" said the baboon. He let go of my hand momentarily and held my chin up, studying my face. "I don't recognize you as one of Sadie-Mae's regulars, and I visit the house quite often."

I lowered my eyes. "My name is Grace, sir." *Can he feel me shaking?* "I'm . . . I'm new."

He laughed. "How refreshing. And young, I see." He looked around as if to challenge any claim over me. "Not to worry, dear Grace. You'll stick with me this evening. You may call me Mr. Bartholomew. I'll take *very* good care of you." His tone sent a chill down my spine. I wasn't sure what he meant, and I did not want to find out. After a few more turns, the tempo picked up a little, and the baboon swung me faster.

Time seemed to be enjoying my anguish, for it was languid one moment, lurching the next. I lost all clues as to its passage.

A soft bell rang; a deep voice announced, "Dinner is served."

The baboon held my hand tightly until we were seated at a table with two other men, both of whom stared approvingly at me through their black leather masks with twisted, curling horns. The baboon introduced them as Mr. Otto and Mr. Jonas.

"We use first names only tonight, isn't that right, boys?" The three of them chuckled as if at some private joke.

The baboon ordered a bottle of wine, then placed his meaty hand firmly on my thigh, pinning me to my seat. I pretended to sip at my drink as he rambled on about the banking industry, real estate, and fox hunting. But all I could focus on were his fingers, trying to squeeze my leg through the many layers of my dress.

A waiter placed a steak dinner, complete with potatoes and greens, in front of Mr. Bartholomew. I glanced around, noticing that only the men had been served. Not that I'd have eaten anyway. The baboon tore into the meat, red juices running down his chin. "Delmonico's steak—fabulous."

When he'd finished stuffing himself, he ran his hand up my arm, his thumb stroking my skin. The other men paid us no mind. Leaning closer, he whispered, "So quiet, dear Grace? No need to be nervous." His voice was thick with the wine.

I'd known this would happen, that I might be treated like a piece of property. But the trail of his touch made my skin crawl and my stomach roil. I pulled the fan out of my purse and snapped it open, knocking his hand away. "Oh, pardon me. It is so very hot in here," I said with a quick smile.

He laughed. "Yes it is, my little sugarplum. Perhaps a place less crowded, shall we?"

"Oh, I didn't mean—"

"I know, I know. Don't fret." He patted his breast pocket. "I am a generous man, my dear Grace." Abruptly he stood, lifting me with him. I scanned the crowd. *Where is Katalina?*

Mr. Bartholomew turned me toward the stair, when a tall crow-guard stepped in front of us. I'd never before been glad to see a crow-guard.

"Excuse me, sir," he said. "Please take your seat. The host is preparing to speak." *Is it Horatio?* I couldn't recognize his voice, muffled as it was under the mask. The guard addressed me. "Miss, if you will . . ." He bowed slightly, and directed me toward the other girls.

Gratefully, I nodded adieu to Mr. Bartholomew.

"Don't worry, dear Grace." Again he pressed his metal muzzle to my hand. "I will come find you later. That is a promise."

"I will keep a sharp eye out for you, sir." *So I can run in the other direction.*

Sadie-Mae's girls gathered to one side of the room, chatting and laughing as the men found their seats. I rejoined Katalina, Mercy, and Delilah.

"Where did you go?" Katalina asked.

"Me? You're the one who waltzed away like you were with Prince Charming."

The music stopped, and a hush fell over the room. Katalina squeezed my hand. "Listen carefully and be calm. You are acting skittish."

I knew both of us felt anything but calm.

From the head table where, presumably, the most important

guests were seated, a large man pushed back his chair and stood. I'd noticed him greeting people all evening. He was hard to miss. It wasn't just his paunch, which was the size of Bessie's rotund belly; it was his commanding presence, like a steam train barreling into a station. His mask was the most terrible and macabre I'd seen all night. It was dark red, with monstrous ram's horns curving down on either side. Whoever he was, he looked like the devil incarnate. But where was Spector? I hadn't seen him at all.

The man removed his mask and cleared his throat. "Welcome, industrialists, financiers, capitalists, and merchants. As you well know, we are at a turning point in the history of our great nation. Consider the American economy a giant web, connected by rail lines and waterways laden with cargo ships, all of which we own, by the way." There was a smattering of laughter as he continued. "At its center sits the city of New York, and we, the people in this very room, are collectively, the spider."

This was greeted with applause.

"Who is he?" I whispered to Delilah.

"Why that's Ogden Boggs. He's a high-powered shipping magnate and philanthropist. He's known for the money he donates to the poor people of the city." Her southern accent made it sound like she was speaking of a kind uncle. She giggled and fanned herself. "He's donated plenty to the House of the Scarlet Ascot, as well."

Boggs. He also donated our water fountain at the factory.

Ogden Boggs smiled and held up a hand. "Not only has

our government decimated the profits from our interests in the cotton industry, but if we are not prudent, the labor unions will empower our own workers. At past meetings of the Commerce League, we have agreed the best way to prevent this is to stimulate division amongst our labor force—using blacks as strikebreakers against whites, hiring Chinese against German and Irish, Protestant against Catholic—for only in their *union* may we be defeated. We've also paid the police and, in accordance with the law, called in the state militia to assault the strikers. And while such measures have successfully forestalled unionization thus far, they are not enough." His voice grew louder as he spoke.

The room responded; men leaned forward in their seats.

"We have already lost control of our streets. We are forced to move further uptown as immigrants and vagrants flood into the city. How many of you stroll in the evenings as you used to do? And how many of you remember the Paris Commune of 1871? Do we want an uprising of the working class here in New York?"

Jeers and angry objections flew around the room.

"The strikes are increasing daily. The rallies are violent." He raised a fist. "It is time to take control of our workers!"

Everyone leapt to their feet. He had the room.

Now he lowered his voice. He knew exactly how to manipulate these men. "I am here to tell you gentlemen, I have a way. My team of scientists, headed by the esteemed Dr. Ignatius Spector, has developed the answer to our problems."

Behind him, Dr. Spector emerged from the shadows. Katalina clenched my hand so tight it hurt. Cold sweat chilled my skin. My throat tightened and a wave of dizziness swept over me.

It was Delilah who saved me. "Take a deep breath, honey," she whispered. "You're positively drained of color."

She handed me a glass of water. Breathing hard, I looked around to see if anyone else had noticed. "It's the corset. It's—" I took a long sip. "It's so tight." I wished I could split the stays and swell my lungs with air.

"Yes, they do take some getting used to." She dabbed a handkerchief to my forehead and whispered, "I always have mine loosened halfway through the night."

Ogden Boggs held out his hand. "Doctor, if you will."

I noticed the men take a step back, shrinking from Spector's hideous appearance. Something strange occurred to me. Spector was like the parasite worm my father told me many confederate soldiers had harbored. And Ogden Boggs was his host.

Dr. Spector's shrill voice snaked toward us. "As you may know," he said, "I am executive director of the Temple of Mind Balance Studies. It is through science that one achieves the ultimate power. Education triumphs over ignorance, as science will triumph over commonality." As usual, he was impeccably dressed, but the warm glow of the lamps above gave his pale white face the greenish hue of liquid absinthe.

I shifted into my second sight. Each time it got easier. All the practice had certainly paid off. But the darkness I saw pervading these men was murkier than the shadows in the room. Boggs had stoked their anger like blowing a bellows over hot coals. I shivered. I let my vision return to normal.

In a gloved hand, Spector held a glass vial, glinting in the light. "Tonight, I give you ultimate power. This serum, developed through years of experimentation, is your answer." He presented it to Boggs.

"Thank you, Dr. Spector. I will take it from her." It seemed he knew Spector's unnerving presence would kill any momentum he'd gained with the men.

Spector bowed as Boggs took the vial and stepped in front of him. For a second his eyes narrowed at Ogden Boggs's back, fixing it with a steely stare, then he retreated into the darkness.

He resents Boggs. But it seemed as though he'd accepted *his* stage to be that of the Tombs.

Meanwhile, Ogden Boggs pointed to something behind him hidden under a velvet cloth. "This past year I have presented most of you with a water source at your place of business." With theatrical flourish, he gripped the cloth and flung it aside. It was a water fountain.

"Katalina," I whispered, "we have one of those at work— the Boggs water fountain. The owner of the Works, Tyber Malice, must be here somewhere."

I scanned the crowd. If he was here I couldn't tell, with all the masks.

Ogden Boggs continued. "A few drops a week of this serum, added to the water, will have a dramatic effect on your laborers. It will restore loyalty and suppress free will." He pinched the dropper on the vial and discharged the serum into the water. "Now when you ask for hard work and lengthy hours, that is exactly what you will get."

One of the men shouted out, "How can we ensure they'll drink it?"

"I'm quite sure you've noticed the lines," Boggs replied. "The question is not *if* they will drink, it is who will direct them *after* they do." He was right—we all lined up for the delicious, clean water daily.

"Yeah! What about that?" another asked. "Someone needs to tell them what to do!"

A short, portly man stomped forward. "This will never work, Boggs." He stabbed a finger in the air. "I want my money back! You promised compliance, and now my men are loitering by this fountain of yours."

Boggs held his hand up again to calm the buzz, like a swarm of bees. "Ah, Mr. Booth, always a pleasure. Let us do a demonstration so you will see exactly how it works. I need one volunteer to drink the water, and since you, sir, are quite the naysayer, I appoint you."

The audience agreed and spurred the man on. "Fine!" he said. "I'll prove this man is swindling us."

Boggs smiled, utterly confident. "I need another volunteer

to act as the monitor—the man you've appointed to stand by the fountain and direct men to their supervisors after they've had a drink."

I recalled the man at the Works who had told us to leave the water fountain. He must be the monitor.

A tall man stepped up. "I'll do it." He bowed, to the crowd's mock applause.

Boggs positioned the man acting as monitor next to the fountain. "Thank you, Mr. Wayne. After Mr. Booth drinks, you may tell him what to do. Be creative," he added. "Say whatever you'd like."

The room quieted as we all watched the naysayer dip the tin cup into the water. He lifted it in a toasting gesture, then drank it down.

Everyone seemed to hold his or her breath. Mr. Booth dropped the cup. "You see? What did I—" He stopped midsentence and looked around the room, as if he forgot what he was going to say.

"Sir, will you please remove your wallet from your pocket?" Mr. Wayne, the monitor, a seemingly playful man, grinned.

Mr. Booth turned to him. "Yes," he answered. *Is he just playing along?* I wondered, as he pulled out a leather wallet.

Mr. Wayne spoke again. "Now, if you will, please distribute all of your money to those men there." He pointed at the gaping faces.

Mr. Booth plodded over and began handing out a

considerable amount of cash. When it was gone, he turned to the monitor as if awaiting orders.

The men laughed and cheered. "Make him do something else."

Mr. Wayne, quite pleased with his role, nodded. "Sir, please give us a round of the polka."

The portly Mr. Booth bowed and held out his arms as if he were paired with a woman. He began to dance on his toes in a sprightly manner, clicking his heels in a dandy display of the polka.

The room erupted into laughter as he twirled around. It was frightful. Now I knew exactly how Spector had compelled Mr. Malice into committing suicide.

Boggs summoned two crow-guards. "Please find Mr. Booth a comfortable place to wait until the serum wears off." As they led the volunteer away, Boggs turned to the men in the room. "Now do you believe? But unfortunately, I am going to ask you to return Mr. Booth's money." He chuckled, then his voice grew serious again. "Gentlemen, I'm sure you are all familiar with the mesmerists popular at the salons. Well, as you have witnessed here today, my experiments have produced a scientific and physical kind of mesmerism. Today we used an increased dosage, and we realize not all employees will drink every day, but they will no longer be able to band together, to unify. We will, in effect, temper the flame, not snuff it out. It is for the workers' own good that we put an end to the unrest." He paused to let his words sink in. "Not only will we save money—we will save lives!"

Murmurs of agreement spread through the men like a virus. They jumped from their seats, applauding loudly.

I leaned toward Katalina so she could hear me. "Bloody hell, Katalina, they're going to poison the water!"

CHAPTER TWENTY-EIGHT
DELMONICO'S STEAK KNIVES

Katalina's eyes were wide as she gripped my arm. "Spector has been experimenting with the seers. What do you suppose is in that serum?"

"I don't know. If we could get the vial, we could bring it to the herb doctor, but Boggs pocketed it." My mind scrambled to understand. These greedy men planned to overpower the commoners—the poor, the immigrant workers, *their own employees*—to take away their free will.

I gazed around the room, bewildered. The standing ovation had morphed into animated conversation. They all wanted to talk with the larger-than-life Ogden Boggs. They were like dogs, and his mesmerizing serum, bloody meat. Some were already taking out banknotes to show their support.

Just then I recalled the conversation I overheard Roland

Malice having. It was surely about this. He'd argued, saying he wouldn't do it. And he was murdered. *Did Boggs send Spector to kill him? Or what if*—the thought was almost too horrible to imagine—*what if his own father, Tyber Malice, had him killed?* He'd drugged Roland to make him lose a fight, but would he resort to murder?

"We have to get out of here. *Now*," I whispered, hand covering my mouth.

While Boggs mingled with his patrons, Katalina and I made our way toward the exit. Loud and lively dance music started up, and the party roared back to life. I pressed my palm to my thumping heart. The people moving about would help to shield us. Out of the corner of my eye, I noticed a crow-guard following us.

"Act natural," I whispered to Katalina. "We're being watched."

She laughed as if I'd said something funny and took my arm in hers. I felt the guard coming closer, felt him reach out and put his hand on my shoulder. I froze.

"I'll go stand by the door. Come in a few minutes so I can let you out." *Horatio.* He swept by us, his long cloak billowing around him.

A few minutes was too long for me, but we moved slowly so as not to attract attention. I glanced over my shoulder, hoping Mr. Bartholomew was nowhere near.

There was one crow-guard at the left of the entrance

already. Out of the corner of my eye, I saw Horatio position himself on the right, folding his arms across his chest.

"Katalina, I just thought of something. If I can get a sample of the water in the fountain, maybe it can be tested. Go tell Horatio. I'll be right back."

"No," she murmured, "we must stick together." But I'd already stepped away, and she had no choice but to keep going.

As I headed toward the fountain, I caught a glimpse, between couples waltzing, of two men in conversation. The large one looked oddly familiar. I had an intuitive feeling that his identity was important.

As I edged nearer, he turned in my direction. *Damn those masks. Who is he?* I had to get closer. With the curtained wall to my back, I angled to get a better view. I heard them talking.

"—unfortunate Norman got arrested," said the small piggish-looking man.

The large one guffawed. "Bale's a fool for getting caught. The Commerce League can do nothing for him now. It's befitting we sacrifice him to mollify the masses."

I couldn't believe it. The rapist and murderer of two young girls had been a member of this club.

"Ah well," said the small one. "I'm terribly sorry about the disappearance of your son. Have you received any new information?"

The other patted his massive gut, chuckling. "I'm afraid Roland was a bit of a boozer. Could have fallen off the docks, for all I know."

The other man looked as shocked as I felt. I knew why I recognized the big man—I'd seen his photograph in the perch. It was Tyber Malice. Roland Malice had his faults, but I'd never, ever seen him drink. Tyber was lying. There was no doubt in my mind *he* was the one who had sent Spector to murder his son.

My mouth dropped open as I stumbled back. I tripped over my dress and collided with a blind waiter, knocking his tray to the floor. His hand flew up, catching in my wig, and the next thing I knew he pulled it from my head.

Someone gripped my arm, steadying me. "Grace!" Sadie-Mae hissed. "Your name most certainly does not suit you. Put yourself back together before you cause a scene."

Behind me, I heard a voice that stilled the blood in my veins. "Her name is not Grace."

Sadie-Mae and I both spun around. He'd materialized right out of the shadows.

Sadie-Mae surprised me by squaring her shoulders and holding her arms out to the side, as if to protect me, but then again, she might have been embarrassed and wanted only to hide me. "My apologies, Dr. Spector, sir. She is new and a bit clumsy."

He smiled—the same smile as when he'd spoken to me in my mother's room at the Tombs. I clenched my teeth as a shiver snaked up my neck. "Either way, she is coming with me. Now, step aside or you will be very, very sorry." He nodded to a nearby crow-guard. Sadie-Mae gave me a mortified look, then rushed over to a group of her girls that had gathered to watch.

I caught Katalina's eye—she and Horatio were ready and waiting. I pushed past Spector and tried to run, but a pair of strong arms grabbed me from behind. The guard's grip was solid and unyielding—I could barely breathe. Pulse racing, I concentrated hard, focusing until I saw Spector's dark shadow. It enveloped him, its tendrils oozing out like creosote oil between railroad ties.

"Another alias, I see." His voice, like nails on a chalkboard, raked down my spine. "I watched you, when you were young. You never showed any sign of possessing ability, but still I suspected you weren't ordinary. You refused to unleash it, didn't you, Avery? You did not want to be like your mother, am I correct?"

Up close, his face was even more frightening—waxy white skin, thin red lips, greasy hair pushed back on his head. At the mention of my mother, I felt the walls closing in, crushing me.

He tilted his head, studying me. "Your mother is as helpless and pitiful as you are."

I had to keep trying. I stared hard at Spector. Our eyes locked. He licked his lips and stared back at me, his thick black energy impassive. I saw no visions, nothing to help me alter the dark cloud swirling around him. *Why?* I wished I could cause another explosion right now.

"You cannot use your tricks on me," Spector said calmly. "I have discovered a way to block deceptive creatures such as yourself."

Everything seemed to happen at once then. Delilah recognized me and rushed over to help. I looked past Spector to Katalina and saw her spin around, swiping something off the table behind her. In that moment, I knew she intended to kill Spector. I prayed her aim was true. But Spector followed my gaze. As Katalina raised her arm, he seized Delilah and hid behind her.

He howled, "Stop that whore!"

Katalina hesitated. We both knew she had no clear shot of Spector.

"Go!" I shrieked. She raced for the door. I watched her energy blazing out like a trail behind her. Her arm swung as she ran. Two steak knives flew from her fingertips, embedding deeply into the chest of the guard next to Horatio. Leaping back, Horatio shoved open the door just as Katalina hurtled toward him. *She killed him. She actually killed him.* I saw dark veins slash across Katalina's energy the moment the guard died.

"After them!" Spector shouted.

But the heavy door slammed shut; they were gone. The stabbed crow fell, his body conveniently blocking passage. Blood pooled onto the white marble floor. A moment ticked by, and then one of Sadie's girls, a petite redhead, let out a scream and collapsed in a faint.

The other crows rushed forward, and I hoped that by the time they pulled the body aside, Katalina and Horatio would have disappeared into the fog.

My father's training kicked into gear. I had a split second to act. I jammed the heel of my shoe into the top of the guard's boot. He jerked back, releasing me. I whirled, reeling back my fist, and punched him squarely in the throat. He doubled over, his mask hitting my chest. I felt a stab of pain from the steel tip of his beak puncturing my skin. I cried out as another guard clutched my arms, pinning them to my side.

"Help me!" I wailed. "Don't let him take me!" The girls shrank away in fear for themselves, and the men in their bizarre masks ignored me, shaking their heads. After all, I was a disobedient harlot. I tried to catch someone's eye; maybe I could convince someone to help me by using my second sight. But no one would even look at me.

Sadie-Mae shooed the girls back into the party, all except Mercy and Delilah. Delilah sobbed, having been thrown to the floor by Spector, as Mercy tried to calm her. Sadie-Mae faced them, nostrils flaring. "I will deal with the two of you later."

Spector advanced on me, so close I inhaled his antiseptic odor. I opened my mouth to scream, but he jabbed a needle into my vein.

The sound of the party was muffled in my ears; all except the *tick-tock* of the grandfather clock in the foyer, its pendulum slicing back and forth like a blade preparing to slit my throat.

CHAPTER TWENTY-NINE
INSIDE THE TOMBS

My lashes were crusted, my lids heavy. I opened my eyes to a dim room, its stone walls absorbing what little light seeped from the flickering overhead bulbs.

How did I get here? I tried to sit up, but a strap around my chest held me tight. Straining my neck, I saw that my hands and feet were tied to the metal side rails of a hospital bed. My clothing had been replaced with drab gray woven pants, a long-sleeved gray tunic, and gray socks. Clearly my mother's white flowered gowns were another part of Spector's hospital illusion.

"Help." My voice was a hoarse whisper.

The door stayed shut. My head fell back on the pillow, tears trickling down my cheeks.

I must have fallen asleep. When I opened my eyes again, there was a wheeled cart next to the bed. On it was a tray of food, a brown stewy mass leaking into a glop of mashed pota-toes and what was once probably a carrot, wilted over the edge of the dish. A spoon and tin cup sat beside the metal plate. The chest strap had been removed, as well as the tie on my right hand. The ones on my feet and other hand were replaced with metal rings, which were locked onto the side rails.

I pushed myself shakily up on one arm. My body felt weak, depleted. Given my restraints, I could do no more than sit up or lie back down. I didn't think I'd have the strength to get out of the bed anyway. My stomach growled; my throat was parched. But I would not touch the stuff on that tray.

Still foggy, I tried to re-create the events of the masquerade. Everything had fallen apart. Spector had drugged me. Katalina and Horatio had escaped, I hoped. I remembered her killing the guard and the dark energy that'd blighted her own. Had she felt it? Did she know she'd scarred her own spirit? I knew I'd been right—our energy was shared. We were all part of the same universal energy.

And what of my mother? Was she still alive? A gripping pressure squeezed my mind as the questions battered it. Had word gotten to my father that I'd been captured? Khan must know, and he would surely have seen to that. I could only imagine the anguish it would bring to my father. I missed him terribly. I almost hoped they *had* kept my mother drugged the past three years. How else could she have survived? My mind would've snapped. Now that Spector knew of our fake names, it was too dangerous for my father to visit either of us. He could not help my mother. *He can't help me. I am totally alone.*

I glanced again at the tray. Maybe just a sip of water. A chemical taste lingered on my tongue, turning my stomach. I swished the liquid around in my mouth and spit it on the floor, then drank a few sips.

The room was smaller than the one I'd seen my mother in, but it smelled the same, like bleach and mildew. The stone walls arched up to a vaulted ceiling above my head. In front of me was a rusty metal door with a square glass window. One wall was covered, floor to ceiling, with a swarm of corroded pipes. They coiled around each other, looping and twisting, and disappeared like snakes into the stone on each side. Aside from a metal clock with a wire cage over its face and a bent pendulum hanging from it, which scraped the wall behind it, the room was barren. I listened. There was no sound except for pings and drips within the pipes and the clock's pendulum scratching a cold smile into the stone.

Pulling the blanket up to my neck, I stared at the ceiling. The hulking tonnage above pressed down on me, squeezing the air from my lungs. This room was a crypt, a tomb. I laughed at the irony. I was buried alive in a tomb. I finally understood the true meaning of the hospital's name—the Tombs. A burning sensation rose from the pit of my stomach up into my throat. My body trembled, causing my breath to come in shallow gulps.

I will go mad in here.

When the panicky feeling passed, tears slid from my eyes. *How could I be so stupid?* I thought I could free my mother. I'd believed I had the ability to help people. *I can't even help myself.* I should've listened to my father and stayed far away from the Tombs and anyone associated with this horrific place. I clenched my teeth against the shiver inside my body.

The party proved Ogden Boggs had support for his monstrous plan and plenty of interest in Dr. Spector's vile serum. I only hoped that Katalina told Khan everything, so he could warn Tony and the other employees at the Works.

At the sound of footsteps, my eyes snapped to the small window. Someone was coming. The darkness outside the door was punctuated by light that brightened and faded as if a lantern was swinging down the hall. A glow appeared beneath the door. A key in the lock; the squeal of metal. I pretended to sleep.

Through my lashes, I watched a woman in the familiar long white buttoned coat and nurse's hat approach the bed. She wore dark goggles over her eyes. Placing the lantern on the cart, she said, "Aw, honey, you got to eat. How else are you going to get well?" Her voice was soft.

She lifted my wrist and took my pulse, scribbling something on a pad. Her hands were warm. Then she adjusted the blanket, smoothing it neatly over my body. "Tsk, tsk, look at this." She massaged my ankles and pulled my socks up, so the metal rings did not chafe my skin.

Maybe I could trust her. I slowly opened my eyes.

"Well, hello there, sleepyhead." She smiled. She looked to

be older than my mother, her brown hair pinned into a neat bun behind her nurse's hat. The snug uniform did not flatter her plump figure, and the goggles looked out of place, but her smile was kind.

"Hello—" My voice was like gravel. I cleared my throat and tried again. "Hello, ma'am."

"Hello, Miss . . ." She glanced at her pad. "Avery Kohl. Lovely name. Are you cold, honey? You're shivering." She pulled another blanket from the lower shelf of the cart and laid it over me. "My name is Mrs. Luckett."

I shook my head. "Please, there's been a mistake. I must get out of here."

She smiled again. "It's all right, honey. Don't be afraid. We'll have you well again just as soon as can be." She scratched her cheek where the goggles pressed against it. "Bet you want to get back to school and your friends, now, don't you?"

"No, you don't understand." I tried to push myself up again. She placed her hand gently but firmly on my shoulder.

"Now, now. You shouldn't exert yourself, dear."

My voice came out louder than I'd intended. "Stop! Let me out of here."

She was unfazed. "This is normal, dear. You're probably disoriented, but you want to get well, don't you? You have to rest." She pushed me back down, and I was too weak to struggle. "I'll give you a little something to help you calm yourself." She took a brass syringe from one of the pouches on her belt.

"No!" I screamed. "Do not give me that!"

"Come now." Putting the needle on the cart, she pulled a long piece of fabric from another pouch. Although I tried to wriggle away, she whipped it expertly around my free wrist, securing my arm to the rail. "I'm sorry about the restraints, truly I am, but it's for your own good." She flicked her finger on the inside of my elbow.

"Help!" I screamed as loudly as I could. "Someone help me!"

But she only smiled sweetly as she pierced my vein and slowly depressed the plunger.

The drug coursed through my body, dragging me down with it. After that, I felt myself drifting—for how long, I couldn't say. Nurses came and went. I never understood what they said; it was as if they spoke in exaggerated slow motion. I spent hours staring fearfully at the pipes, convinced they were squirming and twisting out of the wall. On occasion, I became conscious of being helped out of bed and walked next door to a small bathroom, where the nurses washed me and let me use the toilet. I could not tell the time of day. I ate. I slept. I slept a great deal.

One day, I woke and realized my mind was less foggy. I lay quietly, afraid to make a sound lest a nurse enter with another needle. The room had changed. There was now a chair, a small table, and a lantern—

And I was no longer restrained. Shocked, I sat up. My arms were sore. I pushed up my sleeves. Bruises covered the insides of my elbows. I hugged my knees close to my body. *How long have I been here?* I tried to count the days, but got lost in my muddled memories.

When I felt strong enough, I got out of bed and walked shakily around the small room. There was nothing I could use as a weapon. I stood on tiptoe and peered out the square window in the door.

Segments of yellow light banded the murkiness of the hallway; each marked the point at which an electrical bulb hung from a wire. I watched a few patients escorted by, one pushed in a wheelchair, the others holding on to nurses as they shuffled past. All of them had a glassy, expressionless look on their haggard features.

As I continued to stare through the glass, hoping I would be lucky enough to see my mother, Indigo, or Hurricane, I heard a man's voice approaching, then two. My heart thumped against my ribs. They started to move in my direction. I crouched down. *Hide!* But there was nowhere to go. I flew to the bed and crawled underneath it, scraping my knees and elbows on the stone.

The metal door screeched open, grinding against the floor. Black boots and a pair of leather loafers with a pilgrim buckle entered, then stopped. The boots rushed to the bed. Rough hands grabbed my ankles and dragged me out.

"Get away from me!" I screamed. "Help! Someone help me!"

A guard in a crow mask easily lifted me and sat me on the bed, keeping hold of my arms.

Dr. Spector smiled at me as he slowly shut the door.

"Good day, Avery Kohl. I trust you have been comfortable? Alas, no more medication for you. If we are going to work together, I need you fully decontaminated." His voice grated the edges of my nerves, sent quivers coursing up and down my body. "First I must test your ability, see what you can do." He turned to the guard. "Bring her."

"No. Please no." But the guard hoisted me up. It was walk or be dragged.

In the hallway, I looked around frantically, trying to see a way out, any small detail. There was a nurse and patient down the hall but they disregarded my protest, as if it was commonplace. I counted the doors as we proceeded. At the fifth, Dr. Spector unlocked the door and flicked a switch on the wall. Two globes suspended from the ceiling cast a yellow-green glow.

"Welcome to my laboratory." He lifted his arms proudly.

The small room was packed with machinery, books, glass jars, and beakers. In the center was a large chair, with straps on the arms and a contraption above it that reminded me of the one Spector's cronies had used to test the street urchins. On the wall was a chart of a human head with the scalp divided into small numbered sections.

I cringed at the sight of a real crow standing perfectly still on Spector's desk. When I looked closer I realized the huge bird was stuffed, like the taxidermy animals hunters like to display.

The guard pushed me into the chair, securing my wrists and ankles tightly. My breath came in shallow gulps.

"Why are you doing this?"

Ignoring my question, Spector nodded to the guard. "That will be all."

When the guard exited, Dr. Spector took measurements of my head with a round caliper, occasionally fingering my skull. I cringed at the touch of his bony fingers. Then he lowered the metal helmet to my head, carefully adjusting the fit. "This machine is of my own design. I have a portable one, of course, but this lady is far more sensitive. This invention places me exceedingly beyond my peers at the Institute of Phrenology. Those Fowler brothers, old geezers, will quail in my presence." He turned to a box next to me, fiddled with the knobs and dials, and swung a delicate metal arm to hover over a scroll of paper. The machine began to hum in my ear like an insect.

"Where is my mother?" I imagined her in this seat and shuddered. My voice sounded tinny and small. "Please, can you tell me? Why have you kept her here?"

Spector's eyes flashed with some unreadable emotion. *Contempt?*

"This is where she belongs. This is where all of you belong. Let's just hope you are of use to me as well. Shall we?" He lifted his pointer finger to a small red button.

"Wait!" My mind raced. I had to say something, anything, to keep him from pushing that button. "I'm sure you're right. We do belong here. I'm just trying to understand—"

"Your feeble intellect could never comprehend the intricacies of the science behind my experiments." Spector leered.

That's it. I had to keep him talking. I had to play to his pride.

"Is that why we have no power over you? Why you alone do not wear goggles?"

"As I just said, you underestimate my science. I create my own power." He raised his chin, looking me in the eye. I realized now why his left eye seemed different. This close I could tell it was made of glass. I'd seen a cruder version in my father's workroom, but Spector's was amazingly lifelike.

"You mean the serum?" I blurted out.

Spector laughed. "The serum is for those who have risen to the top and, of course, have the money to buy control over those at the bottom. I provide what they desire and they pay handsomely for it." He shook his head. "No, no, my personal interest is in the science behind the serum, and for that, my name will go down in history."

Heat flushed through my veins. He wants to be famous for his barbaric experiments. *He has not a shred of empathy or compassion.* I'd thought him mad, but this was far worse. The severity of my situation hit me full on. *We are but lab rats to him.* My restrained hands began to shake. Sweat dripped down my face from under the helmet. He observed me with cold, clinical detachment, as if my display of emotion was simply part of his investigation.

Then he grinned and pressed the button.

The hum grew louder and louder until I felt like my brain must be vibrating in my skull. I squeezed my eyes shut, gritted my teeth, and clenched my fists as my body began to tremble. I heard the needle scratching wildly on the paper. I tried to take a breath, but my throat squeezed shut. I felt my eyes roll back in my head. My mouth stretched wide to scream, but nothing came out.

The machine stopped.

Dr. Spector lifted the apparatus as I slumped forward, held in place by the straps. I gulped the air.

Tearing the paper from its scroll, he mumbled to himself, "Yes, yes, just as I'd hoped . . . even stronger . . ."

Then the world went black.

CHAPTER THIRTY
TOXIC FLOWERS

A rush of air filled my lungs as I sat bolt upright in bed. My head swam and the walls of my room tilted. I slumped back on the pillow until the feeling passed.

Fuzzy memories drifted through my mind: Dr. Spector, nurses, an operating table, a needle. I looked at my arm; I saw another large bruise and specks of dried blood.

Spector took blood from me. *I'm part of his lurid experiments now.* I ran my hands through my matted hair. My fingernails snagged, and I realized I'd bitten my nails to the quick. A noise outside my door sparked my attention. Burying myself under my covers, I peeked out as Mrs. Luckett entered with a steaming tin. She placed it on the cart and eyed me warily through her goggles. My mouth dropped open when she lifted the cover: bite-size cubes of red meat in a puddle of red juices, mashed potatoes with a blot of butter, and steamed spinach. I had to pretend to be friendly. "New chef?" I smiled.

Her eyebrows rose up. Her lips stretched into a tight little grin. "Dr. Spector himself requested this meal for you."

I rubbed my arms. Everything hurt. "Mrs. Luckett, I'm very sorry about my behavior when I first arrived. I was scared."

"No need to apologize, dear. I'm glad you're adjusting."

"Yes, I know Dr. Spector is trying to help me. And you are as well. Thank you." I tried to look nonchalant. "Do you know why he has taken my blood, by chance?"

She checked the chart on the end of my bed. I already knew it said nothing, just a bunch of mumbo-jumbo about my psychological condition, and other cryptic notes and dates. "I'm not privy to the treatment specifics, but it indicates here that you are due for another bloodletting on the twelfth and again on the nineteenth. Don't you worry. I'm sure he is doing everything he can to help."

My heart sped up at the mention of more bloodletting. For some reason, I thought of something my mother used to say: *You can catch more flies with honey than vinegar.* How I missed her little quips. My father and I used to chuckle at them, but I'd do anything to hear her voice right now. Or his. "Yes." I kept my voice casual. "I'm quite sure you're right. What day is it today?"

"Today is Monday, November sixth."

"Mrs. Luckett, do you know how my mother is doing? Is it possible to see her?"

Her smile dropped. I'd gone too far. "Now, now. Patient

confidentiality does not permit me to discuss that. Strictly forbidden. Eat up, then get some rest. You need to build your strength. After I collect your dish, no one will disturb you until the morning nurse arrives," she said as she bustled out.

I looked down at my meal. Red meat, spinach . . . of course! Spector was trying to strengthen my blood. All right. I'd play his game. I wanted to get strong as well, to find my way out of here.

Later, I woke to see the tray had been cleared. The clock showed half past eleven. All was dark and quiet in the hall. I raised the wick on the lantern, casting away the shadows.

I had to reach my mother. I had to find Indigo and Hurricane. And how many others was he experimenting on? *This madness must be stopped.*

Lifting my hands, I focused on my third eye. Though I tried to see the energy in my body, the vision would not come. I feared I would lose the ability to control my second sight if I did not practice. Here and now, I vowed to work on it every possible chance. Again I closed my eyes and slowed my breath. I found it helpful to count. *Inhale for four, hold, exhale for four.* When I next dared look, the light flowed around my hands. Somehow, it made me feel closer to my mother.

A flash in the corner caught my eye. A rat. Its energy glowing, it emerged from beneath the pipes and crept along the edge of the room. Turning to keep it within sight, I watched it disappear into a large grate on the wall behind my bed.

I got up and held the lantern up to the grate. Behind it, a narrow horizontal shaft stretched off into darkness. Gripping the edges, I tried to pry the grate free but only succeeded in hurting my fingers. Four screws held the grate in place. I needed a tool.

Looking around the room, I got an idea. Swiftly and silently, I wedged my feet against the pipes on the wall, wrapped my fists around a small pipe, and pulled. It moved slightly. I leaned back, putting all my weight into it. It bowed a bit but held fast. *Damn!*

Getting onto all fours, I lowered my face. Behind the pipes was a dark crevice. Biting my lip, I reached my hand into it, feeling around with my fingers. *Disgusting.* Damp grime, nothing more. I slid my hand out, oily black and caked with dust, and tried another spot.

Exhilaration shot through me. Here were shards of metal. Reaching further, my fingers brushed over something hard and jagged. I pulled out a discarded section of pipe.

This could work. Very carefully, I inserted the edge into the slot of one of the screws. I leaned into it, pressing hard. Slowly, the screw turned. Soon I had all four out, and the grate, hinged on one side, swung open. Behind it was an old stone tunnel just big enough for me to fit.

A few months ago, I wouldn't have gone in there for gold coins. *Desperation breeds courage, I suppose. It might be a way out.* On hands and knees, I entered, pushing the lantern ahead to light my way. As I crawled along, I saw the openings to other tunnels branching off into darkness. *I'll get lost. I'll die in the walls of the Tombs.*

I backtracked to my room. I needed to ensure I could find my way out if I was to explore any farther. I had time, at least until the morning nurse came. *Think, Avery, think.*

Jumping up, I grabbed my extra blanket. Using the rough end of the pipe, I made a hole and worked my way along the fabric, pulling out a long string. I did this again and again until I had a pile of strings I could tie end to end. Then I balled the sheets into the rough shape of a person and laid the first blanket over it.

This time, I tied one end of my long string to the grate. I entered the tunnel with the lantern and pulled the grate closed, trailing the string behind me. Soon I came to an opening on my right. From within came a scraping noise, something moving my way. *Rats!* I braced myself for the vermin, but instead, a snakelike metal tube emerged, sliding forward as if pushed by someone on the other end.

I stared at it in the light of the lantern. Its copper segments created a flexible cylinder. The welder in me was fascinated. On the end was a glass ball inside a wire cage. It reminded me of the periscope device Geeno had run through the door in his crate. I picked it up.

Within the glass was the image of an eye. It blinked. Letting out an involuntary gasp, I dropped it, backing away. The eye blinked again, then vanished; the glass went black.

Slowly, I reached out and picked up the glass ball. It jerked free and withdrew. *Oh no you don't.* I followed it, eager to find out to whom that eye belonged.

The tunnel ended at a vertical stone shaft with a ladder bolted to the side. The air smelled stale, and the dust on the rungs made it clear no one had been here in a long time.

The metal tube continued to recede, tapping a steady rhythm on each rung as it was pulled upward. I tested my weight on the ladder. Sturdy. I had to hold the lantern and the rungs at the same time, making progress slow, but eventually I'd climbed at least thirty feet from the bottom. I couldn't help noticing the welds that fixed the rungs of the ladder in place. Whoever had built it had done it well. As old and rusty as it looked, not one joint had cracked.

My arms and legs ached; my breath felt stifled in the narrow passage. From the echo and the feel of space above me, I knew the shaft continued overhead, but the ladder ended at a large opening in the wall. The air was different here, warm and humid. The stone walls had green algae growing on them.

Hesitantly, I hoisted myself up. There was no one there. Placing the lantern on the floor near the opening, I stood, wishing I had my knife. The first thing I saw was the moon, directly overhead, almost full and serenely beautiful. *Am I outside? It's not possible.*

As my eyes adjusted, I realized I was in some sort of greenhouse. Tall stone walls held a glass roof high above my head. It must've been snowing in the city; each metal frame had a drift collecting in its corners. Spots of greenish glowing light blinked in the night sky; it took me a moment to realize I was looking at the dirigibles, hovering above Manhattan. I tightened my lips, forcing myself to look away. I never thought I'd miss Vinegar Hill, but now I wished desperately that I was there, viewing the sky from my own rooftop.

The smell of soil and sweet flowers drifted through the air. I breathed deep, filling my lungs with clean air. Towering trees and plants and racks of potted flowers surrounded me. Even the continuous dripping of water soothed my soul.

I closed my eyes and focused. Somehow it was easier to concentrate amid all this greenery; my gaze shifted into my second sight. "Oh!" I drew in a sharp breath. Every branch, every twig, every flower pulsed with shimmery white light. I imagined that this was what a fairy world would look like. Like a pearl within an oyster, it was strange that the Tombs should house such beauty within its walls.

With a slithery splatter the tube and ball were pulled through a puddle and across the slate floor. I followed, brushing against the wet greenery, trailing my fingers through the light. Clusters of exotic flowers hung around me, dangling from a trellis above. They glowed in the moonlight, each white blossom, ten or twelve inches long, a delicate bell with ruffled edges. Laughing with delight, I reached out to touch one.

"Don't touch! Don't touch!" a wiry voice yelled down at me.

I stopped, my sight flashing back to normal. "Who said

that?" Ducking below the flowers, I tracked the line of water from the tube up a wooden stairway that rose into the overhead greenery. A tree house was woven into the branches there. The path of the tube ended at an enormous spool wound by a tiny old man, struggling to turn the handle. His face was pressed into a metal cone; all I saw was his bushy gray beard sticking out on either side of his bald head.

At my approach, he turned. I jumped back, nearly falling down the steps. His entire face was an enormous eye, as if a giant peered at me through a round window.

"Oh, heavens, my mistake, my mistake. Please watch your step." He lifted the great bulbous magnifying glass off his face. "Yes, yes, please do come in." He bustled over, chin jutting out to compensate for the weight of the lens on his head.

At two feet taller than him, I had to smile when he reached out, took my hand, and kissed the back of it. Quite the little gentleman. His eyebrows were as unruly as his beard.

"Excuse my manners, please do. I haven't had a visitor in . . ." He tapped his temple. "Forty-four years. Yes, yes, that must be it. Now, what is your name?"

"My name is Avery Kohl, sir. I am looking for my mother. She's being held—"

"Oh yes, lovely woman, your mother."

"You know my mother?" I touched my throat, where my charms used to be.

"Oh yes. But no, not really. I've not actually met her." He

busied himself with a small gas burner and teapot. "Saw a woman brought up to this floor. Her name was Kohl. I peeked in on her once to make sure she was all right. She was quite drugged but lovely, simply lovely." He studied me momentarily. "I do see the resemblance, yes, yes I do. Now where was I, and where are my manners? My name is Hanover Gentry, expert on poisons. Pleased to make your acquaintance." He smiled, his teeth tiny nubs in his mouth. "Would you care for some tea?"

"I . . . I'd love some. Thank you, Mr. Gentry." I watched him flurry about. "But please, can you tell me where my mother is?"

"Have a seat, have a seat, please." He took my hand and walked me over to a wooden table. I sat on the long bench at its side. "You must be tired from the climb, yes? Such a distance. You're a curious one, yes you are."

"Mr. Gentry, please, I have to know where my mother is."

He looked at the floor, shuffling his feet. "Well now." He put a hand on the side of his mouth, as if someone might overhear, and whispered, "You do know she's insane, do you not? Completely barmy, mad as a hatter. Sees things in her head. She's in the padded cell down the hall, poor thing. I'm sorry to be the one to tell you, truly I am."

"She is not mad," I insisted.

He lifted his eyebrows and looked at me as if I was being foolish. I hastily changed the subject; perhaps I could draw out more information another way. "Mr. Gentry, what is that thing, with the eye?"

He brightened. I noticed his bristly beard looked as if he'd hacked at it with a knife and no mirror, and he wore the same prison clothing as me.

"Why that"—he pointed at the giant reel of tubing—"that is my own invention. I call her Sally, Slithering Sally. She's a beauty, eh?" He smiled, puffing up his chest. "They had her fabricated at a big foundry in Brooklyn."

Could he mean the Works? Does my strange connection to this place never end?

Gentry rattled on. "There are a hundred tiny mirrors inside. Bit hard to handle, but Sally sees all, she does. I designed her to see into the pits of this place when it was flooding. Toxic down there it was, yes sirree."

"You mean the prison—the Tombs?" I asked, eyeing Sally, whose copper segments had aged to verdigris green.

"Oh yes, yes indeedy." He tapped his head. "Built back in 1838. It was my job to make sure the toxins didn't kill the prisoners before they were hanged. I had them install shafts to vent the toxic air. Tsk, tsk, built it on a swampy bog, they did. Used to be the slaughterhouse dumping grounds. She's been slowly sinking since the day they set the cornerstone in place. I'm surprised the damp walls don't weep pig's blood, truly I am."

A twitchy quiver ran up my back. "What a horrid thought."

"Yes indeedy. Tea's ready." The kettle whistled, and he poured two steaming cups. I accepted one and held the cup in my hands to warm them.

"If you helped build the prison, why are you a prisoner yourself? Or are you? I just assumed from your clothing . . ." I certainly did not want to offend him.

"You assume correctly, my dear. A long story, it is, but suffice it to say I poisoned my supervisor. Had a bit of a temper as a young-un, I did." Mr. Gentry climbed up onto a metal stool. "Would've been the first one in the gallows, yes I would, but they gave me a reprieve as long as I continued to run the lab. They're always in need of some chemical or other. Been here since I was twenty-one years old, I have." His face drooped as he said this. He rested his chin on his fist. "Where was I? Oh yes, this Spector fellow. He's taken things too far, in my humble opinion, reopening the lower levels and messing with substances he shouldn't."

"Mr. Gentry, I want to ask you about that." I pretended to sip the tea, not wanting to offend but not about to drink a brew from a self-professed poisoner. "Dr. Spector is using something to control people—a serum."

"Ah yes, the serum. It's borrachero extract and blood, mixed with an anticoagulant, of course. Using it on people, you say?" Mr. Gentry looked up, a shocked expression on his wrinkled features. For his age, his bright eyes sparked with intelligence. "Oh no. No, no, no, that just won't do. Told me he was using it on the rats, he did. Never did like that fellow, something malevolent about him. Sounds funny coming from one who slipped his boss some arsenic, but let me tell you, he had it coming, oh yes he did." His shoulders shuddered. "That Spector scares me. Makes my flesh creep, he does."

"Dr. Spector is evil," I agreed forcefully.

He finished his tea and stood. "Now, if you please, follow me."

We returned to the magical fairy grove, the white flowers hanging in beautiful profusion. "Devil's breath," Mr. Gentry said, pointing at one. "Or the borrachero tree, as it's called in New Granada. It's completely poisonous."

These lovely flowers are poisonous? It was hard to believe.

He tightened his lips. "Dr. Spector had me import it for his experiments. Dangerous stuff, it is."

I rubbed my arms, suddenly feeling cold. "Mr. Gentry, if you agree he's gone too far, please help me. I must find my mother and two friends that are being held prisoner. It's urgent." To press my case further, I added, "Dr. Spector has committed murder for his wicked cause." I knew of Roland Malice. It was quite possible there were others.

"Terrible, simply terrible. Of course, there's no way for me to help you. No way. That Dr. Spector will have my head, he will." His eyes blinked rapidly as he shook his head.

I had to figure out a way to get his support. *My second sight?* I slowed my breathing. Again, it seemed easier in this place. Pale light surrounded Mr. Gentry. In my mind's eye, I saw a younger Mr. Gentry cowering before Dr. Spector. "You work for me, Gentry, or you go to the gallows."

I tried pushing energy toward Mr. Gentry, but he seemed lost. He'd just experienced the same memory. Fear was embedded in his bones. I could not alter it.

I felt as helpless as Dr. Spector claimed I was. There had to be another way. I pointed at the glass ceiling. "Couldn't we find a way to go out through the roof?"

"Oh no. Not sure how we'd get you up that high, but even if we could fashion some sort of ladder, you'd be fried to a cinder, woo-hoo, burned to a crisp. They run electricity through the metal framework." The lens of his magnifying glass reflected the green mercury-vapor lamps from the airships above. "Oh dear, oh dear, what a predicament. I've lived most of my life in this very room, yes indeed. Not sure there's hope for your mum, loopy as she is, but a young lass such as yourself shouldn't be in here, no sir. I had a gal once. Her name was Ginny—Virginia, but I called her Ginny. Wonder what happened to her . . ." He stared at the moon, drifting off into his memories.

I couldn't imagine—so many years in the Tombs. "Mr. Gentry, don't you miss the outside world?"

"Yes? Oh, yes. The outside world, you say? I miss my Ginny, I suppose, but what I really miss is Pepper."

"Pepper?"

"My parrot." He placed his hands on his heart. "I do miss talking to him, I do."

"I've never seen a parrot."

Mr. Gentry pulled a woven pouch from his shirt. From

within, he fished out a piece of worn folded paper: a pencil sketch of a bird with a curved beak and long tail feathers. "Taught him to speak, I did. He was quite the chatterbox. I'd do anything to have Pepper here to talk to." He glanced up at the moon. "Oh deary me, look at that. Time to go."

Without another word, he ushered me toward the ladder.

"But—"

"No ifs, ands, or buts about it. You must go. My head will roll, it will, if you are caught here." He smiled crookedly, as if half of him was suspended in dismay, the other half in decorum. "I've enjoyed our visit, though, I have."

I stepped down onto the ladder, into the shaft. A panicky feeling crept into my gut. "Please, Mr. Gentry, can't you help me?"

"No, no, no, absolutely not. There is no way. I'm very sorry, I am," he said as he bustled away.

I took a long look at the moon. *Will I ever see it again?*

CHAPTER THIRTY-ONE
PEPPER

Mr. Gentry had said my mother was in a cell down the hall on his floor. I had to try to find her. The only other opening in this shaft was directly across from the one into the greenhouse. The problem was, the ladder was on this side. If I fell, I'd break every bone in my body.

Leaving the lantern on the floor, close to the opening, I held the top rung with one hand and stretched out with the other. My fingers tried to grip the stone ledge, but it was too slick with algae.

Quietly, I climbed back into the greenhouse. I'd seen a pile of scrap wood that looked like it'd come from the construction of the tree house. I found a thick board and slid it inch by inch across the shaft into the other opening. I held my breath as I gingerly crawled across, pushing the lantern. The board groaned but held fast. I entered another tunnel.

My nerves tingled as I peered through the bars of a small

opening at floor level. My lantern only lit the room so far, but it appeared empty. I continued to the next one.

Lying down, I peeked through. The walls were padded. I sucked in my breath as the light caught a glint of auburn hair in the distance. It had to be my mother's. I realized with dismay that she must be sleeping on the floor.

"Mother? Mother, can you hear me?" I was afraid to speak loudly, but to be so close without being able to communicate with her was agonizing. Then I remembered Mr. Gentry saying she was drugged. After calling out a few more times, I knew it was useless. I had to go.

Using the string, I easily found my way back to my room and closed the grate.

Too agitated to sleep, I spent the rest of the night thinking about my mother. Eventually, a morning nurse came in with milk and bread. When she left, I dozed, exhausted from the events of the night, until the evening nurse entered to escort me to the washroom. Once I was alone for the night, I found myself pacing, agonizing over my predicament.

Mr. Gentry seemed like a decent sort of gentleman murderer, but how could I get him to help me? I wished my second sight was more like Indigo's. Hurricane and I had decided my abilities worked best with people who were doing something that went against their morals. Apparently, that didn't apply here. And I had to think of something else before Spector came for me on November twelfth. The inside of my arm tingled, as if my bruises were alive.

A crazy, probably impossible idea crept into my mind. But I was willing to try anything, and Mr. Gentry was loony enough that he might just go for it.

Again, I made up the shape of a person under the sheets and grabbed the lantern. Once I climbed up to the greenhouse, it was not difficult to find Mr. Gentry. I simply followed the sound of his snores. I placed my hand on his shoulder.

"Oh heavens! Who's there?" He stared up at me, eyes bleary with sleep. "Oh no, Miss Avery. You should not be here. Not again, no sir."

"Mr. Gentry, no one comes to my room at night, so as long as I'm back before morning, no one will know."

"No, no, you must go." He jumped up. "But before you do, care for some tea?"

He couldn't help himself. "Yes, that would be nice." I watched with interest as he struck a match and lit the single-burner kerosene stove, just as he'd done last night. It looked like a lantern, but the wick was circular and set into a perforated sleeve. *I can work with that.*

"Mr. Gentry, would you be willing to help me if I could make you a life-size replica of your parrot, Pepper?" I blurted out. Could I actually do it? I wasn't sure. *Hopefully, yes.*

He stopped, teapot in hand. "Pepper, you say? Oh, deary me, my long-lost Pepper. How I would love to have my Pepper back. But I don't know, surely I don't, how you would do such a thing as that."

"Leave that part to me. In the meantime, will you help me come up with a plan to escape? I have no one else to turn to."

He tapped his head and whirled around in a circle, muttering to himself. "I just don't know. . . . Spector will send me off to the gallows, he will."

"Please, Mr. Gentry. Spector is hurting people. I must get out of here."

Mr. Gentry turned to me, wringing his hands. "Is Spector truly using my serum on people, as you say?"

"Yes, I saw him force someone to jump to his death." I looked down, reliving the memory. Then I lifted my chin and fixed him with a steady gaze. "Mr. Gentry, Dr. Spector is also selling your serum to powerful men who intend to use it against people of every nationality that have come here to work toward a better life. They plan to divide and control them. He must be stopped before it's too late."

"Selling it, you say? My, oh my." His eyebrows pinched fiercely together like two spiky caterpillars, and his face splotched with red. It was the first time I'd seen him angry. "I will, I will help you. I'll noodle it over, but I warn you now, it is impossible, simply impossible, to get out of the Tombs. And if that Spector fellow starts asking questions, I'll deny everything, I will." He folded his hands together in front of his chest, softening his expression. "Will you still make Pepper for me?"

I let out the breath I'd been holding. "Of course. Thank you, Mr. Gentry. Shake on it?" I extended my hand, which he pumped vigorously. "I'll need that stove. And do you have any more kerosene?"

After his kettle boiled, he showed me to his workbench in the back of the greenhouse. Gingerly, he moved a host of jars and vials filled with powders and liquids of various color and density to clear a space for me to work.

"You simply must not touch any of these chemicals," he said. "I have to keep strict inventory, I do, and I will be in quite a predicament if anything is amiss, I will."

Something like trust flickered in his eyes, though, as he placed the sketch of Pepper on the work surface.

Making sure I was not near any of his poisonous concoctions, I set up the stove while questioning him on the types of supplies he had in his space. Then he ran about retrieving the items I asked for: an extra canister of kerosene oil, an old copper teacup, a pair of gardening shears, gloves, a spool of tin utility wire he used to support plants, and some goggles he had for working with chemicals. Lastly, I told Mr. Gentry I needed a small section of Sally; it would not affect her ability to slither, I assured him. We cut off what I hoped was enough and wound her back onto the spool.

"While I work, can you use Sally and try to see where they're holding a Gypsy boy my age, or a blond girl, or a young boy with curly brown hair?" I did not know how many others there were, but I described in detail what Indigo, Hurricane, and the boy from the street looked like.

I hope I can do this. I donned the canvas gloves and set to work. Using the shears, I sliced the copper cup down one side and made a hole in the bottom. I pressed the sides together to form a cone shape, leaving only a tiny opening at the top, and took apart all the thin segments from Sally, cutting them into the shapes I needed, glancing occasionally at the sketch: small feathers for the head and chest; long wing and tail feathers; a wide, curved beak. Wedging the copper cone onto the burner, I lit the stove. If I could concentrate the heat enough, I could melt the tin wire. The Works had taught me well: tin had a very low melting point compared to copper.

I turned up the wick and lowered the goggles. With a copper piece in one hand and the tin in the other, I placed the tip of the wire into the flame coming from the opening in the cone. *Please melt.*

It took longer than I'd hoped, but the wire slowly turned bright silver and then dripped onto the copper. I made a line of the melted tin and pressed another piece of copper to the first. As soon as the metals cooled, the tin would harden, fastening the two pieces together.

The hours slipped away, much as they'd done back at the Works, the familiar actions calming my agitated nerves.

When Mr. Gentry tapped me on the back, I jumped.

"Time to skedaddle, it is," he said. "Is Pepper finished?"

"Don't peek. I need ten more minutes." I continued melting the tin wire and overlapping the copper pieces as Pepper took his final shape. As a finishing touch, I turned a screw from Sally into either side of Pepper's head. Two beady parrot eyes.

Holding up Mr. Gentry's sketch, I compared it to my assemblage. It was remarkably close, even if the body somewhat resembled a falcon. The large head and long tail definitely said "parrot." It was a good thing I knew a lot about birds and their body structure. Although crude in comparison to my father's or Geeno's mechanizations, the overall effect was of smooth feathers with a beautiful patina from the various shades of copper. And, of course, the welds were perfect. I'd even crafted adjustable claws so Pepper could sit upon a branch.

I propped Pepper on the bench and went to find Mr. Gentry.

He took one look at the copper replica and burst into tears. "Pepper! He's wonderful. It looks quite like him, it does. Sally is useful, but she has no personality."

"I'm very glad you like it." I scrunched up my nose and pointed to the table. "Mr. Gentry, I know you said not to disturb anything—and I didn't, I promise—but I accidentally knocked the table. A jar tipped over and spilled. I'm so sorry. I would have cleaned it up, but you said not to touch it."

"Tsk, tsk, tsk. I must get it back in the jar." With a tiny metal spatula, he carefully scooped up every grain, murmuring, "They weigh every substance, they do." When he was done, he breathed out a long sigh. "You were lucky, very lucky indeed. This is iron oxide. Harmless stuff. Good thing you did not knock over the one next to it. A good thing indeed."

I looked at the tiny glass bottle. Inside was a yellow liquid. "Why? What is it?"

"It is sulfuric acid, it is. It'll eat through most anything. It will eat your flesh right to the bone, it will."

I took a step back from the workbench. I had to remember that Mr. Gentry was not only loony but also potentially dangerous. *I hope I can trust him.*

"Sally and I have been busy, too, yes sirree. We have good news and we have bad news." Mr. Gentry picked up Pepper as he spoke, absently running his hands over the metal feathers. "We know where they are keeping this Gypsy boy, but we have seen neither hide nor hair of the one you call Hurricane or the other. But you tell me you need to bust out, hightail it, yes, fly the coop, as they say." Mr. Gentry bounced on his toes, smiling. "Sally and I saw many things." He tapped the hefty lens on his head. "Yes we did, and we saw something that might be of interest to you. It may indeed be possible for you to escape. But you'll only get one chance, Miss Avery, and if you fail, then you will be stuck here forever, just like me."

CHAPTER THIRTY-TWO
RATS

The day stretched into an eternity. If what Mr. Gentry had said was true, there was no way to escape *before* the twelfth. I would have to go through with another of Dr. Spector's bloodlettings and bend myself to his dark experiments, whatever they were. Just thinking about it made my skin crawl.

It occurred to me that Dr. Spector had probably done the same thing to my mother, considering her bruises. Anger surged through me, but there was nothing I could do for the moment except practice my second sight.

I drifted off to sleep in the afternoon and woke at night in a panic, feeling like I'd dreamt up Mr. Gentry, his greenhouse, everything. But the welding burns on two of my fingertips convinced me he was real.

The clock struck midnight. With my lantern and string and

piece of pipe, I plunged back into the tunnels. *Turn left, then second right*, I recited to myself, carefully following Mr. Gentry's directions. They led to the back of a grate, much like the one in my room.

Peering through the slots, I recognized him instantly. His wavy brown hair had grown thicker and longer. He wore a black shirt, open to his waist, above worn leather pants. I thought it strange he was not in prison garb. He was incredibly lean, with sinewy muscles along his arms and stomach. Even from this distance, the raised white skin of his brand stood out on his chest: the brand of the crow. One of his legs had an iron cuff on it, attached to a chain that snaked across the room.

The area at the top of my stomach, where all my butterflies lived, tightened and twisted. I hadn't seen him in three years. *What if he doesn't remember me?*

Indigo sat among a semicircle of rats. The animals crouched while one of their number, a skinny black rat, stood on its hind legs, parading about like royalty. The scene reminded me of when I'd first met Indigo and he'd made the lady from the audience dance. It was so bizarre that I gasped, then quickly covered my mouth.

"What's this?" he asked. "Is one of my rat friends afraid to come closer?" He stared at the grate. After a moment, he said, "I see Dr. Spector is still gathering seers. I'd hoped he'd never capture you, Avery. But you should not have come to find me."

He knows it's me. He must've sensed my energy.

Indigo waved his hand, and the rats withdrew. He bowed his head, hair falling in front of his face. "If you knew what was good for you, you'd go away and pretend you never saw me."

"Indigo, there might be a way to escape. We have to get out of here before it's too late." I put my feet against the grate and pushed. It wouldn't budge. "I have a tool to open this grate, but you have to do it from your side."

But Indigo did not move. "I'll never get out. I'm a monster, Avery. I deserve this." His eyes flicked toward me, then back at the floor. There was hatred in them, but it was directed inward. "I've done terrible things," he whispered, so low I could barely hear him.

"Please just open the grate and let me in."

"No, Avery, it's too dangerous. *I'm* too dangerous."

"Indigo, please. When Spector took you, he took my mother, too. She's been in here as long as you have. And he has Hurricane; he kidnapped her recently. We have to stop him. But I need your help."

Indigo looked up, his radiant eyes catching the light. Their pained expression made my heart constrict. He shifted forward and stood. The chain grated on the floor as he came closer. I stuck the pipe through the bars.

"Use the edge. It worked on mine."

He took the pipe, deftly removed the screws, and swung open the grate. Immediately, he backed away from me and sat down on the floor.

I climbed out of the tunnel, wiping the dirt off my hands and knees. I did not want him to know it, but I *was* afraid.

The tension in the room was solid, like we were on opposite sides of thick glass that could shatter at any moment. Inching closer, I sat down cautiously, slowly. Indigo's shoulders remained hunched, his hands in his lap. I studied him more carefully. He'd grown up from the boy I remembered. Even with him looking down, I could tell his face was leaner, and I noticed a scar cut across one eyebrow.

I wanted to tell him that anything he'd done wasn't his fault. Why would he think of himself as dangerous? But not knowing where to start, I simply took his hand in mine. The moment we touched, a surge went through me. I felt thirteen again. He finally lifted his head, searching my face. Our eyes met, and in that moment, I understood that there was a bond between us that defied explanation. I knew in my heart that he felt it, too. I bit my lip, my insides squirming under his open gaze. His full lips were devoid of their self-mocking grin.

The next moment, he ripped his hand from mine and pushed himself away. Standing, he turned his back to me. The startled rats looked up at him from their huddle on the floor.

"Leave!" he shouted. "Get out of here! Before I hurt you, too."

I didn't know if he was speaking to the rats or me, but we all jumped up as one. The rats darted away—some dove into the tunnel, some disappeared into cracks. In seconds they were gone. I backed up to the tunnel, tears springing to my eyes. I couldn't think of what to say or do.

"Go!" The coldness of his voice shot through me. "What are you waiting for, Avery? I can't help you. I don't want you here!"

CHAPTER THIRTY-THREE
THE PAINTING

Like one of the rats, I scurried away from Indigo, blinded by my tears and the swirl of emotions battering my brain. I crawled under my covers into a tight fetal position, afraid my heart was going to rupture and bleed out. The shock of Indigo's outburst burned inside me as if I'd swallowed a hot coal. My pillow soaked through with my tears, but I didn't care. I cried like I did the night I'd gone back to the Gypsy camp and found Indigo gone. I cried for my mother, locked somewhere in this hell. I cried for my father, who'd lost my mother and now me.

I couldn't eat. I couldn't move. I couldn't even sleep. I'd allowed myself to get my hopes up, to think I might rescue my mother and the others with the help of a crazy old man and a copper parrot. *Stupid.*

Once again, my day passed in a blur. At some point, after

the *tick-tock*ing of the clock took me deep into the night, I heard something scratching in the corner of the room. A rat? Whatever it was, it didn't go away. It kept scratching and scratching; now it was squeaking, too.

"Shoo." I waved my hand. It squeaked again. I rolled over and lifted the lantern.

There, by the grate, was a black rat. It held something in its teeth. I sat up and watched, amazed, as it dropped its burden and ran back into the tunnel.

Tiptoeing over, I picked it up. It was a piece of canvas that looked like it had been chewed around the edges. On it was a note:

> *Avery,*
> *I'm sorry. Please come back.*
> *Indy*

I read it in disbelief. He expected me to literally crawl back to him? *Why? So he can cut my heart out and feed it to his rats?* I never wanted to feel like that again, not ever. I'd been trying to help him. Angry, I threw the note down and got back into bed, covering my head with the blanket.

Some time later, I heard another squeak. Unable to resist, I peeked out from beneath my covers. A fat gray rat sat on its hind legs, staring at me. It also held a small roll of canvas between its teeth.

How does he get them to do it?

Having gotten my attention, the rat dropped the scroll and scurried away. This time, it was not just a note. It was a picture of me, of my face, painted on the canvas. A green mask covered my eyes; the tips of fairy wings were visible at my shoulders. It was what I'd worn on the night of the Midsummer's Eve festival, the night we'd kissed. It was beautiful.

At the bottom was written:

> *Fairy Princess,*
> *Forgive me. Come back.*
> *Humbly,*
> *King of the Rats*

My heart surged with fresh emotion, even as I tried to bury it inside me. My body would not listen to my mind, which was screaming, *Do not go! Do not give in.* I dove into the tunnel before I could think better of it.

When I reached his room and looked through the grate, I did not see him. I pushed, and the grate swung open. Tentatively, I surveyed my surroundings.

Indigo's room was twice the size of mine. Squinting in the dim light, I saw that the stone walls and entrance door were hidden behind tattered canvas drapes.

From somewhere in the darkness, I heard Indigo's voice. "I would have come to *you*, but as you know, they keep me on a short leash."

His chain scraped against the floor. I didn't say anything—I still wasn't sure I should be here. Keeping my back to the wall, I moved toward the sound of his breathing. I passed his bed, a washstand, and a long table covered with jars of paints and brushes. *Why does Spector give him all this?* Finally I saw him, squatting like a panther on a rock ledge that jutted from the dark corner of the wall, the chain coiled at his feet. The other end was attached to an iron ring embedded in the floor.

How has he not gone mad living in this hell for three years? Or maybe he has.

I bit my nails and leaned against the table. He watched me, as if waiting to see what I would do, his blue-violet eyes luminous even in the shadows. I tried my best to glare at him, but felt my anger soften at the sight of his crouched posture and intense gaze.

"Do you like the picture?" he asked.

"Yes, thank you." I nodded toward some paintings on the floor. "I didn't know you could draw." I took a step toward him.

"Don't." He held up his hand. "Don't get too close." He pressed his fists together and took a deep breath. "I'm sorry, Avery. Truly I am. I didn't mean what I said. I do want you here, more than you can imagine."

"Then why—"

"Because . . . I got scared. Sometimes this . . . ability gets away from me. I was afraid I might hurt you."

"You could have said that." I crossed my arms, thinking of how he'd lashed out at me.

"Can you forgive me?" He smiled, one corner of his mouth lifting. That same crooked smile I remembered. Same crazy-sweet dimples. He could have asked me to do almost anything and I would have said yes, just to see him smile again.

"Yes, I forgive you. King of the Rats, huh?" I glanced around in case any rodents were lurking nearby. "It's so disturbing. How do you get them to do your bidding?"

He shrugged. Self-conscious under his gaze, I folded my arms over my chest.

"You should know," I said, "that I don't believe you would hurt me."

"Avery, you'd be surprised by what I'm capable of. I told you the truth. I *am* a monster. There's a demon inside of me that I can't control." He shook his head. "If I wasn't so selfish, I wouldn't have asked you to come back. I would let you go, let you forget about me."

"Indigo, Spector is the monster, not you." I recalled what I'd learned of my mother, that she'd also thought she harbored a demon. "Please, don't give up," I begged. "We can try—"

"No! You can't help me, Avery." He jumped to the floor. "And I don't want to destroy the only good I've seen in the world."

"What are you talking about?"

"I'm talking about you." He paced, dragging the chain with him. "When we were younger . . . when we kissed on the night of your birthday, I saw the world through your eyes. I saw how every living thing is connected, and I thought I could finally forgive myself for what I'd done. Then Spector came, and I realized I was meant to be punished." He laughed and held out his hands. "This—this is my punishment."

"I don't understand." I rubbed my forehead. "What do you need forgiveness for?"

"Let me show you." He turned and raised his arms overhead, taking hold of the curtains behind him.

I gripped the side of the table. What was behind there?

He whisked the curtains open.

The entire wall was covered with a painting. It was of a beautiful woman. From her eyes spread a rainbow, as if she were a goddess. Everything the rainbow touched was covered with flowers and trees and sunshine—except for one thing: a small boy, who stood looking up at her, surrounded in shards of black, a lightning bolt from his raised fist extending into the dark sky above. It was him. It was a self-portrait of Indigo.

But who was the woman? I stared at her face, searching her features for clues. Slowly, it came to me. It was his mother.

Letting go of the curtain, Indigo slumped onto the edge of his bed and bowed his head into his hands. I thought my heart had cracked in two the other night; now it ruptured into a thousand pieces. I pressed my hands to my chest and let my gaze slide into my second sight. When Indigo looked up at me, I saw it. I saw it all.

A bonfire. Around it dances Indigo's exotic and beautiful

mother, laughing and singing, head tilted back, body swaying, giving herself up completely to the song.

Indigo is a little boy, maybe Geeno's age. He and Katalina sit with Mr. Moralis, clapping and singing. Mr. Moralis beams at his wife, devotion in his eyes.

Later that night, the fire is smoldering. Everyone is fast asleep. Indigo's mother slips into the dark night. Indigo wakes and follows. She enters the barn, quietly shutting the door. Indigo presses his eye to the slats and sees her in the throes of passion with another man, a man he has never seen before. Scared, Indigo runs to get his father. Fearing for his wife, Mr. Moralis bursts into the barn and discovers the truth. In a fit of jealousy, he strikes his wife and chases off the other man. Indigo's mother storms away, screaming and cursing at her husband.

Indigo is crying outside the barn, hands over his ears. He chases after his mother as she mounts her horse and rides bareback into the rainy night. Indigo runs, trying to stop her from leaving. Then, clenching his fists, he throws his head back and releases a primal scream. A bolt of lightning flashes from the heavens. His mother's horse rears up and she tumbles to the ground, breaking her neck from the fall.

And Indigo is the only one to see her die.

I didn't realize I'd gone to him, but when I blinked, I was standing inches away. Tears ran down Indigo's face; the cords of his neck stood out, but his expression was that of a child riddled with shock and self-blame.

I'd made him relive his mother's death. I'd made him see it all over again.

"I killed her," he whispered.

Wrapping my arms around him, I gathered him gently to me, stroking his hair, his face buried in my shirt. "Shhh." My tears fell onto his shoulders, which trembled under the weight they bore. "It wasn't your fault. It was an accident, Indigo. You were just a young boy."

For a long time we stayed like that. Then he lifted his face to mine. Everything he had been through, everything he understood about me that no one else did, washed over me.

Gently, he removed my arms from his shoulders and stood. I took a step back as my heart quickened. He'd grown slightly taller than me but had kept the mishievous spark of his eyes. His cheek brushed mine as he whispered, "Thank you, Fairy Princess. But I can never forgive myself." His breath was warm on my ear, sending shivers down my spine. He slowly pulled his head back, deliberately grazing my face with his. I met his smoldering gaze. He looked at me, no into me, as if he wanted to know all my inner secrets. I held my breath, plunging into the blue-violet sea of his eyes.

Like a magnetic pull we drew together, his lips touching mine. I closed my eyes. His mouth pressed harder, parting my lips. His tongue found mine. My nerves, my every cell, vibrated with life. Indigo crushed me against him, our hearts finding the same rhythm, my blood surging through me like a river.

I melted into him and he into me, his kiss wild and untamed. Even with my eyes closed, I felt his dark energy surrounding me, drawing me to a place that frightened me.

I pulled back, pressing my hand to his chest. My lips felt stung raw, my insides shaking.

He swept away from me, crouching again on the ledge like a caged animal. "I shouldn't have done that. You're in danger being here, being with me."

I was beginning to think he was right. He wore a mantle of violence like a heavy cloak he could not shake off. But even so, I couldn't leave him. I'd never met anyone who could do this to me, bring me to the brink of such emotional turmoil, seize me with fear and anger while melting my heart within my chest. I had to be strong. I had to be careful.

"Indigo, there is someone that might be able to help us, another prisoner. He told me that in a little over a week, there is to be a public execution. It seems impossible, but we are trying to find a way to get into the courtyard. It's our only chance." There were so many holes in Mr. Gentry's suggestion; I couldn't imagine how we could pull it off. I only knew we had to try.

Indigo looked up, hope and despair warring in his eyes. Then he nodded. "I'll do anything I can to get you and your mother, and Hurricane, out of this hell."

CHAPTER THIRTY-FOUR
THE EYE

I lay in my bed, stunned at my visceral reaction to Indigo. I remembered my father's concern about the Gypsies; he'd be disappointed in me. *Is that why he'd forbidden me to go, to protect me from such passionate people?*

My thoughts shifted to Mr. Gentry's scheme for our escape; they circled around the problems and possibilities until my head hurt. All we had was an idea, a vague one at best.

The morning nurse and the evening nurse came and went. Still my mind was abuzz with questions.

The first problem was Indigo's iron cuff. If we could not remove it, he was bound to that room. I couldn't imagine how to get ahold of the key. He said only the crow-guards could unlock it. One always lurked in the hallway; if a nurse came to escort him to the washroom, the guard released him. Over the years, Indigo had tried everything to pick the lock or break the cuff. Nothing had worked.

I considered the tools Mr. Gentry had on his workbench. *There must be one that would work.* Another thought occurred to me. *What if it's not a tool?* I sat up. *What if it's a chemical?* Mr. Gentry had said sulfuric acid could dissolve anything. Would it eat through metal? I was determined to find out.

While I waited for the hallways to go silent and the lights to shut down, I practiced seeing the energy around my hands. I had to get better at calming my mind when there was chaos around me—that's when I'd need my ability most.

When midnight struck, I made my way up to Mr. Gentry's greenhouse, skirting the poisonous borrachero trees. I found him pruning roses with a little scissor. Pepper was looking down at him from a nearby tree, and Mr. Gentry was talking to him as if he were real.

"You see, Pepper, we cut just above the bud, like so. Then we—"

"Hello, Mr. Gentry. Glad I didn't wake you again."

"Oh, Pepper, look who's here. Don't sleep much these days, Miss Avery. Used to, but no more." He pocketed the scissor and dusted off his hands. "Did you go to the Gypsy boy?"

"Yes, I found him. Exactly where you said."

"Yes, yes, Sally knows all, she does. Are you sure you want to help that boy? From what Sally and I have seen, he's too far gone for helping. Trouble with a capital *T*, I tell you. Looks like a wild beast, he does."

"He's been through a great deal. Have you and Sally seen anything else? Did you find Hurricane or the boy?"

Mr. Gentry turned his head, closed one eye, and studied me intensely with the other. "You haven't been nipping at my coca leaves, now, have you?"

"What? No. I don't even know what coca leaves look like. I get this way when I'm nervous." I realized I did feel stronger than when I'd first been captured. "I probably have more energy because they're giving me real food instead of mush. Fortifying my blood, I'm told."

"All right, then, all righty. Sally and I have not found them. But we found the board across the tunnel, we did. You saw your mother?"

I hung my head. "Barely a glimpse. It was too dark, and she did not respond." Another thought occurred to me. "Mr. Gentry, now that we are working together, can you please show me my mother though Sally's eye?" Knowing his possessiveness of Sally, I held my breath. "I would love to see Sally in action," I added.

"She's a beaut, she is." His cheeks turned pink. "Sally, I mean. Although your mother is quite pretty as well." He glanced up at the moon. "Not much time, but we can try, we can."

I followed him to Sally's spool. He lifted the heavy glass and strapped it to my head. "Sally prefers to work in the light of day, she does. The sun hits the mirrors and brightens things up quite nicely. But we use a lantern at night."

With the glass orb in front of my face, I stuck my head into the large cone. Mr. Gentry began unspooling Sally's immense length. Then he raised the wick on a lantern hanging directly over us. Shocked, I sucked in my breath.

"I can see." It reminded me of looking into a kaleidoscope. I saw the ringed sides of the tube; at the end was a view out. I was Sally's eye.

My stomach dropped a little as Sally and I went over the edge of the shaft. Then our progress stopped; I heard Mr. Gentry clicking a gear that turned the eye up and into the other opening. He stopped at the grate through which I'd seen the walls of tufted fabric.

The mirrors within Sally reflected a soft light into the space. There, on a mattress on the floor, was my mother.

My view blurred as my eyes welled with tears. She was still sedated, her limbs slack in unconsciousness. Seeing her like this made me feel as if I was breaking inside. I pulled my face away, tears dripping onto the glass. She'd looked so close; I almost called out to her.

"You were right. It's her," I said. Mr. Gentry removed the glass from my head. I rubbed my sore temples. "Thank you, Mr. Gentry."

"You are most welcome, you are. But you must go now. Please hurry." He led me down the steps, waving me along.

"Don't want to get caught up here, no sirree."

I had to find out about the sulfuric acid without arousing Mr. Gentry's suspicion. He was so fearful of coming up even a gram short on his supply levels, I was afraid that if he knew what I was thinking, he would stop helping me entirely. I hated to lie to him, but I had no choice. As he escorted me to the entrance, I took a chance. "Mr. Gentry, the other night you mentioned the deadly properties of sulfuric acid. I'm curious—what could they possibly need it for here in the Tombs?"

"Sulfuric acid, you say?" He puffed up his chest. "Why, how do you think I got them through all the corroded iron doors when Dr. Spector reopened the lower levels? We ate right through them, we did!"

"Of course. Good night, Mr. Gentry," I said, and climbed onto the ladder, my blood tingling in excitement. I couldn't wait to tell Indigo.

Only, as I neared the grate at his room, I heard voices. Someone else was with him.

CHAPTER THIRTY-FIVE
FRESH SOURCE

Quietly, staying in the shadows, I peered through the bars. Indigo stood tensed, holding a loop of the chain attached to his shackle. A guard in a crow mask approached him slowly. When the guard was a few feet away, Indigo whipped the chain up, smashing it into the guard's leg. *Crack*. The guard fell, screaming, then scrambled away, out of my line of sight.

Slow methodical clapping sounded. "Well, well, well." *Spector!* "What's gotten into you tonight, boy? We have work to do, and you are wasting my time."

"I won't do it," Indigo said. "Use someone else's blood."

"But we have succeeded in creating the serum, you and I. And I've told you before, your blood is special, it's stronger. Why else do you think I give you all these privileges, treat you well?" Spector moved closer, coming into my view. Sweat broke out on my brow. My muscles stiffened. *What if he finds me?*

"You're sickening. Why are you doing this?"

"Indigo, haven't we been through this before?" Spector sighed, as if he were speaking to a headstrong child. "I have my reasons; the industrialists have theirs. But our objectives align beautifully."

"If it's my blood you want, let the others go. I heard a guard say you even have a *woman* imprisoned here. You don't need her." The realization hit me hard—Indigo knew I was hiding in the tunnel. He was talking about my mother.

Spector slowly tilted his head to each side, cracking his neck. His eyes sliced over the back of the room. I could tell he didn't like the idea of Indigo getting information from a guard. "You're right, I don't need her. I have a fresh source." *He means me.*

"I won't go with you." Indigo still held the section of chain, and now he began to swing it slowly back and forth.

Spector's voice strained, as if he was trying to stay under control. "Think carefully. I have recently acquired an albino friend of yours. She's quite young, isn't she? In the blossom of her youth. . . . Her face may never heal, but the rest of her will work."

"You swine," Indigo hissed. "She's just a little girl." But he released the chain, letting it fall with a loud clatter to the stone floor. "Don't . . . don't hurt her." Indigo fell still. His eyes flicked in my direction but in the next breath dropped to avoid giving me away.

"You see? You are powerless before me." Spector snapped his fingers. Behind him came two guards, who rushed at Indigo, grabbing his arms. The one he'd hit with the chain hobbled over, too, pulling a wooden nightstick from his belt. I pressed my fist to my mouth so I wouldn't make a sound as he lifted it in the air and smashed it into Indigo's thigh.

Indigo cried out and doubled over. Raising the club again, the guard brought it down onto Indigo's back. Indigo grunted, his whole body jerking from the impact. *No!* I willed them to stop, knowing I was powerless to help. The club cracked down onto Indigo's shoulder.

Did I put the fight back into Indigo, only to watch them beat it out of him?

"Enough," barked Spector, stopping the guard. He bent over, bringing his face close to Indigo's. "Maybe next time you'll make this easier on yourself." Spector spun on his heels and strode toward the door. "Bring him to the OR."

I waited until they were long gone before I dared move. Spector's words sounded in my head. *I have a fresh source.* He had moved my mother to the upstairs room because now he had me . . . my blood. *And he'll keep her as a hostage to use against me, just as he used Hurricane to get Indigo to submit.*

I crawled back to my room and burrowed under my blanket. Every noise in the hallway made me tense, every scratch of the pendulum grated on my nerves.

I watched the clock tick away the seconds. Only five

minutes had passed since the last time I looked. Time, like an evil enchanter, played by his own rules, stealing moments with sleight of hand or stretching them out on a torturous whim. And yet, because my father built clocks, it seemed it was always time that made me feel close to my family.

I rolled to my side and looked at the markings I'd made on the wall, to count down the days to the execution. Today was the eleventh. I had twenty-four hours before my scheduled bloodletting. I had to endure that, since the execution was scheduled for Saturday, November eighteenth.

One week.

A public execution in the prison courtyard was the only time the outside world breached the security of the Tombs. Mr. Gentry thought that maybe, by some miracle, and if all went according to plan, we could slip out with the crowd. And somehow figure out a way to stop Spector's evil plans.

But now Spector was drawing blood from Indigo. Given how I felt after Spector's sessions, would Indigo be capable and coherent enough to help me? And so far, Sally had been unable to locate anyone else.

To distract myself from worrying about the plan, my thoughts drifted to Khan and Indigo. When Khan had kissed me, it felt like home, sweet and familiar. But Khan always had a pretty girl on his arm—he attracted them like bees to honey. I knew he loved me in his own way, but did I want to risk our long years of friendship? And what about Katalina? Where did she fit into Khan's life?

Then there was Indigo. Being with him was like being caught in a storm, thunder and lightning crashing down around me. I felt alive, yes; the danger lit up my soul. Yet I could so easily get burned.

For now, I must restrain my impulses. Until I was out of this prison, I could not think of a future with either of them.

The morning nurse would arrive soon. Again the clock drew my eye. I imagined its inner workings, which Father so loved to show me: the pendulum swinging back and forth, attached to the escapement, which rocked in place, clicking the teeth of the power gears one by one, engaging the timekeeper gears that moved the hands—beautiful in its simplicity. The continuous and flawless motion was fascinating in a way. I heard my father's voice: "Without one part, the clock doesn't work, but together, it's precision and artistry."

It's like our escape plan, I thought. *If all the pieces don't come together, we're dead, or worse . . . stuck here forever.*

CHAPTER THIRTY–SIX
SPECIMENS

As the day wore on, my distress intensified. I was emotionally drained from my midnight excursion, leaving me anxious. The nurses seemed like cruel witches, their callous eyes hidden behind black goggled lenses. Even the food seemed vile. I could not stomach another chunk of nearly raw meat swimming in bloody juices.

Falling into a fitful sleep, I dreamt of Seraphine. She perched on my shoulder as I made my way down the halls of the Tombs. I was following a set of wet footprints. But the footprints changed to blood, and they were no longer made by feet, but by cloven hooves. I stopped, afraid to continue. My only comfort was Seraphine, but then her claws started to grow. They pierced my skin like meat hooks and sent blood running into my hospital gown. When I looked at her in hurt surprise, she opened her razor-sharp beak and plucked out my eyes.

I awoke in a puddle of sweat. The clock said one o'clock. Later today, Spector would come for me. I had to find out how Indigo was before then.

Damp and achy, I opened the grate. Like a giant rat in the tunnels, I knew exactly where to turn. Unfortunately, this was a maze with no exit. How I wished to hide from Spector in here. I could do it, but then all the plans would be ruined, and I would never escape.

When I got to Indigo's room, my heart sank. It was empty. I rubbed my eyes, the dust in the air shaft making them burn.

I turned to go when I heard a rumbling, grumbling noise coming from the tunnel to my left, one I had not yet ventured into. It took me a moment to realize it reminded me of my father's snoring. After checking to make sure I had enough string to keep from getting disoriented, I followed the sound.

Very quietly, I approached the flickering light of a lantern slanting through the bars of another wall grate. When I put my eye to the bars, I couldn't believe who I saw: Nelson Lemming, slumped over a tiny desk in an office of some sort. He was dressed in a rumpled maintenance uniform.

Part of me was desperate to know what had happened to him. Part of me wasn't so sure I could trust him. *But he might know about Hurricane.* I had to risk it.

"Mr. Lemming," I whispered. No response. "Wake up, Mr. Lemming."

"Hmm?" he muttered, eyes still closed.

"Mr. Lemming," I repeated.

He blinked a few times and stretched his arms out wide with a groan.

"Over here. It's Avery Kohl."

He sat bolt upright, looking around as if he were hearing a ghost. "Who said that? Someone there?"

"I'm here, behind the grate in the wall. Avery Kohl."

He lifted the lantern, approaching warily. When he saw me, his eyes opened wide. "Saints alive, what are you doing in the wall?"

"I was captured at the party," I whispered, hoping there were no other guards nearby.

"But how the devil did you get in *there*?" He peered through the grate to see the space beyond.

"I found a tunnel from my cell. I'm glad you're all right, Mr. Lemming."

"Yeah, thought I'd be dead by now. But after some questions, they decided to reassign me to a menial position in the hospital. I really had no choice but to take it. My shift ended a little while ago. I thought I'd slip in a little nap before I left. The bars on the windows of the caravan helped my cause. They thought I was being held prisoner by the Gypsies, which I suppose, technically, I was." He lowered his voice. "They never did find Jason's body."

"Mr. Lemming, do you know what happened to Hurricane, the little blond girl?" I held my breath. "Have you seen where Spector is keeping her?"

"I don't know for sure. But at the far end of Sub-Basement One are some out-of-the-way cells where Spector keeps captives he has no further use for." He shook his head. "Thought I'd end up there myself."

"I have to get back before they notice I'm gone. Can I ask something of you?" *Am I taking a risk?*

He nodded. "Anything." When I hesitated, he added, "You can trust me."

I shifted my sight and saw that he was indeed speaking the truth, but just in case . . . "Do you have pencil and paper?" I asked. He rummaged through a drawer and found something I could use. Using the special code my father and I shared, I wrote out the details of the escape plan. "All right. Please find my father, Edgar Kohl, and give him this." I folded the note, handing it through the bars, and told him the address of the shop. "Thank you, Mr. Lemming."

"Good luck," he said. Then he glanced at the door. "I aim to leave the city soon as I have the chance. And when I get far from here, out west maybe, I'm gonna get me another dog."

I smiled and turned to go, but thought of something else. His outerwear was tossed on a chair in the corner. "Mr. Lemming, if it's not asking too much, may I have your overcoat and hat? They'll come in very handy."

Without hesitation, he stuffed them through the bars.

Once back in my room, the hat and coat hidden in the tunnel, I broke down and cried. I was glad Mr. Lemming would get away from Spector, hopefully soon. But seeing him on the other side of the grate, free to walk out the door, was like seeing the night sky above the greenhouse: a glimpse of an uncertain freedom. If our plan failed, we'd never get another chance to escape.

They came for me at exactly nine o'clock in the morning. I heard the squeak of wheels in the hall and a key in the lock. Mrs. Luckett entered with a crow-guard. My skin tingled, cold and clammy, my breath coming in shallow gasps.

"It's all right, dear. Dr. Spector is in the operating room, all ready to go. It's a simple procedure, don't you worry." She grabbed my chart and nodded to the guard. He came forward and took my arm. I did not resist. My mind flashed to the time my mother ripped the tube from her arm to help me escape. It felt like another life. And here I was, trapped in the Tombs anyway.

"Thank you, Mrs. Luckett. I'm so nervous. How much blood do you think I will lose?"

I climbed onto the gurney, and Mrs. Luckett tucked the sheet around my trembling body.

She shook her head. "I'm sorry, I don't know."

As we moved down the hall, I stared at the wire snaking along the ceiling above my head, at the periodic bare electric bulbs. Inside each was a tiny glowing wire that emitted its feeble light. I missed the warm amber glow of the gaslight.

The crow-guard turned the gurney into the operating room, where Dr. Spector was waiting.

It was a round room of the same damp gray stone as the rest of the Tombs. A domed ceiling allowed for a large, multi-pronged apparatus to be suspended above a wooden table, crisscrossed by two sets of straps. The only light was that above the table.

On one side of the room was an elevated viewing platform shrouded in darkness. Something shifted there. Was someone watching? My skin crawled, and I felt sweat beading down my face and back.

"Sit up, please," the crow-guard said, voice muted behind the mask.

I pushed myself up, and he helped me onto the hard wooden table. Dark stains ran along the edges. A shudder ran through me.

The guard left and Mrs. Luckett transferred a blanket from the gurney to cover my legs as Dr. Spector hovered menacingly to the side. "Lie down, please," she said. The bright light hanging above me glared into my eyes, making it difficult to see.

Spector watched as she secured one strap around my legs and one around my body, pinning my arms by my sides.

"Very good," Spector said. His voice was shrill and scratchy. "It is so much easier when you do not resist. I am ready."

Mrs. Luckett smiled. "Yes, Doctor."

"Good day, Avery. I trust you have enjoyed your meals?" Spector asked, almost cordially.

What have I done? I couldn't stop shaking. Now that I was

here, I wished I'd hidden in the tunnels. "Please don't do this. Please . . . why are you taking my blood?" He'd said he used Indigo's blood in the serum. *Will he add mine as well?*

Mrs. Luckett lifted her chin, eyes widening, as if I was being insolent to the doctor. Spector himself ignored my question. He pulled a small table and chair up next to the operating table. "Nurse, set up the impeller."

She placed a brass instrument on the table. Two glass containers spanned either side of a pump-like device. Each container had a long rubber tube coming out of the top. A long metal needle protruded from the other end of the tube.

"Ready, dear? You'll feel a pinch." She jabbed the needle into my arm. It burned, as if she was pulling on my vein. She pressed the pump. Almost immediately, my blood flowed into the jar. Transfixed, I stared at the bright-red liquid, heard the *drip, drip, drip.*

Dr. Spector sat in the chair, placing his elbow on the table. He rolled up his sleeve. I watched with horror as the nurse inserted the other needle into his arm, as my blood flowed through a connector into the second canister and then on, into Dr. Spector.

"What . . . what are you doing? Why do you want my blood?" I shifted my sight, revolted as the energy surrounding my blood turned dark as it snaked toward Spector. He turned toward me and an image suddenly flashed across my mind: Spector as a young man, lying on the ground; his face and body scorched and smoking, disfigured; fire raging into the sky, enveloping a large mansion behind him; a crow hopping over as he writhed in agony; the crow plucking out his left eye. I squeezed my eyes shut. I'd never seen anything more disturbing, more horrific.

When I looked again, Spector seemed lost in the memory, his thin lips pressed tightly together. *He doesn't know I saw it.* I realized that, for one brief moment, as we shared a blood connection, he was not impenetrable.

I remembered the stuffed and mounted crow on his desk, wondering if it was the same one I'd seen in his memory. My eyelids fluttered and my thoughts fogged. I tried to speak, but my voice came out a whisper. "Nurse, help . . ."

Dr. Spector, leaning forward, murmured to me, "As I told you, science masters sorcery. It is with your very blood, and before you, your mother's, that I am immunized against the power of the seers."

Sensation returned first in my fingertips and toes. I moved them, trying to see if I was still alive. Where was I? Through my closed lids, I sensed a bright light on my face. Then I remembered: the operating table. I fought the urge to snap my eyes open. Someone else was in the room; I heard voices, talking, very near me. My muscles froze. I barely breathed as my ears strained to hear what was being said.

"—you think small, Spector. This serum will shift the balance of power, first in New York and its hinterland, then, in the nation. The waterborne transmission is ideal. I certainly could not have sold the serum in the form of a tranquilizer dart, like your earlier rendition. Although tempting"—a laugh—"we can't very well go around shooting our laborers."

There was no mistaking the contemptible voice of Ogden Boggs. He must have been in the viewing stand all along.

"This the wench that showed up uninvited to my little soiree?" he continued. I felt a warm, fat hand settle heavily upon my arm. It took every ounce of self-control to keep from flinching. I smelled his burnt-cigar breath roll over me, could feel him ogling me. "Pretty. What say you give me a few minutes alone with her, eh?"

Dr. Spector strode toward us, his shoes clicking sharply across the stone floor. "She is a valuable specimen, an anomaly. I appreciate you not contaminating her with your filthy hands." I was never so glad that Spector considered me valuable, specimen or no.

"Shame." Boggs removed his fingers. "Ah well. We are close, Spector. Very soon I'll announce a run for office. And when I win, you will receive the recognition you deserve." He clapped his hands, swishing them together as if wiping off any misdeeds. "No more hiding in the shadows. No more secret meetings of the Commerce League. I will lead us to greatness."

I heard the squeaky iron wheels of a cart and a tinkling of glass. "My science will speak for itself," Spector stated matter-of-factly. "Here is the fresh batch you requested. Next time, give me more notice for an order of this magnitude. I practically had to drain my best specimen, and it is an exacting process to extract the drug from the plant."

"I don't care how you make the serum, Spector. Just remember, you're nothing without me. I am the one people trust, not you." What seemed like a strained silence settled over them as they proceeded into the hallway, taking the cart with them.

My heart wrenched as their words registered. Spector said he'd almost drained his best specimen. He was talking about Indigo. And Boggs was obviously spreading this controlling serum throughout the city. They must be stopped.

CHAPTER THIRTY–SEVEN
THE PADDED CELL

A nurse I'd never seen before woke me with a scowl on her ashen face. "Food's on the side table," she said in a gruff voice as she strode toward the door.

I felt as if an omnibus had hit me. "Wait . . . what is the date today?"

"What do I look like, your personal secretary?" She had her hand on the knob.

"Please!" I sat up as a flash of fear tensed my muscles. What if I'd slept through the execution? "I beg of you."

"Compose yourself, young lady. It's Wednesday the fifteenth. Now if you don't mind, I've got work to do."

I felt a sudden surge of dizziness. Closing my eyes, I slumped back down and took a deep breath. I still had three days, but I was as weak as I was when I'd first arrived at the Tombs.

I have to regain my strength—and fast.

I closed my eyes and tried to focus on my breathing. But I could not do it. I tried to shift my sight; I failed.

What if Spector had taken away my ability? I wished suddenly, fiercely, that I could talk to my mother. My mind slipped again, thoughts still fuzzy. All I could think about was sleep. Before drifting off, I forced myself to eat.

I finally awoke feeling somewhat myself. Hands in front of me, I immediately concentrated on my third eye. Light shimmered around my fingers. I let out a long sigh, as I focused harder. Why couldn't I cause another explosion? It would solve everything if I could blast my way out of here. When I felt my ability sufficiently honed, I watched the clock until all was dead quiet in the halls.

Two nights left. Nothing mattered now but our plan. I had to sneak into Mr. Gentry's greenhouse and "borrow" a few drops of his sulfuric acid. But first I needed to see Indigo.

He was curled into a fetal position on the hard floor, long hair falling across his eyes. If I'd felt weak from a small amount of blood drawn, I could not imagine how Indigo must be faring. While he slept, his face lost its hard edge, the self-loathing he carried in his eyes. I felt sure he'd passed out here instead of on his bed so he'd be nearer to the grate, nearer to me. I wanted to kiss the shadow below his pouted lower lip, the tiny line across his right brow where hair did not grow, and the smooth raised scar on his chest.

I sent him healing thoughts and quietly made my way to the greenhouse, careful not to bang the lantern on the ladder as I sometimes did. Silently, I pulled myself up and waited, listening, until my eyes adjusted. I'd left the lantern hanging in the shaft, so Mr. Gentry would not see it.

Soon enough, I heard snoring coming from the tree house. The moon cast a silver light on the greenery; it was not hard to find the workbench, nor the tiny bottle of acid. It looked so innocent, like golden honey. *How could this eat through iron?*

Wrapping the glass jar in a torn piece of blanket, I carried it, very carefully, back down the ladder.

Throughout the night I practiced my sight, building its strength, increasing the speed with which I could slip into it. My second sight felt as sharp as a hatpin.

Time seemed to mock me with the slow scratch of the pendulum. Friday night could not have arrived fast enough.

This was it. *One step at a time.*

My every nerve tingled as I plumped my pillows into a long shape on the bed and covered it with the sheets and blankets. Pulling the grate closed behind me, I left the room, hoping it was for the last time. With the tiny glass bottle cradled in my hand, I made my way to Indigo's room.

I swung the grate open, gently touching his face to push back his hair. His eyes flew open and he snatched my wrist with bruising strength. I sucked in my breath. If he'd grabbed my other hand, I might've dropped the bottle. As soon as he focused on my face, he released me.

"Avery." He let out his breath, as did I. "I thought . . . maybe Spector . . ."

"Shhh, the guards will hear us." I held up the little bottle.

"What is that?" He sat up, massaging his temples. "My head is killing me."

"Sulfuric acid. Supposedly, it will eat through iron, and you, if we're not careful."

We moved his bed back a few feet and stretched out the heavy chain. *Please don't let me burn off his foot.* I knelt and tentatively dripped the viscous yellow liquid onto the link closest to the shackle.

"It's not doing anything," Indigo whispered.

My heart sank. I'd expected it to work immediately. "Let me think. They used it to eat through the rusted iron doors. Something must cause a reaction." What did the old doors and flesh have in common? A possibility came to me, but could it be that simple? Maybe it was the dampness Mr. Gentry had gone on about. I retrieved the pitcher of water from Indigo's night table.

"Pray I'm right." I poured a small trickle of water onto the iron link. The yellow liquid began to bubble, then turned smoky black. The fumes were horrible, like rotten eggs. "Ugh!" I waved my hand in the air.

Indigo swiped a blanket off the bed. "Quick, put this over your nose and mouth!"

We breathed through the blanket as, little by little, the sizzling acid ate down into the iron. In a matter of minutes, the thick link was reduced to a black puddle on the floor.

Indigo jumped up. "Holy shit! It worked!" He glanced my way. "Sorry . . ."

I covered my mouth to suppress a laugh. "It's okay. Keep your voice down. We don't want to get caught now."

Jubilant, he wrapped his arms around me and pulled me to him. I felt his hand weave into my hair as he tilted my head back and pressed his mouth hard against mine. His touch was like fire, like the sulfuric acid on the iron. Breaking the kiss, he held me out by my shoulders, my lips throbbing.

"Avery, we are going to get out of here."

I smiled at his sudden burst of enthusiasm, freed along with his foot.

He pushed the cuff up his shin to don his boots. We'd have to deal with that later. He gave me his extra pair of shoes. They were big, but better than running around in my socks. He also had a couple of old hooded cloaks and some clothing he'd grown out of over the years. Luckily, Dr. Spector did not want his prized specimen freezing to death in the thin prison uniforms.

"It's strange," Indigo said, as he stuffed the cloaks and clothes, Lemming's coat and hat, and the piece of pipe into a burlap sack. "You've brought time back to me. Days and weeks had stretched into eternity. Sometimes I'd learn entire months had gone by without me realizing it. And now every second is alive. I'd even given up trying to take control of Spector's mind. He has a wall in his brain that I am not able to penetrate. Do you know they wear the goggles to protect themselves from us? All but him."

"I know. His mind is an immoral pit of darkness. There was a moment when I did reach through—but there's so much else to share with you, and now is not the time." I wanted to tell Indigo what was happening, what Spector and Boggs were doing to the people of New York, pitting them against each other . . . controlling them with the serum from his blood. But there would be time to discuss all that later.

We lifted Indigo's bed and set it down over the evidence from the acid. We made a rough body shape on top of the bed, then tucked the dissolved end of the chain under the mattress. We softly closed the grate behind us. Indigo hoisted the sack over his shoulder and followed me on hands and knees through the tunnels. Carrying the bottle of acid carefully, I held the lantern up, lighting our way.

We reached the ladder to the botanical lab. With boots, I had no trouble climbing, and as we ascended, I told Indigo what I knew about his family—that Katalina and his father were well. He grew quiet at the thought of them. I couldn't imagine being alone in this horrific place since the age of thirteen, torn away from loved ones.

We reached the top, and I poked my head into Mr. Gentry's lair.

"Hello, Miss Avery, hello. You're here, just as we planned." Gentry sat cross-legged on the floor by the opening, as if he'd been waiting there all night.

"Oh, Mr. Gentry, you startled me!" I pocketed the vial of sulfuric acid before I ascended further.

He jumped up as we climbed into the room. "You must be Master Indigo. I am Hanover Gentry, at your service." He pumped Indigo's hand. Indigo nodded and looked around, eyes wide and mouth open.

"This is so terribly exciting. Most fun I've had since . . . " Mr. Gentry rubbed his bristly beard. "Fifteen years ago, when a python arrived with one of the specimen plants and escaped into the mess hall. Oh, yes indeedy, must've been six feet long, it was."

"I'm glad *you're* excited. I'm scared to death." I brushed dirt off my pants legs.

"The nurse will come by shortly," Mr. Gentry said. "In the meantime, Mr. Indigo, I must introduce you to Pepper, my parrot."

"You go ahead," I said. "I'll wait here."

They moved away; I dashed to the workbench and replaced the bottle. I hoped Spector would not examine the chain or find the puddle any time soon, and Mr. Gentry would never discover I'd deceived him, or get into trouble because of me. I sprinted back just in time.

"Come, come, quickly now, no time to waste." Mr. Gentry led us to the locked door leading into the hall, popping something into his mouth as we walked. Indigo and I hid behind the nearest trees as he banged on the door. Moments later, I heard a dour voice speak to him through the window. The nurse couldn't possibly see him, as his head was considerably below the height of the glass.

"What's it now, Gentry? Go to sleep. It's late."

"Ah, the lovely Nurse Babbage. I was hoping you'd come. I need your kind nursing skills. I've hurt my arm, I have."

"Go to sleep." She knocked on the glass. "Tough it out till morning."

"Oh dear, I think it's broken." He moaned for emphasis. "How can I work with a broken arm?" He was such a bad actor; it would surprise me if the nurse fell for it. But she did.

"For God's sake." Keys jiggled. The door pushed in. "Now, how'd you go breaking your arm at this hour? I've got more important things to do than swaddle your injuries."

She entered the dimly lit room, the door closing behind her. Mr. Gentry cradled his left arm. She stooped to have a look. But as she got close, he swung his right fist, stabbing her neck with a long syringe. Mr. Gentry stepped back as Nurse Babbage gasped, swiping at the tube of glass embedded into her skin, knocking her goggles askew. Wide-eyed, she slowly stilled and dropped her arms. Her white uniform matched the pale cast of her face.

I stared at Mr. Gentry, aghast. Even though I'd known what he planned to do, he was savage in his execution.

He beamed, waving us out of our hiding spot. I approached

him warily, as he removed his gloves and tossed them aside. "I chewed some coca leaves to get up my courage, yes I did. Didn't want to use the serum, but she's a mean one, she is. Even so, I gave her the smallest dose I could." He fidgeted with his shirt-sleeves. "That should do it, yes sirree."

We'd debated having Indigo use his powers of persuasion to get the nurse to do what we wanted, but we knew he'd have to get her goggles off first. If she screamed, the guards would come running. We'd decided this was safer.

Mr. Gentry spoke to the nurse. "Nurse Babbage, please bend down."

She lowered her head, and Mr. Gentry removed the syringe.

Indigo ran his hands through his hair. "Is this what Spector is doing with my blood?" he snarled.

"Yes, yes it is." I walked the nurse away from the window. "Nurse Babbage," I said, "I'm sorry, but I need you to remove your uniform."

Indigo and Mr. Gentry turned their backs, giving us at least an illusion of privacy. I was terrified the drug wouldn't last, that at any moment she would cry out. But obediently, she removed her belt, hat, and goggles. Unbuttoning her long white coat, she stepped out of it, letting it puddle to the floor. She stood in her shift and drawers, unaware of her surroundings. I wrapped a blanket around her shoulders and asked her to sit down in a chair we had provided. Then I removed her boots.

I got a pit in my stomach thinking about Tony and the other

workers around the city who would do whatever they were told once they drank from the water fountains. And when the serum wore off in the evenings, they would not remember anything odd about their long day of hard labor.

I buttoned Nurse Babbage's long coat over my clothing and replaced my boots with hers. I fastened her belt at my waist, pinned the crisp hat onto my head, and lastly, pulled the goggles over my head.

"I'm ready." Smoothing my hair back, I lowered the goggles over my eyes.

Mr. Gentry clapped his hands. "You look perfect, you do. They'll never know."

One step at a time, I repeated to myself.

I removed Nurse Babbage's keys from her belt and opened the door. The hall was clear. I stepped out. With only night-lights to guide me, I proceeded slowly toward the door at the far end of the hall, almost holding my breath the whole way.

My hands trembled as I fit the key into the lock of my mother's room.

There was a lantern inside the door. I raised the wick just enough to see her. She was still sleeping on the mattress on the floor. The walls were covered with thick cotton batting, just as I'd seen when I looked through Sally's eye. Heart bursting with emotions, I knelt by her side. It seemed like an eternity since I'd resolved to get her out of the Tombs. Now that the moment was here, I almost couldn't move, with the weight of it.

My vision blurred as tears filled my eyes. I pushed the goggles up so I wouldn't scare her.

Gently, I placed my hand on her arm. "Mother, it's me, Avery."

She would not wake up.

CHAPTER THIRTY-EIGHT
THE DARKNESS INSIDE

Mr. Gentry had given me smelling salts in anticipation of my mother being unresponsive. My hand shook as I uncorked the small red bottle and waved it under her nose. Her nostrils twitched. I gave it another pass, closer this time. She lifted her hand and rubbed her nose, then opened her eyes a slit. I could tell she was still far away.

"Mother, it's Avery. Can you hear me?" I rubbed her arm.

She nodded groggily as I helped her to her feet.

"I'm going to walk you down the hall. Don't say a word." Confusion swept over her face, but she let me lead her to the door. I lowered the goggles.

The hallway seemed twice as long now. I had my hand on Mr. Gentry's doorknob when I saw a guard in uniform and mask approaching. I kept my eyes on the floor, silently willing him to pass me by.

Instead, he stopped. "Nurse, do you need assistance?"

"No, thank you. I'm fine."

Through the dark lenses, he studied my face, then gave a careful look to my ill-fitting outfit. "May I ask why you are bringing her in there?" His head tipped toward Mr. Gentry's conservatory—but as he spoke, the door flew open. My mother and I fell aside in a heap as Indigo burst out. I scrambled inside, dragging my mother behind me. Mr. Gentry pushed the door shut. Indigo had his arm around the neck of the guard, and he shoved him into the atrium, slamming the door behind him. Pulling off the guard's mask, Indigo clamped his hand over the guard's mouth.

The guard struggled to push Indigo away, but Indigo never broke his steady gaze. The guard stilled. Slowly, Indigo removed his hand from the man's mouth. The guard walked over to the wall and stood placidly, as if awaiting instruction.

"Why did you do that?" I hissed.

"I had to. I heard him question you. He would've sounded an alarm." Indigo folded his arms over his chest.

"Oh dear. Oh deary me." Mr. Gentry shrunk behind some bushes. "This just won't do. I knew this was a mistake, it was." He stared at Indigo as if he had horns.

"Trust me, these guards are highly suspicious. He would not have let her go." Indigo paced back and forth. "I'll make sure he doesn't remember a thing. He won't give you away, Mr. Gentry."

"Well, it's done now." My mother tried to push herself up.

Swiftly, Indigo lifted her and carried her to the pile of burlap sacks we'd laid out deep inside the greenhouse. I covered her with a blanket. Her eyes were half closed and she still hadn't spoken. Mr. Gentry bustled over, then lifted her eyelids and felt her pulse. Overwhelmed, I sank to the floor, clutching her hand. "Will she be all right? What's wrong with her?"

"Yes, yes, I believe so. I'm not a doctor, mind you, but I've seen the effects of plenty of vile substances, I have. She has good color."

We had to hope she revived soon. While Indigo kept a lookout, I untied my mother's hospital gown, then covered her up with blankets and slid it out from under her. She was so frail.

Next, I nervously escorted Nurse Babbage, in my mother's hospital gown, to the padded cell. The gown was considerably shorter and tighter on her large frame than on my mother's. It gave me a strange feeling, to control another human being, an unpleasant fluttering in my stomach. *How vulnerable and defenseless this serum makes people.*

In my mother's cell, I removed the hospital gown from Nurse Babbage, hoping she wasn't too cold in her undergarments. I tucked her into bed and covered her up to her neck. Then I took out the syringe Mr. Gentry had given me and tapped the needle. Fluid spurted out. I squeezed the nurse's arm until her vein swelled beneath her skin. Just in case she could hear me, I whispered, "Nurse Babbage, this is a harmless sleeping draught. Please don't be afraid. When it wears off, you'll be fine and won't remember how you got here or what happened to you this night."

I punctured her skin and pumped the liquid in. Then I locked the door and left.

By the time I returned to the conservatory, my heart was racing. Now wearing the black pants and shirt of the crow-guard, Indigo led the real guard, in union suit and socks, toward the air shaft. Seeing him control someone with only his mind also unnerved me. It was difficult to comprehend.

Mr. Gentry ran off to make himself some tea. I slid the hospital gown back over my mother's thin, bruised arms and exhaled long and deep. *The first part of our task is done.*

The next one would be harder.

I gently pushed Mother's amber hair back from her forehead. My mind felt jumbled. On the one hand, I felt incredibly grateful she was still alive. On the other, I knew it was up to me to keep her that way. A wave of indecisiveness came over me. *Am I doing the right thing? Am I risking all our lives?* But there was more than our own lives at stake, and I had no choice but to keep going.

The crow mask lay by some bushes. It taunted me with its hollow eyes. Acting on impulse, I went over and picked it up. The leather was smooth and hard. I ran my fingers along the long curved beak, feeling each rivet down to the tip, a sharp metal point. I touched the small scar on my chest where one of these beaks had punctured my skin at the party. My pulse quickened. Slowly, I raised it to my face, pulled the strap over my head, and adjusted it tight. It swallowed me. The darkness inside was complete except for the dim light seeping through the filtered goggle lenses. My trapped face began to sweat. I couldn't breathe.

My fingers touched a seam underneath and pressed it inward, creating a slit for air. I took a deep breath, forcing my heart to calm.

I walked around, testing the weight of it on my head. I felt secretive. I felt powerful. I imagined I was capable of unspeakable acts, hidden as I was behind this mask. *Do all of us have a dark side? Could we lose ourselves to it if we hide behind a mask such as this? Like the Ku Klux Klan*, I thought. My father had taught me about the Klan. Formed by Confederate veterans down in Tennessee, they used fear and violence to terrorize people. They'd never commit such atrocities without the anonymity of their pointy white hoods.

Suddenly, I had to get it off. I pushed the mask up and tossed it away. It stared at me knowingly, its evil birdlike gaze unflinching. I hunched over, breathing hard, my throat still constricted from the stale smell of leather and sweat.

"Avery." Indigo put his hand on my back. "Are you all right?"

I couldn't explain what I'd seen through those lenses. Shaking my head, I scooted over to sit with my mother.

Mr. Gentry returned and joined me, cradling his teacup. "Sally and I went a-searching last night. We think we found your blond friend, we do, just where you said to look."

"What?" I sat up straight. "You mean Hurricane?"

"Yes indeedy. I do indeed."

Mr. Lemming had been right; she was in the abandoned cells. Unfortunately, Sally did not find the boy. We decided Indigo would take the guard's mask and go down through the tunnels to Hurricane's cell. Mr. Gentry gave him some serum darts, in case he encountered trouble.

According to our plan, Indigo also had to get into the morning room where the crow-guards, doctors, and nurses gathered before their shifts, for coffee and tea. Using Boggs's own tactic, Indigo would poison all the water to, hopefully, prevent anyone from being capable of sounding an alarm. In the absence of any direction, Mr. Gentry thought they would wander around placidly, before being summoned to the execution. Indigo would lock the guard whose uniform he took in a cell to be discovered later so that Mr. Gentry would not be implicated.

"Please be careful." I hugged my arms to my chest. "We will be waiting. We must leave here at *exactly* five o'clock in the morning."

"Avery." Indigo took my face in his hands. "Promise me: if I'm not back in time, you will go without me."

"I'm not going to leave—"

"Promise me," he repeated, his voice urgent. "I must hear you say it."

I looked at my mother. Whatever was in her system had weakened her. Curled up on her bed of burlap, she was rail thin, the dark skin under her eyes sunken. I had to get her out of here before the Tombs took her life. I breathed deeply and told Indigo what he wanted to hear. "I promise."

Indigo leaned down and grazed my lips with his, a kiss so light it felt like the wings of a butterfly. Then I watched him disappear down the dark hole of the air shaft, followed by the guard in his long johns.

In his absence, Mr. Gentry and I sat down and went over the plan one more time. He'd secured Pepper to his shoulder, just as I used to do with Seraphine. On occasion, he even brought Pepper into the conversation.

"People are flocking to the city, yes they are." Mr. Gentry pointed up at the lights of the airships clustered above us.

"Mr. Gentry, why do you suppose so many people want to come see an execution?" I shuddered at the thought.

"Well, it is Norman Bale, after all. I even heard about it in here, I did. It was all the talk of the prison yard."

"Norman Bale?" I remembered Khan telling me the rally was because of anger over what he'd done.

"Righty-o. It's not often a wealthy industrialist is sentenced to the gallows, no sirree. Those poor little sisters that worked for him . . . 'Tis no wonder the people of the city want to see him hang, no wonder at all," Mr. Gentry said. "I'd like to watch it myself, if I could."

"Mr. Gentry, tell me again what happens at the execution."

"Very soon, the gallows will be assembled in the machine room on this floor. Early next morning, they pull it out into the courtyard. Quite the contraption, it is. Eight a.m. sharp, old Norman is taken to the Criminal Court Building for formal sentencing, yes sir." He ticked the items off on his fingers as he went. "The gate opens to let in the spectators. Bale is brought back over the bridge, his last look at the world. Might be heckling and flying tomatoes. Then they hang him, yes sirree, and that's about it."

"I hope a lot of people come."

"You know, out on the street, folks sell food and ale like it's a party, they do. You won't get out until it's over, when the crowd is allowed to leave, no way." Mr. Gentry yawned loudly. "Time for some shut-eye. Come along, Pepper."

With the tranquility of the greenhouse enveloping us, I squirreled under the blanket next to my mother, taking comfort in her presence. I watched the green lights of the airships hovering in the sky above us, listening to the *drip, drip, drip* of the lab's watering device and the loud snores coming from the tree house. My mother and I had a lot of lost time to make up. I couldn't let anything go wrong. Tomorrow, I would need all my strength.

My eyelids grew heavy.

The next thing I knew, I opened them to a sense that something was wrong. It took me one second to remember where I was, and another to realize my mother was gone.

CHAPTER THIRTY-NINE
THE GALLOWS

A violent storm of thoughts burst into my head, and I leapt up as if I'd been struck by lightning. *Where is she?*

The storm was not only in my head. Rain battered the ceiling, as if nature were trying to shatter the glass above. Without the moonlight, the lab was a nightmare of shifting shadow, the loud drumming of the rain echoing throughout the space.

What if she accidentally stumbles across the devil's breath flowers?

"Mother? Where are you?" I listened, but the downpour drowned everything out.

As my eyes adjusted, I saw light filtering through the branches and followed a path through the greenery toward it. Pushing aside a thick curtain of leaves, I entered—to my amazement—an outdoor kitchen of sorts. My mother sat at a table, head in her hands. Mr. Gentry bustled about, pouring tea and stirring a pot. He rattled on to her, unaware that her eyes were glazed over and she probably couldn't hear a word he said. It was such a surreal picture that it put me completely out of sorts. "Mother?"

She didn't answer, but Mr. Gentry came over and escorted me to the table. I decided we must be under the tree house where Mr. Gentry slept. A lantern hung from above, lighting the space with a soft amber glow.

"Found her wandering around, I did. Nearly frightened me to death. She looks a little ghostly, does she not?"

She looked to me like a lost little girl, hair hanging down, parted in the middle. It made my heart hurt, I wanted to protect her so. Mr. Gentry placed a steaming bowl of porridge in front of me, which I ate ravenously. My mother did not touch hers.

"Thank you," I said, my mouth full. "How much longer do we have? Has Indigo returned?"

"No," Mr. Gentry said. He sat across from me with his tea. "No, I'm afraid he has not. But we must get you out of here in exactly thirty minutes, no more, no less."

"Mr. Gentry." I turned to face him. "Why don't you come with us?"

He stared at his cup so long I thought he was ignoring the question. Finally, he looked up, first at my mother, then at me. "I cannot; no, this is my home, it is. Sally and I hear about the world beyond these walls. It is no longer a world I understand."

I thought about the Civil War that had torn the country apart. Brothers killing brothers, the newspapers reporting at least half a million men dead, hatred still dividing the nation. And all the while, Mr. Gentry had been cloistered away safely in his greenhouse. I nodded. I understood why he would not leave.

While we waited, I repacked the burlap sack, adding an extra blanket, two pairs of small canvas shoes from Mr. Gentry, and a canteen of water. The seconds ticked by, the three of us staring at the opening where Indigo had gone last night.

"It is time; the time is now," Mr. Gentry said after a while.

We had a little over an hour between the completion of the gallows and the movement of that terrible device into the courtyard. We could not wait for Indigo any longer.

My mother removed the blanket she had wrapped around her body and stood by the door in her hospital gown and knit socks. Her bruises stood out like inkblots on her pale skin. My heart twisted at the thought of leaving Indigo and Hurricane, but a glance at my mother's frail form reinforced my determination to get her out of here.

I adjusted my bun and nurse's cap, neat and tight. Then I pulled the goggles down over my eyes. This was it. We had to go. My nerves were raw, but I felt alive, ready, as if all my senses were on alert.

"We're getting out of here, Mother. Don't talk to anyone. Just go along with whatever I do, all right?"

Her watery eyes searched mine, but she nodded.

"Thank you, Mr. Gentry." I smiled at him. "I couldn't have done this without you."

My mother stumbled forward and gave him a gentle hug. "Thank you," she whispered in a still-groggy voice.

With one last glance at the shaft, I opened the door and looked both ways down the hall. There was one guard at the far end, opposite from where we had to go. When his back was turned, we slipped out into the hall, my nerves sizzling. I held on to my mother as if she was too weak to walk, which was probably the case. We had to be careful not to go too fast, even though the urge to run quivered up my legs.

Our first test came as we turned the corner. A guard was heading our way. I guided my mother to the opposite side of the hall and kept my head down.

"Come on." I filled my voice with forced impatience. "Let's get you washed up. I don't have all day."

It worked. The guard passed with barely a glance. We were almost there. I hoped Mr. Gentry had the timing right. His directions, at least, seemed perfect. One more corner and there should be a set of louvered doors. We turned down the hall. *Yes; there on the right.*

Ahead of us, another nurse guided an old man down the hall, their backs to us. And beyond that, two guards stood talking. We fell into step behind the nurse and patient, perfectly shielded from the guards and thankful for the dim hallway lighting.

The moment we were upon the louvered doors, I gripped the handle and pushed one open. We ducked inside, and I closed the door as quickly and quietly as I could.

We were in a tall-ceilinged mechanical room. The smell reminded me of the Works, all grease and hot steel. If I closed my eyes, I could almost feel at home. Flickering light from an overhead lamp glinted on the metal machinery around us.

Just as Mr. Gentry had described, we stood before the gallows. It was an angry contraption of wood and metal, the top of the platform high above our heads. Two mammoth posts held a beam, from which hung the noose. My body went rigid at the sight. Gently, my mother squeezed my hand in reassurance, but I felt her shaking beside me, from fear or cold I couldn't be sure.

I lifted my goggles. Mother took the sack out from under her hospital gown, and I helped her change into Indigo's old clothes and Mr. Gentry's shoes. I changed as well, lacing Indigo's boots tight, and then stuffed the nurse's uniform into the bag.

The sides of the platform were made of panels of slotted wood. We walked around the perimeter, searching for a way underneath. But there was no opening. It occurred to me that we could pull the lever and open the trapdoor, but what if the noise was heard or we could not shut it once inside? No, we had to find another way.

"I'll be right back." I ran over to a workbench and sorted through the tools until I found what I was looking for.

Next to the bench was a pile of scrap metal. I pulled out two short lengths of L-shaped steel angle iron. Working quickly, I unfastened the bolts holding one of the panels in place. We could easily fit through the two-foot-wide opening. Turning it sideways, I pushed the panel through the hole and laid it on the floor under the gallows. Back at the workbench, I slipped my arms through a work coat someone had left behind, put on my goggles, and picked up a welding gun, still warm from earlier use. I climbed inside the gallows platform with the tools. My mother quietly watched me, her mouth slack.

Gripping a steel bar in one hand, I pulled the trigger, sparking the gun to life. I welded one bar to the top of the steel frame of the platform, and one to the bottom, creating a track upon which to slide the wood panel. Then I returned everything to its place at the bench, except for a small pointy awl and a screwdriver that I thought we might use as weapons. "Come on, let's get in," I whispered hoarsely to my mother.

We crawled through the opening. "Hold that side." I pointed to the wooden panel. On our knees, we lifted it up, slipped it into the tracks I'd created, and closed ourselves in. "Now we wait."

I removed my goggles and wiped the sweat from my face. My mother sat on the floor and held out the bag of extra clothes; I tossed the goggles in. She lifted the canteen and drank heartily. "Avery . . ." She studied the welded steel, her eyes wide in disbelief. "How in God's name did you know how to do that?"

"Mother, I see you're feeling better."

"My head has cleared somewhat but I feel quite weak." She handed me the water and I took a sip.

"One day I'll show you the place I work . . . or used to. You won't believe it." Even as I said this, I wondered if I would ever go back to the Works. Try as I might, I could not imagine what life was going to be like once we were out of the Tombs. *If* we made it out. "Here, hold on to this." I gave her the awl. "I hope you won't need it."

She was about to respond when we heard a sound. I held up my hand and put my eye to a slit between the wood slats. A crow-guard had entered the room, and his evil pointy beak was staring in our direction.

CHAPTER FORTY
THE EXECUTION
OF NORMAN BALE

The guard held a hooded prisoner by the arm. Was Bale being shown his imminent future? Or maybe this was a cruel test to make sure the gallows worked properly in front of the public. I held my finger to my lips and whispered, "Shhh."

At any moment, the outside door would open and the gallows would be pulled out into the courtyard. Footsteps approached our hiding place. We stiffened.

The guard bent down, his goggled eyes searching the darkness below the platform. "Avery? Are you in there?"

It was Indigo. I took a deep breath. *He must have found Hurricane!*

Just then another sound vibrated through the floor, up into my body. The outside door was opening. "Avery!" Panic swept through Indigo's voice.

"This way!" I slid the wood panel open. Indigo pushed his prisoner through and climbed in after.

I closed the panel just as bright fingers of daylight reached into the room, banding the slatted wood of our hiding place like a window blind.

The prisoner let out a muffled cry. Quickly, Indigo lifted his crow mask, letting it hang from his neck, and removed the sack from over the prisoner's head. *Thank goodness!* It *was* Hurricane.

Her face was bruised and swollen, almost unrecognizable. My heart wrenched at the thought of someone doing this to her. I placed a hand on her arm—it was all I could offer at the moment. She lifted her eyes, tears welling in them.

My mother held a hand over her mouth as though she wanted to cry out.

A grinding hum stayed any conversation or questions I had for Indigo, but relief at his sudden appearance comforted me like a warm shawl on my shoulders. I crept to the other side of the platform and peered out. Two enormous doors were sliding open on tracks that resembled those at the barn where my father used to board our horse. I blinked in the gray morning light, but could not peel my eyes from my first real view of the outside world since I'd been captured.

The courtyard beyond was empty, save for a rank of blue-uniformed police officers with guns strapped to their waists and swords across their backs. A soft rain misted the cobblestones.

The officers led a team of horses through the opening and hitched them to a crossbar. Their hooves stomped and scraped on the stones as the officers urged them forward into the court-yard. Slowly the chains lifted off the floor and the gallows jerked forward, its metal wheels squealing loudly in protest. The wood posts and beam overhead creaked and groaned, as if aware of their deathly duty.

Inch by inch, the gallows moved. We moved with it, praying the shadows would keep us hidden. If we were discovered now, we would be trapped, with no way to escape.

The horses were unhitched and led away. Four officers remained, one at each corner of the gallows. Cold air whistled through the wooden slats; rain dripped coldly onto our heads and backs. Our boots sat in muddy puddles, but I was glad for the steady patter, to mask the sound of our breathing. Silently, I handed my mother a wool cloak and gave Hurricane some clothing from the sack. I wished I had another cloak. Instead, she wrapped the blanket around her tiny frame. I tied the other cloak over my shoulders. The crow-guards would sooner recognize me than Hurricane.

Eight o'clock was shrilly announced by a bugle call in the distance, the forlorn notes hanging in the sodden air. Boots pounded militantly from one side of the bridge to the other. They must be taking Norman Bale to the courthouse.

The next two hours crept by achingly slow. Crouching low, I felt my muscles cramp and stiffen. Pain shot up my legs.

I worried my mother or Hurricane would faint from the strain. When Hurricane started to shake in the frigid air, Indigo put his arm around her. Now and then, he and I exchanged a look, his dazzling eyes the only thing keeping *me* warm inside.

Another barrage of stomping boots, closer this time, pricked my attention. A cluster of prison officers passed by; moments later, the shuffling and shouts of the spectators drew near, as if they were jostling for the best view of the scaffold. The rain had not kept folks from coming out to see the infamous Norman Bale.

The gallows platform was engulfed in a sea of commotion, the four of us finally able to shift positions and massage the numbness from our limbs amidst the tumult in the courtyard. Indigo untied his crow mask and shoved it into a corner. He slid his arms into the black frock coat and derby that I'd gotten from Mr. Lemming. Hurricane put on the last pair of canvas shoes. She'd have to hold the blanket over her head like a hood, but even still, I was afraid it would not hide the terrible bruises on her face.

We had to hope for a chance to slip into the crowd. This was the part that had my head spinning. *How will we open the panel and emerge without being seen?*

Another hour must have easily slipped by. No opportunity arose. In whispers, I briefly introduced Indigo and Hurricane to my mother, and Indigo told me what he'd accomplished. Wearing the mask, he'd snuck into the morning room before anyone arrived. He'd poured the serum into every pot and jug he could find. Then he'd found Hurricane, just where Mr. Gentry had said she'd be.

"It must have worked, or we would've heard an alarm by now," I said.

Indigo added, "I looked for the boy you told me about. I'm sorry. He wasn't there."

Just when I felt I would jump out of my skin, I heard shouting somewhere near the entrance gate.

"It bit me!" screamed a woman's voice.

"Kill the bugger," shouted a man. "There, up there!"

More cries sounded. Through the slats, I saw officers rush by to stem the commotion. "Calm yourselves," they ordered. "What's the problem here?"

Amid the confusion, there was a loud knock on the wood. I jumped and looked at Indigo, his eyes as wide as mine.

Then I heard Katalina's voice. I'd know it anywhere. "Come out, quickly!"

How did she know? I took a deep breath, gave everyone a final once-over, and slid open the panel. One by one, we stood up under a black umbrella that shielded us from the crowd. I took the handle, keeping Hurricane tight to my side, and closed the panel. Katalina handed Indigo and my mother identical black umbrellas. *Brilliant*, I thought.

"This way," Katalina whispered, "quickly." She wore a thick black cloak and held a tapestry bag. We followed her toward the center of the throng. Everywhere I looked were similar black umbrellas and capes; I realized the rain was helping to hide us.

We were in a large open space, tall prison walls on two sides, the courthouse on another, and only one gate to the street. Tilting my head, I made out the looming shadows of the dirigibles floating nearby. But the spattering rain quickly forced my eyes down, and the umbrellas blocked my view of the perimeter. *Was Spector or Boggs lurking somewhere nearby?*

"You have no idea how happy I am to see you." I squeezed Katalina's gloved hand as we proceeded. "How did you arrange this? And how on earth did you cause the diversion?" I watched a police officer swatting at something in the air.

"Geeno set his little flying friends loose in the crowd." Katalina grinned. "Nelson Lemming found your father. Your father found us. We came to help."

"Thank you, Kat. Though I do wish you hadn't brought Geeno."

"I tried to talk him out of it, but he is so stubborn. He would hear none of it. He did come up with a good idea to distract them, yes?" Katalina stopped when we were sufficiently surrounded by people on all sides. Then she took Indigo's hand. "Indy . . ." Tears slipped down her cheeks; her eyes tried to say everything in one look. I'd never seen Katalina speechless before.

She composed herself and nodded at my mother. "Mrs. Kohl, I am very glad you are safe."

Last of all, Katalina turned to Hurricane. "I was so worried about you, Hurricane. I will slice that swine. I swear it," she said, touching Hurricane's face. "Here, I brought extra cloaks. Put one on before you draw any attention." Out of her bag, she gave Hurricane and me thick hooded cloaks and stuffed my old cloak and the blanket into her carpetbag.

"Who else came with you?" I looked around to see if I recognized any faces.

"Khan is here," Katalina said. "We did not want to risk anyone else. Horatio and his men are stationed outside the gate."

"Where is Khan? I don't see—" Before I finished my sentence, a gentleman standing a few feet away tilted back his umbrella and winked at me. The sight of him made the words evaporate from my mind. His hair was trimmed short, accentuating the strong lines of his face. He wore a dark brown wool suit, expertly cut to fit his broad shoulders, and a silk waistcoat. To complete the look, he had a matching top hat and wool cape. He was the very picture of a merchant or a trader. His golden eyes searched my face, as if needing to see for themselves that I was alive and well.

I smiled up at him, thoughts buzzing in my brain. Even in the midst of turmoil, I felt the safety of my best friend's warm gaze. He leaned forward and whispered, "This is the last time I give this back to you. Don't misplace it again."

He held out something bound in cloth. I unwrapped the corner to find my knife snuggled inside. The weight of it in my hand gave me courage. My knife was like a trusted friend.

I smiled gratefully at Khan, then scanned the crowd. "Where's Geeno? I don't want him out there alone."

"He will meet us here." Katalina huddled us together. "Khaniferre," she whispered. "I would like to present my brother, Indigo."

The two faced each other, simultaneously reaching out to shake hands. They held the grip through two long breaths, exchanging a look I wished I understood. Khan broke the tension by letting go and turning toward my mother.

"Mrs. Kohl, it's been a long time," he said. "I'm so happy to see you're all right." He bowed slightly, his eyes full of relief. She'd been like a mother to him, too.

Hurricane kept her head down, but she could not hide how badly she'd been beaten. Khan balled up his fist when he saw her injuries. "Those bastards."

With a skimming glance around, Katalina lowered her voice. "We will wait until the gates are open, and stay in the middle of the pack as we exit. Horatio is waiting." She raised her chin up at the sky. "And your father is hovering nearby. He has a ship, ready to get us out of the area."

My father . . . in an airship?

My mother's mouth parted.

"Katalina, are you sure?" I wanted to believe her, but . . . "Sometimes my father says—"

"I saw it myself," she said, cutting me off, and continued in a low voice, "The crow-guards have taken up station at the exit.

They will be watching carefully, so do not attract their notice. Be vigilant."

Just then, a boy pressed his way into our circle. Geeno smiled up at me from under a baker boy hat. He wore knickers and a jacket, and had a bag of newspapers slung over his shoulders.

"Get your paper here," he said out of the side of his mouth. Except that his satchel, unlike one full of newspapers, quivered with movement from within. "They almost squash Harriett," he whispered, "but she get away." Tears sprang to my eyes. I'd missed Geeno terribly.

Khan reached out to take my hand, then caught himself. Instead, he tapped his fist to his heart and lowered his head to my ear. "Avery, I—"

Before he could say another word, a horn blared, announcing the prisoner's death march. The crowd surged with anticipation; we were squeezed together as everyone turned toward the bridge.

"Tell me after," I whispered.

The courthouse door banged open. Out came Norman Bale, marching between two rows of police officers. Jeers rang out; men raised their fists, shouting vulgarities. A ripe tomato flew up toward the bridge and smashed on the rail, showering the unfortunate people below with red pulp.

Finely dressed women held gloved hands to their mouths. I shook my head in disgust. Some in the crowd had even brought their children, who took this as an opportunity to splash around in the puddles. The spectators looked to be a mix of middle-class citizens here for entertainment and working folks wanting justice.

Going through the door on the opposite end of the bridge, the hanging brigade reappeared in the courtyard moments later, just beyond the gallows. Bale ascended the steps to the top of the platform, an officer on each arm. The priest awaited, as did the noose. The officers released Bale and stepped to the side.

The priest spoke softly, "Any last words?"

Bale looked over the crowd. "This is a mistake," he pleaded. "I am an esteemed member of society. Those girls worked for me. They were commoners. . . ." The crowd drowned out the rest of Bale's last words. A chill ran down my back. He was as awful as Ogden Boggs and the others.

The priest placed his hand on the condemned man's shoulder and bowed, mumbling some words. Then he, too, stepped aside, leaving Norman Bale to his fate.

A heavy stomping quieted the crowd as the executioner, wearing the black hood of his trade, thudded up the wooden steps. My pulse quickened. Bale's expression changed to one of fear as the masked man slipped the noose over his head and slid the knot tight. I was never happier to have an umbrella, and I tilted it down instantly. Putting my free arm around Geeno, I made sure the umbrella blocked his and Hurricane's line of sight as well as my own.

The courtyard grew eerily quiet, Bale's labored breathing the only sound. Then a loud metallic clang rang out as the trapdoor dropped open, followed by a quiet swish of fabric. Hurricane, Geeno, and I jumped at the same instant. In the seconds that followed, the only noise to reach my ears, one I will never forget, was the creaking of the beam as the rope swayed with the weight of its burden.

The solemnity was broken by cheers, claps, and a buzz of conversation recounting every detail of the execution.

"Did you see his eyes, how they bulged?" or, "His body twitched once or twice, I'm quite sure of it," and, "Are you aware if the neck does not snap, it takes quite a while to expire?"

The back of my throat went dry and my stomach pulled tight. I just wanted to get out of there, away from the horror of the place.

In a surge, the crowd moved toward the gate, carrying us with it. I kept my head down as we approached the tall stone wall that stood between us and freedom. Geeno walked alone. I had Hurricane on one arm and my mother on the other, afraid one of them would collapse. We did not want to risk pairing either of them with a black man or a Gypsy, so it was up to me to help them. Hurricane could barely stand, and a cut on her cheekbone had reopened, allowing a tiny trickle of blood to run down her face like a red tear.

The sea of people narrowed like sand in an hourglass to pass through the gate. For all their garishness, they were quite civilized as they exited, satisfied with the day's entertainment.

The spikes of the tall iron gate came into view. My knuckles turned white around the handle of the umbrella. We followed Katalina through the crowd. I watched her pass through the gate, my eyes boring into her back.

One step at a time.

My peripheral vision tracked the masked crow-guards lined up on either side, other people avoiding them as much as we. But at least the officer at the gate was from the prison, not the hospital.

As we were about to pass, he looked down at Hurricane.

"What's this? You're bleeding, young lady." He stepped in front of us, extending his hand to Hurricane, lifting her chin. "Are you in need of assistance?"

Her hood slid from her head, and I felt her body stiffen. "She's all right, sir." I kept my face down. "I'll take care of her."

When he saw the bruises covering her face, his eyes narrowed. "Step back, miss. What's happened here?"

No! My heart raced. I concentrated my energy, switching into my second sight. The officer's pale white energy was not what I had expected. He was speaking out of genuine concern. When I met his eyes, I saw his fear of a mob scene . . . his daughter, the same age as Hurricane. He was a worried father, shocked by Hurricane's condition. There was nothing I could do to sway him.

I felt it before I saw it. A tingle at my back—and then I was surrounded by Indigo's powerful energy. The officer looked past me, and I knew he and Indigo had connected. The officer's eyes glazed, and he slowly stepped back to let us pass. I let out my breath and took a hurried step toward the gate.

A black form blocked my path.

CHAPTER FORTY-ONE
FLIGHT

Hurricane screamed. More crow-guards stepped behind the first and slammed the gate shut. We were locked in. The momentum of people behind us forced us into the line of guards. One of them grabbed Hurricane by the arm while the others swooped in like the crows they resembled.

Mass chaos broke out. Not knowing what was going on, people on all sides pressed forward toward the gate, yelling in fear and confusion. An elderly woman tripped and was trampled by the mob. Others tried to climb the wall and fell like stones into the crowd, crushing the people below them. Umbrellas knocked off hats and poked at eyes.

For a split second, I caught sight of Katalina, who had turned to look back, surprise and pain etched upon her features.

Why am I always the one left behind? But I could not have

walked out that gate without my mother—or Hurricane, for that matter, especially given her condition.

I pulled Hurricane to me, but the guard's grip was tight. My mother whipped out the awl I'd given her and drove it forcefully into the crow's shoulder. He cried out, letting go of Hurricane. We dropped our umbrellas and tried to hold on to each other, but we were knocked apart like a living game of knucklebones.

The six of us were the only ones running in the opposite direction from the rest of the crowd. The birdlike masks fanned out into the mob as the police officers tried to regain control. A shot rang out, then another. I did not stop to see whom they were shooting at. We pushed our way back toward the gallows, knowing full well that the only exit was behind us. Rain slicked the stone and pulled heavily at my cloak. Luckily, the officers overseeing the removal of Norman Bale's body didn't notice us in the mass of screaming people.

"Geeno!" I grabbed him as I slammed into the wall of the prison, my eyes searching frantically for somewhere to hide. Then I saw it, a dark alcove ahead. "This way!" I shouted as loudly as I could, hoping the rest would hear me over the sound of the rain and the clamor.

We were at the stairs leading up to the bridge. It was our only chance. I shoved Geeno inside and turned back to find the others. "This way!" I called out again. Hurricane saw me wave before I grabbed my mother's hand and pulled her into the stairwell. Indigo and Khan were sprinting toward us as well, pushing through the crowd.

Up one flight, then another, until we reached the door to the bridge. I yanked it open, only to see police officers running at me from the courthouse. I slammed it shut again. "Keep going! Go up!" I pointed frantically to Geeno, who took off up the steps. A limping Hurricane trailed behind him.

Khan threw himself at the door, his boots scraping the stone as he searched for a foothold. "I'll hold them off!" he yelled.

Indigo rounded the corner. His eyes met mine. A hundred unspoken thoughts passed between us.

My mother stumbled. I slipped my arm under her shoulder and held her up as we began to ascend. I heard Indigo's voice shout, "Khan, help her mother! You have to protect them! I'll brace the door." The pounding of boots echoed behind me, followed by Indigo's desperate cry, "Keep Avery safe, Khan! Please, keep her safe."

"I will!" I heard Khan reply.

It was as if I were running underwater. My head filled with the numbing sound of my own blood surging through my body. Sharp pain stabbed at my lungs. Khan overtook us and, in one fluid motion, swept my mother up into his arms. We burst out onto the roof of the Tombs, rain blinding my eyes. The scene in front of me didn't make sense, even as my legs hurtled toward it.

At the far side of the roof, a wooden ship hung in the air. Above it, a large oblong balloon floated. It was moving past the building, and somehow I knew it could not stop. At the bow of the ship was an enormous clock, its giant pendulum slowly swaying back and forth, and in an instant I recognized my father's work. No one else could have created such an airship.

"Come on, Avery!" Khan's voice cracked like a whip, spurring me on. "Get to that ship!"

I made out Geeno's form in the distance. He was almost there. Men on board were shouting and pointing to a net of rope, which dragged along the surface of the roof. Geeno leapt onto it and climbed frantically toward the waiting arms above. Khan raced ahead, carrying my mother. She was saying something I could not make out.

Hurricane was in front of me but faltering. I caught up to her and grabbed her arm without breaking stride. A loud crack echoed. Something whizzed by us.

Glancing back, I saw a crow-guard standing, legs planted, arms extended out in front of him. The barrel of his weapon pointed directly at me. This was no tranquilizer gun. He took aim. Another crack, a flash of light. Time seemed to slow. Hurricane twisted around, breaking free from my grasp. She dove in front of me. A hole opened up in her shirt as red misted the air, wetting my face and arms. She fell, slowly, slowly, to the roof.

"No! Oh no!" My second sight snapped into focus. A dark swirl enveloped the guard. I felt my knife sliding into my fingertips. Snippets of thought popped into my head: Katalina teaching me to throw; me, failing over and over again. And Hurricane—

The guard aimed his gun again. Instinct took over. I stepped. My arm flew back. I hurled the knife. The trail of light behind it glowed bright and straight and strong, the energy guiding it to its target. It landed with a jolt, sinking to its hilt just above the crow's goggles, in the spot Hurricane called the third eye. The guard's dark energy billowed out and dissipated. His gun clattered to the roof. For a moment, his body froze, fixed in time, and then he dropped backward over the edge of the roof and was gone.

Shaking, I looked down at my hands. They glowed with an oddly beautiful transparent darkness, like volcanic glass. *What have I done?*

I fell to my knees beside Hurricane. "No!" I cried out. "Please, no . . ." But I knew she was dying. Her energy was but a pale wisp.

"Avery, forgive me," she gasped. "I was jealous of your friendship with Katalina." A tiny line of blood trailed from the corner of her lips. "I did see your mother talking with Mr. Moralis, but I never had any reason to believe . . ." Her voice was ragged.

"I forgive you, of course! Shhh, don't talk." I tried to lift her.

"Don't," she whispered, voice raspy with pain. "You must . . . stop Spector." She coughed. "You and Indigo . . . can destroy him." Her voice grew faint and her light faded. My energy grasped onto what was left, and a veil lifted in Hurricane's mind, one that I never even knew was there. Images flooded my brain. Hurricane as a toddler; her mother kissing her, saying, "Forgive me, my little Hurricane. I must go, to free you from the dishonor I have brought to our family. I love you and always will."

I blinked. Hurricane was staring at me, a smile on her battered face. "My mother loved me," she said, as she closed her eyes.

Her energy expanded out in all directions, igniting the sky as it spread. Then it disappeared.

I bent my head. Every ounce of will drained from my body.

Then there were hands on my sides and I was lifted up. Khan stared down at Hurricane. "Is she . . . ?"

I nodded, unable to say the words. "My mother?"

"On the ship. I came back for you." Khan removed his jacket and laid it over Hurricane. "You have to get to the ship. Now. Before it's too late." He shook my shoulders, hard, until I focused on his face. "Avery!"

"No, not without Indigo!" I screamed. Right then I knew. *Indigo is my soul mate. I love him.* Just thinking the words momentarily lit my spirit, even in the midst of this bedlam. *I love him with all my heart. I can't lose him again.*

Khan's golden eyes penetrated mine. He knew as well. His lids closed for the briefest of seconds, and when they opened they had a stern, almost fatherly cast to them. "Indigo risked his life to save you. I promised him I'd protect you. Get to that ship *now*. I'll go back for him." Before I could argue, he turned and dashed toward the stairs. I hated to leave Hurricane here, but I knew I'd never make it if I tried to carry her. I rose shakily to my feet.

Khan is fast; he'll make it back. The ship was moving farther away. I rushed toward it. As I got closer, I saw my father calling out and waving from the deck. *My father!* I didn't know how it was possible that he had done this, but my eyes clung to his figure as if he were my lifeline.

The net dragged to the edge of the roof. A few more feet; I was almost there. But with a scrape of gravel, it slipped over the side and was gone. "Come back!" I yelled up at the ship.

My father's voice cut through the air between us. "Jump, Avery! You can make it."

The net hung from the ship, getting farther away from me with each passing second.

I backed up to get a running start. Shouts rang out. I glanced behind me, hoping to see Indigo and Khan running toward the ship. It was neither of them. Guards swarmed up from the stairwell. My sight shifted; I scanned the murder of crows. In the center, a white face floated toward me. *Spector!* A fury of black murkiness churned around him. It was alive and grasping out toward me. I could almost make out the shapes of black wings along its edges, as if he truly embodied the shadow of his treacherous crows.

The front guards raised their guns and fired. Gravel sprayed up around my feet.

I turned and sprinted, ripping off my cloak as I ran so it would not slow me. The wind clutched the fabric, billowing it out as I pumped my legs faster and faster. I heard more shots. A searing pain bit my left arm, heat blossoming under my skin. My step faltered but I did not stop.

Just then, a *whoosh* of feathers brushed my side. My heart leapt. It was Seraphine, wearing Geeno's magnetic hood. She flew ahead of me, as if showing me what to do. I focused on her with everything I had. Beautiful white energy flowed around her majestic body. The harder I concentrated, the more brilliant it became. Running fast, I approached the edge of the roof.

Somehow, I knew the energy could help me. I had to trust it.

I threw my arms out and jumped, the very air around me quivering with life. Every drop of rain glistened and glowed. The wind shifted and flowed, shimmering like an ocean tide. *This is the life force*, I thought. *It is in the very air we breathe. It is the meshwork that connects us. To see this, to know this, is the gift.*

But a flash of fear cut through my vision. I was too far from the net. A terrible image came to me, of my body smashing to the street below. Seraphine's shrill wailing scream reached out. In that sound, I heard her complete self-abandonment to the flight. It filled me with awe and longing. I arched my back, my heart swelling, and stretched my arms wider.

It seemed impossible, but it was as if the pulsing air itself held me aloft. Wind whipped at my hair. In the next second, I was at the net. I crashed into it and wove my hands through the webbing, grabbing on for dear life.

A shot rang out behind me. I turned toward the sound and watched with horror as one of Seraphine's wings folded up like a piece of origami paper. She dropped below the ship and disappeared.

"No!" I screamed, my tears mixing with the rain.

Above me, my father leaned over the rail, yelling something I could not understand. He drew back his arm and hurled a pinecone-like object through the air; it landed with a metallic clang on the roof.

Boom! The explosion released a tremor, nearly knocking me from my net. The entire ship swayed, as if rocked by a monstrous wave.

I turned to look back. We were farther away from the building now. A plume of smoke billowed into the air, making me cough, burning my eyes. And as I watched, the side of the Tombs caved in.

CHAPTER FORTY–TWO
THE CRYSTAL

One of my father's crewmates scrambled down the net and helped me up onto the ship. I gawked at the scene before me. Jeremiah Thorn sprinted past, shouting, "All hands on deck!"

There was rigging and propellers, a tubular ladder climbing up into the bulky balloon above my head, a giant rudder, and the clock—the beautiful, masterful, enormous clock. We were sailing. We were flying. It was too much to take in all at once.

A pair of arms wrapped me in a bear hug. I looked up into my father's rugged face, goggles pushed up into his hair. My shoulders shook, but no more tears came to my eyes. "You're hurt," he said. "We must tend to that arm." He called to a young man, who rushed over and wrapped gauze around my injury.

Everything was happening excessively fast. Billowing smoke obstructed my view of the Tombs. "We have to go back! Indigo and Khan are still there."

"That's impossible, Avery. I'm sorry. They'll shoot us right out of the sky. Khan and Indigo will find their own way out, I'm sure." My father extended his hand toward the cabin where my mother was huddled in a thick cloak. A large man easily supported her while she drank from a steaming cup. "You did it! You got your mother out. She refused to go down below until you were safely on board."

I glanced toward the Tombs. He was right. If we returned, they'd down the ship. I felt my chest cave in just like the Tombs had.

Geeno threw his arms around me. "I'm glad you all right. But Seraphine . . . she—"

I hugged him to me. "I know."

Geeno's chin quivered, and he ran off as quickly as he'd appeared. I wished I could go console him.

My father checked my bandaged arm. "Did Khan tell you about the assembly?"

"No. What assembly?"

"Khan told me you gave him the combination to a safe in Roland Malice's office. He and Tony snuck in and opened it."

"What?"

"Inside the safe was a letter signed by your old boss. It incriminates his father, Tyber Malice, and Ogden Boggs, among others, in a scheme to poison the water, to control the laborers."

"A letter? This is the answer to our prayers. It's evidence."

"That's correct." My father nodded. "And as we know, the authorities are corrupt, and Tammany Hall probably knew about the plan, so Khan brought it to the newspapers. It has caused quite a furor these last few days. Workers secretly took water samples from around the city to prove what Malice said in his letter was true. They've also reopened the investigation into his death." My father leaned over the side of the ship and looked down to the city streets below.

I stepped to the rail. The rain had softened to a light drizzle, and the building below glistened. Gigantic airships hovered just above ours, and seeing them so close made my legs feel weak, but my father seemed to have his ship under control and I trusted him. The city looked like a rats' maze. Hundreds, no, thousands of people were marching down Centre Street. "What's happening?" I asked.

"Those are the protesters. Ogden Boggs is holding an assembly today to announce his run for office. He's using the death of Norman Bale to demonstrate the perceived danger to the economic elite of being overrun by the common people. He says the newspaper articles are full of lies planted by labor unions. See there." He pointed.

In a square just outside the gates of the Tombs was a stage and raised seating platforms, American flags flapping at every corner. The square was packed with people and surrounded by rows of armed police officers. His voice was faint, but I saw that Boggs was already pontificating from the stage.

I watched the demonstrators advancing toward the square. A dreadful thought came to me. "They'll kill each other. Father! We've got to stop them."

"This is not our fight, Avery." My father folded his arms over his chest. "You and your mother are safe up here."

The boat drifted closer. I heard the stomping feet, angry shouts; saw weapons raised in fists. My mother came up behind us, placing a hand on my father's arm. He immediately put his arm over her shoulder. Whatever they'd given her to drink must be working; her voice was already stronger. "You're wrong, Edgar. It is our fight. And Avery may be able to stop it."

I looked at my mother. A deep understanding settled into my bones. We are all connected. Race, culture, education— none of that mattered. If we hurt each other, we hurt ourselves. *Just as the life I took on the roof of the Tombs has endangered my own aura.* I still couldn't process what I'd done, but this— this coming violence—would affect the energy of so many. "But how? How can I stop it?"

"You need to show them. Even if you can only help a handful of people, it is worth a try." My mother wrung her hands. "I wish Niko had given you the Lemurian Seed crystal."

My father gave her a long look, then nodded to Jeremiah Thorn, who was obviously the first mate on this ship. "Bring the box," he said.

Thorn ran to the cabin and returned carrying the familiar barnacle-encrusted wooden box. My mother ran her hand across the top, a look of awe on her face, then she raised her eyes to my father, questions flooding through them.

My father hung his head. "When I located Khan and the others, Nikolai Moralis came to see me. He told me how he'd convinced you to marry me even though you were afraid to do so. He'd shown you your power was a gift, not a curse. All these years I'd scorned him, foolishly believing he was out to steal your heart, and now I'm eternally grateful to him. He gave me the crystal, for you and Avery."

With teary eyes, my mother opened the lid. Then she commanded, "Thorn, lower this ship, now!"

Jeremiah Thorn let loose his deep rolling laugh.

My father grinned. "You heard the woman! Open the air intakes. Make sure the lateral propellers clear those buildings." He handed Mother off to another strong crewmate and sprinted to the bow.

"I never thought I'd see this again." My mother handed the crystal to me. "I do not have the strength to use it. But you do."

"Mother, I don't!" I shook my head vigorously. "I've tried. I can do nothing with the crystal."

She placed a hand on my cheek. "I can tell you what to do, but you have to believe in yourself."

As she spoke, we flew toward the roof of a building adjacent to the square. If we were lucky, we would get there before the protesters, but I lost track of them as we dropped from the sky.

What my mother had said seemed so simple. *Can I make it work?*

I watched in amazement as my father and his crew maneuvered the ship into position, using air currents as handily as the flow of water. And all the while, the pendulum of the giant clock swung from side to side with ceaseless precision.

Assisted by two crewmates, I scurried down the cargo net to the roof, wincing in pain from the injury to my arm. The building was only three stories high, and when I peered over the edge I saw the assembly directly below. As we were so close to the Tombs, my father was anxious to take to the sky again. I stared down. If Khan and Indigo *had* escaped, I'd never find them now, with all these people clogging the streets.

Ogden Boggs stood on the stage, arms raised to silence the deluge of applause. His enormous ego, as well as his paunch, seemed to have swelled even further since I'd seen him at the party.

As I turned to take the crystal from the crewmen, an eruption of screaming and other commotion broke out in the square. I spun back to see police forming lines, shouting. The approaching mob was a raging river of bodies, like floodwater breaking down a dam.

Angry cries reached my ears. "Tear down the Tombs! No more crows! Stand against the Commerce League! Unite against Boggs!"

I'm too late! But then I thought about what my mother had said. Even if I can help just a few, it will be worth it. As she'd instructed, I squeezed the crystal with both hands. I focused harder than I'd ever done before; my sight shifted immediately. I knew I'd never forget what I saw below. Like thick tar, an obsidian river of energy flowed through the streets of the city.

Possibly due to the crystal, the fury below reached up, touching all of my senses. I smelled the hostility. I tasted its bitter venom. It sucked at my breath and burned my skin. I could not let it consume me.

I turned my attention to the crystal. My fingers found the ridges along one side. I pushed energy into each one, starting at the base of the crystal and moving up, like a pathway toward the top. At the last ridge, I pressed my fingers into the gap and bowed my head, placing my forehead on top of the crystal.

Energy flooded into the crystal, each facet expanding it and multiplying it. The radiant light amplified and grew until I was sure it must rival the sun as it spread across the sky. But an empty feeling enveloped me. *No one can see it but me.* I felt a painful lump in my throat, knowing my mother had been wrong.

In the next moment, a rapid torrent of images snapped through my mind. They flicked by so fast I could barely see them, but I felt every one in the deepest part of my soul. It was limitless. Every misunderstanding, every cruel word, every argument. Feelings of judgment, pride, envy, alienation. Memories . . . memories that held people back, that divided neighbors and made people do hurtful things. Tears streamed down my face. I heard myself screaming, felt myself falling to my knees, and then, the crystal slipped through my fingers.

I tried to grab for it. I flung my arms over the edge of the parapet wall and watched as it hurtled to the square below.

A black man, who'd managed to push through the line of police, saw it. Without thought to his own safety, he threw down his weapon and grabbed a finely dressed woman who was yelling in support of Ogden Boggs. He swung her aside. The crystal smashed to the ground where she'd been standing. It shattered into millions of tiny pieces.

I broke it. I've failed.

The flustered woman, still in the arms of the protester, took a step back. "You . . . you saved my life." She withdrew a fan and waved it desperately in front of her face. "Thank you, sir." The man nodded and turned away with a little smile on his face. Both of their dark auras transformed into light.

Next to them, a man in a cape and a shiny top hat lowered his fist from the air and pointed at the glass shards painting the street. "I haven't seen a projectile like that since the Battle of Bull Run."

A beggar in a wheelchair, who'd been cursing aloud only moments before, nodded in agreement. "Was there myself. Lost my legs at Bull Run."

"I'm very sorry to hear that, soldier." The caped man saluted the beggar and handed him some bills. The same thing happened—their energy brightened.

Although the clash carried on around the square, I saw pockets of light radiating out into the crowd. It was beautiful. Where it touched one person, it spread to another. But while some laid down their arms, listened to one another, others carried on fighting.

Of those whose energy remained dark, two stared directly

at me from the stage—Ogden Boggs and, behind him, hiding in the shadows, Dr. Spector. I was sure Spector had come to take credit for his serum, to get the recognition he craved, but now that he spied me from below, his good eye hardened, dark and inhuman. He had no crow-guards with him, as they'd been run out or captured by the rioters.

My father called down from the ship. "Avery, we must go."

I could not tear my eyes away. Perhaps the police would shift allegiance and arrest Ogden Boggs and Dr. Spector. Some officers were already helping the workingmen, protecting them, directing them away from the square.

I cringed as a band of men climbed over the stands and charged the stage, their energy murky and dark. Ogden Boggs saw them too late. He tried to run but tripped and rolled onto his back. They were upon him, bludgeoning him with sticks and clubs.

"Spector! Help me!" he screamed.

Dr. Ignatius Spector looked down. I would never forget the cold-blooded smile that slipped across his painted lips before he slunk, like the worm he was, into the deepest of the shadows and disappeared.

Ogden Boggs was dragged from the stage. Someone called out, "The gallows!" A chant echoed through the mob. "Hang him! Hang him! Hang him!"

My eyes flew to the courtyard of the Tombs. Already the gates had been cast aside and the walls overrun. The grenade had destroyed the top floors, and the mob was ravaging the rest.

The Tombs would never imprison anyone again, of that I was sure. My only hope was that the other seers and Mr. Gentry would make it out alive.

I watched with shock and repulsion as Boggs was lugged into the yard. He roared as they pulled him up the steps of the gallows.

It was over within minutes. They reset the trapdoor, slung the noose around his neck, and pulled. The mighty beam of the gallows protested its grim obligation but carried it out nonetheless.

For the second time that day, a body hung lifeless in the yard.

The death of Ogden Boggs had a mollifying effect on the mob. As the din quieted somewhat, I heard my name. Across the street I saw Khan waving and yelling for us to go. He was with Katalina and some other Gypsies. My heart jerked. Indigo was not with them.

"We'll find him!" Khan called up to me. They pushed through the crowd. I strained my eyes until I could see them no longer, hoping they'd reappear with Indigo.

Then my father's men were beside me. "Miss Avery, it's dangerous. We must go."

I saw where their eyes were fixed. A battalion of militiamen marched toward the Tombs. One shot would bring the balloon, and the ship, crashing to the street.

Tears streamed down my face as I turned away from the Tombs—away from Khan and away from Indigo.

EPILOGUE
THE *CASSIOPEIA*

We've been drifting for days now. I clutch the rail and look down. Water. As far as I can see, water.

My father stands beside me, scope to one eye. Once again, he refuses to go back. "Do you know what they'll do to me?" he says. "I bombed a government building." He snaps his scope closed and softens his voice. "There's no going back, Avery."

He takes out his pipe and tobacco pouch, pinches and packs the dried leaves, then cups his hand to light them. I catch the cherry-whiskey scent before it wafts away on the wind. The smell reminds me of home. We no longer have a home, or if this ship is it, then we are like the Romany travelers of old who roamed from place to place.

Father returns below to attend to my mother. Her recovery has been slow but steady. She's strong one moment, full of fitful nightmares the next. The important thing is, I have my family back. I tell myself this again and again. I got my mother out of the Tombs.

My eyes are swollen from crying, but there is nothing I can do. I can only watch the endless blue far below.

Not knowing is the hardest part. I fabricate a story in my head. Maybe Indigo used his power to escape. Maybe he ran from the yard before the mob arrived.

Even as I play out the images in my mind, doubt creeps in. Tears roll from my eyes, freezing into ice on my face. I leave them there, relishing the prick of pain. I want to feel pain. I didn't flinch when Father re-dressed the hole in my arm. The bullet went clean through. Pain is better than the numbness that is smothering me.

The memory of Ogden Boggs's murder haunts me, and while that darkness will linger in the city for a long time, there was light in the square, too. People rose up and joined in unity to challenge him. Before my father's men pulled me away, I even saw wealthy spectators standing alongside working-class pro-testers to stop the militia from advancing into the people. The worst part is that Spector escaped, with no one able to stop him.

Seraphine chirps, and I turn to watch her hop along the rail. We'd used Geeno's tracking device to follow Seraphine's erratic descent. We found her half dead on a nearby rooftop. Geeno and my father fabricated an extraordinary mechanical wing that clicks and whirrs as she flies. I think she's still getting used to it, because she tends to fly in circles.

The *Cassiopeia*, named for a constellation of stars and my

mother's nickname, Cassi, flies high and maneuvers nimbly. She is a work of staggering genius. Her rigid balloon, filled with hydrogen, easily carries the sixty-foot wooden ship, an old clipper abandoned in the rear of the navy yard. My father added the steam-driven engine and the clock that helps to power her motion. *The last clock*, I think wistfully. He built the *Cassiopeia* right under the noses of the people who dishonorably discharged him.

I slip into my second sight and am momentarily distracted by the intensity of the ocean's shimmer, but then I see my hands. There's a stain of dark energy swirling with the pale. I don't know if it will ever go away, and part of me does not want it to. I never want to forget the life I took, that I killed a man. *I killed a man*. I think I finally understand the shame and remorse that tore my father apart after the Civil War.

I wish that I could see the colorful spectrum of human emotion that Indigo told me about during our time together in the Tombs, but my sight doesn't work that way. Mine is a simpler view of a soul. I see the subtle shades of our true selves—good and bad, light and dark . . . fear and courage, humiliation and honor . . . the parts that make us human, I suppose. Even as the thought crosses my mind, I second-guess myself. If that was true, then Spector also has some amount of humanity in him. If so, I never saw it.

I've discovered much about my ability since I caused the explosion at the Works, and I fully intend to learn more, now that I have my mother back. I'm told the explosion was a chance occurrence, but I'm not sure. I know that I am an aura healer. I have the ability to help people see for themselves what is causing them hurt, or fear, or anger. And I can push them toward change, toward transformation, toward empathy for others and themselves, but as I've seen, they must be willing participants in order for it to work. If only I could show them the *other* aspect of my ability, the one I am truly mesmerized by: the gift of seeing the universal energy connecting all of us, connecting all living things. Then they would know that to hurt another is to hurt oneself. Things would be different if they saw that.

Questions continue to batter my brain. What will Spector do now? And who will stop him when he emerges, as I fear he will? If I ever get my father to return to it, what will be left of the great and terrible city of New York?

Geeno comes up from below deck and stands by my side. My father plans to adopt him. He will be my true little brother, it seems.

"Avery, tell me again how you escape from the Tombs. Please."

I nod. "All right. Just give me a moment."

His face brightens. He loves the part about the parrot, Pepper.

I laugh at the irony of it. Everyone thought it would be my special gift of sight that would help me save my mother from the Tombs. But in the end, it was my skill as a welder.

As I'd once done from my roof in Vinegar Hill, I stare in the direction of Manhattan Island. It's no longer visible, but I picture my last view of it before we'd drifted out to sea. I'd watched the glimmering lights meld together, until all that was left of the city was a gleam on the horizon.

I thought that if I got my mother out, I would feel complete. Instead, I brood over the ache I feel inside my chest and ask, *What about the pieces of myself that I lost?* Khan. Indigo. Tony. Leo. Oscar. Katalina. Hurricane. Each name brings a stab of pain like a string pulled taut from deep within me. Especially Hurricane. There is a hollow inside of me. I left my living, beating heart behind, as surely as if it had been carved from my body. If only my father could fabricate a heart of metal to take its place—one that does not feel, one that does not hurt. But alas, even Father's genius has its limits.

Still, I wonder, *How can I live without my heart?*

Geeno and I watch Seraphine leap from the rail into the endless blue sky. She has no hesitation, no fear, only her will to fly. I notice she is already adjusting, learning to use her new wing. A flutter of hope flares in my chest. I have my family; maybe together we can face this uncertain future.

Seraphine calls out. I close my eyes and let her shrill cry wash over me. Maybe one day I'll return and heal my broken city . . . and my heart.

Dear Readers,

The word *Gypsy*

In America, most people think of the word *Gypsy* as a term that refers to Bohemian culture. However, today many Romani people consider the word *Gypsy* to be a derogatory term, and *Roma* is often used to refer to all Romani groups. But in 1882, when my story takes place, the word *Gypsy* was most common, and the Romani people referred to themselves as Romany or Romany travelers.

I have opted to use *Gypsy* with a capital *G* to emphasize that it is a proper noun and not a behavior or a slur. I've used *Romany* when members of the group refer to themselves.

The Tombs

The Tombs was a real prison built in 1838. It was modeled after an Egyptian mausoleum and "designed to strike fear into the hearts of potential criminals."

Built over Collect Pond, a dumping ground for slaughterhouses and tanneries, the Tombs began to sink from the moment the cornerstone was set and was gloomy, damp, and leaky throughout its existence until it was torn down in 1897.

It did not house an asylum in the basement! (That we know of.)

Learn more: nyhistorywalks.wordpress.com

The Brooklyn Bridge

The construction of the Brooklyn Bridge loomed over Avery's neighborhood. The project began in 1869 and was a dangerous undertaking. Close to a hundred men suffered from the bends and between twenty and thirty people died during the process. The bridge was completed in 1883.

Learn more: ny.curbed.com/2013/5/22/10241220/130-years-of-brooklyn-bridge-photos-decade-by-decade

Did you know?

There really was a Civil War Balloon Corps.

In 1882, children as young as six worked twelve to eighteen hours a day, six days a week, for a dollar.

Before labor unions, the government supported the use of violence to break a strike and often sent a militia to aid the wealthy business owners. Many died in "the war between capitol and labor."

Learn more: sageamericanhistory.net/gildedage/topics/capital_labor_immigration.html

Peregrine falcons nest atop the New York bridges! (There's a falcon webcam.)

Learn more: www.newnybridge.com/falcon-camera/

While there is much actual history in *The Tombs*, there are also many intentional departures from facts/timing. This is a book of historical fantasy, and I hope you enjoy it as such!

—Deborah Schaumberg

ACKNOWLEDGMENTS

There are so many people I would like to thank for helping me make this dream come true that I hope I can list them all.

Steve, thank you for always believing in me even when I am full of doubt. You help me believe in myself. Skylar and Ryan, thank you for being part of every step of this journey. Your energy is beautiful. Thank you to my mom, for teaching me I can do anything I put my heart to, and my late dad for teaching me to set my imagination free. I'm thankful for my sister Gina, who taught me that life is precious, and my sister Jennifer, who teaches me to put things in perspective. I'm grateful to all my other amazing family members for their support.

Huge thanks to my agent extraordinaire, Dan Lazar, and the talented people at Writers House: Cecelia de la Campa, James Munro, and Genevieve Gagne-Hawes.

Thank you to my brilliant editor, Kristen Pettit, the ultimate seer, who saw this book the way I'd intended to write it and gave it direction and life. And thank you to the talented people at HarperTeen: production editor—Kathryn Silsand; designer—Jenna Stempel; cover artist—Si Scott; publicist—Gina Rizzo; marketing director—Bess Braswell; marketing assistant—Tyler Breitfeller; and Elizabeth Lynch.

Thank you to all the folks at SCBWI. I met my agent at the 2014 Winter Conference in New York organized by Stephen Mooser and Lin Oliver—thank you! Joining SCBWI was the first and best thing I ever did as a writer.

Thank you to my first writers' group—Debbie Levy, Jon Skovron, Pam Bachorz, and Adam Meyer for critiques and friendship. And my new writers' group—Kathy MacMillan, Lisa McShane, Kate Bradley-Ferrall, and Meg Eden Kuyatt—we're on this journey together now.

Thank you to Lois Szymanski and Laura Backes for your help with early edits. Thanks to Gloria Kempton for her Finish Your Novel course and my online classmates, including Donna Matney, for early critiques.

Thanks to Regina Brooks for selecting *The Tombs* as a finalist in her Novel Discovery Contest.

I'm so happy to be a part of the writing community. Thanks to the Electric Eighteens, Binders Full of YA Writers, the Fighting Bookworms, Writer's House Army, an Alliance of Young Adult Writers, and YA Book Central for doing the awesome cover reveal.

Thank you to Mike Dooley, better known as the Universe, for your everyday insights.

Thanks to Erika Satlof for her early website development and continuing graphic design skills. Thanks to Tami Mensh for being my accountability partner, social media helper, and marketing brainstormer. Thanks to all the people who read parts of this book or gave me bookish advice—Tom Schaumberg; Dave, Laurie, Zach and Kyra Flyer; Jordan Janis; Stephen Mazer; Justin and Jordan Mensh; Kim Weinberg; and P. J. Yerman. A big, heartfelt thank-you to all my incredible friends—you've been part of this entire process; I'm truly blessed to have you in my life.

Last but not least, thanks to my future readers, especially my nieces and nephews—Terry and Archie; Madison and Peyton; Parker and Nate; and Mackenzie and Braden—yes Terry, that includes you.